PLAYWRITING SEMINARS 2.0

A Handbook on the Art and Craft of Dramatic Writing
with an
Introduction to Screenwriting

Richard Toscan

A Franz Press Book

Playwriting Seminars 2.0: A Handbook on the Art and Craft of Dramatic Writing with an Introduction to Screenwriting

Copyright © 2011 by Richard Toscan

ISBN-13: 978-0615608211
ISBN-10: 0615608213

Contact the author at richard.toscan@gmail.com

For Sharon

PRAISE: For Playwriting Seminars

"An absolutely essential guide to all aspects of playwriting, covering everything from perfecting plot points to protecting proper percentages, and includes a valuable whitewater raft trip down the rapids of Hollywood screenwriting."
        -*Magellan*

"I have studied the online version for years, which helped me write a Lionsgate movie, two novels, and two nonfiction books. I think the book is even better."
        -*Chuck Hustmyre*

"*The Playwriting Seminars* is a treasure-trove of information, philosophy, and inspiration as well as the nuts-and-bolts of structure and analysis. Toscan's treatment of the subject is excellent, and his Playwright on the Job areas (manuscript formatting, working as a playwright, the business of playwriting) are very useful for giving students a clear plan of action and idea of what to expect after graduation."
        -*Theatre Journal*

"Five Star [highest] rating. Well worth a read for any actor or scriptwriter."
        -*SchoolZone Educational Intelligence* (UK)

"Best of the Net site. A rich, intricately layered course in playwriting. Author Richard Toscan uses both theory and concrete examples to create a terrific learning environment for writers."
        -*WebCrawler Select*

Recommended resource for new playwrights.
        -*New Dramatists* (New York)

TABLE OF CONTENTS

LIST OF DIAGRAMS

CREDITS

People ask me when I decided to become a playwright, and I tell them I decide to do it every day. Every day when I sit down to write, I can't remember how it's done.
   -Suzan-Lori Parks

Many of my colleagues in theatre, film, and television have contributed over the years to the concepts in *Playwriting Seminars 2.0*. Those not credited in the text include Douglas S. Cramer, František Daniel, Athol Fugard, George Furth, Joan Holden, Velina Hasu Houston, John Houseman, Richard Imison, Alex Segal, Ntozake Shange, Anna Deveare Smith, Luis Valdez, and Russell Vandenbroucke.

Playwriting Seminars 2.0 is dedicated to my students at the University of Southern California where I taught playwriting and play analysis for many years and was Dean of the School of Theatre. I initially developed the concepts that eventually grew into *Playwriting Seminars* to meet their analytical needs as they worked with scripts as performers, directors, designers, and playwrights.

While teaching at USC, I also spent some years as executive producer of radio dramas primarily in association with NPR, Lucasfilm, and the BBC. This combination of teaching and producing led me into playwriting and the development of playwriting courses for my students.

I owe a debt of gratitude to Peter Hay and my colleagues at First Stage in Los Angeles for the initial staged readings and critiques of my plays as well as to New Dramatists in New York.

Thanks also to the many writers whose scripts I critiqued as a judge for professional playwriting and screenwriting competitions. Their work increased my understanding of dramatic structure, technique, and "voice" in theatre and film.

Following those years in Los Angeles, my advanced playwriting and screenwriting students at Portland State University prompted me to create the first edition of *Playwriting Seminars* on the Web, a process that continued during my years as Dean of Virginia Commonwealth University's School of the Arts where I founded the Cinema Program.

By 2006 *Playwriting Seminars* had become a widely used resource on the art and craft of dramatic writing in the U.S. and a number of other countries. The positive response has been gratifying. My thanks also for the comments, questions, and suggestions from many students, teachers, and theatre practitioners that have been a great help in preparing this new edition.

When I began the first edition of *Playwriting Seminars*, I wanted to demystify the craft of playwriting as well as its technical issues covering everything from plot structures to such mundane matters as formatting and binding of scripts. My goal was to open up the practice to anyone who was interested in this arcane and marvelous art of the theatre.

FORWARD: Focus of the *Handbook*

There's something very perverse in me that loves trying to do the impossible and put things on the stage that are very hard to stage and that maybe people haven't seen before. Because I think of all the arts, the theatre is the most conservative, because you have that ghastly problem of having to sell all the tickets every night.
　-Tina Howe

Playwriting Seminars 2.0 is intended for a range of users from students exploring the art to playwrights making the transition to screenwriting. Novelists and authors in other genres have found the first edition of this *Handbook* helpful in beginning to write for theatre or film as have theatre professionals working with new playwrights.

Parts of the *Handbook*

This is a professional *Handbook* on the playwright's craft with a focus on the kinds of new plays most often produced by the nearly 500 regional theatres in America.

The *Handbook* is divided into six sections: Content including the importance of the playwright's "voice," themes, character development, and subtext; Structure including plots with supporting diagrams, uses of time, monologues, and theatrical styles; Working including editing of drafts, avoiding writer's block, writing exercises, and dealing with critics; Format for stage plays; Business including the submission process to theatres and competitions, agents, creating a script synopsis and playwright's bio, and self-production; and Screenwriting including craft adjustments from verbal to visual storytelling, screenplay format, writing and placing spec screenplays in Hollywood and the alternative of independent filmmaking.

The Afterword contains a collection of quotes on craft from playwrights, screenwriters, theatre and film directors, and producers. This section has been popular with literary managers and offers mini-lessons in playwriting, screenwriting, and writing for television.

Plays Cited & Examples

The *Handbook* uses examples from many plays to help explain the techniques typical of contemporary practice.

Most of these examples are drawn from the work of contemporary playwrights whose plays have demonstrated their staying power by continuing to be produced by America's regional theatres. Some were first presented decades ago while others were first produced as recently as 2012 as I was preparing this new edition.

Other examples range from what might be called the "classic classics" (Sophocles, Shakespeare, Molière, and Ibsen) to mid-century classics that have influenced the development of our contemporary theatre: Tennessee Williams, Arthur Miller, Harold Pinter, Eugene Ionesco, and Samuel Beckett, to name a few.

In nearly every case I have tried to select plays that are easily available in print or e-book editions. If you haven't read the scripts, the examples drawn from these plays stand on their own in terms of underlining the principles they illustrate. Reading these plays after the discussions here will deepen your understanding of the craft.

Regional Theatres as Entry Point

Regional theatres are the primary entry point into this business of playwriting in America (a similar role is played by noncommercial theatres in the UK). They premiere nearly all new plays produced in the United States and have become the research and development arm of the commercial Broadway and Off-Broadway theatre.

Regional theatres have become reasonably comfortable with their place in the commercial theatre food chain and the result is a very good deal for playwrights and the theatres that produce their plays. If all goes well, playwright and theatre share in the financial gains and if audiences don't respond positively, the producing theatre carries all the risk. Because of their interest in discovering new plays and writers, a number of these theatres offer development programs for playwrights.

The Market for New Plays

For nearly all regional theatres, story and the structure most Western playwrights have been using for the past 2,500 years are givens. But using conventional techniques does not mean that you need to write conventional plays.

David Henry Hwang said it best: *You can't be a playwright without believing there's an audience for adventurous work.*

The theatre offers playwrights considerable opportunity for experimentation in their writing. The conventional techniques underlying your work will help keep audiences engaged with your plays no matter how unconventional they may seem to be.

The compensation for accepting these proven conventions is a large market for new plays.

A measure of this market in 2011: Over 300 regional theatres and 100 competitions with prizes were soliciting scripts, as well as 80 play development programs. All of these opportunities were open to new playwrights. Another 150 regional theatres were soliciting plays directly from playwrights they wanted to work with or from those represented by agents.

Compared with many other art forms including screenwriting, the opportunities available for new playwrights are considerable.

There are signs that these opportunities will continue to expand in the coming years: The 2009-10 season (the most recent analysis available in 2011) saw a 20% jump in audiences for play readings and workshop productions at America's regional theatres. Many of these were presentations of new plays.

Hollywood Options

Hovering over all of this activity is the Hollywood film and television industry. Today, nearly all produced playwrights also work in feature film and television.

Best Practice: *The surest route to Hollywood for playwrights starts with a regional theatre production or recognition in a major playwriting competition.*

The odds of achieving recognition as a new playwright are far better than those faced by novice screenwriters hoping to sell unsolicited screenplays.

Recognition as a playwright nearly always leads to invitations to write in Hollywood. And having that invitation will open doors in the film industry that would require a battering ram to get through if you just moved to Hollywood hoping to sell a spec screenplay.

In August 2011, one of the thousands of overly hopeful novice screenwriters in LA dropped off his unsolicited spec script in a briefcase for a Hollywood agent and within hours it was blown up by the Beverly Hills bomb squad. That's not the usual fate of spec screenplays, but the symbolism is worth noting.

Best Practice Notes

Best Practice notes will be found throughout *Playwriting Seminars 2.0*. They can be taken as "rules," though the first rule of playwriting is that most rules are made to be broken. The notes reduce to a sound-bite my own conclusions about this craft and in nearly all cases reflect the professional practice of most playwrights and screenwriters.

Where to Start in the *Handbook*

If you have experience in dramatic writing or theatre production as a performer or director, you may find it more interesting to begin with Part Two on the structure of plays. Later, it may be valuable to return to Part One, especially Chapter 16 on the critical issue of subtext.

If fiction is your interest, particularly genre novels and their nonfiction equivalents, Part Two (Structure) is the place to begin followed by Part Six (Screenwriting). Genre novels (crime, romance, paranormal, etc.) follow all of the structural techniques of plays, but then rely on the visual storytelling techniques of screenwriting rather than the verbal approach that dominates plays.

PROLOGUE: Starting from Scratch

You have to protect your writing time. The easiest thing to do on earth is not write.
          -William Goldman

Telling stories by getting characters to talk to each other is the flesh of dramatic writing and it's one of those things humans tend to do naturally. For the same reason, the rhythms of dramatic conflict come as second nature to most people.

But the more complicated part of dramatic writing is hidden beneath the surface. The flesh may be willing, even second nature, but the bones are another matter.

The Four Bones of Playwriting

Here are the bare bones of playwriting, or at least the four most important ones.

1. Consequences count. Plays deal primarily with the emotional consequences of events, far more than the events themselves. Stories focusing primarily on events are usually a much better fit for screenplays.

2. Subtext is essential. What characters don't tell us in dialogue is as important as what they do say. If characters tell us everything they're thinking, we'll be bored out of our minds. Mystery is good.

3. Your "voice" matters. How your words on paper sound when spoken (or read silently) is what gets you through the door in this business. Forget about proper sentence structure. Instead, listen carefully to how people actually talk. If you're a talker, don't. Concentrate instead on listening – and later write down what you hear.

4. Plots come in pairs. Playwrights nearly always use a suspense plot as an excuse to hold audiences while they spend most of their time on what's really interesting to them, the emotional plot. Suspense in the theatre is usually not about vampires lurking in dark corners, though it can be that strong. It can also be (and often is) as little as something like: Will they sell the house?

A Note on Dual Plot Structure

The concept of dual or twin plots is one of the core understandings of *Playwriting Seminars 2.0* and was first suggested by the great Shakespearean scholar A. C. Bradley.

This insight has a long pedigree, but the real proof of the concept is in the practice of playwriting: It is nearly impossible to find produced plays by contemporary playwrights who don't use this dual plot structure.

These twins (or pairs) are called *suspense* and *emotional* plots in this *Handbook* since the terms capture the key differences between them, but what they are named matters far less than the impact they have on contemporary playwriting.

Why playwrights use this dual plot structure may owe much more to the way human beings have always told lasting stories than to theoretical understandings. Demonstrating this key part of the playwright's craft is one of the goals of the new edition of Playwriting Seminars.

Reading Plays

The plays used as examples in the *Handbook* provide a reading list reflecting the range of what contemporary playwrights have been writing. Playwriting is primarily a verbal art, so hearing plays is as important as reading plays.

Seeing plays in production helps, but less than you might think. If a production is anything short of terrible, we're usually sufficiently engaged by the story and characters that we have only a hazy memory of the structural techniques the playwright used. Reading scripts is a way to develop professional distance and thus recognize the underlying workings of plays in performance.

Avoid speed-reading of plays. Instead, read scripts out loud or silently in your head, but saying every word. By reading slowly, the technical structure will be easier to recognize as will the playwright's "voice."

PART ONE - CONTENT: What's in a Play

Most writers don't know that actors are never better than in the pauses or in the subtext. They give them too many words. They're useful for the actors, but only that; they aren't the whole story.
-Yasmina Reza

1. VOICE: YOUR SOUND AS A WRITER

I don't write, I listen, and I just take dictation. I was trained as a musician. I'm a terrible speller, and I don't have a sense of prose as a discipline. I only hear people talking, and I put down what they say.

-Michael Weller

The way playwrights put words on paper (their "voice") is a critical part of the content of their plays regardless of the stories being told.

Voice is what makes a literary manager or artistic director of a regional theatre read past page three of a new script. After page three, characters and story determine if they keep reading.

Best Practice: *A play without a "voice" won't work in the theatre.*

Plot can be all that's necessary to make a screenplay work, but that's not the case in the theatre. One of the distinctions between playwriting and screenwriting is that screenplays are read by the pros for story. While voice helps in writing for film, it's not essential. In film, story rules. In theatre, voice rules.

Voice is your personal signature as a playwright and as this develops it will become individual to you. Experienced theatre professionals can often identify the author of a new script by a produced playwright simply by hearing the "voice" on a page of dialogue, and if they're famous, with just a few lines of dialogue.

Playwrights build a physical construction on stage with spoken words. We can move around in it, as the performers do, but it's an invisible construction. That makes it easy to think it's just words, any words that do the job. It's not. Any old words that just do the job are a bore in the theatre. What playwrights do is make us hear things we've never quite heard in that way before and what we hear is their special voice.

What playwrights write is the language as it's spoken, not as it's written. The syntax of spoken language is only vaguely related to the niceties of English composition. Spoken language is governed by the structure of thoughts, not conventional sentence structure.

To be good at playwriting, retrain your ears to hear how people actually speak. No two people speak the language in exactly the same way and that's one of the keys to creating memorable characters.

Quirks of Spoken Language

Voice is built on a base of how people speak in ordinary conversation with all the quirks that involves.

1. Listen for how people actually speak. How they express thoughts in spoken language. It's different from the kinds of linear and logical discourse favored in written language.

2. Listen for the way people really use words. What words are typically dropped from spoken language and which are combined as contractions and how certain sounds within words when "properly" enunciated are typically dropped in speaking.

3. Listen for how punctuation is thrown around in speech. Spoken language often makes a hash of sentence structure and the niceties of nouns, verbs, and all the other paraphernalia of written language.

4. Listen for the odd rhythms of spoken language. People have their own unique cadences and rhythms as they speak and these are often separate from the meanings of the words they say.

If you're a natural borne chatterer, make a sign to put over your desk:

LISTEN MORE talk less

And equally important, start keeping a journal of what you hear. After a morning of eavesdropping on other peoples' conversations, try capturing what they said in your journal. Concentrate on recording the oddities of the way they said things.

Don't record conversations with some electronic device. First, you may end up with a punch in the nose (and may be breaking the law as well). And second, you're not really interested in exactly what these people say and how. What you're after is your own modification of what you've heard and the best way to get that is by writing down what you hear, not by listening to a recording.

Eavesdropping for Art

A good way to start this kind of listening is by eavesdropping on your friends, relations, and strangers on the street, in restaurants, or stores. Be shameless, but don't be obvious.

This sort of thing is not an endearing trait in the normal world unless your day job is with the FBI so whatever you overhear absolutely needs to be kept to yourself. This exercise is not a source for becoming the life of the party. People have a right to what they assume is privacy so you're only doing this as a step toward developing your playwriting voice.

William Saroyan learned to write dialogue by keeping his ear to the upstairs heating vent while his parents entertained – and wrote down what he heard. But most playwrights don't duplicate on paper what they've heard on the street unless what they've heard is especially wonderful.

By doing the work of listening and then writing dialogue, you'll gradually create your own special voice. The way this happens over time borders on pure magic and the best way to speed up the process is to keep subtext out of the mouths of characters by not allowing them to say everything they're thinking.

Remember: Mystery is good. (For a technique that can help develop your voice, see Chapter 41 on Writing Exercises.)

As your ear becomes trained to hear spoken language instead of written language, your natural story-telling abilities will also develop. That skill is probably hidden in our DNA, going back to when humans first began telling stories and drawing them on cave walls 30,000 years ago.

2. SUBJECTS OF PLAYS

Let me just simplify it. Never an idea, never, never, never has an idea led to a play. Every inspiration, every seminal image for a play has been something I've seen on the streets, something I've read in a newspaper, a story that was told to me, always an event external to myself.
        -Athol Fugard

When venturing into the art and craft of dramatic writing, one of the first problems is that most of our experiences with dramatic storytelling nowadays have come from film and television.

There's a simple reason for this: Most people – at least in America – see many more films and watch far more television than the small number of hours they spend seeing plays. The downside is that this volume of experience with film and television conditions and narrows our assumptions about playwriting.

Reading Plays & Play Readings
The best antidote to stories told via media is to begin reading plays, especially contemporary plays written within the last 20 years, and whenever possible listening to them in professional readings or productions at regional theatres. The best combination of all: See a play in production and then read the script.

Regional theatres don't always advertise readings of new plays, so call these operations in your area to see if they're doing these and then get on an email list. That's also a good way to gradually become known by those who run these theatres. There's nothing like having a theatre "know" you to ease the way in for a new script you've just finished.

Play are beginning to be published as e-books – the number of these is surprisingly small for contemporary work – but it's a good idea to read scripts in hard copy form rather than as e-books. The e-book format makes it more difficult to sense the underlying structure of a play – including act lengths and placement of the inciting incident and climax, among other elements – since you're not dealing with traditional "pages."

Plays Are About Consequences

Theatre sounds different from film partly because of the treatment of consequences in plays and screenplays. (See Part Six on Screenwriting for more on these differences.)

Plays tend to be about the consequences of events while screenplays tend to be about the sequence of events. Like all generalizations, this one is full of holes, but it's a helpful way to begin understanding the real differences between these dramatic forms of storytelling.

More specifically, plays tend to be about the emotional consequences of physical events, though that physicality may have more to do with mental activity than external events (Part Two on Structure addresses the impact of this tendency on the plot structure of plays).

Playwrights have a much broader vision of dramatic content and technique than what seems possible in the world of American film and television because regional theatres have a greater tolerance for unusual content and new ways of telling stories.

Family Problems vs. the World

If plays are about consequences – and they are – that leads to the more difficult question, *Consequences of what?*

The answer to that question has bedeviled the American theatre for many decades. As J. T. Rogers says speaking of *Blood and Gifts* (his 2011 play about the involvement of intelligence agencies in Afghanistan during the 1980s), "We're supposed to write three-character plays, with all white people, sitting in a room, talking about Mom." Joan Holden, co-founder of the San Francisco Mime Troupe, made the same point four decades earlier, noting that with all the terrible things happening in the world – economic, ecological, political – the dominant subject on U.S. stages was the American family.

In all those years little has changed on the subject list for American plays – a fact that is often noted with some bemusement by our theatre colleagues in the UK.

Unlike J. T. Rogers, why the majority of U.S. playwrights focus on family problems in America is perhaps unanswerable, though it is curious that UK dramatists embrace a much broader focus. One answer may be that most of the new plays produced by American regional theatres are ultimately family or personal relationship dramas, even if the triggers for these conflicts are external ones.

It may well be that regional theatres mostly select these relationship plays for the new scripts they produce because that's what most American playwrights write – and most playwrights may be writing these because that's mostly what they see being done at these theatres. Then, there's no question that audiences enjoy this subject (admittedly they don't have a chance to see much else) and this reinforces the writing and selection wheel.

What we have in the American theatre may be a vicious triangle maintaining personal family centered plays as the dominant subject of U.S. playwrights.

You can make a reasonably long list (meaning 15 or 20 names) of contemporary playwrights who have broken out of this box – among them Lisa Loomer, Tony Kushner, David Henry Hwang, Velina Hasu Houston, Rajiv Joseph – but they're overwhelmed, at least in numbers, by those who embrace the subject of family and personal relationship problems in America.

The world is full of subjects – social, economic, political, scientific – that could lend themselves to dramatic treatment. A lesson European playwrights have known is that one of the best ways to bring these kinds of subjects to life is to explore them through a core of personal relationships. That emotional center – the relationship piece – gives audiences an entry point to what can be difficult subjects, but the ultimate focus is on the larger issues beyond those relationships.

In considering venturing beyond the family problem subject, you'll certainly have far less competition from other playwrights in terms of subjects. That can be a significant advantage. Admittedly, it's easier to write a play that's solely about an emotional interpersonal issue and there's little controversy about it being much harder to create a play that deals with large issues and to also give it that necessary emotional center. While writing this sort of "large" play may be harder, it's certainly worth all the creative effort it will require.

Writing What You Know

This is the classic advice given by how-to books on writing. While there is some truth here, it's certainly possible – and often much more interesting – to imagine what you know.

Usually when playwrights "write what they know," the thing they know a lot about is only an undercurrent in the play. Michael Hollinger at one point in his life played the viola in a string quartet. That knowledge allowed him to present the inner workings of a quartet and its musicianship with sufficient realism in *Opus* to make us believe we were in the presence of a real string quartet.

But *Opus* is not about how to run a string quartet or how to play the viola. It's about Hollinger's much more interesting inventions of interpersonal relationships between this group of musicians. That's why the play has been widely produced despite its technical hurdles (the performers need to convincingly fake playing their instruments) and is under development in 2011 for a film version.

Doing Research

If you don't think you know anything worth turning into a play, odds are you're wrong. If you're still convinced of that, doing research into a potential subject is a good way to start. What you research becomes what you know.

A playwright wanting to write about a doctor struggling with a cancer patient, could spend a lot of time on medical Web sites and then see if someone they know is a friend of an oncologist, an internal medicine physician, or an oncology nurse who's willing to spend an hour or so talking about what they do. There's nothing like face-to-face conversations to sketch out at least part of the basis for a character.

Most contemporary plays are not founded on research (the exception being plays based on historical figures or events). This is notably different from the world of fiction where novelists – whether they're the literary or mass-market sort – often do research to support the stories they tell. The bottom line: If you have ideas for characters and plots, research doesn't necessarily need to be on your agenda.

While research seems like it must always be good to do, be open to the possibility that the idea you've been exploring may become a bore. If you're bored by a story idea, audiences in the theatre are guaranteed to be bored no matter how much research lies behind the play.

Plays may reflect the truth of life unfiltered by the restrictions of commercial film and television, but they have a very selective lens through which that truth passes. Plays in production last anywhere from 90 minutes (the typical minimum) to three hours, but the stories they tell – with rare exceptions – cover a much longer time period, often measured in days or years. So reducing or distilling the "truth" of life into a play will leave a huge pile of discards on the floor around your computer.

3. USES OF TRUTH & REAL LIFE

*A friend asked, had I heard about the French diplomat who'd fallen
in love with a Chinese actress, who subsequently turned out to be
not only a spy, but a man? I later found a two-paragraph story in
The New York Times. I suspected there was a play here. I
purposely refrained from further research, for I was not interested
in writing docudrama. Frankly, I didn't want the truth to interfere
with my own speculations.*
          -David Henry Hwang

Being faithful to actual events – the "truth" – has little to
recommend it for a playwright.

The truth of playwriting is found in the nature of the
characters you create and the process of the conflict that drives
them.

Playwrights are notorious for bending real life to suit
dramatic ends. Even those who concentrate on docudrama arrange
the material to create a dramatic structure capable of holding an
audience and for good reason.

The most extreme version of not doing this in the wild days
of the last century was an unemployed actor and his wife who
moved out of their apartment and onto the stage of a small New
York theatre with all their furniture, belongings, and an as yet to be
housebroken puppy. You could come in at any hour, day or night
and watch them live their normal lives in front of anyone who'd
buy a ticket. The critics found all this a tremendous bore except for
the fact that the dog wasn't housebroken. This, they said, brought
the only conflict to the hours they spent with these folks.

Docudrama

Docudrama is as close as the theatre usually gets to truth-as-it-
happened. (There's some minor resemblance to reality television in
docudrama, not that this sort of television fare is a good model for
anything in the theatre.)

The key to docudrama or the documentary play is finding
an event or a life that culminates in a natural climax. The creators of

the most successful of these documentary ventures arrange their slices of life to approximate the structure of a traditional play. What ends up on stage may be an accurate recording of real events, but it has the structure of theatrical fiction.

Here are a group of playwrights who have turned documented life into theatre in ways that work for audiences (note that each deals with the consequences of events).

Model Docudramas

Numbers 2-5 below have had a notable impact on the theatrical documentary – the first is intriguing and a first-rate model, though too recent to gauge its long term influence on the genre.

1. *Aftermath.* Jessica Blank and Erik Jensen's play is based on transcripts of their interviews with Iraqi refugees roughly seven years after the U.S. war began. By their own estimate, about 95% of the dialogue is taken directly from their transcripts. Most of the remainder is given to the only composite character (the translator) who leads us as a kind of narrator among the real people whose stories we hear.

2. *Execution of Justice.* Emily Mann's play is based on recorded interviews and the transcript of the trial of Dan White, the assassin of the Mayor of San Francisco, whose attorney successfully mounted the infamous "Twinkie" defense – White was claimed to have become mentally unbalanced from a diet consisting primarily of Twinkies).

3. *In the Matter of J. Robert Oppenheimer.* Peter Weiss' play is based on the transcripts of the hearings that eventually stripped the famous physicist of his U.S. security clearance because of political suspicions raised by his opposition to development of the H-Bomb.

4. *A Few Good Men.* Aaron Sorkin's play is based on transcripts of a near-miscarriage of military justice in a murder trial stemming from events at the U. S. base in Guantanamo Bay.

5. *Fires in the Mirror: Crown Heights, Brooklyn, and Other Identities.* Anna Deavere Smith's landmark play is based on recorded interviews with participants and others impacted by an African American fatality caused by a Rabbi's car and

the investigation that followed. It won the Pulitzer Prize for Drama.

Anna Deavere Smith's creative insight was to base all of the dialogue on her own interviews of those associated with this wrenching event and to then perform all of the "characters" herself. Fires and other plays she has created using this technique led to her winning the $500,000 MacArthur "Genius" Award.

> **Best Practice:** *Write your passion rather than what you think will be liked.*

Follow your passion, even if it feels like you're out of step with what's typical in the theatre today. That was the case when Smith first began developing her technique. The approach she essentially invented has staying power. Many years later, Sarah Jones won Broadway's Tony Award in 2006 with her one-person play *Bridge and Tunnel* using a variant of the technique.

In each of these docudramas, the words of "ordinary people" have a power that comes from the playwright's fidelity to what they actually said and in some cases their physicality in saying it.

4. USING THE WORK OF OTHER WRITERS

You don't have to be faithful to the facts. History has to be faithful to the facts. Drama has to be faithful to the spirit of the facts.
-Milos Forman

There's a claim floating around for more years than are worth counting that there are only 10 basic plots in the world. Don't bet on it.

If you reduce the subjects of most plays or films to their most basic elements, whoever started this rumor probably has a point. If you boil the life out of *Oedipus the King* and end up with "Somebody unintentionally hurts their family" or even more specifically, "A son inadvertently kills his father," there is a long line of writers who've used this subject, and it can be your turn next.

As a general rule, copyright protection does not extend to the barest bones of a story, but the narrative and dialogue writers use to develop their original versions of these stories is protected.

You can't run off to your keyboard with a brainstorm of an orphaned farm boy named Luke Skywalker who gets involved with a princess from another planet and dukes it out with an Arnold Schwarzenegger lookalike whose friends call him Darth. What you can do is a play about a teenager who comes of age by overcoming terrifying odds only to discover his nemesis is his father. Neither you nor George Lucas can get a copyright on that. It's not much of secret that bits and pieces of images from Frank Herbert's *Dune* trilogy float around in the first *Star Wars* films, but in doing this "borrowing" Lucas and his screenwriter were simply operating in a long and approved tradition of appropriation going all the way back in an unbroken chain to Shakespeare and the Ancient Greeks.

The appropriation that contemporary playwrights do is in most cases not a consciously planned borrowing. The stories, characters, and situations from 2,500 years of dramatic writing are "in the air" and filter into contemporary usage though a process of influence that nearly always disguises the source beyond easy recognition.

But there is a far more direct way for playwrights to borrow involving older plays and novels (with some risk): Adaptation.

5. ADAPTING OLDER PLAYS & NOVELS

*Adaptation for me was a way to learn the long form of playwriting.
There might be either foolhardiness or arrogance involved in some
of this, but just to think: Oh wow, you can put your tools on the
same table with that person's cool stuff.*
    -Lynn Manning

A number of American playwrights have turned occasionally to
adapting classic or barely known plays and novels for
contemporary audiences, Tony Kushner and David Ives among
them.

If you're new to the world of dramatic writing, think of
adaptations as a good way to learn the craft. Tony Kushner lived off
the royalties from one of his adaptations until he finished his
landmark play, *Angels in America*.

Against Adaptation
Spending the time to do an adaptation is rarely a practical way to
launch a playwriting career.

**1. Theatres commission adaptations from playwrights they
know.** And if they don't know them, they turn to
playwrights who've begun to have productions of their own
plays. Theatres that accept unsolicited submissions of plays
from unproduced playwrights seldom accept adaptations.
They want to see original work.

2. Most new play competitions won't accept adaptations.
This may be short-sighted on their part, but when you do an
adaptation the result is always a combination of your work
and that of the original dramatist. To be blunt, it's hard to
tell if you've got what it takes or if you're just skating on ice
provided by the original author.

Despite all this (and if you still want to be rash) find an old play –
preferably one first written in a language other than English by a
playwright who's not a household word in the U.S. It does help if
they're a household word or at least of some historical significance

where they came from.

As with adaptations of novels, try to find a play published well before 1900 so the odds will be in your favor of it being in the public domain. That means you might not have to struggle with getting the rights to do this.

David Ives took this approach for his very successful adaptation, *Venus in Fur* (it opened on Broadway in 2011 following its regional theatre premiere). His adaptation is based on an obscure Austrian novel, *Venus in Furs*, first published in 1870. Note the slight change in Ives' title from the original, a typical approach to titling adaptations.

The novel has a 2006 English translation from the original German so while the source was likely in the pubic domain, the translators would have copyright protection for their English language version. A playwright fluent in German could base an adaptation like this on the public domain original and avoid the copyright issue with the recent translation. For that to work, a playwright would need to fastidiously avoid any use of the English translation – the safest approach being never to have read it – and not even to imply that you could have read it by using it for something as innocuous as a coaster for your coffee mug.

Even in this seemingly open-and-shut case of an 1870 Austrian novel, it would be good to seek the advice of an attorney specializing in this field, since Austrian copyright law could also come into play. Do playwrights usually follow this cautious advice? Rarely.

Nobody will give you the rights to a stage adaptation of an older play or novel if you've never had a successful production at a regional theatre, unless of course, you're a successful novelist.

There is a way around this, one that Jeffrey Hatcher took with his 2011 play, *Ten Chimneys* – the title comes from the name of the estate of Alfred Lunt and Lynn Fontaine, the great American actors who are the central characters. The characters are all there to rehearse Chekhov's *The Seagull* and the story in the present begins to mirror the play Chekhov wrote.

Theatres would likely be open to this kind of clever approach from a new playwright since it's not simply an adaptation of an older play. Again, a caution: Hatcher was a produced playwright and screenwriter before he took on America's most famous acting couple and one of Chekhov's greatest plays.

Legal Cautions

When you're involved in adaptations of works under copyright – or that were under copyright in the past – confer with an attorney who specializes in entertainment and copyright law to make sure you won't end up in legal boiling oil.

Remember that a more recent English translation of an older play or novel may still be protected by copyright even if the original work was published centuries earlier and is not itself protected. You don't want to do all that work of creating an adaptation only to discover that you can't get the rights or, if they're nice enough to offer the rights, that you can't afford the cost.

The rights to literary work have monetary value, whether for film, television, or theatrical adaptation. As a playwright, you'll own those rights for your own plays and you won't want other writers poaching off your work without asking (or paying) for the privilege.

Best Practice: *Treat other writers as you'd like to be treated.*

Keys to Adapting Older Plays

The great English director Peter Brook said, "If you just let a play speak, it may not make a sound." The goal of a good adaptation of an old play is to make it speak to contemporary audiences. That's usually what makes a contemporary adaptation work in the theatre.

1. Create the dialogue using your own voice. The prime reason the play needs to be adapted is usually because the original playwright's language now falls flat on our ears. It may also be so removed from our contemporary practice of speaking that it would be incomprehensible to most members of an audience.

2. Find a play with a theme that resonates now. Ideally a theme that is close to what you want to write about in your own work.

3. Reduce the number of characters. Older plays from the 19th Century and earlier (as with most novels) usually have many more characters than today's playwrights keep in their heads. There are contemporary playwrights who create work with large numbers of characters, but you'll stack the odds against your play if the number of characters requires more than about ten performers to play them all.

4. Reduce the length of the play. Playwrights in the good old days took audiences for very long rides, but nowadays audiences like to get home by a reasonable hour so something in the range of 90 minutes to two hours in addition to intermissions is good. That said, there have been a few critically acclaimed and (audience loved) adaptations that have run as long as eight hours or more.

Best Practice: *In playwriting, most rules are made to be broken.*

The "Suggested By" Approach

Making a play speak to contemporary audiences was the initial impetus for Lynn Nottage's very loose mirroring of Bertolt Brecht's masterpiece, *Mother Courage and Her Children* in 2008. She borrowed only a few bones of plot and characters from the original, moved the setting from Europe during the Thirty Years War to the contemporary ravages of war on Congolese women, and titled it *Ruined*.

One of the bones she borrowed: Brecht's incorporation of music and song. And the biggest bone she threw out: Brecht's interest in keeping his audience emotionally uninvolved. Her changes are so significant that "adaptation" is not a description of her real process.

Nottage was recognized as a major playwriting talent well before she took on this daunting project and she was commissioned to create the play by one of America's leading regional theatres. She is not alone in this "suggested by" approach.

Bruce Norris did this with *Clybourne Park*, winning the 2011 Pulitzer Prize for Drama with a play prompted by Lorraine Hansberry's classic, *A Raisin in the Sun* which had won the Tony Award for Best Play in 1960. He set Act I in 1959, the year of Hansberry's play, borrows a character with the same name who in both plays attempts to prevent an African American family from buying a house in a "white" neighborhood. But while the situation and a character is borrowed, all else is Norris' invention. His point of view in Act I is the white family selling their house in the same neighborhood rather than the black family buying it. And he moves the time of Act II from 1959 to the present with a white family attempting to move into the same house, now in a gentrifying

African American neighborhood. (The title is taken from the name of the white neighborhood in Hansberry's play.)

Like Nottage, Norris had established his playwriting credentials before he ventured into his mirroring of Hansberry's classic.

If adapting other people's plays or novels seems of less interest now, there's always the option of using other people's lives. You may sense the red flag of risk already.

6. USING OTHER PEOPLE'S LIVES

*The play is my contribution to piercing the silence around
Armenian history. There was so much anguish and pain attached
to this history. I decided that my play would be like a boat that had
to ride the river of those tears until I got docked somewhere and
had the proper writer's perspective.*
      -Leslie Ayvazian

Thinking about people you know – or wish you knew – can be a
good way to develop characters and subjects for plays.

When selecting a real person to be a central character in your
play, it helps if their life has followed a dramatic arc. Is there some
major event that was the capstone of their lives? If they led a
relatively ordinary (even if somewhat interesting) life, it will be
difficult to structure a full-length play around them that will work
in production. If their life had no climax, you'll be hard-pressed to
come up with a convincing ending to the play.

Legal Cautions

What follows here on the right of privacy and right of publicity
represents a conservative approach to these legal issues, one that
most playwrights ignore. From a practical standpoint, they're
probably right to do so. The possibility of an aggrieved party being
able to argue successfully that the production of a play besmirched
their good name or harmed them financially is unlikely. There
simply aren't enough people going to see even the most successful
play (musicals excepted) to have a significant impact – negative or
positive – on public or private personalities. (Screenplays are an
entirely different matter.)

This should not be taken to mean that if you annoy someone
sufficiently by how they're portrayed that they won't go after you
out of spite. Even if they have little hope of prevailing in court, they
can still cause you an immense amount of grief.

If you're determined to use real people either living or dead
less than a 100 years as actual characters in a play, see a lawyer,
preferably one who specializes in this kind of law. Nobody needs

legal entanglements complicating their writing lives.

If you're thinking of basing a play on private individuals – anyone who's not a "household name" reasonably well known through media coverage – the legal doctrine of Right of Privacy may apply. This literally means they have the right to protect their privacy and you'll be flying in the face of that if you make them an identifiable character in a play without first getting their permission to do it.

In 2011, this issue was demonstrated with accompanying national notice as a result of legal action brought against the author of *The Help*, the highly successful novel and its subsequent film adaptation. The claimant was the long-time maid of the author's brother and alleged that she was used as the model for a central character without the author having asked permission to do so. The case was dismissed – don't be emboldened by that – because the maid filed her claim after the one-year statute of limitations had expired.

For well-known public personalities, the legal doctrine of Right of Publicity may apply. This means they may have the right to control exploitation of themselves, especially for financial gain. Exploiting them is really what you're doing when you create an identifiable character from a well known figure.

Both of these legal issues become particularly important if you intend to shine a highly unfavorable light on either public or private individuals. If you're writing a love letter to them – or at least a balanced letter – you may be able to get them or their estates to bless your plans, or at least leave you alone if the play is a success. But don't count on it.

Recreating Actual People

Basing characters on real people runs through at least three options, each with its own pitfalls.

Anna Deavere Smith uses the actual words, gestures, and speech patterns of the "ordinary" and famous people she's interviewed for her plays, but she gets their permission to recreate them in her scripts. If you try this approach, it's likely that most people (especially if you know them) would think it's a lark to be put on the stage without actually having to be there in person. If you don't know them and this is to be your first play, you'll either have to be a marvelous bluffer or wait until you've had some success as a playwright.

Creating Versions of Public Figures

Tony Kushner used a version of the well known (and some would say, infamous) attorney Roy Cohn as a character in *Angels in America*.

Public figures – people like Cohn who were or are widely talked about in the news media – are generally fair game for playwrights. It helps if they're dead. If your version of one of these figures is distinctly unflattering – as Kushner's was – it's a good idea to add a disclaimer in the preliminary pages of your script. This won't necessarily keep the lawyers away from your doorstep, but it may help.

Here's how Tony Kushner handled this in his script for *Angels in America*:

> DISCLAIMER: Roy M. Cohn, the character, is based on the late Roy M. Cohn (1927-1986), who was all too real; for the most part the acts attributed to the character Roy, such as his illegal conferences with Judge Kaufmann during the trial of Ethel Rosenberg, are to be found in the historical record. But this Roy is a work of dramatic fiction; his words are my invention, and liberties have been taken.

While Roy Cohn (the character) was important in *Angels in America*, he was not the central focus of the play. A real person can be the central character and usually is for a good reason. If you're going to wrestle with all the rights issues that may be involved in using real people, it usually doesn't make sense to put them in service as a minor character.

There's a fascination to using real people as characters. From a PR standpoint, you may attract a lot of attention – separate from the merits of the play – from potential audiences who seldom go to the theatre, but know of the person you're presenting and will buy tickets for that reason alone.

Recent "Icon" Characters

That added lure of celebrities works best by using an icon as a character, preferably one who's life and work has created either a large following or at least an image of historical significance.

1. David Auburn's *The Columnist*. Scheduled to premiere in

New York in 2012. His play focuses on the famous mid-century American journalist Joseph Alsop and the attempt by Soviet agents to set him up for blackmail. Auburn established his playwriting credentials with the acclaimed play Proof as well as screenplays focused on fictional characters before taking on the very real Joseph Alsop.

2. John Logan's *Red*. Focusing on the great mid-century American painter, Mark Rothko. Like Auburn, Logan established his credentials first with produced plays and screenplays before taking on Rothko as a character. The resulting script was the winner of the 2010 Tony Award for Best Play on Broadway.

Getting Back at Your Parents

As Edward Albee did in one of his first plays, *The American Dream*, though he was later dismayed that people thought his theatrical version of his mother was intriguing rather than the negative portrait he intended.

It's a well-worn cliché that writers are known for miserable childhoods, but this last approach raises some tricky liability issues – issues that most playwrights who draw on their families for character inspiration ignore. As elsewhere in the *Handbook*, what follows here is a very conservative reading of these legal issues.

Technically, you can't expose your mother or old Uncle Joe to ridicule in your play in a way that would allow others to recognize them – and as a result think poorly of them – without putting yourself at some legal risk. No matter how much you hate them and regardless of how nasty they were to you, people who are not public figures may have a right to maintain their privacy, even from a playwright in the family. (Tracy Letts partially modeled the vicious matriarch in *August: Osage County* on his grandmother, but after seeing the play his mother concluded he was nice to her in his portrayal.) The same right of privacy is also true for your next-door neighbor or your roommate at school.

Accomplished playwrights and screenwriters agree on at least one thing: If they use autobiography as a source, they typically disguise the remnants to such an extent that only they can recognize the sources in the final draft of the script.

If you're still determined to take on the parents, consider writing a tell-all memoir instead. Book publishers have an insatiable appetite for nonfiction memoirs marked by family misery. Regional theatres and commercial theatrical producers seem (so far) not to share that interest.

Of course, if you want to make your play a love letter to Aunt Minnie you probably don't have to worry about whether she'll call her lawyer, but it doesn't hurt to ask before you write.

If this is your first venture into playwriting, you'll have enough craft issues to keep in mind without having to deal with lawyers. Go with an original fictional or well-disguised batch of characters now. Once initial recognition has come, you can think about the possibility of using real people as characters.

If "borrowing" is still of interest, a lot of playwrights have done this with popular songs – they're much easier to borrow than people.

7. INCORPORATING POPULAR SONGS

The springboard for my work is an image – a theatrical image – that can give birth to an entire play. For Tongue of a Bird, the image was of a woman in a 1920's flight suit – leather jacket, helmet, goggles – hanging in the air. There's something sinister and inscrutable about it.
>   -Ellen McLaughlin

When playwrights use popular songs today, they quote only a small portion of the lyrics, usually not more than half a dozen lines.

Remember, you're not writing a musical, a wholly different dramatic form from the full-length play. The reason – separate from rights issues – that popular songs are not used in their entirety in plays is that it takes forever in stage time for a character to sing a basic pop song. Three minutes may seem like the blink of an eye on your iPod, but it will feel like three days in the theatre. Even if the singing and the band is well above average, the more serious problem this will cause is that the conflict driving the play will be forced to a halt and with it the audience's engagement.

As an aside, it's tough to find theatre performers (other than musical comedy stars) with the vocal chops to take on a whole pop song at a level that competes well with the original singer. Great acting ability and great singing ability are not necessarily two sides of the same performer, at least outside of musical comedy. Even if they can do it well, the audience may spend those three minutes comparing their singing to that of the original pop star rather than focusing on the story you're telling. That's a distraction you don't want to encourage.

Ways of Using Popular Songs

Selections from pop tunes can add an intriguing thematic feel to a play or simply offer practical information – with many options in that range.

1. Allowing characters to speak their subtext. And do it without making us cringe. Musicals do this with great abandon. This is what Wendy Wasserstein did for the end of

Act I of *The Sisters Rosensweig*. She has one of her characters sing four lines of Frank Sinatra's old hit, "Just the Way You Look Tonight."

2. Providing an ironic comment. Especially in relation to the character singing a few telling lines of the song. A variant of this is David Henry Hwang having his lead character in *M. Butterfly* describe the plot of Puccini's *Madame Butterfly* as we hear a collage of arias from the opera. All of which helps establish for the audience how much the diplomat has been blinded – unknowingly of course – by Western stereotypes of Asian culture and Asian women in particular.

3. Establishing an attitude toward the theme. Particularly at the beginning of acts or scenes. When songs are used for this at the opening of the play, a recording is used rather than having one of your characters sing it. Edward Albee goes to the opposite end of this approach in *Who's Afraid of Virginia Woolf*. He has George sing a few lines of the old children's tune, "Who's Afraid of the Big Bad Wolf," as part of the resolution of the play, substituting the name of the experimental British novelist Virginia Woolf for the critter with all the fur and teeth. The reference to the novelist, though obscure, relates to Albee's theme of the need to cut through the veneer of what appears to be reality to the genuine reality beneath that surface of people's lives.

4. Indicating the time period of the play. For this to work, the words to the tune or its musical style need to be well enough known for audiences to get what you're trying to tell them. Charles Fuller does this at the beginning of *A Soldier's Play* by using the Andrews Sisters' hit tune of the 1940's, "Don't Sit under the Apple Tree," a song from the era of the play's main action. Its bouncy up-tempo also creates a strong contrast with the murder that suddenly happens as it's playing.

5. Helping create the mood and emotion of a scene. This is one of the many devices film borrowed from the theatre a century ago and it's still used occasionally by contemporary playwrights. Tennessee Williams incorporated the blues tune, "I Just Can't Stay Here by Myself" in the so-called

"Broadway" Act III of *Cat on a Hot Tin Roof* to accentuate the lull in tension just before the climax of the play. He may have gotten the idea from Shakespeare who had Desdemona sing the haunting "Willow Song" for the same purpose near the climax of *Othello*.

Permissions for Using Popular Songs

If your characters insist on breaking into song – and occasionally characters do take on a life of their own, insisting on doing things you'd rather not have them do – you'll need to get permission to use these tunes in your play.

Rudyard Kipling long ago captured what contemporary playwrights fervently wish the legal situation here to be (I've paraphrased a bit):

> *When Homer smote his bloomin' lyre,*
> *He'd heard men sing by land and sea;*
> *And what he thought he might require,*
> *He went and took – the same as me.*

The Ancient Greeks may have invented a lot of things with or without help from the Egyptians, but one of them was not our modern approach to copyright protection for the lyrics and music of popular songs. While Homer could swipe whatever he wanted, he's not a great role model for contemporary playwrights.

There's no problem if you're snatching the "Willow Song" from *Othello*. But if it's a tune you've heard on the radio (or your grandparents could have heard out of their old AM set), taking without asking is not in order.

The songs that feed Tin Pan Alley and its equivalent nearly anywhere else in the world are protected property. That goes for the lyrics of a song as well as the music, even if you only want to use a line or two. The exception is folk tunes passed from generation to generation, though that means you can only use the original tune and words, not for example, the contemporary Carolina Chocolate Drops' version of it.

When playwrights use lyrics of popular songs in the first drafts of their plays, they are obligated to get the rights to do so before duplicating the script. Do most of them do this? No. Should they – and you? Yes.

For better or worse, it seems like the common practice is to wait to jump through these rights tangles until a theatre commits to taking on the play. The downside of waiting to get the rights – especially if you feel the song you've used is crucial to the play – is that when you're ready for production, the owners of the rights may not agree to grant permission to use the song.

It goes without saying that getting the rights to use popular songs in a play will in most cases cost you or the producing theatre money. On the positive side, getting these permissions is usually a fairly simple affair, and you owe the song writers the same favor you'd like from others about your own work.

If you want to avoid the whole ethical issue, don't quote the lyrics in your script at all. Just say in a general stage direction something like: (Julie sings the opening lines of Dylan's "Like a Rolling Stone.").

When you do need permissions, you can find out who to contact if they're penned by U.S. tunesmiths from ASCAP, the American Society of Composers, Authors and Publishers. (www.ascap.com).

There's enough of a hoop to jump through in borrowing a song that playwrights don't do this lightly. There needs to be a compelling reason to borrow anything, and that compulsion (at least for playwrights) can usually be traced back to a play's theme.

8. THEMES: MEANING IN CONTENT

One theme I trace through all my work is this kind of fluidity of identity. In a lot of my plays, people become other people. It has a lot to do with the nature vs. nurture question. To what degree do you have an inherited identity, and to what degree is your personality shaped by the influences and environment around you? This question is intimately related to my own desire to know myself.

        -David Henry Hwang

Plays nearly always tend to be about something that matters.

Screenplays have the luxury – assuming you want that – of only needing to be about what-happens-next (for more on this issue see Part Six on Screenwriting). But plays need this something of consequence. Being about something that matters guarantees that a play comes with a theme.

Themes develop from a playwright's personal values (moral, social, or political) expressed through a play's plot and characters. In a sense, the theme is your moral or ethical position about the story you're telling.

Integrating Your Personal Values

Playwrights don't often think consciously about their themes as they write. Their personal values tend to be so integrated into how they see the world that their themes flow into each play as the dialogue goes on the page. That's why the same theme often shows up in a writer's work from one play to the next.

If you're new to dramatic writing, spend some time thinking about what matters to you socially, politically, and ethically as you look at the world and the people around you. Write about this in your journal as a way of clarifying your thinking.

    Best Practice: *What matters deeply to you will matter to your audience.*

Some Intriguing Themes

A sampling from plays currently in the seasons of regional theatres, ranging from an American classic to recent premieres.

1. David Henry Hwang's *M. Butterfly*. Believing in racial stereotypes will blind you to reality.

2. Wendy Wasserstein's *The Heidi Chronicles*. A heavy price was paid by women who were the professional career path-makers and breakers of the 1970's.

3. Beth Henley's *Crimes of the Heart*. It's a crime not to follow your heart's desires.

4. Tennessee Williams' *Cat on a Hot Tin Roof*. Overly sensitive people are crippled by the lies of the world we live in.

5. Michael Hollinger's *Opus*. Staying together emotionally is even harder than playing together harmoniously.

6. Tracy Letts' *August: Osage County*. Parents who can't release their children create havoc in their lives.

Most playwrights express their themes with considerable subtlety. That's the difference between having a theme and a message. If your primary goal is get across a message, there are probably more effective ways of doing that than writing a play, though one of the attractions of docudramas is that they can carry a significant message with ease.

Cautions on Writing from a Theme
Nearly all contemporary playwrights would say it's a fool's errand to try writing a play driven consciously by a predetermined theme or message. But it can be tempting to try.

Doing this seems especially intriguing since it can be argued that Shakespeare did it with his political tragedies (*Hamlet* and *Macbeth* among them) and his history plays, probably to help support the monarchy that allowed his theatre company to operate. If the Bard could make this work, why not try?

The poster-boy for why this practically never works is the German playwright Bertolt Brecht, one of the major dramatists of the 20th century. He tried writing from a theme in most of his great plays including his masterpieces, *Mother Courage and Her Children* and *Galileo*. One of the liabilities he had in attempting this was the misfortune to create such compelling characters that they obscured his intended messages, but those characters were only part of the problem.

The main obstacle for Brecht (and contemporary playwrights) is that a playwright's real themes – those deeply held and integrated personal values – always end up being infused into the play whether they want them there or not. As those values enter the play, they overwhelm and finally bury any consciously intended themes. Brecht's overriding personal values – the way he lived his entire life – centered on a belief that wily survival skills were essential in the world. It's no surprise that his major plays have title characters incorporating that same belief toward living and survival.

In *Mother Courage*, he wanted us to take away the message that the title character was a stupid (his word) woman who never learned that the loss of her children and her own near ruin was being caused by her pursuit of capitalist ideas. That intended theme was overwhelmed for audiences by Brecht's internalized theme: They always saw Mother Courage as a wily survivor fighting to make it against nearly impossible odds. Instead of seeing her as stupid, audiences always saw her as worthy of admiration. Despite reworking the ending of Mother Courage in subsequent years to make his intended theme clearer for audiences, he could never get it to break through his internalized theme.

Best Practice: *For messages to work in plays, they need to coincide with your deeply held values.*

A second danger in writing from a theme is that it can lead to unconsciously manipulating characters and plots to make the point rather than allowing the conflict between the characters to logically drive the play. The artificiality that nearly always results from this risks turning off audiences, primarily because the logic of the play's climax and resolution won't make sense to them.

The best approach with themes is to allow them to flow naturally into the play as you write. Since it is nearly impossible to prevent your personal values from flowing into a play (if you take your characters seriously) it makes sense to just let this process happen.

If you're uncomfortable simply leaving this to trust and the greater forces of playwriting, then it may be time to employ an authorial spokesperson.

9. USING AUTHORIAL SPOKESPERSONS

The great advantage of being a writer is that you can spy on people. You're there, listening to every word, but part of you is observing. Everything is useful to a writer, you see -- every scrap, even the longest and most boring of luncheon parties.
        -Graham Greene

When the theme is really important and there's serious doubt that audiences will get it, playwrights usually turn to an authorial spokesperson.

"Attention, attention must be finally paid to such a person," Linda tells her sons in *Death of a Salesman* after her husband Willy has veered dangerously close to what audiences may think is the jerk of all time.

That's the function of an authorial spokesperson: Telling us the theme if you think we'll miss it or – as in the case of Miller and *Death of a Salesman* – come to the opposite conclusion. It's also true that audiences can often be more perceptive on this score than playwrights sometimes think.

If the theme is complicated – or not part of the currency of the nation's moral landscape – and you wonder more than a few times while writing if the audience will really understand it, you may need the help of a spokesperson.

Candidates for Spokesperson

Generally, playwrights don't use a minor character as a spokesperson because it's important for the audience to "know" the spokesperson. That knowing comes from the character being given a reasonable amount of stage time and in turn that makes us willing to believe what the character tells us about the meaning of the play.

1. The central character. Though often the central character doesn't really "understand" the theme and – if it's not a comedy – this is often why they come to grief. If you use the central character for this role, they either need to get the theme from the beginning or, even better, have a moment of realization later in the play.

2. The narrator of the story. Narrators usually open and close a play by introducing us to the situation or characters at the beginning and summing up the theme as the authorial spokesperson during the resolution. That may be all you need a spokesperson to do, but nearly all playwrights who use a narrator as a play's bookends, doubling as authorial spokesperson, also bring them back periodically to talk with us as the story progresses. (See Chapter 23 on Narrators.)

3. A significant secondary character. Secondary characters as authorial spokespersons don't need to speak directly to the audience. Linda does a fine job making Arthur Miller's theme clear to the audience by giving her sons hell for looking down on their father.

Michael Hollinger demonstrates one of the more subtle combinations of direct address to the audience by a central character at the end of *Opus*. The character, now an authorial spokesperson, tells us about a vision he has and – assuming we understand the vision – that leads us to understand the play's theme. Hollinger begins the play having all four members of the string quartet (the four major characters) lined up across the stage speaking to us in alternating lines that gradually come together, giving us a hint of the theme.

There are times when this sort of approach is too oblique for the nature of the theme and direct address to the audience may be the only way to be sure we'll understand it. Charles Fuller took this approach in *A Soldier's Play* which on the surface comes across as a gripping murder mystery. Davenport, the narrator and one of the central characters, tells us in his final monologue that the conflict we've just seen was a result of "the madness of race in America." He tells us this so we won't go home thinking it was only a grand murder mystery we've been watching – which it also happens to be.

10. TITLES: DESCRIPTIVE & METAPHORIC

Some people were quite shocked by the fact that there was no nudity, no swearing, no sex in Bedroom Farce. The joke I wanted was: Let's write a play about three bedrooms, and the first thing you expect to happen in that bedroom never happens.
                    -Alan Ayckbourn

Script format (see Part Four) may be the first message literary managers get about the professionalism of a dramatist, but the title is the first message you send them about the worth of the play and its content – and also your voice as a playwright.

The best titles often come as flashes of insight in the process of writing or even before you put that opening stage direction on page I-1. When a title really catches fire, it's often an intuitive response to the play you're creating.

Titles come in two basic flavors, either descriptive or metaphoric. Most playwrights opt for the metaphoric kind because of the added messages they can send through them to readers and audiences, but a good descriptive title can still carry a lot of interest.

Dangers of Descriptive Titles
The downside of descriptive titles is that they can be a bore, lacking any additional resonance. They're the kind of thing much of commercial television still thrives on. TV audiences like to know what they're getting before they get it, and who can blame them given the huge number of options pouring out of their cable systems.

Obvious & Intriguing Descriptive Titles
As always, most rules are meant to be broken in this game of dramatic writing and some great classics of the theatre have used descriptive titles.

1. *The Tragedy of Hamlet, Prince of Denmark.* Bad things happen to this Danish prince. No mystery about that.

2. *Death of A Salesman.* A salesman dies. But it's still a

grand and powerful play over six decades later. And there is a metaphoric meaning lurking beneath what seems to be pure description: The questioning of America's belief in selling yourself as the ticket to success.

3. *The Persecution and Assassination of Jean Paul Marat Portrayed by the Acting Company of the Asylum at Charenton Under the Direction of Mr. de Sade.* Still the ultimate descriptive title in the Western theatre. It's a great, crazy, brilliant play by Peter Weiss, even though you'd never need to see it to know what happens. It won Broadway's Tony Award for Best Play.

4. *Other Desert Cities.* Partly a hybrid title from Jon Robin Baitz, capturing the description of the play's Palm Springs setting, but also a glancing metaphoric reference to the relationships among the family members.

5. *August: Osage County.* An absolutely descriptive title of the time and place of Tracy Letts' Pulitzer Prize winning play. But it has a great sound.

Advantages of Metaphoric Titles

Metaphoric titles have excitement built into them. They resonate through symbolism, double meanings, and general cleverness, what a play might be about and often focus on the play's theme. Most playwrights prefer these over their descriptive cousins.

That's why it takes a bit of work to find examples of those straightforward descriptive titles in the contemporary theatre. Partly this is because theatre audiences seem to have a great tolerance for ambiguity and symbolism in their dramatic fare.

Inspired Metaphoric Titles

Each of these titles has a resonance with the story of the play and its theme, encouraging us to think about issues beyond the script itself.

1. *Death and the Maiden.* Ariel Dorfman's brilliant examination of a political torture victim's chance for vengeance uses as its title a piece of music critical to the play's action: Franz Shubert's string quartet, "Death and the Maiden." The victim is a woman who finally gets to decide if death is the vengeance she'll deliver to the man who may

have been her torturer many years ago. It won London's Olivier Award for Best New Play.

2. *The Mountaintop*. Katori Hall's intriguing play about the last night of Martin Luther King Jr.'s life, set at the Lorraine Motel in Memphis on April 3, 1968. If we didn't know the subject of the play, the title is unassuming. But once we connect it to the central character, the metaphor gains considerable power: It's from the famous sentence King used in his last civil rights speech earlier that evening in Memphis ("Because I have been to the mountaintop."). And the title's metaphoric meanings multiply as we read the script or see the play in production. It won London's Olivier Award for Best New Play.

3. *Crimes of the Heart*. Beth Henley's comedy about three alienated sisters learning to be supportive of each other uses a play-on-words, or rather a play-on-a-cliché (a crime of passion). And there is an actual crime at the heart of the play, though it's more a crime of dis-passion. We also discover all three sisters have committed crimes of the heart by ignoring their emotional desires. It won the Pulitzer Prize for Drama.

4. *As Is*. William Hoffman's wrenching comedy about a man who finally accepts his AIDS-afflicted companion as is – as they say on used car lots when there's no guarantee that comes with that heap of your dreams. It won the Drama Desk Award for Outstanding Play.

5. *'night, Mother*. That's *'night,* as in "Good night." Marsha Norman's portrait of a daughter's decision to commit suicide in her mother's home, a plan she does not keep secret for long. It went on to win the Pulitzer Prize for Drama.

6. *M. Butterfly*. David Henry Hwang's darkly humorous chronicle of a French diplomat who claims never to have realized in twenty years that his Chinese bride is a man, played against the plot of Puccini's opera, *Madame Butterfly*. His first version of the title was "Monsieur Butterfly," but his wife thought it was too obvious so he shortened it in the French style to "M. Butterfly" which he felt was "far more mysterious and ambiguous." That is, metaphoric. And it won Broadway's Tony Award for Best Play.

Hybrid Titles

Then there are those really good titles that seem not to fall comfortably into either category.

These hybrid titles work exceptionally well in drawing in audiences because they sound so good and curious to our ears, even if we don't know what they mean. Or more to the point, we may not know what these titles mean, but we want to find out.

Strong Hybrid Titles

Typically, hybrid titles combine both descriptive and metaphoric aspects of the play.

1. *Farragut North.* Beau Willimon's inspired title for his presidential campaign play is obscure to say the least unless you know the metro system in the nation's Capitol (it's a good stop for the folks who work DC's K Street lobbying firms). If you know what it is and where it is, it sends off a suggestion of the political sleaze lying at the center of the play's plot. For those who don't know DC, the playwright provides a glancing reference in the script to the title as a transit stop favored by political consultants. The stop is actually named for the captain of that Union Civil War ship who cried, "Damn the torpedoes, full speed ahead." If you push that metaphor into a pretzel, it captures a life-changing decision made by the main character at the climax of the play. George Clooney's subsequent film – a distant version, but with Willimon still involved as one of three screenwriters – changed the title to *The Ides of March*, a reference instead to the date Julius Caesar was assassinated in Ancient Rome (the logic of that new title is obscure, to say the least).

2. *The Fifth of July.* One of Lanford Wilson's most compelling plays, set well into the aftermath of the Vietnam War and the radical opposition to it. If he'd called it "The Fourth of July" (it takes place over that weekend), it wouldn't resonate with us because our American ears are so accustomed to hearing that phrase. Adding one day makes it

strange and intriguing.

3. *4000 Miles*. Amy Herzog's title captures both the journey a grandson makes across the country to visit his grandmother and the metaphoric distance initially between their generations and social and political attitudes. If she'd called it "3000 Miles," odds are we'd just take it to be a play about crossing the country since that number is associated so closely with the width of the United States. That extra thousand makes it sound odd – and interesting.

Because these hybrid titles sound so good and unusual to our ears, they create their own suspense. We want to know what they mean as we pick up a script or sit in the theatre waiting for the curtain to go up.

Using Act Titles

Giving a formal title to each act of a three-act play is a good way to focus your energies and intentions as you're writing each of these movements of the script (doing this informally for a two-act play may also be helpful).

Whether you use these titles purely for your own guidance as you write and then remove them from the final draft is up to you, but if they have been useful to you as a guide, odds are they will be helpful to your readers as well.

Notable Act Titles

In each of these three-act plays, the act titles telegraph what happens in each act, sometimes directly ("Exorcism") and sometimes metaphorically ("In Vitro").

1. In *Who's Afraid of Virginia Woolf*, Edward Albee's three acts are titled: I. Fun and Games – II. Walpurgesnacht – III. Exorcism

2. In *Three Hotels*, Jon Robin Baitz's three acts (each composed of a single long monologue) are titled: I. The Halt & The Lame – II. Be Careful – III. The Day of the Dead

3. In *Angels in America, Part I: Millennium Approaches*, Tony Kushner's three acts are titled: I. Bad News – II. In Vitro – III. Not-Yet-Conscious, Forward Dawning

Playwrights who work in three acts tend to use act titles while those who work in two acts seldom do. As with play titles, act titles are generally more effective – and useful to in writing – if they are metaphoric rather than purely descriptive.

If titles are the first thing literary managers see in a new script, the page they often turn to next is the list of characters.

11. CHARACTERS: IN MODERN DRAMA

I'll keep writing about the decreasing power of the individual and the increasing responsibility of the individual. I'm in pursuit of something, and it's a long-term notion.
    -Jon Robin Baitz

The major shift in character development that marks most interesting plays since the turn of the 20th century is buried in the question, *Where's the villain?*

In the kinds of new plays regional theatres do, you usually can't find a real villain to save your soul. But they are there – embedded in the central characters.

Clichés are deadly in the theatre, but in this case there's a lot of support for at least two of them to describe "modern" characters: "He's his own worst enemy" and "She's her own worst enemy." That's where the villain has gone.

The Internalized Villain
Technically, that's what is modern about modern drama: The internalized villain. There are many other issues that mark modern drama, but from the perspective of playwriting, this is the most critical one.

This kind of villain skulks within each character, or at least the central characters. That's Hedda, Stockman, Mrs. Alving and all the descendants from Henrik Ibsen's great characters.

At the transition to this new drama, sometimes even Ibsen couldn't resist using a real villain in addition to a modern central character, so he added Dr. Rank as Hedda's nemesis. Though in this case, Dr. Rank wouldn't have been successful as a villain if Hedda hadn't been her own worst enemy.

In the good old days of the 19th century when things were simpler for playwrights, a play's conflict nearly always hinged on a triangular relationship between three characters: The absolutely good Hero, the absolutely purely good Heroine, and the absolutely villainous Villain. Nobody had flaws. Nobody had doubts. And they all wore their subtexts on their sleeves.

With internalized villains, the hero and heroine are gone, replaced by those ordinary people who are their own worst enemies. This is partly what led David Mamet to say that good drama is "a depiction of a human interaction in which both antagonists are, arguably, in the right."

The internalized villain is what makes contemporary characters "complex." The complexity comes from these warring – or at least competing – traits within the central character. The current excitement about Scandinavian detective fiction is partly driven by the complexity of the detectives these crime writers have developed: Their internal demons (villains) often come close to preventing them from solving the cases they are investigating.

Impact on Endings

The internalization of the villain has a key impact on the endings of contemporary plays. The "Good" no longer have guarantees of living happily ever after while the "Bad" are no longer guaranteed to suffer as the curtain comes down. Or as Tom Stoppard said, "The bad end unhappily, the good unluckily."

These changes mean that audiences often leave the theatre thinking in deep ways about what they've seen, thoughts often prompted by the play's theme. But traditional villains haven't vanished. Like vampires and werewolves, they never die – they've just moved around the block to film and television. Most contemporary playwrights don't miss them.

12. CREATING & NAMING CHARACTERS

The character I'm creating is coming from me, has been nourished in whatever I am. And I would assume – I hope – there's a plethora of them, thousands of them in there. And I want them to be as totally whoever they are – as young men, or old men, or young girls, or whomever – as they can be.
              -Ntozake Shange

It doesn't matter if you're writing the gloomiest tragedy or the wackiest off-the-wall farce. Take your characters so seriously that part of you goes into each of them. Drop any character you can't do this with.

If you can't take your characters seriously, you'll end up making fun of them or creating little more than stick figures (this holds for comedies as well as serious plays). When that happens, subtext vanishes and the forward movement of the play feels like molasses on a cold day – and half the audience starts thinking about how much they're paying the babysitter.

Complex Characters & Internal Conflict

Taking characters seriously is also the only way to insure that you're developing complex characters, the kind contemporary plays thrive on. There's a key question to ask about central characters: What are the conflicting drives inside each of them?

Central characters without internal conflicts won't do well in contemporary plays. These traits do not need to be balanced and in equal competition. In fact, unbalanced and competing traits are often more effective. Eddie in *A View from the Bridge* wants desperately to protect his young niece from the dangers of the real world but he also – mostly unconsciously – is driven by an inappropriate love for her. Those competing traits (his love for her being the dominant one) lead to his doom. In a similar way, Steve in *Farragut North* mostly embraces the sleaziness of political campaign management, but a small part of him would still like to be a decent human being. That decency is a very small part of him – but it's enough of a trait to lead to his own professional doom.

Meaning in Character Names

The old days of Lydia Languish and Tom Trueheart wandering through plays are long gone when playwrights thought they always had to hang a character's subtext around their necks with a name. But despite the passage of centuries, remnants of this tradition persist in the contemporary theatre. That doesn't mean that all character names needs to be fraught with meaning today, at least based on how audiences may perceive them.

One of the most visible results of banishing villains to Hollywood is the approach of contemporary playwrights to character names where being subtle is the watchword. But enlightened as we like to think we are, character names still do carry meanings, even today – at least they do for many playwrights, even if you can't count on audiences always sharing those implications. Stereotypes in names still have power, even subtle ones coming only from the sounds of the names.

Think of renaming the central character of one of those action movies "Wendell" instead of the classic, "James Bond." As a fine demonstration of how odd this meaning in names subject is, Ian Fleming lifted the name of his famous spy from the American author of a field guide to birds, wanting, "the simplest, dullest, plainest-sounding name I could find."

Arthur Miller called his central character, the failing salesman, "Willy Loman" for a reason instead of a name like "Creed Lancer" and there aren't many spies or masked avengers called Elmer or Gladys in Hollywood films for the same reason, unless they're in comedies. On the surface, it makes no sense that Wendell couldn't be as effective as James in the secret agent business. If anyone ever did a study of the first names of CIA and MI5 agents, they would most likely find the same frequency of names inside those agencies as in the general population, but that tends not to be the case in film or theatre.

If in the good old days, playwrights painted a sign on characters with their names by drawing on a dominant trait, that's a bit obvious for the contemporary theatre.

But occasionally, obvious is good as in what Tennessee Williams did with character names in *Cat on a Hot Tin Roof*:

BRICK For the favorite son.

GOOPER For the "wimpy" un-favored son.

MARGARET (also called Maggie) For the strong sister-in-law married to Brick.

MAE For the weaker sister-in-law married to Gooper.

Note the sound of these names when spoken aloud: The strong (or seemingly strong) characters have hard and clipped sounds in their names while the weak characters are given soft and sliding sounds. The villain in Ibsen's *Hedda Gabler* is Dr. Rank with that hard "R" and even harsher "k" while Hedda's husband, the ineffectual Tesman, is given one of those sliding names. It's interesting that this naming tendency seems to cross language borders.

Contemporary Character Names

August Wilson said what many playwrights experience in developing characters and their names: "Someone says something to someone else, and they talk, and at some point I say, Well, who is this? and I give him a name. But I have no idea what the storyline of the play is." In most cases for contemporary playwrights, characters begin to form first and then their names come.

Most playwrights don't use the full name for designating a character in the dialogue pages of the script. Instead, they select either the first or last name either as a matter of habit or based on the one that seems to say more about the character. (Using only one name in the script also means fewer keys to pound as you write.)

Names from Well Known Playwrights

The selections these playwrights made for character name designations in the scripts are in all capitals.

1. From Charles Fuller: Richard DAVENPORT, Vernon C. WATERS, Tony SMALLS.

2. From David Henry Hwang: Rene GALLIMARD, MARC, Comrade CHIN, HELGA.

3. From Wendy Wasserstein: HEIDI Holland, PETER Patrone, SUSAN Johnston, SCOOP Rosenbaum.

4. From Tony Kushner: BELIZE, LOUIS Ironson, PRIOR Walter, ETHEL ROSENBERG.

5. From August Wilson: SETH Holly, ZONIA Loomis, Rutherford SELIG, BYNUM Walker.

6. From David Mamet: Shelly LEVENE, Dave MOSS, Richard ROMA, James LINGK.

7. From Lisa Loomer: VICTORIA, FORGIVENESS From Heaven, WANDA, OLIVER.

When Tracy Letts uses the title plus the last name SHERIFF GILBEAU, it's a way to quickly define for us a character we see only briefly (to make this naming business murkier, the Sheriff is called "Deon" in dialogue). If a character is given one of those double first names popular in some parts of the country like Sara Jean or John David, that's typically what is used throughout the script.

There are no rules or even common practices here other than to say it's unusual for a contemporary playwright to use more than a single name in the script and when they do, there's usually some significance (at least to them) for doing it.

Names help bring characters into focus, but what drives them and fascinates audiences is conflict. That's what makes them seem real.

13. CONFLICT: CHARACTER DEVELOPER

Is there a good argument going on? It all starts with a fight, a disagreement.
            -John Guare

John Guare was right, but he's also crammed half the craft of playwriting into that word, good.

Best Practice: *Argument is not dramatic conflict.*

At least not the special kind of conflict that drives plays. Arguments in real life are usually circular with no one getting anywhere when they're over except having blown off some steam. As in real life, in the theatre arguments are a bore for everyone except the people doing the yelling.

Dramatic conflict draws from a much deeper vein, rooted in the subtext of the central characters and is driven by fundamentally opposing desires. Marsha Norman may have Mama argue with Jessie about Snowballs and her nails, but what drives *'night, Mother* is Jessie's ultimate desire to commit suicide that evening and Mama's desire to prevent her from doing it. That's the stuff of dramatic conflict.

Conflict as Overcoming Obstacles

Conflict is often said to be created by overcoming obstacles in the path of a character, though dramatic conflict in plays is often more subtle and complex than this may suggest. It can be argued that the approach may make more sense in screenplays where obstacles external to the central characters are a common device.

This way of thinking about the source of conflict is worth considering (if it makes sense to you) since almost any source of dramatic conflict can be converted into a sequence of obstacles that characters need to overcome in the course of the play.

In *'night, Mother* Jessie's conflict with her mother can be framed as a series of obstacles she must overcome in order to achieve her ultimate goal – the most significant being her mother's attempt to prevent her from doing that final act. In this case, the playwright has given Jessie an actual list of most of the "obstacles" she needs to overcome including doing her mother's nails, each characterized by varying levels of conflict.

This kind of obstacle analysis is often used in U.S. actor training programs and may have something to do with the number of performers who have successfully turned to playwriting and screenwriting in recent years.

Killers of Dramatic Conflict

Dramatic conflict in plays happens between characters and it's in that dynamic where things can go wrong, draining the sources of conflict.

> **1. Characters agreeing about everything.** In this case, they may have a warm and cozy life together, but we won't be interested.

> **2. Characters turning-the-other-cheek.** In real life, that's a great way to reduce conflict, but that's exactly what you don't want to have happen in the theatre.

> **3. Characters speaking all their subtext.** Spoken subtext drains the conflict between characters and inhibits character development. That's how you can end up with an argument instead of real dramatic conflict (see Chapter 15 on Subtext).

Triangular Conflict Problems

Dramatic conflict only happens when each character has a stake in the outcome. If those characters with a stake don't confront each other directly, you'll end up struggling with the problem of triangular conflict. If the dramatic conflict is between Joan and Larkin, but the scene takes place between Joan and X who has no stake in the outcome, there will be no dramatic conflict. Perhaps an argument, but no genuine conflict.

Make sure you've got the proper side of the triangle on stage. If the conflict is between B and C, you won't get anywhere with a scene between B and A if old A is just curious, helpful, thoughtful, and sympathetic and if A won't face any real changes if C jumps off the bridge or not.

If you find yourself in this situation, there's a simple solution. Reshape the scene so it's between the two characters who have a real stake in the outcome: C and B. Send A to the bathroom, or to answer the phone, or to Pago Pago. When the wrong side of this kind of triangle has the stage to itself, tension drains out of the dialogue and after a page or two the whole enterprise comes to a halt.

Great listeners may be nice to know in real life, but they'll make life miserable if you let them into your play.

14. THE PLAYWRIGHT'S POINT OF VIEW

I didn't consciously decide I was going to write the play from the point of view of the women. But my mother was a feminist in her time, and she always made me feel that I was somebody. Japanese men were very chauvinistic, especially in those days, but women had a way of adapting things, of handling the men. That's one of the things I wanted to show.
        -Wakako Yamauchi

A play's point of view is determined at the moment you decide who your primary character will be. It's through this character that you'll be telling the story and it's through this character that the audience will be watching the story unfold. That decision is critical.

Tennessee Williams tells his story in *Cat on a Hot Tin Roof* (at least in his original version of the script) from the point of view of the character he's most interested in: Brick. To enhance this, he establishes the setting as Brick (and Maggie's) bedroom for all three acts, forcing all of the other characters (and conflict) to come to Brick's lair.

If you decide to use a narrator to lead us through the play, that doesn't necessarily mean that this guide establishes your point of view. A narrator may have a point of view that is different from yours. Arthur Miller uses the lawyer as the narrator of *A View From the Bridge*, but Miller's point of view is through the longshoreman, Eddie. Even though the lawyer is telling us the story, Miller doesn't accept his narrator's attitude that "It's better to settle for half." Eddie's refusal to settle for half is why the playwright wants us to see the story through Eddie's eyes, not the narrator's point of view.

Once having established this point of view through the selection of a major character, it's important to stay with that character as the major focus. If as Act I goes forward this character begins to recede from the action, in effect being displaced from that central role by another character, it's time to rethink your point of view. There may not be anything wrong with allowing your point of view to transfer to another character, or to several other characters, but if this begins to happen you may be moving toward a "group" point of view.

The Group Character Alternative

It's not necessary to limit a point of view to a single character. If a group of characters are your primary interest, they'll collectively set your point of view. This is what Beth Henley did with the three sisters in *Crimes of the Heart* and what Chekhov did long before her in *The Three Sisters*.

These group characters usually develop in plays where the writer is more interested – or at least equally interested – in what happens to the group as compared to the outcome for one member of that group.

Henley goes to the extreme with this approach in *Crimes of the Heart* where she halts development of the play's suspense plot just short of a climax, thus never resolving for us what will happen to the sister who tried to murder her husband. Despite short circuiting the suspense plot, Henley's emotional plot does end in a kind of climax when the sisters as a group finally achieve what they've wanted in their relationship among themselves.

For Henley, that outcome was of far more importance than the practical matter of what would happen to her would-be murderess. Audiences would have liked knowing what happened to this near-murderess, but plays – even successful plays – don't always give audiences everything they want.

15. LANGUAGE: FOUL & OTHERWISE

We tend to believe people when it costs them something to say whatever it is they have to say. It almost takes the form of a mathematical equation, the more it means to a character, the more difficult it is to say. More to the point: no restraint, no inhibitions, no guilt, no shame, no drama.
-Robert Towne

If you take your characters seriously – as you must to write them well – the words coming out of their mouths will be how you genuinely hear them speak. That's all that matters. Forget about what's proper or "nice."

Best Practice: *Write dialogue how you hear it.*

Having said that, gratuitous nasty language (foul, scatological, or profane) doesn't win you many points any more if it's not essential to the characters you've created.

Not so long ago, you could occasionally find a literary manager who thought audiences wanted that sort of language in the theatre – the kind that would still be bleeped today by PBS and the commercial TV and cable networks – even if it seemed inappropriate to the characters involved. A few would even encourage playwrights to spice up their dialogue to meet these expectations. We've gone through that phase now and come out the other end to an openness about less than polite language in plays. (More than one current cable TV series has discovered that pushing this sort of language to the kind of extremes the theatre used to revel in pays dividends – or at least raises ratings.)

Again, the general rule here: Take your characters seriously and the language they use will make perfect sense, regardless of whether it's fair or foul. Rajiv Joseph even has the Tiger use foul language in *Bengal Tiger at the Baghdad Zoo*, but it makes perfect sense given where the Tiger has to live (and later be a ghost).

Language that doesn't flow naturally and logically from the nature of your characters is deadening to a play and the ears of your audience, regardless of whether it's naughty or nice.

The Naughtiness Factor

The talk of the New York theatre world in 2011 was Stephen Adly Guirgis' play with an unprintable title usually altered by mainstream media to the incomprehensible *The ___ with the Hat* (the more "daring" press called it *The Mother___ with the Hat*). While the media felt compelled to edit the title for family consumption, it was nominated for Best Play in Broadway's Tony Awards. The English playwright Mark Ravenhill had done something similar with the title of his first full-length play back in the late 1990's. But in both cases you could argue (as the playwrights believed) that the titles came out of themes and characters in the plays.

While the playwrights would probably object to this conclusion, these unprintable titles also gave their plays a landslide of publicity unrelated to what they'd written. It's worth mentioning that these "unprintable" titles are not just a guy-thing: Suzan-Lori Parks did the same in titling her riff on Hawthorne's *The Scarlet Letter* at the turn of the millennium. No family media said or printed the offending part of that title either.

The latest envelope of this sort being blown apart is the importing of the sex and nudity typical of R-rated Hollywood feature films to the far more circumspect theatre. This was not unusual in the experimental theatre of the 1960s, but had fallen out of favor by the end of that decade. Now its back with the leading practitioner currently being Thomas Bradshaw with *The Ashes* and then *Burning* in 2011 – though most critics found more of interest to talk about besides the sex scenes. In his scripts, the general stage directions for those scenes are no more graphic that those in feature screenplays aiming for R-ratings. How portable these on-stage graphic depictions can be outside of New York (where the plays opened), San Francisco, LA, and Chicago is a question yet to be resolved.

Best Practice: *The naughtiness factor still works in the theatre.*

Clichés: The Great Ear Closers

Audiences have ear-lids as well as eyelids. Nothing closes those ear-lids quicker than clichés, especially dialogue that behaves as though clichés really mean something.

Characters can be clichés, plots can be clichés and occasionally you can get away with these, but clichés in dialogue don't even buy you death on the installment plan. Use them more than a few times and it's over.

These things are phrases, sayings, and aphorisms that have become so overused that they have virtually lost all significant meaning. We know them too well and as a result they have no impact on us. As language, they're like grandma's old clock clacking away in the living room. After a while, you don't "hear" the ticking. The sound is there, but it's so familiar, your brain doesn't even bother to register it anymore – or more correctly refuses to recognize it anymore.

Perhaps the worst aspect of using clichés is that our minds move much faster than sound so audiences flash to the end of a cliché long before it's left the performer's mouth. That means the audience ends up hearing these twice, first as their minds automatically complete the phrase and again when the sound of the performer's voice reaches their ears.

It's one thing to hear something interesting twice. We'll put up with that within limits. But to hear something boring twice? That's in a class with water-torture.

As a reminder, here's what these look like on the page. The words in boldface are what the audience leaps to long before their ears register the noise: *Let's run it up the **flagpole**. Strong as an **ox**. Pretty as a **picture**. Dead as a **doornail**.*

You can use clichés to advantage, but only under very controlled circumstances. One option is making them a defining trait of a character. If a character continually uses clichés and is the only one who does so in the play, you'll quickly establish that we're dealing with an air-head.

An alternative is to twist the ends of clichés so they end up defying audience expectations and don't land like a marshmallow. What we hear then is no longer a cliché, even though it starts out that way. Oscar Wilde built a playwriting career on twisting clichés, most famously with "Her hair has turned quite gold from grief."

Writing in Accents

When a character walks into your head speaking in an accent that seems to demand phonetic reproduction in your script, resist.

Even if Eugene O'Neill did it, that approach drives readers to clean their glasses or water their contacts far more than you'd ever want. And the harder you try to duplicate accents with combinations of letters and punctuation marks, the more indecipherable your script will become.

The key to rendering accents is to remember that a script on the page is mostly about plot, character, your voice, and theme. That's what's important, not the odd and accurately reproduced accents of your characters. Literary managers can always ask you what your characters really sound like in your head.

Decades ago, playwrights labored over this sort of phonetic duplication as Sean O'Casey did with Irish accents back in the 1920's for his masterpiece, *Juno and the Paycock*:

> JOHNNY: Bring us a dhrink o' wather. Tay, tay, tay! You're always thinkin' o' tay. If a man was dyin', you'd thry to make him swally a cup o' tay!

Nowadays, most contemporary playwrights write dialogue for a character who speaks with an accent by simply capturing the rhythm and odd word order of the accent. If the accent is particularly dense and obscure in real life, they'll add an opening stage direction explaining what it should sound like, but the dialogue will be written as if it's nearly conventional spoken English.

Here's what Martin McDonagh did with Irish accents (seven decades after O'Casey) in *The Beauty Queen of Leenane*:

> RAY: Are they a bit stale, now? (*Chews*) It does be hard to tell with Kimberleys. (*Pause*) I think Kimberleys are me favourite biscuits out of any biscuits. Them or Jaffa Cakes.

An exception to the rule and an extreme one: David Lindsay-Abaire has a character (a stroke victim) in his highly successful *Fuddy Meers* whose dialogue is written phonetically and is incomprehensible to mere mortals like us. To solve that problem, he adds a long note at the end of the script with a translation into standard English of every line of dialogue this character has.

What made *Fuddy Meers* work in New York and regional theatres across the country is that this character's dialogue can't be understood by most of the characters in the play either. That's the point, and that makes it intriguing to us instead of an annoyance. But reading the script – as opposed to seeing it in production – is serious work until you realize that understanding what this character is saying is not essential to understanding the play, at least not until the end. And in the obligatory scene, other characters help us figure out the important bits.

The playwright includes the translation of that distorted phonetic dialogue for the director and the performer playing the character because it contains the subtext of that character. It was a daring move for Lindsay-Abaire to write his script this way. Most playwrights would have settled for the easy way out by writing the stoke victim's dialogue in the script in near normal English, and adding a stage direction saying it's delivered in such a slurred and mangled way that we can't understand it.

Best Practice: *Taking extreme risks in writing can lead to professional recognition in the theatre.*

In Lindsay-Abaire's case, the playwright was taking his characters seriously and writing them as he heard them speak. He probably didn't think of this as a risk as he was writing the play.

Writing characters as you hear them is critical, but there are some things you don't want them to say.

16. SUBTEXT: WHAT YOU DON'T TELL US

There's nothing there except lines of dialogue. If they're sketched correctly and minimally, they will give the audience the illusion that these are "real people," especially if the lines are spoken by real people – the actors are going to fill a lot in. So a large part of the technique of playwriting is to leave a lot out.
-David Mamet

Subtext is what you leave a lot out of in dialogue. Pushing subtext just beneath the surface of the dialogue is what makes plays exciting and helps keep audiences in their seats.

Subtext is the unspoken thoughts and motives of your characters – what they really think and believe, but don't say. In well written dialogue, subtext seldom breaks through the surface except in moments of extreme conflict. At other times, it colors the dialogue by helping the director and performers develop your characters in production.

Another way of looking at this: Subtext is content underneath the spoken dialogue. Leaving it where it belongs gives performers something to do. If you let your characters tell each other everything they think or feel, performers can't do what they're trained to do best (and paid to do): Revealing through gesture, movement, intonation, and expression, the real essence of their characters, the real meaning behind what they say.

A Subtext Example

With a debt to Woody Allen (stopping just short of plagiarism), a graphic depiction of subtext in relation to spoken dialogue. In the following scene, the subtext is shown in italics below each line of spoken dialogue.

(*The two of them on a roof-top patio with a safe 10 feet between.*)

HER: Hi.
Oh, God, nobody cool says Hi.

HIM: Hello!
I'd love to take her out. I hope my deodorant's working.

HER: Nice view.
He's talking to me! And he'll hate my silly dress.

HIM: Just look at the clouds over there.
I've got to find out who she is.

HER (*Taking a step toward him*): I'm…Leslie.
What a stupid name. He'll hate it and hate me.

HIM: Neat dress.
I just love her name.

(Note that this scene and all subsequent examples in the *Handbook* – except those in Part Four on Format – are in publishing format, not standard script format.)

Characters Speaking Subtext

Keeping subtext below the surface of the dialogue helps build tension and suspense – and that maintains audience interested. In the following scene, here's what happens when every shred of subtext is spoken by characters.

(*Nikki and Stu's family room. The smoke still curls in the aftermath.*)

NIKKI: So? What have you got to say for yourself after this horror of an evening. You always manage to get us into things with people I hate.
STU: What? Why are you landing on me for this? I don't know why you don't get along with any of my friends. They're just not people you like. Nobody's people you like.
NIKKI: You're so amazingly unimaginative. Is that all you can say? You just don't understand anything about me. After this – I don't know what's keeping us together.
STU: You know that's not true. Nik – I love you more than I can say.
NIKKI: Don't call me that name, Nik. I hate you when you do that. How can you be so stupid to keep calling me that.
STU: I don't know why you're so upset. It's just a nickname.
NIKKI (*Exploding*): You make me sound like a man! Is that what you want?

(*Blackout.*)

Cutting Spoken Subtext

Spoken subtext is marked with strikethrough for cutting in the following version of this scene:

(*Nikki and Stu's family room. The smoke still curls in the aftermath.*)

NIKKI: So? ~~What have you got to say for yourself after this horror of an evening. You always manage to get us into things with people I hate.~~

STU: What? ~~Why are you landing on me for this? I don't know why you don't get along with any of my friends.~~ They're just not people you like. Nobody's people you like.

NIKKI: ~~You're so amazingly unimaginative.~~ Is that all you can say? ~~You just don't understand anything about me.~~ After this – ~~I don't know what's keeping us together.~~

STU: ~~You know that's not true.~~ Nik – ~~I love you more than I can say.~~

NIKKI: Don't call me that ~~name, Nik. I hate you when you do that. How can you be so stupid to keep calling me that.~~

STU: ~~I don't know why you're so upset.~~ It's just a nickname.

NIKKI (*Exploding*): You make me sound like a man! Is that what you want?

(*Blackout.*)

The Edited Scene

A final edited version of the scene follows with nearly all (note that it's not all) subtext removed; the actors will express what's been cut.

(*Nikki and Stu's family room. The smoke still curls in the aftermath.*)

NIKKI: So?
STU: What? (*Pause*) They're just not people you like. Nobody's people you like.
NIKKI: Is that all you can say? After this –
STU: Nik –
NIKKI: Don't call me that.
STU: It's just a nickname.
NIKKI (*Exploding*): You make me sound like a man! Is that what you want?

(*Blackout.*)

When accomplished playwrights allow subtext to be spoken, it's usually at moments of high tension and conflict. Even in real life, that's usually when the truth comes out among people who would rather never say what they're really thinking.

It may seem sensible to use more spoken subtext in the opening scenes of a play and then decrease it as the play progresses – when audiences should know more about the characters – and we can more easily understand the subtext without hearing it. That may seem logical, but as we'll see the more spoken subtext is allowed into the dialogue, the less dramatic conflict the play will have regardless of where this happens.

Subtext in *'night, Mother*

Marsha Norman's play was a ground-breaking work when first produced at a major regional theatre with later productions following across the country and eventually a film version.

The play is particularly notable for its careful pacing of subtext and eventual revelation of spoken subtext as the script progresses. The opening of the play gives us another way to understand the importance of subtext.

In the opening lines of Norman's play, tremendous subtext lurks just beneath the surface of the dialogue as Mama's 40-ish daughter, Jessie, asks a seemingly innocuous question. Under that question is several decades of emotional baggage about to come home.

Jessie's first line asking if her mother has any old towels she doesn't want, is an odd request, one that we find curious, but we have to spend eight more intriguing pages with her before we understand how ominous it really is. That's because Jessie's subtext is kept beneath the surface of the dialogue.

This is what would have happened if Jessie had been allowed to speak all of her subtext in that opening line of dialogue (Marsha Norman would never write dialogue like this):

> JESSIE: Do we have any old towels, plastic sheeting or foam rubber padding? I'm going to commit suicide in the bedroom tonight with Daddy's pistol as soon as I get everything done for you and I need the towels so all the blood won't make a mess on your floor.

Done this way we would know too much and know it too soon.

And we'd be much less interested in knowing more, because it would seem like there wasn't any more to know about Jessie.

How Spoken Subtext Kills Plays

Put away your television and Hollywood film spectacles for a moment since spoken subtext can be much less damaging in those venues. But plays are highly susceptible to this virus.

1. It destroys any sense of mystery. Loading Jessie's subtext into her spoken dialogue removes any suspense about why she's making her odd request about old towels and the more odd requests that follow.

2. It undercuts the development of conflict. If Jessie spoke her subtext, the playwright's ability to build conflict between the characters is undermined.

3. It collapses pages of the script. In Norman's play, that would be eight intriguing pages gone – and those vanished pages would come out of the minimum of 90 needed for a full-length play.

Technically, one of the many things playwriting is about is using up time and time is pages. Keeping subtext below the surface of the dialogue forces playwrights to take time telling the story and that makes the result far more interesting for audiences.

Settings as Visual Subtext

Think of the setting as the visual content of a play.

Another way to look at this: Most playwrights think of the setting as the visual subtext of their central characters or as the subtle expression of the theme of the play even if they can't fully visualize what that may mean on stage (that's why scene designers exist).

The setting for *August: Osage County* shows us three floors of rooms, each with all its windows and shades taped shut. The characters can't see out and no light comes in. This sealed house is the subtext for the family with its hidden secrets that eventually come to light – and in Act III where the key emotional "unsealing" happens among the characters, the act opens with all the windows unsealed for the first time.

The setting of *Cat on a Hot Tin Roof* shows us Brick and

Maggie's bedroom dominated by their huge bed with the bedroom and its bed implying the subtext of their relationship – and the key problem with that relationship.

There are a few playwrights who imagine the entire set down to the geranium in the corner before they start writing. If you think in a highly visual way, that may make sense, but doing this is not necessary or even helpful before starting to write.

What you do need is an idea of the visual feeling of the setting. Sensing that will help drive the subtext of your characters and will provide a visual benchmark for the tone of the play.

The best practice is usually to lay out what is essential to begin putting words on paper. Don't do more than that. The visual elements of a play as described in the script have subtext just as dialogue does so the more elaborate your set description is, the less interesting it often becomes. Just as mystery is good in dialogue – mystery that comes from keeping subtext below the surface – that same kind of mystery is helpful when allowed to exist in the description of the setting.

The typical practice nowadays is to say little about the setting. A number of playwrights use the David Mamet approach where you assume you'll deal with all this when you go into production. Here's all Mamet indicated for the setting of *Oleana*: (The play takes place in John's office.); and here's all Rajiv Joseph indicated for the setting of *Bengal Tiger at The Baghdad Zoo*: (Baghdad.); and what David Lindsay-Abaire did for the first scene of *Rabbit Hole*: (A spacious eat-in kitchen.).

Keep in mind that the real work of developing the setting will happen in collaboration with a director and scene designer once a theatre takes on the play for production.

No-Subtext Plays

It's probably worth a moment to say that a play can be written without subtext, meaning the characters tell us nearly everything they're thinking, and thus nearly everything we'd rather not know. In most cases, that also means the characters stand around yelling at each other or – the reverse – idle and desultory conversations.

No-subtext plays can work if they have strong and intense suspense plot (see Chapter 25 on Plots) on the level of a body stashed in the closet, a vampire looking in the window, or a nuclear device stored in the oven. These sorts of plays are so rarely produced that you'd have to travel the country many times to find one. It used to be much easier to find their equivalent on TV, but even there with the marked rise in the quality of dramatic television over the past decade, it takes a lot of channel surfing to find their equivalent.

A seeming exception to this rule is the successful (and controversial) playwright Thomas Bradshaw who makes a point of claiming that his plays are all spoken subtext, that his characters say exactly what they are thinking and are "acting on pure id." He's the only current American playwright to make this claim. But in fact, his dialogue still contains subtext – much as he attempts to have it all spoken – and thus dramatic conflict. What he really creates are characters who freely express and act on urges most "normal" people would want to keep under a manhole cover.

The reason for the lack of no-subtext productions is that – no surprise here – spoken subtext drains conflict between the characters and conflict is what makes characters vivid to us.

Best Practice: *No subtext, no meaningful conflict, no play.*

17. USING DRAMATIC IRONY

If I read one more article about how we all have to steer ourselves away from narrative and realism because TV and film do that, and our job is to "push the envelope," I'm just going to throw up. This elitism is driving audiences away.
  -Theresa Rebeck

Dramatic irony makes an audience feel both privileged and engaged in a play through the creation of an environment where they know more than the central character does (or at least will admit to). Good use of subtext can help make this work.

Dramatic irony is called that for a reason. It began as a technical device when Sophocles decided to have Oedipus attempt to run away from being the guy who (unknowingly) murdered his father and will (unknowingly again) sleep with his mother. The irony: We're almost certain Oedipus can't avoid either – and we think he should know this long before he does.

Sophocles plants that awareness in the opening scenes when he has Oedipus told that he's the murderer he seeks, something he refuses to accept. But we do – though we hope it's not true. We now know more than Oedipus and thus wouldn't do what he's doing, which among other things consists in forcing a series of reluctant witnesses to eventually reveal the evidence that convicts him.

The result of this dramatic irony is a marked increase in our tension and concern. We're sitting there yelling (in our minds, anyway) "Don't do that, you fool, don't you see where this is leading?" And yet until the end, Oedipus has very good reasons – which Sophocles has him share with us – for believing he is innocent.

Irony vs. Being Stupid

Characters who see the yellow caution signs proclaiming Personal Calamity Ahead, but do what they're going to do anyway, may just be idiots and we could care less. But if these same characters forge ahead out of ignorance of facts that would be difficult for them to know – or have logical reasons not to believe – that's Oedipus. And that's interesting.

Dramatic irony is primarily a device for tragedy, not surprisingly since that's where it was invented. Later, playwrights like Moliere also incorporated it into classical comedies where we sense the pending humiliation of the central character – a character who refuses to admit such a possibility. Since it's a comedy, we enjoy the dramatic irony rather than dreading the outcome.

By letting us sense the truth of a situation in plays rather than telling us directly, we'll buy into the dramatic irony in the script without hearing the creaking of a mere theatrical device.

When establishing the conditions for dramatic irony, you can skate very close to the edge of spoken subtext. Sophocles has that minor character tell us directly that Oedipus is the murderer he seeks, but it's done in a way that allows us to believe this might not be the truth. He tells us, but at the same time he allows us to believe – as Oedipus does – that this can't be true. That's the key to compelling use of dramatic irony.

Contemporary Dramatic Irony

In the theatre of Ancient Greece where this all began, central characters nearly always knew the truth of what lay in store for them even though they didn't believe it.

In contemporary plays, the approach is less complex. Typically, the central character simply doesn't know the truth. It's also typical that the audience will know that secret the central character doesn't know – yet – and know it without a doubt.

The build toward the revealing of that secret within the play creates a version of dramatic irony. It's a less complex approach because we usually only learn of the "secret" shortly before it's revealed, in contrast with Sophocles who feeds us the secret close to the inciting incident. So with *Oedipus*, we're caught in the grip of dramatic irony throughout the play, while in contemporary usage playwrights seldom put us in that situation for more than a few scenes.

Unlike Oedipus who is the driving force of his own slow discovery of a truth we already sense, practice today often delivers the truth to key characters as external thunderbolts rather than their being the agents of their own discovery. The removal of personal agency by contemporary playwrights technically knocks most of the pins out from under the classical device of dramatic irony, but the shreds that remain still work because we fear what will happen when the character who doesn't know the secret finally is told.

Tracy Letts uses this to great effect in *August: Osage County* in the build (in Act III) to Ivy finally being told that her lover – who has brought happiness to her for the first time in her life – is in fact her half-brother. The playwright could have saved this bombshell and had it delivered in a single line to Ivy. But he took the more effective approach of establishing dramatic irony by revealing it to us earlier, letting us know before Ivy knows, so we'd have to go through that tension of realizing the secret will come out, but hoping somehow that it won't.

This brings us back to that issue of the subjects of American plays. Classical dramatic irony works best with larger than life characters and large issues. While *Oedipus* can be reduced in a nearsighted way to a family problems play, that was not the subject that fascinated Sophocles. He was intrigued instead by the character trait that led Oedipus to his doom and the play can be seen as a cautionary warning to the rulers of Ancient Greece – who seem not to have gotten the message.

18. SERIOUS COMEDY & THE REVERSE

All along my characters cracked jokes, which I tried to suppress. People were in the process of expiring, and here I was laughing. I mean, this was supposed to be a serious play. I was having dinner with my friend who was a hospice worker at St. Vincent's Hospital in Greenwich Village, in the heart of New York's gay community, when it finally dawned on me that maybe humor was a key to my play. She said, "We tell a lot of jokes in my line of work." I permitted the play to be funny.
                    -William Hoffman

Nowadays, playwrights don't even try to write tragedy – comedy has not suffered that same kind of neglect – but most are attracted to "serious" plays.

Most contemporary playwrights work in a hybrid form that is sometimes – and unfortunately – called "dramedy," an awful name, but one that does capture the nature of plays that combine comedy with drama. In these plays, we laugh but in the end nothing good may happen for at least some of the central characters – or to turn that on its head, we cry and in the end something good happens for those characters.

Bertolt Brecht was well ahead of his time in the last century with his counterintuitive insight: *All theatre educates. Good theatre entertains.*

This hybrid is what practically everybody is writing now. The mixture of seriousness with laughter produces very fine contemporary plays and generations of playwrights continually rediscover that incorporating humor in serious plays helps audiences connect with difficult themes and stories.

Laughter is Everywhere
Humor is a good way to heighten the impact of serious issues, even life-and-death issues. Laughter picked up a bad rap for too many years, most likely from the annoying use of laugh tracks on sitcoms, sending a message that laughter equals being frivolous, but it certainly doesn't have to in the theatre.

Before the advent of modern drama, tone in plays was much simpler for playwrights. You wrote a farce if people ran into doors, a comedy if they waved handkerchiefs, a drama if somebody unimportant died, and a tragedy if the same happened to the hero (or heroine).

The idea of mixing comedy with serious subject matter was frowned on if it went beyond the gravedigger chucking skulls out of a grave for a few minutes in *Hamlet*. It's a lot more interesting now. Contemporary playwrights have taken this mixing of styles that Shakespeare sometimes used a thousand miles further down the road. It's the way of the world and how they hear the world, so what they write are two ends of the same keyboard: Comedies with serious themes or serious plays with humor. That doesn't mean the style requires a serious play to be a laugh-fest.

This mix of styles has influenced screenwriting as well and is particularly easy to see in romantic comedies where it's now more common to find serious themes woven through films in the genre.

PART TWO – STRUCTURE: Parts of a Play

Getting people on and off stage from that living room set was a challenge. You can't always have the phone ringing.
-Wendy Wasserstein

19. THE SHAPE OF TWO-ACT PLAYS

I've always had to invent some kind of form for my plays that will take the place of the form that plays usually have. I know for a fact that the only reason one watches something for more than 15 or 20 minutes is because it has a plot and you're curious to know what happens next. But having no talent for the regular type of plot development, I have had to struggle to invent an equivalent that would be equally gripping.
-Wallace Shawn

A play is a construction of parts and the shape or structure of a play shares equal billing with the story you're telling. As the old song says, it's like a horse and carriage: You can't have one –.

Well, you can have one without the other, but odds are you won't be able to hold an audience for more than those first 15 or 20 minutes. And that's a generous assessment of the patience of audiences.

If structure strikes you as a pointless exercise, one-act plays might be more to your liking. Keep them under 10 minutes and you can get away with almost anything (see Chapter 38 on Writing One-Acts). There are even playwriting competitions for one-acts.

Caution on Experimental Structures
The envelope can be pushed a considerable distance with subjects, but audiences and literary managers alike are usually less willing to be adventuresome with structure. You can play with structure as long as you also provide a way for the audience to have a general idea of where they are in the story. If they loose the thread of the story completely, then you've lost them completely.

> **Best Practice:** *The more experimental the structure, the more you'll need to be responsible for producing the play.*

Much as it may feel good to blame the audience for being too conservative, it's never the audience's fault if they can't follow the play because of its complicated and unusual structure. That structural invention puts an added burden on you and the play to find those specialized audiences that can understand it. And keep in mind that this unusual and complicated structure you've invented may make much more sense in the script than it will to audiences in performance.

The Two-Act Play Standard

Part Two on Structure focuses on the two-act (full-length) play since that's the form most playwrights use today. The only significant difference when moving to a three-act play is that the script – and thus its running time in performance – is usually longer.

At the opposite extreme are playwrights who prefer constructing a play as one long continuous act, the equivalent of a two-act play without an intermission. In either of these three alternatives, the internal structure of the resulting plays remains essentially the same.

20. STRUCTURE OF A TWO-ACT PLAY

First, the play was going to be sold to television, and then it was sold to the movies. It became a hit at Playwrights Horizons. It won the Pulitzer Prize. It was almost too much to believe. It was the first play I had ever written! I didn't know what I had done exactly. I still don't, but you never do.
                    -Alfred Uhry

The diagram below is a visual approximation of the typical structure of two-act plays, showing the sequence of the key parts. While comedies follow a similar structure, the diagram reflects the kinds of serious plays most contemporary playwrights create (those "dramedys" discussed in Chapter 17).

STRUCTURE OF TWO ACT PLAYS

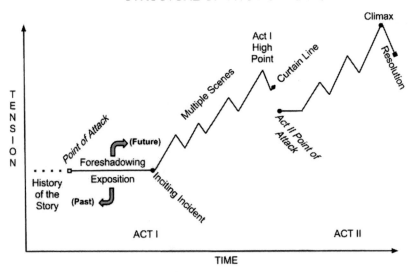

If you've found that pure comedy with at most only a slight dash of melancholy is your style, keep in mind that in place of rising tension as the play progresses, the level of laughter and comic complications intensifies, ideally reaching its highest point at the climax.

The following chapters detail the parts of the construction used by contemporary playwrights, the *–wright* part of the playwright's craft.

21. POINT OF ATTACK: THE BEGINNING

Affecting the audience is why one writes a play to begin with. You don't write it for yourself, the actors, or the director. You're there to do something to the audience.
-Lee Blessing

Plays don't begin at the beginning. It's only a slight overstatement to say that *plays begin at the end.*

HISTORY OF THE STORY & POINT OF ATTACK

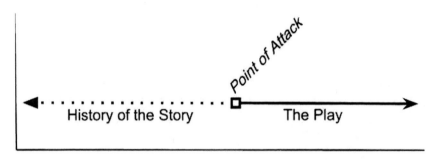

The point of attack is that first thing the audience will see or hear as the play begins. It's the first decision that can make or break a great idea for a play.

In James Michener's *Hawaii,* that famous novel begins with steam bubbling up out of a crack in the ocean floor as the first volcanic island begins to form miles below the surface of the Pacific. That's a point of attack at the very beginning of a story if there ever was one.

Unlike novelists, successful playwrights know never to start a play at the beginning of the story. Novels have the luxury of unlimited time – there's no clock running over the novelist's keyboard. Plays don't have that luxury of time that allows you to begin at the beginning. In thinking about where the point of attack should be, keep in mind that every story and its characters has a history. The problem is to decide where in that history to begin telling the tale.

Plays need conflict to fuel their dramatic action, so from a technical standpoint this "fuel" needs to catch fire a few pages after the point of attack – and this tells you where the point of attack should be in the history of the story.

Since contemporary playwrights use a very late point of attack, their plays cover only the last few hours or days of the story's history prior to the climax of the major conflict generated by that history. Robert Schenkkan may have covered 200 years from point of attack to resolution in one of his plays, but he's at the end of a very short line of playwrights who've tried that.

Points of Attack in Notable Plays

Plays typically begin at a point just before the primary conflict erupts out of the history of the story.

> **1. *Opus*.** Michael Hollinger's play begins shortly before the members of the string quartet are invited to perform at the White House and before one of their founding members is fired for erratic behavior. The point of attack comes several decades after the members of this now internationally famous quartet met and then began playing together.
>
> **2. *'night, Mother*.** Marsha Norman's play begins as Jessie puts in motion her plan to commit suicide in her mother's house 90 minutes later. The point of attack comes about 40 years into Jessie's history and that of her relationship with Mama.
>
> **3. *Bengal Tiger at the Baghdad Zoo*.** Rajiv Joseph's play begins a few minutes before the tiger is killed. The point of attack comes two days after the lions escaped from the zoo and were killed, and soon after the initial U.S. invasion of Iraq. While actual events following the invasion are included in the play (the tiger and lions, the killing of Saddam's sons), the timeline of the real history of the story is compressed and rearranged to enhance the play's conflict.
>
> **4. *The Mountaintop*.** Katori Hall's play about Martin Luther King, Jr. begins as he comes into his motel room after having given his famous "I've been to the mountaintop" speech in Memphis the evening before he is assassinated. The point of

attack comes 13 years after King came to national attention following his first major civil rights action.

5. *Death and the Maiden.* Ariel Dorfman's play begins at the moment the lights of the car carrying Paulina's husband and the doctor who may have tortured her flash through the living room windows. The point of attack comes about 17 years after Paulina was arrested for political activity, then tortured and released. The point of attack is also the day the first democratically elected president of this Latin American country has offered her husband the position of chair of its new Human Rights Commission with the charge of resolving the past issues of torturer and tortured in this unnamed nation.

6. *Crimes of the Heart.* Beth Henley's play begins a day or so after one of the three Magrath sisters failed at murdering her husband. The point of attack comes years after the other "crimes of the heart" committed by her two sisters.

7. *Cat on a Hot Tin Roof.* Tennessee Williams' play begins the evening Big Daddy realizes he must decide which of his two sons should be the heir to his 40,000 acres of the richest land this side of the Valley Nile. The point of attack is 65 years into Big Daddy's history, 49 years after he got the plantation, and 5 years after his favorite son Brick's rocky – and still childless – marriage to Maggie.

8. *August: Osage County.* Tracy Letts' play begins several days before the patriarch of the Weston family disappears, a disappearance that finally triggers revelations of the family's dark secrets. The point of attack comes about 38 years after an event that's the darkest of those secrets, the revelation of which comes at the climax of the play.

The Teaser Point of Attack

The complexity or richness of a story may sometimes demand development through as much as 10 or more pages of the script before the major conflict of the play can be introduced in a clear enough way to hold the attention of audiences. A teaser or false point of attack can hold the audience's attention while you gradually draw them into the background of the conflict that will eventually erupt.

These borrowed scenes are false or teaser points of attack because the following scenes cover portions of the story's history prior to the teaser's actual place in that story. They're a technical trick to hold the audience's attention while the years or days prior to the onset of the play's real conflict are filled in. This can also be done effectively using a strong visual image in place of dialogue.

Teaser Point of Attack Techniques

Playwrights who use a teaser point of attack still keep that moment where it belongs in the play's chronological history, giving audiences a sense of revelation when they finally discover how that teaser moment fits into the overall story of the play.

1. Borrow a small part of the climax. This can be the actual moment of the play's climax from the end of Act II. When a teaser borrows from the climax, playwrights do this sparingly, usually taking such a small portion that audiences are still surprised when that excerpt from the climax arrives in its proper context.

2. Excerpt a short section having considerable tension. But well before the climax. This is particularly effective when drawn from the last scene or curtain line of Act I and avoids the problem of giving away the climax at the beginning of the play.

3. Use a narrator. For narrators to provide the teaser, they need to speak directly to the audience at the opening of the play. As they talk to us, they hint at the conflict to come in a way that generates enough suspense to keep the audience engaged until the central conflict builds sufficiently to support the play. (See Chapter 23 on Using Narrators.)

A teaser point of attack usually requires that the play be structured in a series of formal scenes. Formal scenes are necessary because the use of a teaser means you're actually altering the time structure of the play with what is technically a flash-forward: After the teaser is over, the play drops back in time to a period prior to the teaser.

Notable Teaser Points of Attack

Currently, the majority of playwrights prefer linear structures over using a teaser, even though some great plays exploit the device.

1. *M. Butterfly*. David Henry Hwang's play begins with the French diplomat addressing the audience from his prison cell where he finds himself as a result of the history of the story related in the rest of the play. After this teaser point of attack monologue and a following scene occurring at roughly the same time, the play drops back to the true point of attack 41 years earlier. What follows are scenes from the diplomat's history prior to his talking to us from his jail cell.

2. *The Heidi Chronicles*. Wendy Wasserstein's play begins with Heidi's end-of-term lecture to her art history students delivered complete with slides to the audience in the theatre. The true point of attack comes in the following scene when Heidi was in high school, 24 years before the lecture we've just seen.

3. *A Soldier's Play*. Charles Fuller's play opens with the murder of Sergeant Vernon Waters in 1944, a scene that won't make sense to us until we see it again in context at the play's climax. This teaser draws the audience along through the initial subdued reaction of his platoon to the killing and the early stages of the murder investigation. The investigating officer is the play's narrator. Fuller could have had his narrator tell us about the murder as the teaser, but in this case showing us the teaser is far more effective in capturing the audience's attention.

4. *Equus*. Peter Shaffer's play begins with the psychiatrist (as narrator) drawing our attention to a teenage boy embracing a stylized horse, saying he must start at the beginning for us to understand the story. The image of the boy and the horse won't make sense until we see it again in context at the end of Act I. (It won Broadway's Tony Award for Best Play.)

These playwrights concluded during the writing of their plays that the stories would not hold audience attention if they began them at the real point of attack. The resulting plays using a teaser point of attack were great successes in the theatre and all were subsequently adapted for film versions.

22. EXPOSITION & FORESHADOWING

*Nobody's life – certainly not mine – is ipso-facto, word for word,
stageworthy. In the end, we must improve almost everything we
live, before opening the curtain. What we call Realism has very
little to do with what we call Reality.*
     -Israel Horovitz

The sound bite version of these technical terms: Exposition is what
happened before the point of attack. Foreshadowing is what *may*
happen after the point of attack.

EXPOSITION AND FORSHADOWING

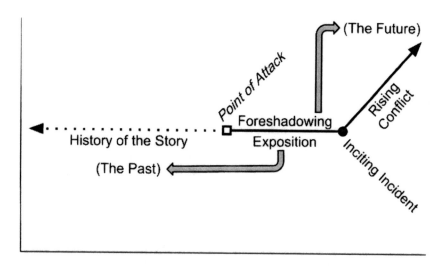

Exposition is giving us information about the past. Since the
point of attack in most contemporary plays comes very late in the
history of the story, there's a premium on weaving in enough
information about what's happened before that so we can get our
bearings.

Exposition – unlike foreshadowing – tends to deal in facts.
Occasionally, playwrights will have their characters mislead us
about what's happened in the past (Tennessee Williams famously

has Big Daddy lie to us in *Cat on a Hot Tin Roof* about how he got that plantation), but typically the majority of information given to us as exposition is true. And if we're initially misled (as with Big Daddy's story), eventually we learn what really happened prior to the point of attack.

Why Exposition

Exposition is like awful medicine. We need it, but nobody wants to know it's going down, so in the contemporary theatre you need to do this without our realizing what you're up to.

A century ago, playwrights could just send the maid on stage with a feather duster and have her chatter on about all the terrible, mysterious, scandalous things that had befallen the family during the last 50 years before the point of attack. For a change of pace, you could shove the butler out instead. This doesn't cut it anymore (though you still might make this work if you're writing a wacky comedy).

Best Practice: *Give us what we need to know, when we need to know it.*

For centuries, playwrights have been using that just-in-time approach to manufacturing invented by the Japanese auto industry a few decades ago.

Fortunately, exposition is something else about structure that you don't have to think about much – at least that's true if your central characters have a shared past and if you've controlled the amount of subtext allowed into the dialogue. Then the exposition needed will usually flow off the characters' tongues seemingly on its own and we won't mind.

Deliberate Elimination of Exposition

Since most playwriting rules are made to be broken, here's the most famous exception to that exposition rule.

Harold Pinter rose to fame and eventually fortune (and the Nobel Prize for Literature in 2005) by among other things taking the daring step of removing nearly all traces of exposition in his early and great full-length plays including *The Birthday Party* and *The Caretaker*. Audience don't normally enjoy this sort of thing, so don't take this as a solution to the exposition issue.

With the Pinter approach to exposition, we have no way of

knowing if any of the characters should attract our sympathies. When we have no idea if the sweet piano player in *The Birthday Party* hiding at that boarding house is being hounded by two guys from the mob because he saw something he shouldn't have, or by two guys from Scotland Yard because he burns down orphanages, you've got no way to get your bearings. Or to be crass about it, we don't know who to cheer for.

Pinter always argued that most of the time that was exactly the way we experienced events in real life: We come upon them after they've started, have little or no idea about the past history of the people involved and what may have triggered the issues between them, and have no clues about how it will end. Pinter eventually developed a large following in the U.S. and Europe with his later plays – and not incidentally, plays in which he incorporated more exposition – though still not nearly as much as most playwrights use today.

If you want audiences to care about your central characters but they don't, you've probably got the answer to the question of whether your play has enough exposition.

> **Best Practice:** *The more we know about what characters have been through in the past, the more we'll care about them.*

Role of Foreshadowing

Foreshadowing is the laying of hints or clues about what may happen in the future of the play's story and particularly what may happen at the climax of the play.

Early in the play, these lines of dialogue or events typically suggest a wide range of possibilities to the audience, but as we move forward in Act I and then on into Act II, the range of potential outcomes narrows.

The ultimate goal with foreshadowing is to have the audience be surprised by the play's climax and yet to find it a logical outcome of the story. Foreshadowing provides the logic of the climax.

In Chapter 25 on Plots, we'll examine the two intertwined plots nearly all contemporary playwrights use. At this point it's enough to know that if the suspense plot (the what-happens-next of a play) is integrated into the play's structure, you should be adding foreshadowing almost automatically. Those continual reminders to the audience about this plot will prompt most of the foreshadowing the play needs.

Specific foreshadowing hints can fall anywhere in the script, but are usually more effective if they begin occurring earlier rather than later. While there are lots of exceptions to this practice, foreshadowing is nearly always more effective when there is some distance between that first hint and the climax of the play.

The Key to Foreshadowing

Unlike exposition and its focus on facts, foreshadowing is much more oblique.

If as a way of inserting foreshadowing, Tennessee Williams had Big Daddy in Act I of *Cat on a Hot Tin Roof* pull Big Mamma aside and say, "If only my son Brick's wife would get pregnant, I'd give him the plantation" he would have given away the whole game. We'd be unsurprised by the play's climax – and relatively uninterested. Instead of this ham-handed approach, the playwright foreshadowed the climax by gradually showing us Big Daddy's extreme dislike of his other son's kids as well as his close identification with his favored son's internal struggles.

By hinting at the outcome through what we learn of Big Daddy's attitudes towards his two sons, the climax is both a surprise to us and also makes perfect sense once it's happened – that foreshadowing has established the logic of the play's climax.

Beau Willimon uses a similar approach to foreshadowing in *Farragut North*, his play about sleazy political campaigning. By letting us know the range of dirty political tricks the opposition campaign manager intends to use, it's a surprise – but a logical one – when at the climax this guy suddenly withdraws his offer of employment to the young political operative of a rival campaign. The devastating withdrawal of that job offer fits into the campaign manager's behavior patterns that we've seen through foreshadowing. While we're stunned by his doing this, it makes perfect sense that he would do such a thing.

A test to know if you don't have enough foreshadowing: If more than a few readers or audience members are scratching their heads and saying, "I don't get the ending," you've got the answer. If there's not enough foreshadowing, audiences won't understand the logic of the play's climax or the logic of how your characters ended up in the resolution following the climax.

Deliberate Withholding of Foreshadowing

Playwrights nearly always use foreshadowing as a way of leading audiences to a realization rather than shock at the climax of the play. We may be startled by the outcome, but the logic put in place by foreshadowing leads us to say, "Oh yes, now I understand." But there is a place for shock in the theatre.

Creating shock instead of realization can have a real impact – if it's done deliberately.

The situation for shock is created by not allowing foreshadowing of the event that will finally happen or the truth that will finally be revealed. That's what produces the reaction of shock. This nearly always works best if at least some characters in the play are as shocked by the revelation as we are.

Tracy Letts uses this kind of shock to great effect in *August: Osage County* by withholding foreshadowing that Ivy's lover is (unknown to either of them) her half-brother. When that fact is first revealed, we're as stunned as another character who hears it for the first time, but given how dysfunctional the family is, our shock leads to a realization that anything is possible with these characters. Because Letts was intent on creating shock, he's careful to mislead us as well on his script's Character Page about who the parents of Ivy's lover really are.

If shock is the goal, it's essential not to telegraph it in the preliminary pages of the script – literary managers and readers for competitions need to have the same sense of shock in reading your script as audiences will have seeing it in production.

23. USING NARRATORS

Although knowledge of structure is helpful, real creativity comes from leaps of faith in which you jump to something illogical. But those leaps form the memorable moments in movies and plays.
    -Francis Ford Coppola

Narrators are great storytelling devices and they're good shortcuts for providing exposition and foreshadowing.

In contemporary plays, narrators are nearly always a significant character, not the chatty maids of yesteryear, but when they open the play with a monologue to the audience, they serve the same function.

Narrators Have a Stake in the Outcome

The best way to make this device work is to weave exposition into the personal concerns of the narrator.

Narrators need to have a serious stake in the consequences of the events in the story. Contemporary playwrights hardly ever use impartial and uninvolved observers for this job, even when they have their narrators claim to be impartial and uninvolved. When narrators do make that claim (as in Arthur Miller's *A View from the Bridge*), they usually end up having their own personal views deeply shaken by the outcome of the story. That personal disruption is normally what prompts the narrator to tell us the story.

Narrators are often put into additional service as authorial spokespersons (see Chapter 9 on this use) to clarify thematic issues, something that usually happens toward the end of the play. In the meantime, they serve up exposition and foreshadowing at important breaks in the play's action.

Key Places for Narrators

Narrators are nearly always first used to open a play and audiences will expect these guides to keep them company on the rest of the journey.

1. Act I point of attack. Providing both exposition and foreshadowing.

2. Opening or ending short formal scenes. Offering observations and foreshadowing.

3. Giving the last speech of Act I. Thus including the curtain line. If they do this in Act I, they'll need to do the same at the end of Act II in a three-act play.

4. Act II point of attack. If there's an intermission after Act I (there usually is), giving us exposition about what happened during that time break and adding foreshadowing of what's to come in the next act. They'll provide the same before Act III, in a three-act play.

5. Resolution of the play. Usually summing up the meaning of the play (its theme) and sometimes telling us what happened to the characters after the play ends.

A note on time: Narrators exist with the audience in the present even if the play is set in the past. They're telling us a story they've already been through so when they are talking to the audience they're doing this in the present but when they're in the events of the story, they're back in the past.

To make this more complicated, the present time of the narrator may be in the audience's past depending on the year in which the opening of the play is set. What narrators do technically is to make us automatically feel that whatever year you've chosen to begin telling us the story is the "present." Fortunately, audiences don't see this as some sort of a strange psychic phenomenon.

A Few Good Narrators

Any character can be used as an effective narrator as long as they spend sufficient stage time with us.

1. A jailed diplomat. In David Henry Hwang's *M. Butterfly*, telling his own tale of how he got there.

2. A disaffected son. In Tennessee Williams' *The Glass Menagerie*, telling the story of his sister's decline and how he got away from the family.

3. An investigating Army officer. In Charles Fuller's *A Soldier's Play*, telling the story of how he identified the murderer and the motive and what it meant to him.

4. An attorney. In Arthur Miller's *A View from the Bridge*, telling the story of his client's downfall and what it meant to him.

5. A psychiatrist. In Peter Shaffer's *Equus,* telling the story of a disturbed boy's therapy and what the successful treatment meant personally to the psychiatrist.

6. A teacher of the hearing impaired. In Mark Medoff's *Children of a Lesser God,* telling us the story of how he destroyed his relationship with a student and the impact it had on him. It won Broadway's Tony Award for Best Play and London's Olivier Award for Best New Play.

Each of these narrators is far more than a story-teller. Good narrators, like these, are deeply impacted by the events they relate and that personal impact is their subtext for why they have "decided" to tell us their story today.

24. INCITING INCIDENT: CONFLICT FUSE

For me the opening moments of a play are most important, in terms of form. I might begin a play a hundred times until I get it absolutely right. Because if I don't get you in those first few minutes, I've lost you. I want to get you caught up as fast as possible. You hear something, you see something, there's enough to drag your butt into that play. Once I'm dead certain of the opening moments, the rest is a lot simpler.
　　　　-Charles Fuller

The inciting incident introduces the suspense plot, the source of the major conflict of the play.

INCITING INCIDENT

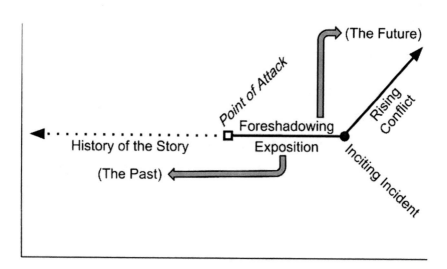

Most contemporary playwrights don't wait longer than four pages into Act I to introduce the inciting incident of the suspense plot and often do it on the first page.

A century ago, Ibsen could wait until the end of Act I of *A Doll's House* before giving us the inciting incident, but today's audiences won't sit still that long without knowing why they're there. Neither would Shakespeare's for that matter, or the Ancient Greeks. And contemporary theatre critics – at least those based in New York – are quick to point out when a play falls short in this regard.

Flagging the Inciting Incident

The inciting incident is so important in contemporary plays that most playwrights wave a flag just before they introduce it.

The flag they use most often is a pause in the action or dialogue – the "(Pause.)" stage direction. As an alternative they'll describe a physical action in a General Stage Direction that implies a pause in the dialogue. In the extreme, the inciting incident will be followed by another pause – either a physical action implying this or that stage direction again – so it stands out in the audience's ears, bracketed by silence.

Inciting incidents can knock us out of our seats like the sudden shooting of Waters in Charles Fuller's *A Soldier's Play*. Or they can be so mild you'll miss them if you scratch your ear at the wrong moment as when John whispers that his wife might want to buy Ken's house in Lanford Wilson's *Fifth of July*.

Forms of Inciting Incidents

Inciting incidents come in two varieties (that's another of those playwriting rules that's meant to be broken, but few dramatists do).

1. A single sentence. Or a phrase within a line of dialogue.

2. A physical action. Usually a simple and direct one.

In practice, most playwrights prefer using a line of dialogue for the inciting incident rather than a visual image. It can be dropped on the audience like a sledgehammer or a daisy petal (that's the so-quiet-they're-hardly-there variety). Either kind works. You just need to have one. That's a rule with some notable exceptions, but wait until you're famous to tinker with this one.

Of the two, there's an advantage to the daisy petal approach. By using a first vague reference as the inciting incident, you can gradually clarify that initial hint over a number of pages, using up time (and thus pages) in an interesting way for audiences.

Notable Inciting Incidents

In the history of dramatic writing, the placement of inciting incidents has always been early – with a few notable exceptions – and for nearly all contemporary playwrights, that has become a rule.

1. Paula Vogel's *How I Learned to Drive*, on page 1 (the first line of dialogue): Li'l Bit tells us, "Sometimes to tell a secret, you first have to teach a lesson." And we wonder what the secret is. The play won the Pulitzer Prize for Drama.

2. Tracy Letts' *August: Osage County*, on page 4: Violet asks in the play's Prologue, "Are the police here?" And we wonder why that would be necessary. This is almost a false inciting incident, though there's a reason her husband might have called the police. Then on page 8 (and the first line of Scene 1): Mattie Fae says, "Beverly's done this before." That's the real inciting incident. And we wonder what he's done again.

3. David Lindsay-Abaire's *Rabbit Hole*, on page 5: Izzy says, "Hey, I'm still coping, too, Becca. I know it's not the same, but it's still hard." And we wonder what they're both trying to cope with. The play won the Pulitzer Prize for Drama.

4. Yasmina Reza's *Art*, on page 1: Marc tells the audience his friend has bought "This white painting with white lines." And it's clear he doesn't like it, making us wonder why someone would buy it and also wonder at his friend's decision. It won London's Olivier Award for Best New Play and Broadway's Tony Award for Best Play.

5. Beth Henley's *Crimes of the Heart*, on page 1: Chick says something "awful" has happened. And we wonder what that awful thing was.

6. Edward Albee's *Who's Afraid of Virginia Woolf*, on page 15 (an exception to the inciting incident rule): George in deadly earnest warns Martha not to "start on the bit." And we wonder what the "bit" is.

7. Ntozake Shange's *For Colored Girls Who Have Considered Suicide/When the Rainbow Is Enuf*, on page 1: The Lady in Brown tells us of a woman "never havin been a girl." And we wonder why she never had a childhood.

8. Richard Nelson's *New England,* on page 3: Harry takes a revolver out of his desk drawer and cocks it. The build continues in the next 15 seconds of stage action as he puts the barrel to his head, his wife walks in, and he kills himself. And we wonder why and what will happen now.

9. David Hare's *Skylight,* on page 1: Kyra unlocks the front door of her apartment and leaves it open as she exits to the kitchen. And a young man appears in the doorway, standing there, listening, uncertain. Within a few moments, we discover through exposition that this is her former step-son she has not seen since he was a boy. But the tension remains around this stranger.

10. Tina Howe's *Pride's Crossing,* on page 3: Mabel says, looking at a bill, "The Beverly Visiting Nurse Service? Eight hundred thirty three dollars? What next?" And then stuffs it away in a pile of junk. And we realize, or think we do, that this 90-year-old lady hasn't been paying her bills, and we wonder what will happen to her. It won the New York Drama Critics Circle Award for Best American Play.

11. Warren Leight's *Side Man,* on page 2: Clifford says to us, "And even if there are no clean breaks, I swear, tomorrow morning I'm out." And we wonder if he'll really be able to do this. The play won Broadway's Tony Award for Best Play.

12. Martin McDonagh's *The Beauty Queen of Leenane,* on page 8 (another exception to that rule): Mag says, "The fella up and murdered the poor oul woman in Dublin and he didn't even know her." And we see that she's in her seventies. And Maureen responds, "Sure, that sounds exactly the type of fella I would like to meet, and then bring him home to meet you, if he likes murdering oul women." And we wonder what will happen to these women. It won the Drama Desk Award for Best Play.

13. Rajiv Joseph's *Bengal Tiger at the Baghdad Zoo,* on page 1 (the first line of dialogue): The Tiger says, "The lions escaped two days ago. Predictably, they got killed in about two hours." And we're concerned about the danger permeating the city and what may happen to the tiger.

14. Katori Hall's *The Mountaintop,* on page 1 in a stage direction following the first line of dialogue: Martin Luther King deliberately and carefully locks the deadbolt on his Memphis motel room door, then just as carefully secures the safety chain, and then pulls the window curtains tightly shut. And we sense his fear. Hall's play is a special case since it comes with an external suspense plot. Because of its setting and time (the Lorraine Motel in Memphis, Tennessee, on August 3, 1968) most audiences will know that the civil rights leader was assassinated standing on the balcony of that motel room the next evening. While the play uses a traditional introduction of the suspense plot, that external suspense plot hovers over the audience even before the curtain goes up.

Regardless of how it's handled, the function of the inciting incident is to introduce the suspense plot – and thus the conflict – that drives the play forward.

25. PLOTS: THEY COME IN PAIRS

I used to think that you could just start to write and see what happened. Now I find that if you do that, it doesn't turn out; you may not get anywhere that's interesting. There are drives to plays. Sometimes I think of them as pieces of machinery.
        -Marsha Norman

Plots come in pairs. Successful playwrights instinctively know that and have for centuries.

SUSPENSE AND EMOTIONAL PLOTS

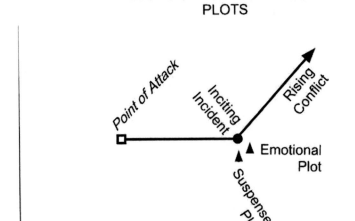

A Note on Dual Plots

The concept of dual or twin plots was suggested many years ago by the great Shakespearean scholar A. C. Bradley. This insight has a long theoretical pedigree and a far longer one in terms of practical usage by playwrights.

But the real proof of the concept is in the practice of contemporary playwriting – it is nearly impossible to find produced plays today that do not use a form of this dual plot structure. The reason playwrights use this structure probably owes more to the way human beings have always told lasting stories than to theoretical understandings of dramatic structure.

Suspense & Emotional Plots

A. C. Bradley pointed out that we sit through those four hours of *Hamlet* because we want to find out if Hamlet will kill the King before the King kills Hamlet. Even Shakespeare knew about the critical function of a suspense plot, but that was not what the Bard wanted to spend much time on.

Shakespeare knew – as with nearly all playwrights before or since then – that he needed an excuse to hold audiences in their seats (or in his case, on their feet). Having accomplished that, he could then spend most of the play exploring what he really wanted to write about: The emotional (and political) consequences of Claudius having killed Hamlet's father (the rightful king) and then taken his place on the Danish throne and in the King's bedchamber.

The purpose of the suspense plot – the what-happens-next of a play – is to provide an excuse to write about what really interests playwrights: The emotional plot. As Lynn Nottage said about writing her play *Ruined*, "I believe in engaging people emotionally, because I think they react more out of emotion." She's right.

Emotional Plots Are Why You Write

Emotional plots are why most playwrights do what they do: They want to focus on the consequences of events, the emotional ramifications of the suspense plot. This is what the suspense plot allows you to spend your time on.

Since the emotional plot typically takes up about 90% of a play, it leads most playwrights to assemble characters who have a shared and emotionally complicated past. This is usually a past that has been simmering beneath the surface of their relationships for some time. The inciting incident of the suspense plot provides the catalyst for this simmering past to finally come to light.

While screenwriting will be treated in detail in Part Six, it's worth noting here that screenplays often bring together central characters with little or no shared past, an approach made possible by suspense plots that can dominate scripts. Many successful screenplays are simply about the what-happens-next of the story (the suspense plot).

Some Notable Emotional Plots

While emotional plots take up most of a play, they are typically simple and uncomplicated to describe.

1. Can Maggie get her husband to sleep with her again – and preferably love her (assuming he ever did)?

2. Can the three sisters learn to be supportive friends?

3. Why is the Sergeant's relationship with his troops so antagonistic?

4. How will the Diplomat handle the exposure of the true nature of his relationship – with the person he thinks is his mistress?

No matter how intriguing the emotional plot may be, it's nearly impossible to hold an audience for more than about 20 minutes without that suspense plot doing the dirty work.

Suspense Plot Function

Even though a suspense plot uses up only a small fraction of the script, here's why playwrights go to all that trouble.

1. It keeps the audience engaged with the play. While you concentrate on the emotional consequences of the suspense plot's events.

2. It triggers and justifies the eruption of the emotional plot. Allowing the audience to understand why all of this emotional baggage is coming to the surface now – as opposed to five years ago or next week or next year.

It's true that Maggie could have walked into that bedroom and out of the blue said, "Listen Brick, we have just got to deal with our problems." Therapists might applaud her initiative, but audiences would sit on their hands – assuming they came back after intermission.

But Tennessee Williams knew how to use these paired plots. The suspense plot (*Who gets the money?*) forces Maggie to raise her very personal and emotional issue today. She launches the emotional plot with motivation from the suspense plot, knowing that if she fails with this emotional issue, her husband (and she) won't get the money.

Best Practice: *Emotional plots don't float well on pure coincidence.*

Here's another way of looking at this: The suspense plot is like a railroad flatcar. Its purpose in life is to carry the emotional plot from the inciting incident to the climax of the play. Once it's done that, you can coast without it to the end of the resolution.

And here's the mechanism: The suspense plot is the trigger that unleashes the emotional plot and the climax of the suspense plot (the climax of the play) leads directly to the resolution of the emotional plot.

Suspense Plot Techniques

The goal with a suspense plot is to get as much as you can with as little as possible. This plot is critical, but your energies need to be invested in the emotional plot.

For most playwrights, suspense plots hinge on practical, physical, issues:

1. Will Ken sell his family home?

2. Who killed the sergeant?

3. Will Tess get to go to college in America?

4. Who's going to get the money?

5. Can Mama stop her daughter from committing suicide?

If the suspense plot is about a person rather than the more typical practical issue, it's still "practical," but something like: *What's happened to Beverly who's vanished?*

Since plays are about consequences more than the events themselves, suspense plots are kept in the background, but stretched as far as possible.

Evolving Suspense Plots

Playwrights usually evolve or transform suspense plots as the plays move forward. They often begin with a hint at the inciting incident and then make these plots clearer as Act I progresses.

1. What's the disgusting thing the in-laws are up to?
Becomes: Who gets the money? (*Cat on a Hot Tin Roof*)

2. Who killed the Sergeant? *Becomes*: Can Davenport find the killer? (*A Soldier's Play*)

3. Why does Jessie want towels and a gun? *Becomes*: Can Mama stop Jessie from killing herself? (*'night, Mother*)

4. Why would the police have been called? *Becomes*: Where's Beverly? *Becomes*: Did he kill himself? (*August: Osage County*)

In more subtle approaches, there is often an initial process of clarifying the suspense plot instead of giving it to us straight at the inciting incident. Here's how Tennessee Williams did this:

Clarifying the Suspense Plot in *Cat*

Step One: Introduction of the Suspense Plot.
Margaret tells Brick that his brother and sister-in-law are up to something disgusting.

Step Two: Partial Clarification of the Suspense Plot.
Brick asks what those two are doing. Margaret tells him he already knows. Brick denies knowing.

Step Three: Making the Suspense Plot Clear.
Margaret tells Brick they're trying to get his father to leave nothing in his will to Brick.

Here's the annotated inciting incident and clarification of the suspense plot as Tennessee Williams wrote it:

Step One: Introduction.
MARGARET: Of course it's comical but it's also disgusting since it's so obvious what they're up to!
BRICK (*Without interest*): What are they up to, Maggie?

Step Two: Partial Clarification.
MARGARET: Why, you know what they're up to!
BRICK: No, I don't know what they're up to.

(*He stands there in the bathroom doorway drying his hair.*)

Step Three: Making It Clear.
MARGARET: I'll tell you what they're up to, boy of mine! --- They're up to cutting you out of your father's estate, and ---

(*She freezes momentarily before her next remark.*)

Williams managed the clarification of his suspense plot in less than a page of the script while Marsha Norman stretched the process of clarification over nine pages in *'night, Mother*. Both approaches work.

Reintroductions of the Suspense Plot

Nearly all playwrights remind us of the developing suspense plot about once every four to eight pages of the script. Those reminders can vary from a seemingly casual mention of the suspense plot to an entire scene devoted to it.

Another way to look at this: If the suspense plot is like a railroad flatcar carrying the emotional plot for the audience, we want to know periodically that the wheels haven't fallen off. The reminders keep the level of concern (or suspense) high enough for audiences to maintain their engagement with the play.

"Red Herring" Suspense Plots

Red herrings offer another way to stretch a suspense plot by providing an opening bridge that leads us to the introduction of the real suspense plot.

These kinds of suspense plots come few and very far between in the work of contemporary playwrights. Their most famous use was in the classic *James Bond* films (with Sean Connery as 007) but they can work in the theatre, too.

By using a red herring, the play begins with what appears to be a suspense plot, but one that has no direct connection to the play's actual suspense plot. Its primary purpose is to hold us while the characters are introduced and the setup is established for the inciting incident of the real suspense plot.

One of the benefits of red herrings is that they use up pages on the way to the minimum length needed for a full-length play. That's also one of their dangers. These red herrings are a great way to damage the opening of a play. They can do that by pushing you to accept a point of attack that's nearly always too early in the history of the story.

Red herrings only work well when introduced at the beginning of a play. Done that way, audiences will ride through the transition from the red herring to the real suspense plot and accept the fact (usually happily) that they've been conned.

This is an issue where Aristotle was absolutely correct: His rule of unity of action matters. Audiences like one story at a time and the red herring suspense plot technically gives them that: We get the fish first and then get the real thing. If the red herring is introduced later in the play, you'll be interrupting one story to tell another. It's possible to make this work, but there is also a message in the fact that it's hardly ever done by playwrights today.

A classic example of a red herring suspense plot is the opening of Edward Albee's *Who's Afraid of Virginia Woolf.*

> **1. The Red Herring:** Who are these guests coming at 2:00 a.m.? Albee holds us with this issue for 16 pages until:

> **2. The Real Thing:** "Just don't start in on the bit, that's all." Albee uses the fish to keep us involved until the actual suspense plot hooks us. By then, 16 pages in, we know a lot about how George and Martha behave and some of the tensions between them and this gives impact to the real inciting incident.

It's not that the red herring suspense plot is untrue. There are guests who've been invited to George and Martha's home. It's just that the red herring about the guests is not the suspense plot that will support – and drive – the remainder of the play.

Repetitive Activity as Suspense Plot Substitute

Repetitive or mundane physical activity can serve as a temporary support structure, especially for scenes verging on pure discussion. The structure of the physical activity itself provides shape and a sense of forward movement, even if there is little conflict in the dialogue. This device can work for short segments of a play, in a way like a suspense plot for the entire piece.

The technique has been around the theatre at least since Shakespeare's Grave Digger carried on that philosophical discussion with Hamlet while shoveling up dirt and bones.

There's nothing particularly interesting about digging a grave, or doing the dishes, or taking photos, or cooking dinner, or getting dressed – in real life, but in the theatre they take on an interest they don't really deserve. These kinds of routine physical activities do have a structure to them, having a beginning, a middle, and an end and they heighten the sense of tension when woven through a scene.

Notable Long Mundane Activities

These repetitive mundane activities have even been used to considerable effect for the entire length of a play, though it's been a long time since a contemporary playwright tried this.

> **1. Arnold Wesker's *The Kitchen*.** The mundane activity: Making an elaborate Greek pastry from scratch throughout the play.

> **2. David Storey's *The Contractor*.** The mundane activity: Erecting a huge tent for a wedding reception throughout Act I and taking it down throughout Act II.

Most contemporary playwrights still do what Shakespeare did and use this device sparingly. In *Red*, John Logan does this by having Rothko's studio assistant attach a large sheet of painters' canvas to a wooden frame (a "stretcher") using a heavy spring-loaded stapler during a monologue by the central character. The loud crack – almost like a gunshot – of each staple going in punctuates the painter's long speech and the process of attaching the canvas (in reality a boring activity in painting studios) provides an intriguing underlying structure to the scene and its monologue.

A fine example of the technique is Tony Kushner's second scene in Part One of *Angels in America*: Roy Cohn is on a multi-line phone continuously making and receiving calls. This repetitive activity, including his end of the phone conversations, keeps our interest as we learn about him and the man who's come to see him – all of which takes about four pages of the script. Viewed in isolation, the mechanics of this repetitive activity have no real significance, but in the play's context it tells us volumes about Roy's attitude toward underlings.

26. ELEVATOR PLAYS: BISQUICK PLOTS

I'm an emotional writer. I write a play because I do not want to stay where I am. It's an uncomfortable place and therefore very powerful.
    -John Patrick Shanley

All plays are elevator plays, at least in the technical sense. The central characters have to be kept in the same place long enough for the conflict between them to generate 90 to 120 pages of dialogue. If one of those key characters simply decides to opt out, the whole enterprise falls apart.

A practical example: What if Prince Hamlet at the end of Act I decides that these ghostly goings-on, coupled with his uncle marrying his widowed mother, are just too much for him to wrap his brain around? So instead he goes back to finish his university degree. If Hamlet did that, he could look forward to a long and happy life, but the play he's in would be dead.

In most plays, it's the suspense plot that keeps the characters together, even if cold logic tells us they could leave at any time. The twist to the elevator version is that we know the characters physically can't leave.

The elevator gimmick often gets a bad rap in the theatre. The reality is, the theoretical concept of an elevator play is what earns it the bad rap, not the plays that result from it. Critics (and audiences) seldom register a complaint when an elevator is in operation.

Elevator Principles

The original elevator play concept sounds ridiculous when it's torn down to its basic elements.

1. Cram a group of characters in an elevator. They don't need to know each other. A crowd of 10 is good with a mix of ages, genders, social status, and emotional problems.

2. Close the doors and stick it between floors. When that happens, one of the passengers turns out to be a lunatic.

3. If nothing happens, turn off the vent fan. So it gets hot in there and if that still doesn't produce the goods, turn off the light.

An elevator play is a fake play in a way, but sometimes as with classics of the form they go on to lead charmed lives. Mark Medoff's *When You Comin' Back Red Ryder* is a classic elevator play where the elevator is a guy with a gun. John Huston's moody, *Key Largo* is a classic elevator film where the elevator is a hurricane and a guy with a gun (Humphrey Bogart make a great elevator operator).

When they work well, the elevator becomes the suspense plot, most often evolving into a variant of "Will they survive?" or more likely "Who will survive?"

The advantage of this technique is that there's no need to worry about a suspense plot. That's the elevator. The point of attack is when the characters get in and the inciting incident is when it sticks between floors. The conflict is driven by the aggressive lunatic picking on everybody. The climax hits when the lunatic loses it, and the resolution is of course when the elevator finally –.

An elevator play can be set practically anywhere as long as its location is (or seems) sufficiently isolated so the characters can't – or just think they can't – leave. And at least one of those characters, if not a raving lunatic, is at least borderline.

Tracy Letts borrows from the elevator concept in his Pulitzer Prize play, *August: Osage County*: The whole strange family (10 + housekeeper) is stuck in the parents' home for the funeral of the patriarch. The windows are taped shut, it's August on the boiling plains of Oklahoma, and the air conditioner is turned off. Then the matriarch turns out to be a little off and mean as a snake.

Notable Plays with Elevators

Some of the great plays of the last century are held together by elevators.

1. Harold Pinter's *The Dumb Waiter*. The elevator: The Organization that sent Gus and Ben to wait in this room. There's even a real elevator: The dumbwaiter of the title through which the organization sometimes communicates with these two.

2. Samuel Beckett's *Endgame*. The elevator: "Something that's taking its course" outside, forcing Clov, Hamm, and his parents to stay inside this small building.

3. Jean-Paul Sartre's *No Exit.* The elevator: They're in Hell – or some version of it – so the three characters are confined to this living room forever.

4. Edward Albee's *Who's afraid of Virginia Woolf.* The elevator: The demand of Martha's unseen Daddy that these two couples spend the remainder of the evening together, though the play has much more than this elevator: There's the red herring suspense plot plus the actual suspense plot and that's certainly a way to guarantee audience attention.

The elevator form can also be a cure for writer's block since most of the hard work is instantly done for you by selecting the elevator and those odd characters inside it.

27. HIGH POINT OF ACT I

*It's been less crucial for playwrights to fulfill audience
expectations. I don't mean Broadway, where there's often an
economic downside if you don't fulfill rules, and where people
usually want to see things that reassure them. But those who
tinker off Broadway are freer of that. And we were off-off
Hollywood! With a low budget, we could make the movie exactly
as we wanted.*
-Neil LaBute

The high point is what Act I has been heading for from the moment
the inciting incident was introduced about 60 pages earlier. This
moment doesn't need to be very high in terms of tension and
conflict. It can, but it doesn't have to and being subtle can be good
for an effective high point.

The Act I high point stops short of becoming a climax since
that has to be saved for the end of Act II. But it is usually the highest
point of tension in Act I – unless a teaser point of attack was used,
borrowing this moment for the point of attack.

Think of this high point as something that could have
developed into a climax of the suspense plot under slightly different
circumstances, but one that can't be allowed to happen for the most
boring of technical reasons – the annoying *Hamlet* Question (see
Chapter 33 for more on this): There's still an Act II that needs to be
written to make this a full-length play.

Notable Act I High Points
In each of these, the high point is limited to providing tension and
revelations for the audience, but not enough to resolve the suspense
plot.

1. Loomis is terror stricken by a vision, but his vision
doesn't resolve the suspense plot in August Wilson's *Joe
Turner's Come and Gone*. It won the New York Drama Critics
Circle Award for Best Play.

2. Howie screams that Becca must stop erasing their child,

but that only shows how far apart these two still are in David Lindsay-Abaire's *Rabbit Hole*.

3. Babe reveals how she tried to kill her husband, but we still don't know what's going to happen to her in Beth Henley's *Crimes of the Heart*.

4. The Diplomat attempts to roughly seduce Song, but it doesn't get us much closer to understanding how he ended up in jail in David Henry Hwang's *M. Butterfly*.

5. Stanley's wife offers to get him all the women he wants, but that doesn't resolve the conflict in Pam Gems' *Stanley*. It won London's Olivier Award for Best New Play.

Technically, the high point usually happens within the last five pages of Act I and sets the stage for a strong Act I curtain line – the device that brings audiences back for Act II.

28. CURTAIN LINES FOR ACTS & SCENES

Words should taste good in the mouth; they should sound good,
too, have the right weight and heft to them; the more dangerous,
alluring, mysterious, inflammatory, the better; the more we feel
that they are driving us to the edge of some dangerous place,
someplace that we've never quite been before, the better.
-Robert Auletta

Jason Miller ends the first act of *That Championship Season* with a character yanking a loaded shotgun off the mantle and threatening to blow the head off an old friend who has been sleeping with his wife. As he holds the gun steady, the curtain comes down on Act I. (The play won Broadway's Tony Award for Best Play.)

That's the concept of a curtain line, but most contemporary playwrights handle this in more subtle ways.

ACT I HIGH POINT & CURTAIN LINE

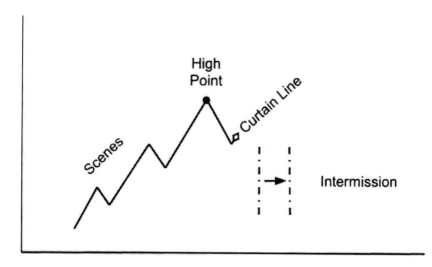

Technically, a curtain line is an inciting incident that is not allowed to build through further dialogue. Whatever its form – whether a spoken line of dialogue or physical action – this is the last thing the audience hears or sees before the curtain comes down or the lights go out on Act I.

Curtain Line Options

These lines are a key technical device for keeping audiences engaged in a play.

1. The last line of dialogue. Even though contemporary plays seldom hang together only on what-happens-next, in this case the curtain line is a what-happens-next moment.

2. The last physical action by a character. A visual image can be as strong as what we hear.

3. The last sound we hear other than dialogue. Sound effects can be highly evocative.

That something needs to be strong enough to make us want to know what the outcome will be in the next movement of the play. If the curtain line ends a formal scene but not the act, then its job is to propel us into the next scene. If it's at the end of an act, its job is to make us want to come back after intermission for the consequences.

The milder the curtain line, the more its power depends on the build to it. Softer curtain lines can't stand on their own or they'll seem to be drifting onto us from the sky and we may not notice them. When they are weak or simply not there at the end of Act I, audiences often ask themselves the worst possible question: *Is there any reason to come back after intermission?* That's the last thing playwrights want audience to be asking.

Best Practice: *Curtain lines need to leave us with something unanswered.*

A curtain line that doesn't come easily may be a signal that there's a structural problem with the act or scene. These lines usually grow out of the conflict that's been building since the beginning of the play. When that's happening, they'll come naturally. If you can't find a curtain line, you've probably allowed the play's conflict to resolve itself too soon.

Some Notable Act I Curtain Lines

A good curtain line typically lives – if it does at all – in a context with what's happened or been said just before it, but even as a single line it needs to deliver a punch, even if it's a gentle one.

1. From Tom Stoppard's *Arcadia* (winner of London's Olivier Award for Best New Play):

VALENTINE: Well, the other thing is, you'd have to be insane.

(*Valentine leaves. Hanna stays thoughtful. After a moment, she turns to the table and picks up the Cornhill Magazine. She looks into it briefly, then closes it, and leaves the room, taking the magazine with her. The empty room. The light changes to early morning. From a long way off, there is a pistol shot. A moment later there is the cry of dozens of crows disturbed from the unseen trees.*)

2. From Wakako Yamauchi's *And the Soul Shall Dance*:

EMIKO: Because I must keep the dream alive...the dream is all I live for. I am only in exile now. Because if I give in, all I've lived before...will mean nothing...will be for nothing. Because if I let you make me believe this is all there is to my life, the dream would die...I would die.

(*She pours another drink and feels warm and good. Fade out.*)

3. From Terrence McNally's *A Perfect Ganesh*:

KATHERINE: Please, someone help!
MARGARET: I can't hear you...Kitty, Kitty...
KATHERINE: I've lost someone, a young man, he's not well, he may have fallen.

(*She blows and blows the whistle, as Margaret continues to call down from the balcony. The roaring [of a vast multitude] is almost unbearable. Ganesha claps his hands together. Once and all sounds stop. Twice and the others all freeze. The third time and all the lights snap off for the end of Act One.*)

4. From Tracy Letts' *August: Osage County* (for Act II of this three-act play):

VIOLET: You can't do this! This is my house! This is my house!
BARBARA: You don't get it, do you? (*With a burst of adrenaline, she strides to Violet, towers over her*) I'M RUNNING

THINGS NOW!

(*Blackout.*)

It's possible to have a curtain line fall from the sky with no relationship to anything in the scene or act, but few playwrights have tried this except in farce or the wildest of comedies.

That fall-from-the-sky approach can occasionally produce something as inspired as the Saturday Night Live classic: *Missiles headed for New York! News at eleven.*

29. ACT II & ITS PROBLEMS

The director had definite reservations about the third act. He felt
that Big Daddy was too vivid and important a character to
disappear from the play except as an offstage cry after the second
act curtain; he felt that the character of Brick should undergo some
apparent mutation as a result of the virtual vivisection that he
undergoes in Act Two. He felt that the character of Margaret
should be, if possible, more clearly sympathetic to the audience. I
was fearful that I would lose his interest if I didn't reexamine the
script from his point of view. I did.
 -Tennessee Williams

Act II is seldom a problem if you haven't been moving too fast in
telling the story in Act I.

STRUCTURE OF ACT II

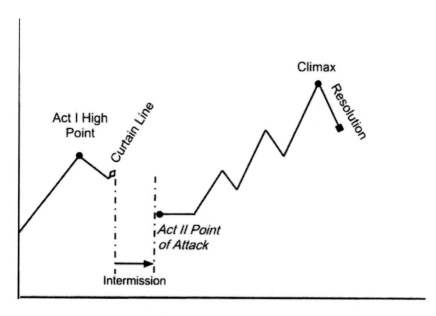

If you have been moving too fast – and there's a great
temptation to do this – Act II will be your worst nightmare. If you're

writing a very long play in three acts, then Act III will be the one haunting your dreams.

Best Practice: *Take time telling the story.*

Allow the conflict between characters to set the storytelling pace and resist the tendency to summarize and compress the forward movement of the story. Playwrights have an advantage over novelists in resisting the compression urge: Novelists can quickly summarize what should be large movements of a story in a few narrative paragraphs. The preponderance of dialogue in plays helps playwrights avoid this trap, but it's still simple to go from a blackout to the next scene – and in the hitting of that return key, skipping over necessary story development.

Keep in mind that it's much easier to edit down a script that seems to be too long for its story than to expand a script that ends too soon.

Saving Conflict for Act II

The key to a healthy Act II is to save a large portion of the source of the conflict for the play's second movement. That's where the climax has to be – unless the script is going to end up being nothing more than a long one-act play.

If you've found that on more than one script that you've finished telling the story by the end of Act I and an Act II refuses to follow without considerable agony, then you're rushing the telling of the tale. A potential solution for this tendency is to try outlining the next play – giving as much weight to Act II as to Act I – before starting to write. This approach should force conservation of enough conflict for an Act II.

While outlining may solve the problem of rushing, it may also lead to some negative incentives: See the section on Outlining in Chapter 40 before trying this.

Act II Realities

There are two technical realities that help in launching Act II.

1. Act II usually has to start at a lower level of conflict than the end of Act I. The audience has been away from the play during the intermission, perhaps for as long as 20 minutes. They've been out in the theatre's lobby talking about your play (we hope) and other topics having nothing to do with your work. They simply won't return to their seats after the intermission with the same level of tension and connection to your work as they had at the curtain line of Act I. But if that was a good and compelling curtain line, they will be back for Act II.

2. There can be a long time break in the story between acts. That means Act II can start with a combination of foreshadowing and exposition (as did Act I), but this time moving much faster. This means selecting a new point of attack for Act II and determining its place in the history of the story.

Intermissions & Story Time Breaks

The break created by an intermission in the timeline of the story can offer a source of new conflict to help drive Act II.

If there's a long time break in the story between Act I and Act II, it's best to have something important happen in the interval whether that time break is an hour or 30 years. What happened during the time break should be something that has the potential to increase the level of tension or the development of the suspense or emotional plots in Act II.

Nearly all contemporary playwrights take advantage of this time break device if they've conceived of their play with an intermission. Tennessee Williams was unusual – even reckless – in not doing this. He started each new act of *Cat* with no time break at all: His curtain line of the previous act and the point of attack of the next act were identical.

If the play is structured in three acts and thus does not have a formal intermission between Act II and Act III, there can still be a time break in the story during the pause, even though the curtain may only be down for a minute. There's no relationship in playwriting between the actual length of an intermission or pause between the acts and the length of the time break that's possible in the story.

Economics of Intermissions

Regional theatres like intermissions (as do the owners of commercial theatres) because the audience buys food and drink while they're standing around waiting for Act II. This is an income stream that helps support the theatre's operations including the production of your play.

It's highly unlikely that any theatre would decide not to do a play if it doesn't have an intermission, but it is a win-win device: The theatre gets help with keeping the lights on and the playwright gains the opportunity for increased conflict in Act II. If it feels right to have a break in the story at the end of Act I, then definitely opt for a formal intermission.

If you've conceived the play without a time break during the intermission – and nothing significant happened in that time break – be prepared for a director to suggest the option of going without an intermission, especially if the script runs in the 90-100 page range. The suggestion will probably be made because the director believes the loss of dramatic momentum that always results from an intermission will significantly dilute the impact of the play.

30. CLIMAX & THE OBLIGATORY SCENE

The climax is that point beyond which everything is extraneous.
Now, this can be violent physical action, or it can be someone
turning silently away.
  -Edward Albee

The obligatory scene is what the script has been heading for since the point of attack began Act I.

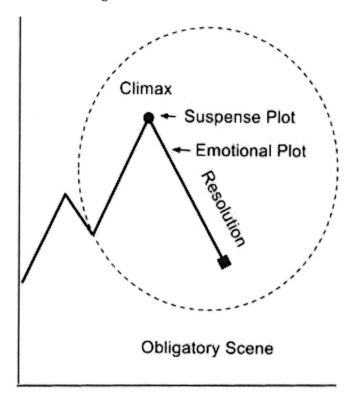

Odds are you've sensed the shape of that peak of conflict and tension from the point of attack of Act II – conflict so intense it has to snap. It doesn't matter if it's a farce or a serious epic, the climax within the obligatory scene results from the same forces and produces the same impact.

The Climax from Narrowing of Options

The best kind of climax for a play is one where you feel as a playwright that you just need to get out of its way.

That may be overstating the degree to which the central characters have taken over the writing process, but it's not unusual for playwrights to feel like they're racing to keep up with what's happening between the characters.

By this point in the play, all of the forces of conflict and tension triggered by the inciting incident at the start of Act I have been steadily narrowing your options – and the characters' options – until the climax is the only door left open. Because of the high pitch of conflict now, it's possible for some kind of physical action to mark the climax, but it's not required.

Notable Climaxes

The climax of most contemporary plays is nothing but words – often intense ones – but still, words.

1. **Maggie lies to Big Daddy that she's pregnant**, in Tennessee Williams' *Cat on a Hot Tin Roof*.

2. **Peterson shoots Sgt. Waters**, in Charles Fuller's *A Soldier's Play*.

3. **The Angel crashes through Prior's ceiling**, in Tony Kushner's *Angels in America, Part I*.

4. **Peter confronts Heidi with her lack of commitment**, in Wendy Wasserstein's *The Heidi Chronicles*, winner of the Tony Award for Best Play.

5. **George tells Martha their "son" has been killed**, in Edward Albee's *Who's Afraid of Virginia Woolf*.

6. **Babe tries to gas herself (comically) in the oven**, in Beth Henley's *Crimes of the Heart*.

7. **Jessie pulls the trigger (off stage)**, in Marsha Norman's *'night, Mother*.

8. **Bernard and Chloë reject each other**, in Tom Stoppard's *Arcadia*.

9. **Ivy learns her boyfriend is her half-brother**, in Tracy Letts' *August: Osage County*.

Role of the Obligatory Scene

The climax comes as the cap of the obligatory scene. Another way to look at this: The climax is wrapped inside the envelope of the obligatory scene. It's obligatory because the audience wants to see it. They want that final confrontation between the main characters, coming out of the conflict set in motion with the Act I inciting incident.

Not only do audiences want to see this final encounter, but they also want to see it carried through to a resolution (that's the job of the obligatory scene). And if you disappoint them in this regard, that will color their whole experience of the play. (In Chapter 31, we'll talk about an exception to this obligatory scene "rule" when using open endings.)

Here's the simplest technical way to get the obligatory scene started: Bring the two most opposing characters face-to-face and keep them there until this storm of conflict breaks. Keep in mind that there have been two interconnected plots operating through the play and it's nearly always the suspense plot that generates the climax.

In the heat of that moment, one or more of the central characters will have their lives and relationships altered in some meaningful way because the climax of the suspense plot nearly always triggers a climax in the emotional plot within the next several pages.

The Obligatory Scene Sequence

1. Main characters come face-to-face, *Building to*:

2. Climax of the suspense plot, *triggering*:

3. Beginning of the resolution, *followed by*:

4. Minor climax of the emotional plot, *leading to*:

5. Completion of the resolution.

There's nothing mysterious about this process. The climax of the story has been reached. It's a big moment and it has taken a lot of effort to get there, so now take a breath or two before going on. That's the beginning of the resolution and you're ready to take on the minor climax of the emotional plot.

Annotated Obligatory Scene

This is the sequence of the obligatory scene as Marsha Norman built it for the end of 'night, Mother, a classic lesson in how to do it:

1. Climax of the Suspense Plot:

MAMA: Jessie! Please!

(*And we hear the shot, and it sounds like an answer, it sounds like No.*)

2. Resolution begins:

(*Mama collapses against the door, tears streaming down her face, but not screaming anymore. In shock now.*)

3. Climax of Emotional Plot:

MAMA: Jessie, Jessie, child...Forgive me. (*Pause*) I thought you were mine.

4. Resolution continues:

(*And she leaves the door and makes her way through the living room, around the furniture, as though she didn't know where it was, not knowing what to do. Finally, she goes to the stove in the kitchen and picks up the hot-chocolate pan and carries it with her to the telephone, and holds on to it while she dials the number. She looks down at the pan, holding it tight like her life depended on it. She hears Loretta answer.*)

MAMA: Loretta, let me talk to Dawson, honey.

(*Curtain.*)

Note how the impact of that last line would evaporate if it had been written as: "Loretta, Jessie's shot herself, let me talk to Dawson, honey." The power of the playwright's final line comes from the incredible amount of subtext kept beneath the surface of that short line of dialogue. Yet even with keeping her foot on the subtext, the story is fully resolved at the end.

As with all stories, the history of this one could continue on past Norman's ending. We could imagine a sequel or an Act II (or Act III) driven by the relationships between the remaining family members, now unbalanced by what Jessie has done. That's not an interesting idea—and that's why the playwright didn't do it.

Best Practice: *Knowing when to stop writing – when you've finished telling the story – is as important as selecting the point of attack.*

31. THE RESOLUTION & ENDINGS

Why write the play if you know the end?
            -John Guare

The resolution is the final summing up of the consequences of the events that triggered the conflict (and the play) all those many pages ago.

Even though the climax is over, this is no time to relax because the resolution is on its way and that's the last image audiences will carry away as they leave the theatre.

Resolutions can be very short. Marsha Norman's for *'night, Mother* has one 8-line stage direction followed by a single line of dialogue of only seven words and they are practically never longer than a few pages. There's a good reason for that: The climax has drained the conflict from the play by resolving the suspense plot and then the emotional plot. Once the climax happens, the play has to resolve itself fast or it will become a bore.

Avoiding Tying It All Up

Resist the temptation to tie everything up with a neat bow in the resolution. That's just old-style television tugging at your sleeve. Theatre offers the luxury of leaving some secondary issues for audiences to work out on their own. Let them. Theatre audiences enjoy having some complex questions to consider after the play is over.

Here's what Tennessee Williams left for the audience to work out, but only after resolving the suspense plot at the climax of *Cat on a Hot Tin Roof* (Who gets the money? Brick and his wife, Maggie, do). And we also know that Brick is willing to have a sexual relationship again with his wife – at least briefly – thus resolving the major driver of the emotional plot.

The questions Williams leaves unresolved are notable: What if Maggie doesn't get pregnant tonight? And if so, what if Big Daddy lives long enough to discover she lied to him about being pregnant with Brick's child? If Big Daddy dies tonight and thus before he can execute his will, what will Big Mamma do about the estate? Can Brick really have a relationship with Maggie for the long term or even for a night?

Leaving issues like these unresolved – essentially allowing the audience to resolve them to their own satisfaction – is typical of what nearly all contemporary playwrights do. In *August: Osage County*, Tracy Letts leaves unresolved the questions of what will happen to the matriarch now that she's been abandoned by the family and whether Ivy will be able to sustain her romantic relationship with Little Charles now that she knows he's her half-brother.

The Last Word

Usually the character with the last word in the script is the one the playwright is most intrigued by or who is put through the most extreme changes. In some cases, that may not be the same character the audience finds most compelling despite the playwright's best efforts.

Best Practice: *The central character nearly always has the last word at the end.*

A recent example of this is the last word in *August: Osage County*. That's given to the matriarch and the housekeeper (with overlapping dialogue). The oddity is that the mother changes only slightly in the course of the play – that's one of the interesting things about her – while the other female family members go through notable changes. Because of those changes, the other characters are the ones most likely to capture audience attention and sympathy.

The last word rule assumes the central character is still alive or still functioning. If they're no longer alive, often the character given that last word uses it to refer to the central character who's gone. Shakespeare nearly always ended his tragedies and histories this way.

For a classic demonstration of the last word, compare the original and what's known as the "Broadway" Act III endings of *Cat on A Hot Tin Roof*. In the original script it's Brick's play (that's the play Williams intended to write and the character he was most interested in) and Brick has the last word. In the revised script (that's the play his director wanted him to write), it's mostly Maggie's play and she has the last word – though her last word refers to Brick (Williams wouldn't give up everything for his director).

If a narrator has been leading us through the story, that character needs to be given the last word and invariably a narrator refers to the central character in this final summing up.

Open Endings

If you want to push your luck to the limit with how much the audience is left not knowing at the end, an open ending is the device to use. Be prepared to be disliked by audiences.

In June of 2011, the popular cable television series *The Killing* ended its first season without resolving who the murderer was. The series writers and executive producer thought they were being clever by taking this risk and that the show's audience would enjoy it. Instead they were deluged by a boat-load of furious comments attacking them for using what in technical terms was an open ending. They caught all that grief for an interesting technical reason. Audiences are accustomed to open endings for each weekly episode of a multiple-episode series (though most episodes will offer some partial closure). What they hated here was having an open ending in June knowing they would have to wait through the whole summer to find out who did it. The very popular Julian Fellowes series – the BBC's *Downton Abbey* – produced similar audience grumbling for the open ending of its first season.

Open endings are a great way to infuriate an audience whether in theatre, film, or television. As a story-telling technique, open endings are unsatisfying for audiences because the payoff of the play's conflict never arrives. Audiences – even the most sophisticated – want closure. Defy them at your peril.

Despite the antagonism open endings may produce, playwrights using this device often do so for a very good reason: They doubt there is a solution to the conflict they've been exploring since the point of attack and they take the risk of using an open ending because they believe strongly that this is the only logical way to end the play.

Open endings may not be an ideal choice for most plays, but the positive side is that by leaving the major conflict initiated by the suspense plot unresolved, audiences can be force to confront a play's theme in deeper ways than they might with a traditional "closed" ending.

As a result, we are left with both the suspense and emotional plots unresolved. Audiences used to more conventional storytelling in film and television (and even theatre) don't like open endings even when the compensation offered for this is the intellectual challenge of working out possible endings for themselves. It's probably not appropriate to write this off as an intellectual failing on their part. It could be that the same DNA issue driving the storytelling skill also drives the desire for story closure.

Notable Open Endings

Technically, an open ending is created by not allowing an obligatory scene to take place. That automatically means the play won't have a climax or resolution. It will just stop.

> **1. Shelagh Delaney's** *A Taste of Honey.* A moment before the anticipated climax as Jo goes into labor, her mother walks out on her daughter because she's just learned the baby's father is Black. There's almost a climax, but as distaste for the mother grows, she stops and turns to the audience. Becoming the playwright's authorial spokesperson, she asks us what we would do in her situation. And the play is over.

> **2. Eugene Ionesco's** *The Lesson.* An exception of sorts: There is an obligatory scene with a climax, but the resolution ends with a scene nearly identical to the once at the original point of attack, implying that nothing has been resolved by the climax, and that the play (and its story) will continue to repeat itself indefinitely.

> **3. Samuel Beckett's** *Waiting for Godot.* There is no obligatory scene or climax and the play ends with the two tramps convinced – as they were at the end of Act I – that Godot will surely come tomorrow. Like Ionesco's play, this ending suggests the story will continue repeating forever, or at least for the lifetimes of the tramps.

For what it's worth, Shakespeare never used an open ending.

Happy Endings

Happy endings are the perfect caboose for pure comedies. There are not a lot of these written or used anymore in the theatre outside of musical comedy. They don't fit well on the ends of those "dramedys" most playwrights are creating today.

Best Practice: *Satisfying endings grow organically out of the conflict and characters of the story.*

Forget about what you think audiences would want, or literary managers, or critics, or your significant other, or what Aunt Minnie and Uncle Bert will think if they see the play with the ending you know is right.

There's nothing wrong – and in fact everything good – about a happy ending if that's the logical outcome. The problem with happy endings is that more often than not, they defy the logic of the story.

The Dreaded "Refrigerator Question"

The danger of happy endings is that they can easily become fake endings clamped onto the ends of stories that logically can't support them. That's a serious negative in the theatre and when that happens, audiences may experience the moment Alfred Hitchcock called "The Refrigerator Question." They arrive home from the theatre, decide to have a late night snack, and as they open the refrigerator door one of them suddenly says, "Wait a minute! It doesn't make sense that –."

The idea of having things end if not well, at least better, is a human urge difficult to resist. The hazards of tacking happy endings onto stories that can't support them became a national issue in the summer of 2011 when a major regional theatre announced it was attaching "a more hopeful" ending to an adaptation of the classic, *Porgy and Bess* (the original has a partly open ending which opened the door for this). The change to the ending, among other alterations, generated a ferocious response from Stephen Sondheim and many others, but in this case audiences had the last word: The happy ending was cut during previews, the original "less hopeful ending" reattached, and the result met with substantial success on Broadway in 2012.

This happy ending issue can lead to an intricate dance when a Hollywood producer asks to bring your play to the screen – assuming the play doesn't have a cheery ending. Know that giving happy endings to otherwise "unhappy" plays is a Hollywood tradition, though at least some Hollywood producers seem to be recognizing that if a play has value, its ending is part of that value.

32. EMOTIONAL PATTERNS

Translating and adapting classical plays is a great way to learn craft. Most new plays, by and large, are dramaturgically quite simple and, I think, similar. This has something to do with the need to write only two and three characters, and so the way of crafting the scenes and the structure of the play, is pretty much set by this. But if you want, as I did, to write scenes with six or eight or nine people, suddenly it's a very different exercise.
-Richard Nelson

Shakespeare was a great fan of emotional patterns. So were Sophocles, Molière, and everyone else who filled their pockets from playwriting in centuries past.

EMOTIONAL PATTERNS

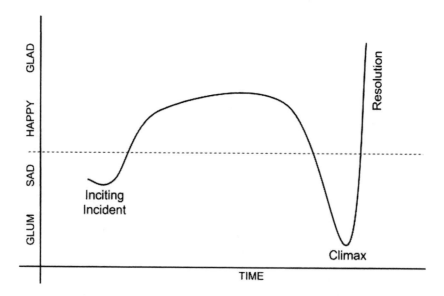

These patterns work like a charm – literally – on audiences, but despite that fact, most contemporary playwrights demonstrate little interest in them. The same is not true for screenwriters. If you're thinking seriously about making the transition from playwriting to film, this is an important device to understand.

Emotional patterns manipulate our emotional responses through the story's sequence of events. This manipulation heightens audience reaction by deliberately alternating positive and negative events, particularly during the obligatory scene and resolution.

The technique sounds more complicated than it is. The goal is simply to present a sequence of events that puts the audience through an emotional roller coaster.

The Hollywood Cliché Pattern

Nobody gets very excited if boy meets girl and they live happily ever after (clichés, after all, are nearly always true), so Hollywood adopted the formula Shakespeare always knew and that has become a cliché of these kinds of stories.

1. Boy doesn't have a girl (We feel sad for his sorry state).

2. Boy meets girl (We feel happy).

3. Boy loses girl (We feel glum).

4. Boy gets girl (We feel…).

This (not surprisingly) may seem silly, but flip that diagram on the previous page upside down and it's what Shakespeare used in his tragedies. It's also the version (right side up) that works particularly well in comedies.

Use of Patterns in Serious Comedy & Tragedy

Following are examples of the device in very different sorts of plays, a contemporary serious comedy and a classical tragedy.

Emotional Pattern in *The Fifth of July*

1. The central character, Ken, doesn't have what he thinks he wants. We feel emotionally negative about his situation because we'd like him to have what he does want (assuming he even knows what that is).

2. It looks like he may get what he wants. Because this is what he wants, we feel emotionally positive about his situation.

3. At the climax, it suddenly looks like he definitely won't get what he wants. This reversal makes us feel emotionally negative about his situation – we feel badly for him.

4. And then it all works out for him in the resolution. And for nearly everyone else – even better than we expected – and we feel emotionally positive about the outcome.

Emotional Pattern in *Othello*

What's intriguing about these emotional patterns is that they share characteristics independent of the subjects of the stories being told.

1. Desdemona sings "The Willow Song." There's a faint glimmer of hope that everything may work out after all so we experience a flicker of positive emotional feeling about her situation with Othello.

2. At the climax, Othello strangles her. This is not good, emotionally or otherwise, and we feel terrible.

3. Othello has remorse and suddenly believes Desdemona still lives! We feel great about this, though with obvious misgivings (because we know this apparent happy ending doesn't seem possible).

4. Othello realizes his mistake: She's dead. We feel really awful.

In plays with definitely unhappy endings, it's that flash of positive emotion or hope just before the final ax falls that does us in. In pure comedies, it's a flash of negative emotion or despair just before everybody gets what they want (or think they want) that sends us gliding out of the theatre on Cloud 9.

Shakespeare does something with emotional patterns in his tragedies that contemporary playwrights hardly ever do. After dumping us in the gutter emotionally, the Bard nearly always has a secondary character end the play with that last word, telling us that as a result of the tragic death of the central character good order has been returned to the world. Now we realize our hero (Hamlet, for example) has not died in vain. We feel a little better emotionally for that.

33. LENGTH OF FULL-LENGTH PLAYS

*That sound you hear is the shutting of theatre doors and the
slashing of art subsidies. Consequently, the smart playwright is,
no doubt, busy churning out those easily producible two-character,
single-set plays. So why then am I writing a two-part, six-hour,
nineteen cast-member epic?*
  -Robert Schenkkan

Technically one of the many things playwriting is about is using up
time – and thus script pages – regardless of how long the play is
intended to be, and at a minimum to use up enough time to tell the
story and have the play last for 90 minutes in performance. That's
the typical minimum for a full-length two-act play.

The next step up in length is the three-act play where
minimums are less established, but something close to 120 pages is
typical.

MOVEMENTS OF A FULL LENGTH PLAY

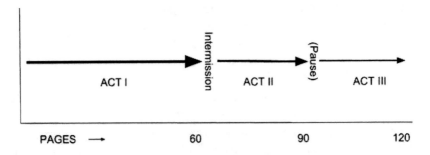

Estimating these lengths while writing is one of the reasons
why using professional manuscript format (see Part Four on
Format) is important: Each page of a script in format equals about a
minute of playing time on stage.

The 90-Minute Rule
As with everything else in playwriting, there are exceptions to the
90-minute rule for a full-length play.

Steve Martin's *Picasso in the Lapin Agile* runs only 75 minutes in performance, but if you're not Steve Martin –. It's also true that Harold Pinter's *Ashes to Ashes* only ran 45 minutes in London and New York and thus holds the record for the shortest full-length play in the history of the world. That's only what you get to do when you're famous throughout the Western world. Otherwise, they'll just call what you've done a long one-act play and most regional theatres won't be interested.

In the last several decades, a few contemporary plays have been keeping audiences in the theatre for much more than this 90-minute minimum. Part One of *Angels in America* runs about three hours, not counting time for its two intermissions which add another 30 minutes. Then there was Robert Shenkkan's *The Kentucky Cycle* clocking in at six hours.

Length: The *Hamlet* Question

While length is another of those rules that's made to be broken, this issue leads to The *Hamlet* Question, *Why doesn't he just do it?*

There is a serious technical question lurking here: Why doesn't Hamlet kill the King in Act III of this five-act play when he stumbles on him praying? "Now might I do it pat," says Hamlet while flashing his blade, "Now he is a-praying. And now I'll do it...." But he doesn't.

A boatload of psychological reasons – and even a religious one – have been developed to explain why the Prince doesn't do it then, but these are simply excuses tossed in our eyes by the playwright (and subsequent critics) to make us overlook the real technical reason: If Hamlet killed the King then, the play would be over – and it would be over in just under three acts in an age where the five-act play was the norm. (This obvious but often overlooked technicality was pointed out by the noted Shakespearean scholar G. Blakemore Evans, editor of *The Riverside Shakespeare*.)

This same constraint the Bard faced has haunted every playwright since plays were first written. Audiences want satisfaction for the price of their tickets, and a play's running time is one of those items on the satisfaction checklist. While 90 minutes feels reasonable, much less than that raises questions playwrights would rather not have audiences ask.

Best Practice: *A play can't be over until it's gone on long enough to be over.*

Acts and Intermissions

Length is also an issue with acts, particularly Act I. Act I tends to be the longest act in both two- and three-act plays, usually running close to about 60 pages in manuscript format. In practice, this typically means an Act I of about an hour and an Act II of about 30 minutes in length.

In three-act plays, Act I again runs about an hour followed by the two remaining acts at about 30 minutes each. While there is no rule here for internal lengths of a three-act play, the general practice is for each of the last two acts to be shorter than Act I.

Think of the structure of a play as a series of decreasing arcs or movements: The first movement is the longest (Act I). Then comes an intermission, followed by the shorter concluding movement (Act II). In three-act plays, Act III provides the final movement.

For nearly all playwrights today, the maximum number of acts in a full-length play is three while most opt for only two. The most compelling reason for this is a technical one.

Plays running about 90 pages usually have only two acts with an intermission between them because that length simply makes for too short a performance time to be broken into three acts.

No Intermission Plays

A few playwrights opt for one very long act without an intermission. That's what Marsha Norman did with 'night, Mother where an unbroken 90 minutes of stage action continually intensifies the play's conflict and the resulting tension felt by the audience. Michael Hollinger's Opus also does the 90-minute sprint as does John Logan's Red. In all three cases, this allows the action to build to the climax without the problem of having to partially start over with the audience after an intermission.

While few playwrights would admit this, that 90-minute sprint is also a good way to keep audiences in their seats if the suspense plot is a particularly mild one (as is the case in Opus and Red). This avoids giving the audience the chance to ask that awful question about whether there's a reason to come back after intermission – though in Opus and Red the combination of a mild suspense plot and no intermission resulted in plays audiences loved.

General practice suggests that 90 minutes is the appropriate length for a play without an intermission, but like most playwriting rules, this one is ripe for breaking. Stephen Karam pushed this limit to just below two hours in 2011 with *Sons of the Prophet*, a likely Pulitzer Prize contender. Despite that, playwrights going much beyond 90 minutes are basically hoping audiences will put up with the discomforts of typical theatre seats far longer than they'd like. And they run the risk of losing audience interest – not because the play isn't good, but because the audience is simply too uncomfortable physically to care about it anymore.

Three-Act Plays

Long full-length plays (over 110 pages) often have three acts with an intermission between Act I and Act II while there's usually just a "Pause" of a minute or so between Act II and Act III, not an actual intermission. (Even with such a short pause where the audience stays in their seats, a time break in the story can still be introduced to help gain added conflict.) Very long plays (over 140 pages) usually have an intermission between each act.

Sometimes a long three-act structure can allow you to write the equivalent of three related one-act plays sharing the same central characters or similar situations. One of the best known of these is Alan Ayckbourn's *Absurd Person Singular* with each act taking place on three successive Christmas days. That's not unlike an American three-act play that called itself what it really was: *Same Time Next Year*. Recently, Bruce Norris did this with only two acts in *Clybourne Park*: Act II takes place 50 years after Act I with a new set of characters facing nearly the same conflict those Act I characters did many decades earlier (each act is set in the same house).

Having a maximum of three acts is another one of those rules that's made to be broken: In Part Two of *Angels in America*, Tony Kushner opted for Shakespeare's structure with five acts plus an epilogue.

34. TIME STRUCTURES

Wherever there is a present moment, the past is also present, although it's usually invisible. That's what draws me to theatre – the ability to put different times on stage and see how they collide or how they resonate with one another – how the past tells a story within a present story.

>   -Naomi Wallace

Time can be a great asset in storytelling, though it can also complicate the writing process.

The structural complications of time can be ignored – and most playwrights do – by using the simplest time arrangement possible: Start the story's clock with the point of attack in Act I and turn it off at the end of the resolution in Act II (or Act III).

With this approach, the plot's events are presented in the linear order in which they occurred and even with an intermission at the end of Act I, little or no story time goes by while the audience is out in the lobby.

Continuous Time Examples

Continuous time may be simple, but it's a very effective storytelling method and some interesting variations are possible in an approach that would seem to allow no variation.

> **1. *'night, Mother*:** No intermission. Marsha Norman's play is the ultimate continuous time affair. She has no intermission. A number of clocks are incorporated into the setting – all running and large enough to be visible to us – and all showing about 8:10 p.m. as the curtain goes up on the point of attack, approximately the time the play will actually start for most evening performances. All of these clocks run in real time, heightening the play's realistic style and the pressure of passing time on the two central characters.

> **2. *Cat on a Hot Tin Roof*:** Intermissions with replay. Tennessee Williams' classic is the great example of halting the story's clock during intermission. Time freezes at the

curtain line of Act I and again at the end of Act II of this three-act play, but it's then reset back about 10 seconds at the points of attack of Act II and Act III, thus replaying the last moments of the previous act. This is done by having the curtain line of the prior act become the first line (and thus the point of attack) of the next act. It's also a fine exception to the rule that the point of attack of Act II needs to begin at a lower level of tension than what held us at the curtain line of Act I.

3. *That Championship Season*: Intermission with frozen time. Jason Miller does it straight in this play about lost dreams and the 20-year reunion of a high school basketball team. Time freezes at the curtain line of Act I, stays that way through the intermission, and starts running again with the point of attack of Act II. It's no accident that this is the way time is structured in basketball games.

Using Flashbacks

If exposition doesn't seem to do a sufficient job of telling audiences enough about the past, flashbacks can show us the actual events from that past.

Until the 1960s, this was usually only done in films. Somebody would say, "It must have been 40 years ago that I first saw Old Joe –" and the screen would turn wiggly and when it clears we're close on the license plate of a 40-year-old Plymouth showing the year of the flashback.

We're all wiser now. Flashbacks in film and theatre happen without warning, often without clear verbal or visual clues about how far back we've gone in time. Occasionally, there will still be a film flashing one of those "Five Years Earlier" titles, but not in the theatre. Playwrights hang their hats on exposition and the context of the scene to do this job for them.

Adding a Scene Breakdown Page (see Part Four on Format) to the script can help clarify a particularly complicated version of flashbacks, but you can't rely on audiences remembering the crib notes even if you've put it in their programs. Besides, they're sitting in the dark while the scenes go whizzing by so they can't read those notes.

Best Practice: *Flashbacks work best in chronological order.*

Most playwrights interweave those scenes in the present with flashbacks from the past, but each set of scenes moves chronologically through its own time – present or past.

Adding a Third Layer of Time

Adding a third level of time involving the use of multiple pasts is the most complicated time structure of all. Charles Fuller is practically alone in trying multiple pasts – and making it work. In *A Soldier's Play,* he uses three levels of time.

> **1. Present:** The central character, Davenport, speaks to us as the narrator. Because the narrator is speaking to us, we assume we're in the present with him, even through he's wearing a WWII officers uniform. In reality, this "present time" is at some point after the events of the play's suspense plot and most likely after the end of WWII, but certainly not the actual present the audience is living in.

> **2. Past:** The murder investigation Davenport has been assigned to run.

> **3. Past-Past:** The actual murder and events leading to it. This past-past runs through the play and is made up of a series of flashbacks-within-flashbacks (from "past" to "past-past"). It's a cinch in production and even in reading the script. It's only the theory that seems complicated.

The formal scenes of each time period are essentially arranged in a nested structure that might be expressed this way as if it were a mathematical equation: (Present (Past (Past-past))).

Going into Hyper Time

Then there's the option of indeterminate time: By mixing both past and present simultaneously – and even mixing several different pasts – a kind of hyper time can be created. It's neither past nor present, but a limbo that can embrace centuries without blinking an eye.

When this is done without the use of formal scenes to contain each time frame, something that is simultaneously now and then is created – or now, then, and then.

Notable Uses of Hyper Time

Hyper time is easy for playwrights to create, but it's the most complicated for audiences to follow.

1. Tom Stoppard in *Arcadia*. After six scenes of doing it the usual way (with formal scenes containing distinct chunks of the 1809 story and the present), the final scene of the play blends characters from both times. But they don't acknowledge anyone who is not from their own time period.

2. Lisa Loomer in *The Waiting Room*. Characters from different times come together in the same location and interact with each other. It works because her theme stresses the similarities across time periods rather than the differences.

3. A. R. Gurney in *The Dining Room*. A number of different and unrelated pasts mingle in the same dining room. Scenes are not formally indicated, but they are there. During the transitions between these informal scenes and time periods, the same sort of cohabitation-without-acknowledgment that Stoppard uses takes place.

Using Formal Scenes

Building a play from a series of short formal scenes provides a technical advantage in using time. If you're a bit short-winded as a writer for the demands of a full-length play in continuous time, this may be a way to solve that problem.

Formal scenes provide the screenwriter's luxury of moving the action of the story through multiple locations – a good way to create new conflict with each change.

These short scenes can be very short – sometimes as little as half a page – though if you find yourself writing a scene pushing 20 or 30 pages, using formal scenes may not be the right solution for telling the story.

Technically, each time a new formal scene is started, a new secondary point of attack begins the scene. Doing that offers the potential for a jump in time between these scenes, providing the same advantage as an intermission between acts: What's happened in that break in time can refuel the conflict between the characters.

Plays put together this way usually have a minimum of 4 scenes to a maximum of about 10 in Act I. Since Act II is invariably shorter, it will often have at least one scene less.

With each new scene, there's the chance to begin what is almost a new play with the same characters. That's not really what's happening, but the freedom you probably felt as you began Act I – from all that conflict waiting to be released – can be partially recreated by the use of this short scene structure.

The majority of playwrights working today are using this technical device. Partly, they've been influenced by film, but audiences also respond to this storytelling technique. Just as film has influenced the way playwrights structure their plays, it has also influenced the way audiences understand dramatic stories.

35. CHARACTERS: NUMBER & CAUTIONS

For me, it's always a question of trying to whittle things down to what the central question is and also what are the fewest number of characters I can have to make it fully dramatic. A play shouldn't have more characters than it needs at minimum and it shouldn't be any longer than it needs to be.
          -Lee Blessing

What matters – or should matter – is how many performers are needed to handle the number of characters in a play, not how many characters it has. Even if a script has 33 characters (as Robert Shenkkan did in one of his plays and winning the Pulitzer Prize for Drama) you're home free if those 33 can be played by about 10 performers playing two, three, or four roles apiece.

While that's absolutely true, it's also true that literary managers become increasingly nervous the longer that list on a script's Character Page gets. There's a simple reason for this: Each character equals a performer who equals a weekly salary and living expenses. Even with the performers doubling parts, those additional characters will need costumes and costumes equal money. No matter how this is analyzed, the practical number of characters in a play aimed at U.S. regional theatres is driven by the economics of production (European theatres are less sensitive to character quantity).

The Magic Number 10

The magic number is 10 for characters. More than 10 and the weekly financial burden of employing the actors will make most regional theatres think twice about producing your play. Sad, but true.

If there's no way to avoid a character list of 15 or 20, add a sentence before the list on your Character Page explaining that they can all be played by a cast of 10 performers or even less, and highlight that fact in your letter of inquiry to theatres.

Before making this doubling claim, make sure the play is structured to allow this: Check that there's enough time for those doubling performers to change costumes and that the doubled characters are never on stage at the same time. This may sound incredibly obvious, but the logic and conflict driving the story may have made this difficult to achieve – especially if the solution of doubling came after that first draft was finished.

To avoid this numbers problem, Amlin Gray deliberately structured *How I Got That Story* so that 21 of his 22 characters could be played by one performer. To be fair, the economics of production was only a small part of his motivation. The rest was thematic: All those 21 characters represented the "Event" confronted by his central (other) character. For Bruce Norris, the doubling of parts was likewise important for thematic reasons in *Clybourne Park*, but also solved an economic problem by requiring only 7 performers to play its 15 characters.

This sort of doubling of roles by performers is seldom seen as a negative for scripts that are structured to allow it: Norris' play won the 2011 Pulitzer Prize for Drama and London's Laurence Olivier Award for Best New Play. Despite the success plays with doubling can have, prudence suggests that 10 remains the magic number of characters until you've gained recognition as a playwright.

One-Character Plays

At the other end of this character scale is the bare minimum. Plays with only one character – and one performer – are about as minimalist as possible and still have a play when all the dust settles, though Samuel Beckett once wrote a short play that had no characters, only the sound of breathing.

One-character plays are probably the most difficult to write. The technical problem faced with only one character is how to find a source for the conflict that drives typical plays with two or more characters. If monologues don't come easily, this is not the kind of play to try.

One-character plays are the ultimate monologue, but instead of structuring a typical monologue running anywhere from 10 lines to a page, this will require writing about 25 pages of one character talking. It's "only" a 25-page monologue since solid dialogue by a single character in format roughly drives the playing time from one minute to four minutes per page.

Keep in mind the old Zen question: *What is the sound of one hand clapping?* The sound of one character talking for all those pages can become no sound at all for audiences, especially if a source of conflict hasn't been found to drive all that talk. There are several solutions to this problem.

Celebrities as Characters

If the character is famous enough, that fame can substitute for at least some conflict. It helps if the celebrity has gone through some tough times – that's a typical source of the minimal suspense plots these "celebrity plays" generally use. It's tough to create one of these in a way that will hold an audience if the celebrity led a fine life from the moment they were born with nothing but love and happiness and then died in bed with no regrets at 105.

It helps even more if the celebrity kept journals or wrote lots of letters in the days before disposable e-mail, sources that can then become the basis for dialogue. That's how *Lucifer's Child* was created, the successful one-character play about Isak Dinesen (of *Out of Africa* fame).

Some other celebrities who've been featured in one-character plays: Janis Joplin, Joan Didion, Paul Robeson, Edith Piaf, Gertrude Stein, Isadora Duncan, Mark Twain, Virginia Woolf. It's worth noting how many of these are women.

Invisible Characters in One-Person Shows

In one-character plays, these invisible creatures actually exist for the central character and for the audience even if we can't see them. They're used by the playwright as a source of conflict with the real character on stage. Audiences accept that they are really there, but just out of sight off stage. The only way we seem to "hear" them is when what they have said is interpreted for us by the on-stage character:

> CHARACTER (*Looking off stage*): What do you mean, "I can't?" (*Pause, listening*) Just you try and stop me.

One-character plays are often written with a particular performer in mind, usually a performer the playwright knows and sometimes playwrights will involve the performer in creating the play.

A caution: The one-character play usually doesn't float to the top of new play competitions. The style is also not high on the list of what literary managers are looking for. That makes the one-character play a difficult sell until you've already gotten recognition as a playwright.

One-character plays are worth serious consideration for established performers who are interested in playwriting, especially performers who have professional relationships with artistic directors of regional theatres. The economic incentives for regional theatres to program one-character plays are considerable and a noticeable number are producing these on an occasional basis.

Solo Performance

If you're daring and you're also a performer you can combine writing and acting in your own script. Solo work won't get you past the door of many regional theatres, but there's a market at more adventurous small theatres and clubs for these. Regional theatres with small second or third stages in their facilities are also becoming more interested in the form.

In solo work, the playwright is the performer, presenting a number of stories – or one long continuous story – in monologues held together by a shared theme. It's tough work, if you can get it.

The most successful of these tend to be highly autobiographical: You become the subject of your own play with the focus on your involvement with some event, person, or even an object. The play ends up being about these subjects as you experienced them.

Among the most recent of these is Mike Daisey's 2011 take on the iPhone he happily lives with (*The Agony and the Ecstasy of Steve Jobs*), colored by the much darker attitude he developed after talking with workers in China where Apple's devices are assembled. As with Daisey, It's rare that solo performers elect to be neutral and external observers of events that have no impact on themselves.

Much of the power of solo work comes less from structure than the inventiveness of the performance compared with multi-character plays or even one-character plays. While structure is less critical, keep in mind that the audience still likes to know when it's time to go home.

A key element in the success of this kind of work is how compelling you are as a performer. The best way into solo work is to read solo performance scripts, then see solo performers in the flesh or on DVD if you can't find the real thing. The American grandmaster of this form – even after his death in 2004 – continues to be Spalding Gray and several of his autobiographical monologues including his classic *Swimming to Cambodia* can still be found on DVD.

Kids as Characters

Hollywood films make kids look easy, but they're not – and they're expensive. When real kids are needed as characters, they come with a lot of baggage: Tutors, nannies, parents, strict limits on rehearsal time, and the producing theatre has to foot the bill for all of this.

Best Practice: *Kids less than 13 don't work well in the theatre.*

That practice is regardless of all the nannies, tutors, and parents you may have in the wings. They're best left to film where the camera does most of the work of controlling their performances. The Trapp Family in *The Sound of Music* aside, the safest way to deal with kids is to boost their ages so an 18-year-old performer can play them. It's fairly easy to find performers who are 18 or a bit older who can do a fine job of playing as young as 12 or 13 in appearance as well as vocal impression, though the odds are better in finding actresses than actors who can pull this off.

If you can't resist, limit kids played by real kids to a maximum of one. Having said all this, David Mamet made it work in *The Cryptogram* with a 10-year-old as a significant character and played by a kid. It is possible, but should you do it if you're not David Mamet yet? Only if you're so driven by the story you want to tell that you can't think of writing anything else.

Animals as Characters

Elephants and horses – the real kind that snort, chomp, and do other natural acts – were all the rage in 19th Century British and American melodramas until film came along.

Nowadays regional theatres seldom take on more than the occasional dog, usually the small and useless variety. So take a cue from *Equus* or *Bengal Tiger in the Baghdad Zoo* or *War Horse* and have human performers play animals, in furry suits if you must, or preferably more symbolically.

Best Practice: *Real animals work even less well in the theatre than kids.*

They're one more thing best left to Hollywood where the camera makes Fido seem as professionally reliable as Meryl Streep or Jeremy Irons.

The safest way to deal with animals: Stuff them. A small stuffed critter bought from an upscale toy store can be held by a performer and made to seem alive to an audience. This is the best way out for your basic cat (they sleep a lot) or small dog. If you absolutely must have the real thing, rely on a performer's pet dog. This way, you may avoid the cost of a handler and it might even follow directions. And if they're real, get them off stage as soon as possible. Animals can work just as well unseen as seen.

As with kids, only do this if you're driven to it by the story you want to tell and can't think of writing anything else.

David Rabe used a large and very real dog in his play called – what else? – *The Dog Problem*. The dog was played by a very compliant Labrador Retriever and Rabe was clever enough to only give him one scene. All the dog had to do was sit on a park bench and "listen" to a monologue by the central character.

Another tip with dogs: The performer (human) needs to keep the performer (canine) on a leash so the beast can't take off into the audience.

36. MONOLOGUES: THEY'RE MINI-PLAYS

My writing isn't actually guided by issues. I know it seems that way, but I don't sit down and think, Oh, there's this issue I'm bothered about. I only write about things that directly impact my life. When I write, there's a pain that I have to reach, and a release I have to work toward for myself. So it's really a question of the particular emotional circumstance that I want to express, a character that appears, a moment in time, and then I write the play backwards.
　　　　　-Paula Vogel

A monologue is a tiny play with a beginning, a middle, and an end. It's not just continuous talk by a single character. It tells a story, usually a short one, and it does this with a point of attack and inciting incident followed by a middle portion leading to a climax – and if not a climax at least the equivalent of a curtain line. It's the climax or curtain line of the monologue that catapults us into the next scene or the resumption of the play's dialogue.

The Monologue as Aria

Think of the monologue as an operatic aria. When the emotion and complexity of a character's subtext becomes overwhelming, a monologue is a good solution and that's why monologues usually contain spoken subtext. Within the context of a monologue, spoken subtext works well, especially if there's a build to it, culminating with the climax of the speech.

We've all met people who can talk a blue streak with no real structure to the words pouring out of their mouths. That may be a monologue in real life, but not in the theatre.

A century ago, playwrights had characters speak in paragraphs so the transition from dialogue to monologue was not an earth-shaking event. Now, with characters often only speaking in short phrases, the monologue is a significant event, especially because there are usually only one or two in a contemporary play.

Since they are used so sparingly by contemporary playwrights, the stakes are high for making them have an impact.

That makes it essential that the character being given a monologue has something of value to say – and a compelling way of saying it.

Keys to Writing Monologues

The story typically told through a monologue is either of an event in the past or an emotional realization – ideally, it does both of these at the same time.

1. Put the inciting incident in the first sentence. Since monologues are tiny plays, there's no time for the more leisurely gap between the point of attack and the introduction of the inciting incident that "grabs" the audience. Very long monologues running two or more pages can afford a slightly longer gap between the point of attack and the inciting incident.

2. Establish internal conflict. Once a monologue begins, the source of the conflict driving the play through dialogue between the central characters is suspended until the monologue ends. That puts a premium on the conflict becoming internal to the character speaking all those words.

3. Make the story significant to the character. The more it means to the character saying it, the more there will be a good source of internal conflict to drive the monologue.

4. Tell us something we might never know otherwise. By the end of the monologue, we should have a much deeper knowledge of this character, far more than we could get through dialogue between characters.

5. Give it a strong curtain line or climax. The ending of the monologue needs to throw us back into the conflict between the characters in the play so it should end with a verbal punch that drives the play forward. If it's intended to be a comic monologue, then its curtain line needs to be a strong laugh line. If audiences don't laugh, rewrite until they do.

The exception to the one or two monologues in a play rule: If a narrator is being used, this character speaks to us in a series of monologues – there may be many of these narrator-monologues in a play, but each needs to be written as a mini-play.

Length of Monologues

A character needs to say at least 10 lines in format for a speech to be considered a monologue. If a character doesn't have at least 10 lines to say about an issue, then the event or realization is probably not significant enough to support a monologue.

At the other end of the scale, a whole play can be written as a single monologue complete with acts and intermissions – or three long monologues by different characters, one filling each act of a three-act play as Jon Robin Baitz did in *Three Hotels*.

Monologues are such a natural part of theatrical storytelling that you may be writing them without realizing it, unconsciously concealing them in what appears to be dialogue. (See Chapter 46 on Finding Hidden Monologues and Chapter 47 on Turning False Monologues into Dialogue.)

37. THEATRICAL DEVICES & STYLES

When I saw my first naturalistic play, I was shocked. I thought:
This is like a movie or TV show. This is not what theatre is
supposed to do.
  -Moisés Kaufman

Audiences will accept almost any theatrical convention as long as the device is established early in the play – no matter how bizarre it may seem compared to what's "real."

Once the audience sees that those horses in the opening scene in *Equus* are actors wearing openwork masks of metal tubing and hoof-like platforms on their shoes, but otherwise dressed in brown turtlenecks and slacks, they'll react as though real horses are on stage. So much so that they'll let out a collective gasp when the boy stabs the "eye" of one of those horses.

Four decades later, *Bengal Tiger at the Baghdad Zoo* has a tiger as the play's narrator – played by an actor – and the playwright insists that nothing in his costume or movement should suggest a tiger. Audiences happily accept this "tiger" as real.

Use It & Own It for the Duration
The key to the audience's heart in this is introducing non-realistic devices early in the play, ideally within the first several pages. Once having taken the trouble to introduce a stylistic device, most playwrights continue to use it throughout the remainder of the script, at least partly because the audience expects to see it again.

Saving these devices for the end of a play doesn't seem to work as well, or at least contemporary playwrights practically never do this. But there's Ariel Dorfman's final semi-ghost scene in the otherwise realistic *Death and the Maiden* where the device has no early preparation, but it still works. Katori Hall does something similar in *The Mountaintop*: Projected images of the "future" (after the 1968 assassination of Martin Luther King) suddenly fill the stage a few pages from the end of the script. One reason this works well is that Hall introduces occurrences of "magic" – cigarettes lighting themselves, flowers growing from the carpet – in the second half of the script and she does this slowly at first so we have a chance to adjust our stylistic expectations.

Devices Needing Early Use

Early introduction of these techniques insures that audiences will buy into them without second-guessing their use.

1. Short formal scenes. When using these kinds of scenes that last anywhere from half a page to five or so pages, a particular rhythm is being established for the play. If far longer scenes follow, that interrupts the rhythm set initially. While the audience may not consciously realize what's happened by altering the scene rhythm, on some level they'll sense it and be uncomfortable with the change.

2. A narrator. If a narrator is used, then the narrator is telling us the story and needs to begin doing so with the opening scene, then becoming a guide who leads us through the rest of the play.

3. Non-realistic symbolic techniques. A caveat: Holding this kind of device until the end can produce a tremendous reaction in the audience, as the angel does crashing through the ceiling in Part One of *Angels in America*.

4. Language style. If you're driven to write a play in verse, do it from the very first line of dialogue, but don't expect regional theatres to leap at the script. Having said that, Ntozake Shange wrote her landmark play *For Colored Girls Who Have Considered Suicide/When the Rainbow Is Enuf* in verse, but she was a recognized poet before she turned to playwriting.

Theatre allows – even encourages – the creation of highly theatrical realities through the use of stylistic devices that audiences accept as real even when they clearly are not. There's an argument that has been made over the last five decades that this kind of symbolic approach to dramatic writing is what playwrights ought to be doing, that it's what theatre really should be. Few produced playwrights embrace this position today.

At the other stylistic extreme, there's a case to be made for not using theatrical or symbolic devices at all and striving instead to show us something that looks as much like real life as possible.

Contemporary Naturalism

American literary managers, directors, and playwrights sometimes use "naturalism" as a contemporary playwriting style, but what they mean has little to do with the movement Émile Zola was credited with founding more than 100 years ago. While these pros might seem to have their theatre history mixed up, they know what they mean and it's usually not a compliment. Despite that, a large number of playwrights have had major success borrowing features of the style, among them August Wilson, Sam Shepard (*Buried Child*), Jez Butterworth (*Jerusalem*), and Tracy Letts, among many others.

Naturalism may be a bit of a dirty word in the contemporary theatre, but a noticeable number of plays in the style are produced by regional theatres for a disarmingly simple reason: Audiences like them and they can have real dramatic power.

Contemporary naturalism assumes that the best way to show the reality of life is to literally show us something very close to the appearance of real life. That's what Tracy Letts did in *August: Osage County*, though he only borrowed what he wanted from the style: A highly realistic setting showing three floors of the family home along with supercharged interpersonal dysfunction among the characters. But – and it's a big "but" – unlike the focus of historical naturalism, all of his characters are respectable middle class types, most of them professionals with reasonable incomes and several with their own businesses.

"Rules" for Using Naturalism

If this slice-of-life style seems attractive, here are four rules – all having reams of exceptions – for making it work.

1. **Use highly realistic interior settings.** With everything including the kitchen sink and running water (these used to be called "kitchen sink" plays). Keep the same setting for each act – it's far too expensive for most theatres to build two or three of these kinds of sets for one play. A similar approach to exterior settings also works well. Since this sort of replication of reality is unusual in the theatre today because of the economics of production, audiences are usually amazed by it.

2. **Use a continuous time structure.** The naturalistic style

doesn't work well with flashbacks. Rely on a two- or three-act structure with the only time breaks (if any) at intermissions. A multitude of short formal scenes will undercut the slice-of-life feeling of the style. If you must have scenes, try making them long enough so no more than about three or four will fill each act.

3. Focus on personal relationships. The more dysfunctional (by normal middleclass standards) the better. Plays using this style often focus on characters living at or near the bottom of the economic and social ladder and who are thus particularly vulnerable to slight changes in their physical or economic environment.

4. Stress personal themes. With a focus on interpersonal relationships. Think of these as family-problems-in-America (or fill in your country of choice) plays. Larger political, social, or economic issues explored beyond a glancing reference add clutter to what the style does best. Keep this sort of theme as part of the play's subtext. If those political, social, or economic issues are what's driving you, put them in the mouth of a central character.

Many literary managers still like to say that this sort of duplication of reality works best in film and television. For the theatre, they're after that real reality beneath the surface reality of everyday life. (You might not know that by looking at the contemporary plays presented by regional theatres).

Representation vs. Presentation

A key stylistic decision faced by playwrights before starting to write is whether to actively admit that they know the audience is sitting out there. Technically, the answer to this question marks the difference between representational and presentational techniques of storytelling in the theatre.

Representation is what most screenwriters do: They don't let characters talk directly to the audience. Or to put it another way, they don't let them make eye contact with audiences in those seats.

This is the old "fourth wall" device in the theatre. Just before the curtain goes up, some idiot with a bulldozer rips off the front wall of that living room set – and the characters inside never notice that we're staring at them through the resulting hole. It's the ant farm approach to theatre, or so those say who prefer far more theatrical styles. It's also the style that's essential for contemporary naturalism.

In contrast, presentation admits the obvious. There's an audience out there watching, so you might as well use that fact in telling the story and at least one of the characters talks directly to us. Technically, this can be done with a narrator while the rest of the characters don't acknowledge us or any number of characters can take us into their confidence – even all of them as John Guare did in *Six Degrees of Separation* and Michael Hollinger did in *Opus*.

Wendy Wasserstein used a variant for *The Heidi Chronicles* by having her central character address us at the beginning of each act in the guise of giving an art history lecture. She talks to us, but she doesn't acknowledge us as a theatre audience, but we understand we're her students sitting in a lecture hall.

Making a choice between representation and presentation is not as simple as pulling one kind of pen or another out of a playwright's tool bag. You may find that you're hard-wired for one of these styles and practically incapable of using the other. If you're stylistically ambidextrous, representation can be a better choice if your primary interest is the psychological interplay between characters.

38. WRITING ONE-ACT PLAYS

With my plays, when the lights go down, at least the audience isn't thinking, Oh, God, two more hours of this.
 -David Ives

Short plays, or one-acts, start at about 10 pages. The Actors Theatre of Louisville became famous for among many other things the production of 10-page plays with a $1,000 prize. There's no bottom limit on one-acts – there are even occasional competitions for 1-minute (one-page) plays.

A more usual length is about 20 to 30 pages for a one-act. Much beyond that and you begin to limit chances of finding a production. A 60-pager is a real outlier and more than a few literary managers will see a play running about an hour as falling in a limbo between a one-act and a full-length play – too short for a full evening and too long to be easily produced as part of a bill of multiple one-acts.

Related One-Acts

Creating a series of related one-acts offers a solution for playwrights attracted to the short form. David Ives took this approach, calling the result *All in the Timing* and won the Outer Critics Circle Award for Playwriting with it.

Related one-acts are often made up of five or six (or more) short one-acts from 5 to 20 pages long or as few as three of these about 30 pages each. Individual length is not critical as long as the total length of the script reaches the minimum for a full-length play. Usually, there's a balance in length within these sets of related one-acts – it's nearly unheard of to find a 60-pager followed by six 5-page or three 10-page plays.

Unifying Related One-Acts

A set of related one-acts is always presented under a single title, held together by some vague (or sometimes obvious) unifying force:

1. A similar theme. Or related themes in each play. Even if the characters are different in each, the repetition of similar ideas reinforces the sense that we're watching a unified play.

2. The same characters. Or at least one central character appearing in each play. This is the simplest way to unify a group of one-acts. With this approach, the themes can be different from play to play.

3. Similar subjects. Or at least appearing to be similar subjects. A group of related one-acts might have each focus on a couple having relationship problems. That may sound like a cliché (it is), but it's a simple way do the job.

What's essential is a way to let the audience know that these short plays are all connected in some reasonable way – beyond simply the fact that you wrote them all. That often means the final one-act of the series has the greatest punch or climax, giving the series the feel of a full-length play.

One of the problems of writing related one-acts is finding a way to let the audience know when it's time to go home – other than simply having the curtain come down. With more traditionally structured plays, the climax and resolution usually lets us feel that the play is over so we're not startled when the curtain falls or the stage lights come up again on the curtain call. At the end, playwrights never want audiences saying: *What? Is that it?*

Tips for Writing One-Acts

There's not an overwhelming interest among regional theatres for one-acts. Even related one-acts masquerading as a full-length play rarely make it into a theatre's season, one reason being that very few playwrights are attracted to writing in this form.

One-acts may be helpful writing exercises, though the quirks of the form don't necessarily make these good training for the long-windedness required for writing the full-length play.

Keep in mind that the shorter the one-act, the less emphasis you can have on:

1. Character development. This takes time and that's what you don't have in a short one-act.

2. Subtext. Something else that takes time for the audience to understand. Too much subtext beneath the surface and we may be left totally confused when the play ends after 10 or 15 minutes.

3. The consequences of events. Consequences also need time to explore so try centering the play on an event – short event. It can even be an event that just happened prior to the point of attack, but contained enough so that you can deal with the consequences and end with a climax within a limited number of pages.

There is a mild connection between one-acts and screenplays: What happens next is often a driving force in one-acts, so a strong inciting incident helps and the climax often comes as a punch. Subtlety in one-acts is not always the virtue it can be in full-length plays.

PART THREE – WORKING: The Day Job

The work is a good deal more than just consecrating so many hours of the day to sitting at a desk writing words – it is living in the midst of the artificial world one is creating, and letting no detail of everyday life enter sufficiently into one's mind to become more real than or take precedence over what one is inventing.
    -Paul Bowles

39. WRITER'S BLOCK & INSPIRATION

*It is definitely unhealthy to sit in front of a silent [keyboard] for
any length of time. If, after you have typed the first sentence, you
can't think of a second one, go read.*
-Marsha Norman

Writer's block and inspiration are at the opposite ends of a very
short scale.

For all writers, regardless of medium, the goal is to avoid the
first and get the second and while that sounds obvious, it may not
be in the process of writing.

Writing is Work

Playwriting and screenwriting are not what you do after the dishes,
walking the dog, feeding the fish, washing the car, and vacuuming
the rug. All of that comes after writing. Or it should, but the
discipline to do so takes practice for most people.

Writing is hard work, so avoid falling into the trap of getting
all the unimportant things out of the way first so you can
concentrate on writing. By then your back will hurt or you'll feel
like going out to the local coffee shop. Make writing the most
important thing you do and let it come first. The dishes can wait.

Most professional writers treat putting words on paper as a
job. They usually set aside at least four prime hours every day and
do it – the hours where they feel their best and most energetic.
Often they set a daily goal for the number of pages or words. You
can take the weekends off if you must.

That's the ideal, but few people starting out in playwriting –
or any other form of creative writing – have the luxury of adopting
the life of a professional writer. Most playwrights early in their
careers need a day job and that complicates the writing life – but the
same rule holds. Among all the hours when you're not working,
allocate the best ones that are left to writing and try to do it every
day.

Writing is no different from playing tennis or basketball or
any other physical skill: The more you do it, the better you get – or

at the very least, more efficient. It's in the air now to say it takes 10,000 hours of practice to become an expert in any activity, mental or physical, but on the way to racking up those hours you may end up writing a fine play. The early plays of many playwrights often end up being among their best work (though not necessarily that very first play).

Writer's Block

Prevention is the best cure for writer's block. Graham Greene came up with a nearly fail-safe inoculation: Stop writing when you still know exactly what the next line or even the next scene will be. If you'd really just like to get that one last line down: *Don't*. Avoid writing until you simply run out of dialogue. Instead, jot a quick note about the next line if you're afraid you'll forget it by the next morning, but not the exact wording.

This line that's been waiting to be written, primes the creative pump the following day since those first words are ready to go the moment you face the monitor or – if you do it the old-fashioned way – that piece of paper the next morning.

The odds of inviting writer's block to come live with you go up considerably if you write until you're too exhausted to put another word on that page. Those odds reach the moon if you keep writing until you don't know what words to write next.

If Prevention Fails

If you think writer's block has come to roost, forget about the play you're writing (at least for the moment). Pick two new characters with no connection to what you're working on. Then make them talk to each other.

It doesn't matter how dumb the dialogue is as long as you get words coming out of their mouths. Odds are this simple exercise will generate the urge to go on from where you hit the wall. If that fails to work, try setting up an elevator play (see Chapter 26 for more on this). If you don't have the energy yet for either exercise, dip into the *Handbook's* Afterword of Quotes on Craft. These can be a good substitute for a supportive writers' group if there isn't one near you and they may rekindle the desire to write again.

Technical Blocks to Writing

Keep in mind that the wall you hit may not be writer's block at all.

It could very well be the result of technical problems peculiar to playwriting.

1. Not having a suspense plot. Or not having one strong enough to support the story you're telling. Or forgetting to remind us (and the characters) at least every four to eight pages that the suspense plot is ticking away. Remember that emotional plots need a support structure to keep them afloat and to keep the play moving forward.

2. Using up the suspense plot too quickly. This usually results from having lost (or never having had) that roughly 90%-10% balance between suspense and emotional plots. If the suspense plot has been allowed to creep up to being 30% or 40% of the play, that may be why you've run out of gas, and that has nothing to do with writer's block.

3. Resolving the suspense plot too soon. Go back and see if you've allowed the climax to occur without realizing it. Pay close attention to what was happening in those last few pages before you thought writer's block grabbed you.

4. Letting dramatic conflict drain away. This often happens when the emotional issues between the central characters aren't serious or deep enough to keep generating conflict. It may also be that there wasn't enough shared – or complex enough – history between the characters at the point of attack.

5. Getting bored with the central characters. If you're bored by them, think how your audience will feel being locked in the dark with these folks for at least 90 minutes. If boredom is the problem, it may trace back again to that shared history issue.

6. Worst of all, losing interest in the story. There's no cure for that except starting over with a completely new idea and new characters, but those pages you've written are worth saving. Resist the temptation to burn them in the barbecue. Someday, you may be hit by an inspiration for the story those characters really needed.

Getting Inspiration

Inspiration comes from the act of writing. That's often where (and when) the best ideas for the next play will come from – or the next scene, or the next line of dialogue. Inspiration may also hit when taking a break from writing for a meal or walking the dog – or even while at your conventional day job.

Newton may have had an apple bounce off his head while he was sleeping and then changed the emerging field of physics, but for playwrights he's not the best role model for getting inspiration. You'll get some great ideas that seem to fall from the sky, but most of the inspired ones will probably come the old fashioned way – while putting words on paper or on the screen.

Best Practice: *If you're not writing, write in your journal; if you're still not writing, read plays or novels.*

40. KNOWING WHEN TO START WRITING

A few hours and a couple of unsatisfactory pages later, I would give up in frustration. Something essential was missing. I could not figure out, for instance, who the woman's husband was, how he would react to her violence, if he would believe her. Nor were the historical circumstances under which the story developed clear to me, the symbolic and secret connections to the larger life of the country itself, the world beyond the narrow, claustrophobic boundaries of that woman's home.
> -Ariel Dorfman

Most playwrights do at least some mental research in their heads before they're ready to start a new play. Many writers have learned that putting words on paper is a good way to explore potential ideas for plays and screenplays. These exploratory ventures may never find their way into a script – at least not in a way that would be recognizable to anyone other than the author – but they've helped clarify characters and plot. This practice of exploration through writing also keeps your writing engine warm so when those ideas do come together, you're ready to go.

The "Good to Have" List

Everyone's working methods (and writing superstitions) are different, but there are some signals that can indicate when it's time to begin putting words on paper.

> **1. Names and a sense of at least two central characters.** And what some of the key emotional issues are between them.

> **2. The point of attack.** Where this will be in the history of the story and what happened prior to the opening of the play.

> **3. A suspense plot.** That's what justifies the whole enterprise happening so have it locked down. There's a good reason to have this clearly in hand. Suspense plots are extremely difficult – and in many cases impossible – to insert into a play after you've written pages of an emotional plot without

one, so know what's triggered the emotional plot before you start.

4. A feeling or image of the climax or resolution. Many playwrights discover the real makings of the climax and resolution as they write the play, so don't let a lack of specific details of a potential ending postpone writing. (Screenwriters nearly always know the shape of these in detail before they start writing.)

At this point, don't worry about the curtain line of Act I. It will usually begin to take shape in your mind about half-way through the act or even as late as a few pages before intermission.

While this list may be good to have in hand, some playwrights have a very different working method, one that starts with a single character, perhaps even one without a name. Then they essentially let that character talk on paper until they begin to "know" the character. Once they have what is now a central character, they move on to assembling the pieces of the play including other characters.

Outlining: Why (and Why Not)

Some playwrights – and nearly all screenwriters – swear by outlining as the bedrock of their scripts and careers. This is a case where you simply have to see if the shoe fits (that's another of those clichés that's true).

A reasonable guideline: Find a balance between having some sense of a general direction for the play while still allowing leeway for the unexpected. After all, among those things that makes playwriting exciting are times when characters seem to take over and carry you off in directions you'd never planned.

There are playwrights who don't ever begin writing dialogue until they know all the pieces of the play and where they'll go. Athol Fugard relies on a journal to help shape the scenes in the order he's after and nearly always knows what will happen in each scene – and how it will happen – before he starts writing dialogue. Edward Albee says he composes the first four or five drafts of a play in his head before putting the "first" draft on paper.

When thinking about outlining, a middle ground is worth considering. There's a real difference between planning where you're going in a scene – that is, what will have been accomplished by the end of the scene – and how you're going to get there. If you need the security of an outline, try focusing it on the where-you're-going part and leave the "how" for your fingers to discover in the process of writing the scenes. That at least opens an option for characters to come up with more interesting ways to get there than you may have originally planned.

A Caution on Outlining

For many playwrights, doing a detailed outline drains away the urge they originally felt to tell the story. Others find outlining, sometimes scene by scene, gives them the confidence of a road map. A few even sketch a biography of each of their characters before they begin.

There are also more than a few writers who do an outline and then stick it in the back of a drawer and never look at it again once they start that serious work of writing. But pay at least some attention to Steve Tesich's take on this sort of pre-planning:

> So I made an outline. Well, you know, days are going by, and I am not writing anything because this thing is laid out in front of me. It's as if you get every brochure for a trip you are going to go on and you get the minutest details of every step along the way. Well, I really doubt you're going to then get in the car and go. You know, it's like, why bother if it's all laid out in front of you?

David Mamet claims with some vehemence that it's a lot of nonsense that characters can take on a life of their own, one that you can barely control. You created them, he says, so make them do whatever you want. He's a bit of a loner on this point.

A lot of playwrights have had the experience of getting into that groove where the play (and its characters) seem to write the script with you hanging on by your fingernails as the recorder. Those in the non-Mamet camp enjoy being astounded by what sometimes comes out of their characters' mouths and the unplanned directions they often create.

If you begin to feel that characters are writing the play for you, let them and stuff that outline back in the drawer. You can always go back to it, but the play your characters seem to write may be far more interesting than the one that follows those predetermined building blocks.

41. WRITING EXERCISES: TO DO OR NOT

I just sit down and write, and I don't think. And the characters just do it. Sometimes they won't, and that's a bad day. I assume if I keep myself open and don't take myself too seriously, they'll keep talking. I live for those unexpected moments. I don't really know when they will come out – I just know what I want to say. Control so you can lose control – that's what writing is. Disciplined control. If you can sustain that for ten pages, you're lucky.
    -Eduardo Machado

Playwriting Seminars 2.0 is based on the idea that the best way to learn the craft is to write something real: A full-length play suitable for professional submission to competitions and regional theatres.

Writing exercises can certainly work, encouraging creativity, an understanding of dialogue written to be spoken, and overcoming the fear associated with putting words on paper. There are all kinds of ways – other than working on a script – to develop as a writer, everything from psychoanalysis (the poster boy for this is Woody Allen) to working on an assembly line. The process of dramatic writing is not a science. Whatever works for you, works. But finding what works – assuming simply writing a script doesn't – is far less easy to prescribe.

Following are three exercises that should have an impact on understanding key playwriting concepts.

Exercise One: Getting Rid of Spoken Subtext
Go through Chapter 16 on Subtext before you start.

> **1. Write two pages of dialogue.** With only two characters and without allowing any character to say more than *three words per line*. The limitation on words per line will automatically remove spoken subtext from dialogue. Think of this as like wringing out a washcloth – the water is the subtext. A caution: The sparse result will probably not be in your voice as a playwright and may make you sound like Harold Pinter.
>
> **2. Do this once more with two different characters.** Use the

same three-word limitation per line of dialogue.

3. Now experiment with line length. Find that point where subtext remains below the surface of the dialogue while allowing your voice as a playwright to come out.

Exercise Two: Combining Suspense & Emotional Plots
Go through Chapter 25 on Plots before you start. Then do these steps in order:

1. Select two characters with a shared past. A shared past means they worked together, lived together, grew up together, were in jail together, anything as long as they did it together.

2. Give these characters names. Ideally, names that seem "right" for each of them, even if you don't have a clear idea about why these seem right.

3. Pick an emotional issue that lurks between them. Ideally one they've never spoken about before and an issue with considerable depth to it.

4. Find a reason for them to start talking about this emotional issue. Other than coincidence. Something that forces them to start talking about this issue now.

This reason (#4) is your suspense plot. The issue (#3) between them is the emotional plot. Now start writing the first pages of the play you've just formed.

Exercise Three: Keeping a Journal
This is less an exercise than what should be an on-going fact in your life as a writer.

Nearly all writers keep journals. Some intend them for eventual publication and think of them that way. Others view what they say in a journal as an intensely private affair – many mark their journals as off-limits even to their significant others.

Keeping a journal gives you a practical way to note down intriguing ideas for plays, character names, bits of conversation or possible dialogue, physical appearances and behaviors you've observed, and ideas for suspense and emotional plots.

It's good to include thoughts about plays or screenplays

you've read and the same for plays or films you've seen.

Write in your journal about issues that are important to you, what you think about the world, how you view people. Get to know your beliefs. This process will help you understand the themes that will come into your plays.

Best Practice: *If you're not writing a play, write in your journal.*

A lot of writers like to do this the old-fashioned way with a pencil or pen in a notebook rather than on a computer or iPad. Carry the notebook with you and that way you won't have to try to remember that strange overheard exchange until you get back to your desk. Often while writing in your journal is when you'll get the inspiration for that next scene or that next play.

42. EDITING: THE HARD WORK

A play can feel too long because of three lines. You try and hold things to a point of maximum tension, if you miscalculate you lose the tension in a moment, as though a piece of elastic has snapped. To win back that moment you might find that you are taking out (or even in some cases re-inserting) an amount of writing which would be completely unnoticeable in a novel.
  -Tom Stoppard

More than a few playwrights use their first draft simply to find out what the play is really about. For them, half a dozen drafts (or even more) may follow before the script has the right shape.

Editing is a middle ground between the foolish assumption that the first draft is the greatest play ever written – and therefore not a word should be changed – and the equally rash impulse to burn the whole thing in the nearest fireplace. Just because D. H. Lawrence used the first draft of *Lady Chatterly's Lover* for firewood, doesn't mean you should.

It helps to have a little distance in time between dropping the curtain on the last act and going back to edit the script. For most playwrights, it's been a long ride in writing a script so you're due a vacation from it for a while – a few days at a minimum. Then go back and see what you've really done.

The Play in Your Head vs. on the Page

There's usually a difference between the play in your head (the one you're sure you've just written) and the play that actually made it to the page. One of the jobs of effective literary managers and directors in play development and workshop programs is to help playwrights come closer to that play in their heads. The best of these pros can look through the script as if it's a one-way mirror into the play you thought you were writing.

If you've developed an association with a theatre or a writers' group, this is the time to have a first reading of the script – not a formal staged reading, but a very informal one that allows you simply to hear performers saying your words. Many playwrights –

including the most accomplished – find this a valuable way to assess what they've created. And then they tackle the job of editing and rewriting the draft.

43. EDITING CHARACTERS

*I had a very linear story line for this particular play, and I wanted
to open the piece up a bit, so I started doing that with my writing.
I would describe fragments of scenes on index cards, then move the
card around to see how it changed the piece.*
    -Philip Kan Gotanda

The key question to ask about characters when the first draft is
done: Do each of those characters matter? Or to put it another way,
are they all essential to the story being told? If not, the script is
better off without them.

This may seem harsh and you may even feel these characters
have become friends after all the time you've spent with them and
they shouldn't be treated unkindly. But be ruthless. In this case, a
play is like a small boat – the more people it's carrying, the slower it
goes.

Keep in mind that magic number 10, the typical maximum
number of characters in contemporary plays.

Characters Needing the Ax
Be particularly suspicious of any character who feels uncomfortably
like at least one of these:

1. They show up for less than a page. In the entire script.

2. They don't say anything when they're on that page. Or
nothing important. Unless that's an essential part of who
they are.

3. They have little or no connection to the conflict. That is,
to the suspense or emotional plots. These are folks who just
happen to drop in to say hello.

4. They're just a technical device. Like waiters and
waitresses who say things like, "May I take your order?"
and are never seen or heard from again.

Be ruthless with these hangers-on and write them out of the play,
the only exception being if you've got three or four of them that can

be handled by the same performer – and they're essential to the forward movement of the script.

The second key question to ask: Does each character have a reasonably distinct way of speaking? Watch for anyone who:

1. Uses the same odd expressions typical of another character. Unless that's a key point in the story. If these sharing characters seldom show up on the same page, it's possible you've created identical twins who need to be put back together again as a single character.

2. Has the same subtext of another character. Again, this can work if it's a key point of the theme (David Mamet exploited this in *Glengarry Glen Ross* to fine effect and won the Pulitzer Prize for Drama). Otherwise, it's the identical twin issue again.

If two characters strike the audience as being clones in the way they speak or think, both lose impact. Make sure each character brings something new and essential to the script.

44. EDITING STAGE DIRECTIONS

> *The historical figures I've chosen to write about are extreme individuals – Marcel Duchamp and the Marquis de Sade – and to serve them in a way that felt honest and true to the spirit of their own lives, I had to write plays that were as extravagant in style as their own work was in its time. Research is crucial, but indulging in it to excess can be dangerous. It quickly becomes a terrific excuse not to write.*
>
> > -Doug Wright

Like other parts of a script, stage directions can be overwritten – and when they are, they become particularly annoying to theatre professionals. Of course the audience won't notice if this sort of overwriting is allowed to stand, but literary managers and other first readers will.

Specific things to look for in editing stage directions (see Chapter 54 for more on kinds of stage directions) follow.

Opening Stage Directions

The usual problem here is telling us too much about the setting of the play. The cause is simple: As a playwright it may be helpful to know what the setting looks like in considerable detail, but we don't need to know all that.

Here's an over-written opening stage direction marked for editing with strikethrough:

> *(NIKKI and Stu's family room. ~~There's an oriental rug on the floor, two chairs on either side, matching, with grey striped upholstery. Between the windows is a couch with matching end tables, each with a brass table lamp with a cloth shade. The curtains on the windows in the center of the rear wall are light cream. There are framed paintings on the walls. The~~ door to the kitchen ~~is to the left.~~ The living room ~~is to the right.~~ It's 2:00 a.m. ~~on a warm evening in summer~~ and the smoke still curls in the aftermath of a party ~~they've just given.~~)*

You may need to know all of that to write Act I, but here's all we really need to know from this opening s.d.:

> (*NIKKI and Stu's family room. Doors to the kitchen and living room. It's 2:00 a.m. and the smoke still curls in the aftermath of a party.*)

Give us the bare essentials. Make sure we know what's in the setting only if those elements become important later in the conflict driving the play.

General Stage Directions

While writing dialogue, you may visualize the central character coming in the front door on the right, moving toward the sofa against the back wall, then drifting toward the kitchen on the left. That's important to you, but not to us.

All we need to know is that the character enters and wanders around the room. Make sure you're telling us only what we absolutely need to know – what we need to know may not be any more than the character is on stage. Leave all that stage business to directors.

In screenplays, the equivalent of general stage directions makes up the majority of a script and thus become an essential target for editing in the same way that dialogue is the essential target in stage plays.

Character Stage Directions

These are the most important over-writing culprits to look for: Stage directions telling us repeatedly how characters says lines of dialogue or where they move as they're speaking. If there are more than two of these on a page, cut the excess.

When there are too many character stage directions, they clutter up the script and continually get in the way of your readers' eyes. More importantly, they interrupt the flow of the dialogue, making it harder for readers to "hear" your voice as a playwright.

A scene with overuse of character stage directions (none of these are necessary):

> JOAN (*Smiling*): Isn't this a nice change.
> LARKIN (*Frowning*): I don't know.
> JOAN: If you think about it. (*Quietly*) There really isn't anything to (*Whispering*) complain about.
> LARKIN: So you're leaving? (*Loudly*) Giving it all up?

JOAN: Not at all. (*Adjusting her glasses, softly*) Not at all.

Performers often take such a dim view of these performance tips that it's not unusual for them to cross out nearly all character stage directions in their parts before rehearsals begin.

45. EDITING DIALOGUE

*There's nothing like encountering the problems of costume,
lighting, set design – What do you mean by this? Where is this?
Where is the window? – which make you more aware of the totality
of what you're doing. I discovered with Fences that I had a
character exiting upstage and coming back immediately with a
different costume. That's really sloppy but I was totally unaware. I
never thought, "The guy's got to change his costume." I've become
conscious of things like that and it's made me a better playwright.*
                -August Wilson

Since dialogue comprises most of the script of a play, that makes it
the prime candidate for editing. Be careful doing this. Dialogue is
the real heart of a play, so while you can hack away with abandon
at stage directions, take much more care with what characters say.

Red Flags in Dialogue
There are six key warning signs for potential dialogue editing, each
of them fairly easy to spot in the early drafts of a script.

   1. Hidden monologues: disguised as dialogue (see Chapter
   46 on this).

   2. False monologues: that condense dialogue (see Chapter
   47 on this).

   3. Spoken subtext: giving away what characters really think.

   4. Talking to yourself lines: critiquing what you've just
   written.

   5. Transition lines: telegraphing where you're headed next.

   6. Variant lines: trying out versions of the same line.

All of these have a double impact: They drain the script of interest
and they prevent performers from doing what they do best:
Communicating subtext to the audience.

   Also watch for unintended clichés, those great ear-stoppers
for audiences (see Chapter 15 on this).

Even the big guns have done this sort of editing, sometimes with a vengeance, as Eugene O'Neill did with this part of a monologue from one of his masterpieces, *More Stately Mansions*:

> But you ~~lie! You~~ distort and exaggerate, as you always do! You know I do not take [it] ~~that daydream~~ seriously. I am lonely ~~—desperately lonely—~~ and bored! I am disgusted with watching my ~~ailing,~~ revolting body ~~go from day to day~~. Anything to ~~divert my mind and~~ forget myself ~~to wile away the time~~.

Take a second look at the script's opening scene. If this is your first play, odds are you were still discovering your voice during the opening scene or the first dozen pages of Act I. Now that your voice is more established, go back and rewrite those opening pages so they will match the level of the rest of the play.

Spoken Subtext

Subtext spoken by characters as dialogue – except at moments of high tension – is like sand tossed into an engine. It has the same effect on the conflict driving a play.

Best Practice: *Trust the intelligence of your audience.*

They'll get the subtext of the characters. If you're afraid they won't, it may mean you're not allowing your characters to talk with each other in scenes long enough for us to sense their subtexts. It takes time for audiences to "hear" subtext.

Likely culprits for spoken subtext editing:

1. Speeches composed of several sentences. Other than real monologues. Often one sentence or phrase will be the real dialogue line and the rest will be spoken subtext.

2. Lines where characters say exactly what they're thinking or feeling. But keep in mind that spoken subtext can work well near or at the climax of the play or during other high points of conflict, usually near the curtain lines of scenes or acts.

For detailed examples of editing spoken subtext, see Chapter 16.

Talking-to-Yourself Lines

Deep in your subconscious somewhere this side of the Id, lives a voice that tries to set you straight about what you've written. Since this beast can't talk directly to you – maybe because you won't pay attention – it speaks to you through your characters. Listen: This voice may know more about playwriting than you think.

There's a simple way to spot the lines where characters suddenly become a mouthpiece for your subconscious literary manager. When they do, they're often pointing out some playwriting transgression you'd instantly spot in someone else's play.

These talking-to-yourself lines have basic traits that make them easy to spot:

1. They're not related to the character. They don't come out of the character's subtext.

2. They have no prior preparation. They come out of the blue, to use a cliché.

3. They express dissatisfaction. Or frustration. With your writing, with your plot, with what another character says or does – even sometimes with their own dialogue – or with something that's happened.

And they always refer to portions of the script that come just prior to the line, telling you what to cut or what to rewrite.

Typical Talking-to-Yourself Lines

Why are you telling me all this?
Why are we talking (arguing) about this?
What a lot of drivel.
How did we get off on this tangent?
You said that before.
Can we get back to the subject now?
I can't believe you said that.
This is really boring.
Let's change the subject.
How many times do we have to go through this?
Before we got distracted, you were telling me about –
Nothing's happening here.
I'm getting confused.
Why are you behaving this way?

Cut these lines, but don't kill the messenger. Follow the directions instead. They're nearly always right.

Transition Lines

Transition lines and words are a playwright's inadvertent way of holding the audience's hand and leading us from one movement in the dialogue (sometimes called a "beat") to the next. These transition devices smooth the texture of the dialogue, eliminating surprise and reducing our interest.

Just as with spoken subtext, transition lines also prevent performers from doing the job they're paid for. Non-verbal transitions are what performers live for.

Since these devices plaster over the cracks between movements in the dialogue, they can nearly always be replaced with a (Pause.) stage direction with an immediate increase in the level of tension and interest in the scene.

Likely culprits for this kind of editing often begin with the same sort of throwaway words we fall into using in casual conversation – but just because we often use these transitions in real life, doesn't mean they work well in the theatre.

Transition words and phrases to cut (a small sample):

Besides…
And then…
Let me tell you…
What happened was…
The next thing that…
Well…
So…
Anyway…
As I was saying…
Whatever…

Another way to look at this: Transition lines or phrases are really saying to your audience: *OK, get ready. Here we go. Be warned. We're about to start a new subject. And the subject is –.*

Variant Lines

When characters repeat the same idea with slightly different phrasing in the same speech, there may be a candidate for editing. This kind of repetition may simply be your attempt to try several versions of the same thought and then, rather than using the best one, the trial version has also been left in the dialogue. When that happens, usually the last version is the best. Cut variant lines if:

1. They don't establish rhythm: in a character's speech pattern.

2. They don't build tension: in the scene or between characters.

Be careful with this since you don't want to edit out the special vocal rhythms of characters that may depend on verbal repetition for their impact. That's a subtle distinction, but keep variant lines when they're a deliberate part of a character's speech pattern. Tennessee Williams and David Mamet are famous for this kind of repetition and they use it to build toward moments of great intensity.

Using Apparent Repetition

There's another special case where considerable impact can be gained by using repetition in dialogue, though it's actually apparent repetition, not the kind that begs for cutting. Apparent repetition is a subtle way of waving a red flag for audiences that significant subtext waits for them if they compare version #1 with later versions of what appears to be the same story.

This kind of deliberate repetition is usually based on at least two monologues that seem at first hearing to tell the same story, but the similarity is a ruse. The impact of apparent repetition comes from the fact that we think the playwright is telling us the same old story we heard earlier in the play. But the variation in facts in the last version – usually the true version – suddenly tells us a great deal about the character who conned us the first time around.

Tennessee Williams created a classic example of apparent repetition in *Cat on a Hot Tin Roof* by having Big Daddy tell two versions of how he got those 20,000 acres of the richest land this side of the Valley Nile:

Version #1: Horatio Alger pays off. Big Daddy tells this first tale in front of the whole family including his wife and daughters-in-law. He worked hard, lived clean, and got the plantation as his just reward when the two men who owned it died.

Version #2: "Leaving a lot unspoken." The old goat tells us the "How I got it" tale, but this time only to his son, Brick. In a character stage direction, the playwright warns us to watch for the differences by telling us (in the script) that Big Daddy is "Leaving a lot unspoken." And what a difference. Listen carefully, and we understand why Big Daddy is so sympathetic to what he assumes is his son's conflicted sexuality. It falls to the director and performer playing Big Daddy to alert us to that "leaving a lot unspoken" stage direction that audiences can't "see" in production – but they can sense it through the subtext.

The advantage gained with apparent repetition comes from letting audiences discover the truth through their own detective work. The facts and subtext come to light by our comparing the contradictory versions of an event presented by the same character. Using apparent repetition to reveal these discrepancies is usually more powerful than taking the easy way out by having another character tell the real story.

Foreshadowing

If the goal is for audiences to have a revelation at the climax rather than shock, it's a good idea to check the level of foreshadowing woven into the script. Keep in mind that foreshadowing doesn't require more than subtle hints, but the hints – at least one – need to be there, otherwise shock at the climax will be the result. (See Chapter 22 for more on revelation vs. shock and foreshadowing.)

Fact Checking

Fact checking is a final review playwrights need to do when their characters make comments about real events. That's important because if characters unintentionally get their facts wrong, it's guaranteed that someone – probably lots of someones – who know these facts will be sitting in the audience. Worse, they'll probably whisper the mistake to their companion in the next seat and talk about it at more than a whisper during intermission.

An incorrect fact about something real can undermine the play by distracting a portion of the audience from what you're really writing about, and there's a good chance they'll assume if one fact was wrong then there are probably other mistakes as well.

As an example, if the 50-year-old father in a play set in 2011 tells his daughter that seeing the Beatles on the *Ed Sullivan Show* changed his life and led to him divorcing her mother, that only works if the daughter confronts him later with the real fact: That he was only three-years-old when that actually happened. For this approach to gain force, it helps if we gradually discover the father lies to his daughter about everything – and rather than being told by someone else, his daughter is the one who finally realizes this.

One of the advantages of working on new plays is that it's a collaborative process and that allows many sets of eyes to help spot issues for fact checking, but the safest way to handle this is to do it first.

46. FINDING HIDDEN MONOLOGUES

*In many of my plays, there was a kind of autobiographical
character in the form of a son or young man. The purpose of it, of
course, was to write about myself. That character was always the
least fully realized. Eighteen years later, you realize, "That's what
he was about."*
        -Sam Shepard

Hidden monologues ought to be monologues, but instead have
been written so they look visually like dialogue on the page. When
this happens, tension, conflict, and forward movement drain from
the scene at a rapid rate. The reason: This section of dialogue has
degenerated into essentially a one-sided conversation devoid of
conflict.

The most common red flags warning that a hidden
monologue sits within a section of dialogue:

1. A series of dialogue lines telling a story. The lines are
spoken by only one of the characters and tell a single
coherent story with a beginning, a middle, and in most cases
an end.

2. These lines are fueled by internal tension. There's little
or no external conflict between characters in this portion of
the script. If there's conflict, it's internal to the character
telling the story. Thus the progression of these lines
develops independently of a second character who is
present.

**3. These lines are consistently longer than those spoken by
the other character.** Not only are they consistently longer,
they're a lot longer – often by a factor of 10 or more.

**4. The "listening" character punctuates these story lines
with upscale versions of grunts.** Typical (and meaningless)
response lines:

Uh, huh.
And then what did he say?

Oh.
Mmm.
Wow.
I can't believe it.
She said that?
What did you do then?
That's amazing!
Really?
I never knew that.

Hidden monologues can be brought to life by cutting these *Uh, huh* lines along with any insignificant responses to those "grunts" by the character telling the story.

These "Uh, huh" lines were probably written to give your fingers something to do while puzzling out the next movements of the monologue you intended to write – and when it was finished, you didn't realize what you'd accomplished.

Hidden Monologue Example (Still Buried)

JOAN: Snow White in Brooks Brothers. And you missed it.
LARKIN: I didn't!
JOAN: Oh, yes you did. You always do.
LARKIN: We'd come out of the clinic that morning. Biting cold. I'd forgotten the sound of cold like that.
JOAN: Sounds miserable.
LARKIN: Burgess was oblivious, as always. We could've been in the West Indies for all it mattered.
JOAN: What did he say?
LARKIN: Oh, he talked about theory and strategy. The Gobi, Hudson's Bay. He was doing it again with White Alice.
JOAN: And then what happened?
LARKIN: I'm hearing my breath freeze as it comes out. Sun driving off the snow. I could barely see where I was. After all those weeks inside. No warm up. "Got back your clearance," he says. Just – Bam.
JOAN: Really?
LARKIN: Uh, huh. Like it was doing laundry. Which for him I suppose it was. I knew he wasn't doing it for old times, no matter what you think. "This is my ticket to the Home Office."

JOAN: That's amazing.

LARKIN: That's how he put it. Like everybody gets one. Above a certain level. Beyond a certain point. So I asked him, What's my ticket?

JOAN: I can't believe it.

LARKIN: Well, he stops and he looks at me. I know that look. And he says, "You don't need one. You've got me."

JOAN (*Gently*): Do you get it now?

(*Lights out.*)

Scene Edited for Cuts Including Transition Lines

JOAN: Snow White in Brooks Brothers. And you missed it.

LARKIN: I didn't!

JOAN: Oh, yes you did. You always do.

LARKIN: We'd come out of the clinic that morning. Biting cold. I'd forgotten the sound of cold like that.

JOAN: Sounds miserable.

LARKIN: Burgess was oblivious, as always. We could've been in the West Indies for all it mattered.

JOAN: What did he say?

LARKIN: Oh, he talked about theory and strategy. The Gobi, Hudson's Bay. He was doing it again with White Alice.

JOAN: And then what happened?

LARKIN: I'm hearing my breath freeze as it comes out. Sun driving off the snow. I could barely see where I was. After all those weeks inside. No warm up. "Got back your clearance," he says. Just – Bam.

JOAN: Really?

LARKIN: Uh, huh. Like it was doing laundry. Which for him I suppose it was. I knew he wasn't doing it for old times, no matter what you think. "This is my ticket to the Home Office."

JOAN: That's amazing.

LARKIN: That's how he put it. Like everybody gets one. Above a certain level. Beyond a certain point. So I asked him, What's my ticket?

JOAN: I can't believe it.

LARKIN: Well, he stops and he looks at me. I know that look. And he says, "You don't need one. You've got me."

JOAN (*Gently*): Do you get it now?

204

(Lights out.)

Hidden Monologue Brought to the Surface

JOAN: Snow White in Brooks Brothers. And you missed it.
LARKIN: I didn't!
JOAN: Oh, yes you did. You always do.

(Pause.)

LARKIN: We'd come out of the clinic that morning. Biting cold. I'd forgotten the sound of cold like that. Burgess was oblivious, as always. We could've been in the West Indies for all it mattered. Theory and strategy. The Gobi, Hudson's Bay. He was doing it again with White Alice. I'm hearing my breath freeze as it comes out. Sun driving off the snow. I could barely see where I was. After all those weeks inside. No warm up. "Got back your clearance," he says. Just – Bam. Like it was doing laundry. Which for him I suppose it was. I knew he wasn't doing it for old times, no matter what you think. "This is my ticket to the Home Office." That's how he put it. Like everybody gets one. Above a certain level. Beyond a certain point. So I asked him, What's my ticket? He stops and he looks at me. I know that look. And he says, "You don't need one. You've got me."
JOAN (*Gently*): Do you get it now?

(Lights out.)

The hidden versions of monologues are often well written – once they're unearthed from the apparent dialogue that has buried them, but that won't be clear until they're pulled out of that black hole of seeming dialogue.

47. FALSE MONOLOGUES TO DIALOGUE

It was a roller-coaster process. For a long time I had no idea what I was doing. I wasn't writing with an outline. And, rare for me, I wrote scenes out of sequence. I didn't understand the play when I wrote it. It was something I'd given in to. It happens to me periodically. I give over and write whatever comes to me and I don't know what it means and then I do. It's thrilling.
  -David Rabe

False monologues are exactly that. At first glance, they look like short monologues, but are actually a series of minimally connected thoughts that will gain strength by being threaded together as alternating lines of dialogue.

They are a good source of dialogue when they're broken apart into individual lines. This is made easier by the odd fact that false monologues are often written in pairs. The solution is to interleave the lines, alternating between each of the characters.

The surest way to spot false monologues is to look for a sequence of speeches by two characters that are far longer than your typical lines of dialogue. Besides being noticeably longer, each will usually contain multiple sentences and those sentences won't tell a coherent story or even lead logically from one thought to the next.

A False Monologue Pair

JOAN: Well, I don't know. I mean – you know he could be anywhere. Anywhere at all. That's what these guys are like. You didn't think of that?
LARKIN: Where could he be? He can't be anywhere. He has to be some place he would've been before. That's common sense. That's what I've been thinking.

The first step in untangling a hidden monologue is to try converting each sentence into a single line of dialogue.

The False Monologue into Dialogue

LARKIN: Where could he be?

JOAN: Well, I don't know.

LARKIN: He can't be anywhere.

JOAN: I mean –

LARKIN: He has to be someplace he would've been before.

JOAN: He could be anywhere.

LARKIN: That's common sense.

JOAN: Anywhere at all. That's what these guys are like.

LARKIN: That's what I've been thinking.

JOAN: You didn't think of that.

Since you wrote the dialogue to begin with, there's no reason to necessarily organize the lines in their original order. They may have a stronger impact by altering the sequence. One of the interesting mysteries of false monologue pairs is that interweaving these lines usually creates some level of conflict between these two characters where there was none before.

If a false monologue doesn't come with an obvious twin, the solution is to write new lines for the other character and interweave these between the lines of this problem-child, though there still needs to be enough conflict to support the exchange.

48. EDITING STRUCTURE

The first scene of the play is the first scene that I wrote. I wish I could say that I planned it, but I didn't; people kind of showed up doing whatever they were doing in whatever time they were doing it. Then, once I had a first draft, I could look at it and say, What does this want to be about? and focus it.
　　　　　-Lisa Loomer

Editing may be too strong (and hopeful) a word for what can really be done at this point with structure when the first draft of the script is finished. Tinkering with beginnings and endings may be a better way to talk about what is possible.

For the most serious (and most common) structural problem – lack of a suspense plot – rewriting the play from the beginning is the only real solution. That hardly qualifies as "editing."

Inserting Suspense Plots

Going back into a script and inserting a suspense plot after the fact is nearly impossible. A suspense plot can be grafted into an already written emotional plot, but it will never be integrated into the play the way it would have been if you'd started out writing with the suspense plot in hand. If you suspect this may be a problem, take another look at Chapter 25 on Plots.

When the structure is all there, the suspense plot is integrated into the subtext of the characters and leads directly to the play's climax. That's why patching in a suspense plot in bits and pieces after the fact and having it build to a convincing climax and resolution hardly ever works.

The solution for a missing suspense plot: Bite the cap of your pen – hard – and write a second draft of the play from scratch, this time with a suspense plot launched by the inciting incident. The resistance you'll feel to doing this will be strong, but the second draft will be much easier to write since the conflict created by the suspense plot will help drive the new draft. The alternative is a high probability of having a script that generates little or no interest at regional theatres or competitions.

Here's what can be done if the suspense plot is in place. All of these structure edits focus on beginnings and endings, the transitions into or out of each structural element of the play.

Beginning of the Play

Look carefully at the first scene or at least the first five pages. Do this whether the play is structured in short formal scenes or continuous acts.

The question to ask: *Is the point of attack one scene too early?*

If the opening pages seem "soft" (meaning little conflict is evident between characters) and it feels like it's taking a very long time to get to the inciting incident, that's an important message: Scene 1 may only have been a warm-up for writing the real play.

Beginnings of Scenes & Acts

The opening of the first scene of a play is the most obvious place to find an initial softness in the writing, but each subsequent scene and act can be affected by the same problem.

The question to ask: *Have you started later acts or scenes too early?*

Look at the first half-dozen lines of dialogue following the beginning of each formal or informal scene and see if these openings were just warm-ups for the real beginning of each scene.

Warm Up Lines

Warm up lines are one of the most common structural problems, because they rob scenes and acts of a firm start. Their impact is like jamming the gas peddle to the floor on sand: There's a lot of noise, but nothing's happening.

Warm up lines are literally that – you needed to go through the exercise, but they're of no value after that. If they're left in the dialogue, they weaken the scene mostly because they are usually full of spoken subtext and unnecessary exposition.

Warm-up Lines Scene Marked for Cuts

JOAN: ~~How could you be so careless? I told you never to take the gun with you until you knew how to use it properly. So now you've killed someone, and for no good reason. And someone very important.~~
LARKIN: It went off without me doing anything. I didn't –

JOAN: Do you have it with you?
LARKIN: No. (*Pause*) I don't know. Maybe. I –
JOAN: How many times have you –
LARKIN: Perhaps it's all right. Maybe it doesn't matter.
JOAN: How could a death not matter? Especially his.

(*Pause.*)

LARKIN: I didn't mean to do it.

Cutting warm up lines always strengthens the opening of acts and scenes, increasing the level of tension and interest.

Endings of Scenes and Acts

The question to ask: *Do acts and scenes end with a curtain line?* And do these propel us into the next movement of the play?

Look at the last line of each scene and consider how it feels. Every scene doesn't need to end with a ferocious curtain line, but even the mildest of these should at least catch our attention. If there's no curtain line, look at the last two or three lines and see if you've let the dialogue resolve the conflict instead of pushing us into the next scene or act.

Climax of the Play

The question to ask: *Does the climax fall within the last four pages of the play?*

If not, cut the pages following it to a maximum of four, a typical length in contemporary practice.

Alternatively, see if the climax has come too early. Be careful if it's too early. That may mean you've imposed an arbitrary climax on the characters rather than allowing it to grow directly out of the conflict between them.

Resolution of the Play

If the resolution runs on for more than three or four pages after the climax, the play is just being pushed when it's out of gas. Briefer is better at the end, but if there is a lot of conflict still in the resolution – and it makes you want to keep writing – then the play has probably been ended too soon.

The advantage of a short resolution: It usually leaves audiences with something to think about when they've left the theatre because you've left us with some partially unresolved issues.

49. CRITICS & ADVICE FROM FRIENDS

Don't talk about your play while you are writing it. Good plays are always the product of a single vision. A play is one thing you can get too much help with. Don't talk the play away.
        -Marsha Norman

Beware of advice from your friends. Nearly everybody who wants to write a screenplay – that's almost everyone – will often settle for a stage play, if they figure out you know how to write one. They may not intend it, but they'll try to get you to write their play. That's the one they'd write, if only they had the time, the [fill in the blank].

They will see this as offering helpful advice, but if you take them up on the offer, you'll soon be a thousand miles away from the play you wanted to write – and thought you had written.

Literary managers and professional directors more often than not have the knack of commenting on the play you've written, as opposed to the one they might like to write themselves, though this professional process of play improvement is far from foolproof.

There's a joke (first told by a literary manager) that's worth keeping in mind as a quiet caution: A literary manager comes to Hamlet's line, "To be or not to be" and scribbles in the margin, *Bill, why is he talking to us again???*

Theatre Critics

There's a very long line of American playwrights who have learned not to pay a lot of attention to professional theatre critics. Some like David Mamet simply refuse to read reviews.

Basically, all professional critics can do is make a noticeable dent in the potential size of a playwright's wallet (either thick or thin) and there's nothing you can do about their power anymore. In the 19th Century, theatre producers sometimes put critics on their own payroll. That helped.

The problem is not that critics don't understand the craft – many of them do - it's just that most of them are not writing for playwrights. They're writing for your potential audience, those people thinking about putting out $60 a ticket to see your play at a major regional theatre or $100 or more if you've made it to Broadway. What they want to know is if they'll have an interesting time – if the babysitter, the drive back to town, dinner out, drinks at intermission, and the tab at the parking garage, will all be worth it when the curtain comes down on your play. That's a lot different from the craft issues you're dealing with.

Don't blame the audience for wanting this assessment, given the total of that tab beyond the cost of the tickets. You're lucky. You'll often get complimentary tickets when you want to see your own play. Besides, you may have a far more serious problem.

Self Criticism

Being your own critic is a millstone you don't need to cart around, though most artists do, especially before they've gotten that first recognition for their work – though sometimes recognition makes self criticism even worse.

There will be enough critics and would-be-critics ready to hammer on your head without you leading the chorus. There's a difference between clear-headed thinking about how you might strengthen the first draft of a play and self-criticism which is usually nasty, mean, brutish, and sly. Unlike talking-to-yourself lines written by your internal literary manager, that self critic is not your friend.

The goal of this kind of internal criticism is to make sure you don't write anything at all.

Muffling Your Self Critic

Carting around a particularly nasty self critic can do more to undermine your work as a writer than the most ignorant and mean-spirited of critics.

1. Beware the pitfalls of advice from your friends. If they're not theatre professionals, they'll mostly be shooting in the dark. In doing so, they'll be providing boxes of ammunition for that self critic to hurl at you.

2. Spend time with other writers. Preferably ones at about the same stage of a career as you are. It helps to have support and interest from writers who know what it's really like to put words on paper. Many cities have playwrights' organizations. Ask at local theatres about whether there's something like this in your area and check the DG and TCG listings (see Chapter 62 on Professional Support). Doing a Web search with the name of your city and Playwrights may also provide leads to writers' groups.

3. Never criticize your own work to others. This sort of behavior reinforces what that self critic is up to and most people won't like hearing you do this. Especially don't do this around anyone who might be thinking about presenting your play. After all, if you're telling the world your play isn't any good, why should anyone take the time to see if you're wrong?

4. Never allow your self critic to introduce your work. A surprising number of playwrights allow their early efforts to be undermined at readings and workshop productions by a drum roll saying some variant of, "It's just OK, it's only a first draft, I'm not sure about it." One of the reason new playwrights allow their self critic to say these foolish things is that they're trying to buy insurance against looking like an idiot if the audience doesn't like the play. If you're not sure about the play, keep that to yourself – at least until after you've heard the audience response.

Best Practice: *The play your self critic hates the most may be your best.*

The object of your loathing may be a significant breakthrough especially in developing your voice as a playwright.

50. WHEN TO STOP REWRITING

Until a script is ready for a director, it is self-defeating to give it to him. If it is not your play yet, you can't blame him for making it his.

-Terrence McNally

When to stop editing and rewriting is probably the hardest decision of all for a playwright to make. There are no real guidelines for making the decision any easier.

If you're in previews and audience reaction is far from what you and the director hoped for, you may need to keep rewriting all the way up to opening night and even into the run of the show.

There's a long tradition of doing that with scripts in need of "fixing" in the theatre (there used to be a class of professionals called "play doctors" who specialized in rescuing scripts that weren't working with audiences). It's debatable whether doing surgery on scripts at this stage will produce more than modest gains. That sort of rewriting is much better done in workshop environments, but if the first draft is still on your desk, there are two key questions that may help.

1. Are you still making progress with this script? Don't total up the number of edits. This is an emotional call, relying mostly on gut feeling.

2. Do you have a new play that's burning to be written? Or not even burning yet, but just tugging at your sleeve enough to be a distraction.

If the answer to the first question is No or Maybe, it's time to check the spelling and ship it out to theatres and competitions. Or show it to a director. Or bring together a group of performers to do a reading. Or put it in a drawer until you have enough distance from it to see if it has legs.

If the answer to the second question is Yes, then as Nike likes to say, *Just Do It*. It's another indication that it's time to move the play you've finished from inside your computer to the world of the theatre so you can start on that next play.

It's especially important to move on to the next play if the one you're revising now is the first you've written. The amount learned from writing this first play is probably far greater than you realize and you'll only see the proof of that in the next script.

PART FOUR – FORMAT: Play Scripts

There are so many rules about playwriting. I'd have a nervous breakdown if I followed them.
-Terrence McNally

51. PROFESSIONAL FORMAT FOR PLAYS

*Usually, the faster I write, the better it is, so I was probably
writing five or six hours a day. I can write about five pages an
hour when I'm going good. The original script was about 180
pages long, but when we ended up doing the play it was reduced to
around 90 pages. So I cut about half the original script.*
        -Tom Noonan

It may seem like the maximum in un-creativity, but using standard professional format is important.

How that first draft is put on paper is nobody's business but your own – pencil in a notebook, magic marker on a role of butcher paper – whatever works is all that matters. But once you're ready to submit a play to regional theatres, directors, literary managers, and competitions, using professional format is essential.

Advantages of Using the Format

Many playwrights do nearly all their writing using the standard format because it provides a quick way to estimate the running time of the script in performance. This timing device also provides alerts for when to start thinking seriously about the curtain line for Act I and the obligatory scene in Act II.

Most importantly, it's literally the first impression literary managers and their readers will have of the script and your professionalism. Using the format sends a signal that you know what you're doing.

Writing a play in format can be annoying or just exasperating and distracting even if it's easy to do once you sort it out. For more than a few playwrights it can keep being just as annoying when they are on their 10th play.

Getting It Done for You

But the alternatives are not great.

1. Hire a secretary to do it. The playwrights who do this usually make enough from their plays that they never miss the money it takes. And if you don't live in New York, Los

Angeles, or London, it won't be easy finding someone who combines flying fingers on the keyboard with knowing how to do script format.

2. Get screenwriting software. It's much cheaper than a secretary. The leading screenwriting programs also provide the format for stage plays. If you're thinking of writing for film or television as well, this is the only way to go. (See Chapter 72 on Screenwriting Software.)

If you're new to playwriting, try formatting the old-fashioned way first and save the investment in technology for when you're ready to make a real commitment to the form.

Even then, most contemporary playwrights who don't also write regularly for film or television – that's hardly anyone nowadays – don't bother with software for putting their scripts in format. That's a measure of how easy it is to do with a word processing program.

Traditional & Modern Format

What is presented in the *Handbook* is "traditional" format. For those who have been writing for a decade or more, the "modern" format is nearly identical to the traditional one, with two exceptions:

1. General stage directions: (but not Character s.d.'s) are typed without parentheses and now begin at the center of the page, going to the right margin, the way the Opening s.d. always did.

2. Times New Roman is the font of choice: instead of the old Courier. (Courier remains the font of choice for screenplays.)

There is no firm rule on being modern or traditional. Use whichever format feels most comfortable, but use one or the other in terms of #1 above. Don't mix and match the handling of stage directions.

A number of theatre pros (including Tony Kushner) prefer the traditional format – perhaps because the theatre has never been a fan of change.

Publishing vs. Script Formats

Nearly all published plays in book form use a format that has little relationship to the standard script format used in the theatre. The most noticeable differences in publishing format are placing character names at the far left margin and italicizing stage directions. The *Handbook* uses publishing format for its scene examples.

Publishing format uses less space (and thus less paper) and is a compatible style for e-books, but it's not as easy for performers and directors to use in rehearsals. That's why new scripts use the format described in the following chapters.

52. FONTS & FORMAT BY THE NUMBERS

I was working on a more filmic approach to my playwriting. I knew from the beginning that it was a play with a lot of filmic elements, like fades. I move freely from one location to another and there are many locations in the script. There are moments that dissolve into other moments, and these juxtapositions add to the sense of connection in the play.
　　　　　-Philip Kan Gotanda

The best way to understand the standard format for scripts is to look first at the reduced dialogue page in format on page 223. A visual idea of a page in format will help in understanding the details that follow. A full-size dialogue page example is on the Web (www.vcu.edu/arts/playwriting/adobeformatpage.pdf).

Paper Weight & Color
Always use white 20-pound 8.5" x 11" paper for all pages of the final draft of the script. This is typically what's used in most copy shops, but ask to make sure before giving them the green light on that copy machine.

Duplicate scripts for theatres and competitions on three-hole punched paper so you don't have to do the hole punching yourself – it's usually more expensive per ream than un-punched paper, but will overcome an awful chore.

Font & Type Size
The type font used by most playwrights today is Times New Roman, though Currier is sometimes still favored by those old enough to remember what an IBM Selectric was. Always use 12-point type for all pages of the script.

Script Format by the Numbers
There's more to the format of a script's preliminary and dialogue pages than a ruler provides, but this is a place to start. Note that screenplay format is a very different world from what's standard for plays (see Chapter 71 on Screenplay Format). Keep in mind that

what matters in stage play format is the general appearance – the physical relationship between character names, dialogue, and stage directions on the page – not the exact fractions of an inch.

The page categories are listed in the order they should appear in the final bound script. More detailed discussion of each page follows.

1. Title Page
Center on the page: PLAY TITLE & Your Name.
Left Margin at bottom of page for copyright notice:1.5" - 2.0"

2. Character Page
Left Margin: 1.5" - 2.0" & Right Margin: 1.0"

3. Setting & Time Page
Left Margin: 1.5" - 2.0" & Right Margin: 1.0"

4. Scene Breakdown Page [Optional Page]
Left Margin: 1.5" - 2.0" & Right Margin: 1.0"

5. Quote Page [Optional Page]
Left Margin: 2.5" - 3.0" & Right Margin: 2.0"

6. Dialogue Pages
Top Margin: 0.75" - 1.0" & Bottom Margin: 1.0" - 1.5"
A. Character Names & Opening Stage Directions:
Left Margin: Center of page, thus 4.25" & Right Margin: 1.0"
B. Dialogue:
Left Margin: 1.5" - 2.0" & Right Margin: 1.0"
C. General & Character Stage Directions:
Left Margin: 3.5" & Right Margin: 1.0"

Dialogue Page I-1 of a Script in Format
The following Dialogue Page, reduced in size, is useful for understanding the relationships between the elements of the format. Keep in mind that scripts are printed on 8.5"x11" paper (and in 12-point type) noticeably larger than the pages in the *Handbook*.

ACT I

SCENE 1

(A courtyard. Joan and Larkin surrounded by a
pool of light. Larkin only in a sweater and scarf
– he's freezing. They are alone as it's possible
to be in this business.)

JOAN

How are you?

LARKIN

Fine . . . fine.

(Pause.)

JOAN

That's not what I was asking.

LARKIN

No?

(Joan takes out a phone, checks the number. He watches
her, glances around, sees nothing.)

LARKIN

Everyone who matters in this is dead. Or nearly so. At least we accomplished that
much doing nothing.

JOAN

That's good?

(Larkin won't face her. Sound of a car door slamming,
close. Joan looks up at the sound.)

LARKIN
(Quietly)
Doing nothing is the brass ring in this business.

JOAN

And Annie? Our Annie.

LARKIN

Our Annie. That's a funny way to put it.

53. TITLE & PRELIMINARY PAGES

I knew I wanted to make a film about a writer whose talent has grown stagnant. The idea for a writer finding her roots came first, and then I discovered the apartment – and made the connection. Sometimes for an idea to cement, you have to see a place.
-Ismail Merchant

The title page and preliminary pages are things of value, the first glimpse, other than the cover, that a literary manager or director will have of the script. And these pages provide important information for readers.

Title Page & Example
Center the title in all capital letters about 3.5" - 4" down from the top. Insert one space after the title and also before your name:

TITLE OF THE PLAY

A play in two-acts

by

Your Name

In the lower left corner, add the copyright notice with your contact information:

Copyright © 2012 by Your Name
Mailing address
Phone number
Email

Note that some play competitions will require that your name and contact information appear only on a separate unbound title page and not on the title page bound with the script. Competitions do this to help level the playing field so that playwrights known by the readers and judges won't gain an edge over unknown writers.

Character Page & Example
Most playwrights list their characters in descending order of

importance. Usually the descriptions of these characters are brief, sometimes but not always giving their ages. Character names are always in all capitals here and in the dialogue pages.

A typical character page looks like this with one space inserted between each name and description:

CHARACTERS

JOAN   She's been on the inside around Langley, VA. 40's.

LARKIN   A structural engineer and wishes that was all. 40.

BURGESS   Heavy, but still mostly muscle. 58

ANN   Near 30.

BILLINGS   Has a crew cut. Late 20's.

Setting & Time Page & Example

Don't stay up nights pondering the intricacies of the play's setting. Lose sleep over a very general sense of where the play is happening and how to capture the essence of that in a brief description since scene designers and directors won't pay much attention to a playwright's detailed set description and neither will professional readers.

Give us just enough information to know where we are and to create our own rough picture of what this might look like. Then let the designers do what they're paid to do.

Literary managers, directors, and designers don't need to know where the doors and windows are, the lamps, and where that old standby the couch is. Or chairs and that other standby, the dining table.

But if the setting is suggestive or symbolic rather than realistic, we do need to know how you imagine this abstract space and more importantly the atmosphere it should create. A third of a page should be ample for this.

Center the headings, but align the descriptions flush left. Here's the Setting & Time Page for a reasonably realistic setting:

SETTING
Nikki and Stu's family room in a tract home on the edge of Santa Fe. They tore a page out of *House Beautiful* years ago. And later, a mesa somewhere in Arizona.

TIME
Evening. And the next evening. Winter, 2011.

Scene Breakdown Page

This page is optional and most plays don't need one. It provides useful information only if a play is structured in a series of many formal scenes taking place in different locations and time periods. List the scenes numbered as they are in the script, flush to the left margin and give each a very brief description of the location and time period.

This page can also be used to make a very complicated time structure clear to readers.

If the play has fewer than about six scenes (perhaps three per act) taking place in different locations and time periods, it works as well to list them under each act on the Setting & Time Page. Don't list individual scenes if they take place in the same general setting. So if the set has a living room and dining room in the same house – and both are visible on stage – there's no need to list the scenes regardless of how many there are.

Quote Page

Some playwrights acknowledge an influence on the play by placing a quote on a separate page within the preliminary pages. Usually this page comes just before the first Dialogue Page. In nearly every case, the quotes playwrights use are short.

Notable Quotes on Quote Pages
1. Lines from a well-known writer:

A solitude ten thousand fathoms deep
Sustains the bed on which we lie, my dear;
Although I love you, you will have to leap;
Our dream of safety has to disappear.
　　　　-W. H. Auden

2. A lyric or phrase from a song:

"I could escape this feeling
With my China girl..."
        -David Bowie & Iggy Pop

3. A folk or common saying:

ALWAYS BE CLOSING
        -Practical Sales Maxim

Here's why the playwrights used each of these quotes:

1. Craig Lucas' quote: from a poem by W. H. Auden practically summarizes the plot of *Reckless*.

2. David Henry Hwang's quote: captures a variant of his theme in *M. Butterfly*.

3. David Mamet's quote: summarizes the code of his characters in *Glengarry Glen Ross*.

Only include a quote if it means something significant to you and the script. If you're just fond of the quote and are simply looking for a way to use it, don't. The odds are 99 to 1 that a literary manger will ask you what the significance of the quote is and you won't earn points by saying you just liked it.

A recent exception to quote length: Tracy Letts has a 230-word quote from Robert Penn Warren's *All the King's Men* on his Quote Page for *August: Osage County* and thus holds the record for the longest quote page in living memory – it works because it relates directly to the theme of the play.

Numbering of Preliminary Pages

Preliminary pages are often left unnumbered, though numbering can help in making sure these pages are ordered correctly in bound scripts. If these pages are numbered, use lower case Roman numerals (i, ii, iii) starting after the Title Page (thus the Character Page will be page i).

Experts at word processing – not a skill playwrights need – know how to keep both Preliminary and Dialogue Pages in the same file with different numbering for each. If that's not a burning interest, skip the preliminary page numbering or go back and struggle through the Help menu.

54. DIALOGUE PAGES

Early in my career my work was partially disguised autobiography. After I got through that phase I had this realization that the role of the outsider was more universal. I began dealing more with the problem of how whole cultures are unable to interact harmoniously.
                    -Ping Chong

Dialogue pages are your primary investment and invention as a playwright. They are also your primary intellectual property in the script so it's worth treating them kindly and presenting them in the best way possible. What follows are descriptions of each element of the format for these pages.

Page Numbering
Page numbers are essential for estimating the running time of a script as well as checking the relative balance in the lengths of acts. Numbering begins with the first page of dialogue in the upper right-hand corner of each page (placing numbers flush right in the header is a simple way to handle this).

Each act is numbered consecutively in the sequence: I-1, I-2, I-3 through the last page of the act. The numbering for Act II begins again from scratch in the sequence: II-1, II-2, II-3. And for an Act III: III-1, III-2, III-3.

Plays structured in short formal scenes without act designations are numbered consecutively with numerals only. If act designations are also used with formal scenes – and most playwrights do this – follow the numbering system for plays in acts without regard for the scenes within each of those acts.

Act & Formal Scene Designations
Each act or scene begins at the top of a new dialogue page of the manuscript. The act and/or scene number is placed at the top of the initial page of the act or scene. They begin at the centerline of the page, just as character names do. These are always in all caps and

appear only on the first page of dialogue of each act or scene. Thus, ACT I only appears on the first page of Act I; SCENE 2 only appears at the top of the first page of that scene. Scene designations are only used if the play is structured in a series of formal scenes.

Acts are usually designated by Roman numerals or with the number spelled out: ACT II or ACT TWO. Numbers tend to be saved for scenes: SCENE 2 rather than SCENE TWO.

Opening Stage Directions

The opening stage direction needs to get to the point. A few playwrights feel compelled to write paragraphs here, but most tell us only very briefly where we are, who's there, and when it's happening.

If you feel the urge for paragraphs, put them on the Setting & Time Page and keep your opening s.d. to a brief summary. A long opening s.d. only makes sense if the play begins with detailed physical action that's essential to understanding the story.

The opening s.d. is flush left to the centerline of the page (not to the left margin or the margin for general s.d.'s), just as character names are. The easiest way to do this is with the Indent function.

Act II (and Act III if it's a three-act play) also has an opening stage direction. If the setting is identical to Act I, there's no need for more than a brief reminder of where we are and if important, the time of day.

Character Names

Character names begin at the vertical center line of dialogue pages and continue in all capitals toward the right margin. They are not centered on the page so don't use the "center" alignment command for names: Use the tab key.

Character Stage Directions

Character stage directions are placed under the character name or between the lines of dialogue of a single speech. The left margin for these is about 1" to the left of the centerline of the page and thus that much to the left of your capitalized character names.

Remember that most playwrights use this kind of s.d. sparingly. If you're averaging more than two per page, you're cluttering up the dialogue with unnecessary noise. As with everything else in manuscript format, the visual structure is designed for ease of reading. In this case, clearly separating stage directions from dialogue.

Save character stage directions for those moments when you have an overwhelming need to tell us what the dialogue can't. Here's what they're good for:

1. Physical action to be done by the character: as the line is being spoken: (Filling the glass)

2. Action implying a (Pause) s.d.: (Shaking her head)

3. Tone of voice or the emotional quality of the line: (Distraught)

4. Clarifying who the line is said to: when more than two characters are on stage: (To Joan)

These character stage directions are very brief. Note that there is no period at the end of the phrase, unlike general stage directions.

You should use a general stage direction instead of a character s.d. if the character s.d.:

1. Is so long that it's not finished when you hit the right margin.

2. Describes more than one physical action.

3. States what a another character is doing.

Dialogue Spacing

Saving trees in admirable, but don't compromise the script by using a narrow left margin for dialogue pages. That 1.5" - 2" left margin is needed to leave room for the holes in 3-hole punched paper. If you use a narrower margin, the left hand words will get lost in what's called the gutter of the script when it's bound with a cover, and that makes it a pain to read.

All dialogue is single spaced and runs across the page from the far left to the far right margin. Insert a line between the end of a line of dialogue and the next character name. There's no space between a character name and its dialogue.

(Pause.) Stage Direction

(Pause.) means just that: A brief silence. Harold Pinter claimed that the only real communication between characters happened, not when they were speaking to each other, but in the (Pause.) – a stage direction he made famous. The (Pause.) s.d. comes in handy for:

1. Signaling the start of a new "beat" or movement: in the conflict between the characters.

2. Signaling the introduction of the inciting incident: of the suspense plot.

3. Those moments when silence can have far more emotional impact on audiences than words.

When (Pause) is used as a character stage direction within a speech by a single character, there's no period (Pause) – but when used as a General s.d. it's (Pause.) with the period.

(Overlapping) Stage Direction

When two or more characters are speaking at the same time, use the (Overlapping) character s.d. under the name of the second of the pair doing this.

Lots of variants on (Overlapping) can accomplish the same thing. We'll get the message as long as the phrase suggests the delivery you want. Some options: (At the same time), (Riding over), (Simultaneously). Unlike the other variants, (Riding over) implies that the second character is much stronger – or at least louder – than the first of the pair.

In the old days when playwrights used typewriters, another option was one Lanford Wilson made famous: Running dialogue of the two overlapping characters in side-by-side columns down the page. To get a word processing program to do this, you'll need to read the manual and that's why the (Overlapping) s.d. is a simpler choice today. If it really matters which specific lines overlap between characters instead of relying on chance, the Help menu is in your future.

(Continued) Character Note

(Continued) means just that: A character's speech is too long to finish at the bottom of the previous page so the dialogue has to carry over for that character to the top of the next page. The

(Continued) character note – as in JOAN (Continued) – alerts readers and performers that this is not a new speech when they turn the page.

General Stage Directions

General stage directions within acts or scenes stand alone in the manuscript. They're single spaced and usually deal with physical action or a combination of physical action and lighting or sound effects.

These general s.d.'s use the same left margin as character stage directions and continue across the page to the right margin. If this s.d. runs more than one line, use the Indent tool to maintain a flush left margin. Insert a space before and after general s.d.'s.

Act & Formal Scene Endings

The endings of formal scenes and acts are usually indicated by a stage direction that often ends with a statement of the lighting change – typical usage is (Blackout.) or (Curtain.) – and this s.d. can also serve as part of the curtain line.

Since a lot of theatres don't have an actual curtain, contemporary playwrights typically use lighting indications instead. Some other common phrases for these lighting changes: (Lights fade.) or (Lights dim.). Lighting designers won't feel you're treading on their turf when you indicate these cues. Whether this ending s.d. stands by itself or simply follows the final stage direction as if it's a new sentence, is your choice.

55. COVERS & BINDINGS

I'll keep writing about the decreasing power of the individual and the increasing responsibility of the individual. I'm in pursuit of something, and it's a long-term notion.
-Jon Robin Baitz

After duplicating multiple copies of the final draft of the script on 3-hole punched paper, this is what holds it all together with the SASE stapled inside the back cover (see Chapter 59 on Submitting Scripts).

The simplest way to bind a script is with standard term paper covers, the kind made with a pliable cardboard back and clear plastic front with built-in brads. One of the advantages of these is that the Title Page shows through. Solid color covers need a label centered in the upper half of the cover with the title and your name as on the Title Page.

The "Never Use" Bindings List

Never use 3-ring binders. They're more expensive, bulky, tough on readers, don't stack well, and pros in this business hate them. Don't spend the money on any kind of permanent binding, spiral or otherwise (they are also the sign of an amateur).

Once you move into readings and workshops or productions, you'll be rewriting and replacing pages at an alarming rate and that can't be done with a script welded together in some sort of permanent binding.

Being Kind to Your Readers

For scripts noticeably over 90 pages, prefab covers usually won't have brads long enough to keep it all together. The solution is to use three-hole punched 8.5" x 11" card stock with brass brads (about 2" long) or the silver-colored ACCO two-piece fasteners (make sure the ACCO prongs will line up with the top and bottom holes of 3-hole punched paper). ACCO fasteners reduce the potential hazards to your readers compared to the sharp points of brass brads.

Maybe it's the nature of Hollywood, but screenwriters and film producers don't mind dealing with scripts that may draw blood from the sharp ends of brads sticking out the back. Literary managers at regional theatres don't think this is a such a great idea.

Be kind to potential readers by looking for a cover that folds over the sharp parts of metal fasteners. It's fine if a play makes readers bleed in their souls, but anything other than metaphorical blood won't earn you any points. Don't do this act of kindness with a screenplay (see Chapter 71 on Screenplay Format).

Best Practice: *Apply your creativity to your script, not to its format or binding.*

A note on duplicating scripts: While a tree can be saved by using two-sided duplication, most theatres don't like scripts done that way and may not accept them. Always be sure to check the submission guidelines for regional theatres and competitions – some may even ask for scripts to be sent without bindings and a few may only want electronic submissions.

PART FIVE – BUSINESS: The Next Steps

There are three primal urges in human beings: food, sex, and rewriting someone else's play.
　　　　-Romulus Linney

56. THE BUSINESS OF PLAYWRITING

What am I looking for in a play? If I knew before I read them, I'd write them myself. Of course as an artistic director I sometimes have antennae out for, say, a role to stretch an actor in the company or a theme and presentation that could be immediate for audiences in a projected tour. But mostly what I want is for the playwright to persuade me as I read that what they're doing is what I need to produce.
     -Sharon Ott

Playwriting is an art and a craft while you're doing it, but once you've put a cover on that draft, it becomes a business. That's a tough concept for artists to accept, but it's the way it is.

When you've attracted real notice with productions an agent may take care of some of the busywork, but until then, there's no one but you to do it. None of this is hard, it's simply tedious, and the best time to work on it is after you've done that serious writing for the day.

This grunt work of playwriting provides a marvelous excuse not to write. It may even feel like a relief not to start that next play. One way to solve this problem is to give yourself a reward for having put the binders on by taking a "vacation" from playwriting. But instead of going to the beach, spend the time writing a synopsis, updating your bio, preparing script packages and making trips to the Post Office. But keep writing in your journal during this vacation and don't let the break go on for more than a week. At that point, the heavy lifting should be done and what's left can be squeezed in after you've done that real writing for the day.

Copyright Protection for Plays

The first order of business for all writers is protecting all those words they've just put on paper. The good news is that nobody steals unproduced plays. Or maybe somebody has, but it's hard to find a case of that happening in the last 50 years. The FBI and Scotland Yard have special agent details focusing on fine art theft, but there's no law enforcement equivalent for stage plays. That's because an unproduced script has little or no monetary value and there is no future in copying someone else's unproduced play.

The theatre is still a very civilized business, but it's a good idea to help keep it that way by always including the copyright notice on your title page in the proper form:

Copyright © 2012 by Your Name

The © needs to be in the notice (word processing programs create this through the Insert and Symbol menus). If you're a Neo-Luddite using one of those things we dimly remember called a typewriter, try faking it with (c). Technically, the tops and bottoms of the ( ) around the "c" need to be connected to resemble a circle.

The work of playwrights (or novelists for that matter) is protected the moment the words leave their fingers and hit the screen or printer. Technically, playwrights don't have to do anything but write plays to have protection in the U.S. But note the fine print that follows.

U.S. Copyright Office

Entertainment lawyers recommend getting a formal Certificate of Registration (no surprise there) for plays. They have a good point: If the script isn't registered, you won't be able to enforce your rights as an author in court against anyone who "steals" a script or get a court award of monitory damages including reimbursement of your attorney's fees.

For all of that, registration with the U.S. Copyright Office is essential. It's easy to do, but may not be worth the fee ($35 and up in 2011) until a theatre has committed to producing your play. If you have the cash and aren't ready to start that next play, there's no reason to hesitate, but if you're strapped, play the odds. The money is probably better spent on duplicating and mailing scripts to theatres and competitions.

Note that copyright registration is essential when a play is published in either hard copy or electronic form.

For everything on getting a Certificate of Registration from the U.S. Copyright Office, go to www.copyright.gov and then enter Dramatic Works in the search box.

Having added that copyright notice on the title page, you're ready to start the rest of the business of playwriting.

57. COMPETITIONS & DEVELOPMENT

Reading the story of the sisters Christine and Lea Papin, maids who, one cold and bitter February afternoon in 1933, murdered the mistress and daughter of the house they worked in, I became completely obsessed. The same obsession took me through countless readings, rejections, and revisions until My Sister in This House won The Susan Smith Blackburn Prize and was produced at Actor's Theatre of Louisville's New Play Festival.
-Wendy Kesselman

New play competitions are a good way to begin building a bio as a playwright. Winning or even placing is nice, but not necessary. Simply making it into the semifinals will send a signal to literary managers that your play is worth serious reading.

Most competitions let playwrights know if their plays make the semifinals. If you do, you're in very select company: These are the small number of scripts that competition readers think have potential for the top two or three prizes. Typically, semifinals are limited to about 1% of the total number of entries. First prize awards for competitions range from a lovely certificate to a substantial dollar number so they're worth the postage. A few playwrights have even discovered that by assiduously entering competitions they can generate enough income from prize money to cover anything from their coffee habit to car payments.

A Caution on Entry Fees
A small number of competitions have been charging playwrights an entry or submission fee. While this may be typical for poetry and fiction competitions, it's not in the theatre and the Dramatists Guild frowns on this.

Best Practice: *The higher the fee, the greater the reason not to submit your play.*

An exception to the entry fee rule: The Eugene O'Neill Theater Center's National Playwrights Conference (www.theoneill.org), one of the leading competition and play development programs in the country. The O'Neill has probably launched more playwrights' careers than any other program in the U.S. and they accept electronic submissions so the entry fee is partially offset by the postage and duplication costs you'll save.

New Play Development Programs

The play development process run by many regional theatres and other organizations for playwrights provides something essential: The chance to hear professional performers say the dialogue you've put on paper, to hear it in front of an audience, and most importantly to revise the script based on what you've heard. That's a very different kind of editing from what's possible based only on what your eyes can see on the page.

What playwrights gain from this simple act is worth all the grief that may come with it as you pull your play apart – at the urging of literary managers, performers, directors, and even the audience – and stuff it back together in revisions.

Most playwrights find the development process helpful and it comes with a significant side benefit. These programs usually last from several weeks to a month, long enough for to make professional friendships – especially with directors – that can pay dividends for years to come.

Negatives of Play Development

Play development is not all sunshine and roses. Edward Albee despised the process – he never went through the experience – charging that its goal was to reduce scripts to a bland lowest common denominator. There's no question that being absolutely clear about what you intended in the play is essential to making sure that intention is still intact at the end of the process.

A chorus of playwrights feels they were (or are) trapped on a never ending development treadmill – always being "in development" and never "in production" – and think some theatres run these programs without any real interest in moving those developed plays into full production.

Viewed from the other side of this wall, what seems like a treadmill may be less than a conspiracy theory. In some cases, there may not have been a good match between playwright and theatre – that elusive thing called "chemistry" may be the culprit. If there's no spark between you and the theatre that's developing the play, you need to be somewhere else. If you end up feeling that development treadmill sensation, it may be time to consider producing the play yourself (see Chapter 65 on doing this).

The Play Development Process

The development process for new plays moves through three initial stages, each taking you closer (hopefully) to the fourth stage – a full production.

1. Reading. Just that. The actors sit on chairs in a rehearsal room or on stage facing a small audience and read the script, sometimes with no rehearsals. A stage manager or another performer reads the descriptions from your Character Page and Setting & Time Page as well as essential stage directions during the reading. The goal at this level is for the performers and director to become more familiar with the characters and to ask you questions about character motivations, theme, and structural issues.

2. Staged reading. The performers have several rehearsals with a director who establishes entrances, exits, and other key movement as well as basic character interpretation. The goal now is to provide a chance to see and hear how the play works when the performers are beginning to do the job they love. They haven't had enough rehearsals to show you the full deal, but they'll give you a real sense of how subtext has been handled, the builds of scenes and acts, curtain lines, and most importantly the climax and resolution of the play. You may have a chance to revise dialogue during the very short rehearsal process for this kind of reading.

3. Workshop production. This is a production usually following a week or so of rehearsals, employing effective but minimal costumes, modest lighting, a very minimal setting, and possibly sound if that's critical to the play. In some cases, rehearsals may happen over several weeks to give you a chance to do revisions that can then be incorporated into performances. It's the real thing, but in a small theatre usually seating less than 100. The actors have their lines down (in the best case) so there may not be a script in sight. Some theatres may give you a small royalty at this level. In some programs, a workshop production may not be part of the mix either because the sponsoring organization doesn't have the facilities for this or those running it don't think a play is ready yet for that step. For most development programs, acceptance of a script is a commitment on their part to moving it through these first three phases of the process.

4. Mainstage production. This is the *real* real thing on the large stage of a regional theatre, usually seating 400 to 600. With a little luck and good critical response (and ticket sales), the next stage after this one may be productions at other regional theatres around the country, a commercial production in New York, and a film deal.

Don't hold your breath. Instead, get back to work. Now is the time to be well into that next play because the first – or maybe second – question you'll get from everyone is, *What's your next play about?* And then with barely a breath taken, *When can I see it?*

58. READING YOUR AUDIENCE

There are three ways, I suggest to deal with critics. The first, most sensational, slightly dangerous but highly successful if carried out with sincerity, is to hit them.
-Sir Alec Guinness

There are two very different phases when it's critical to carefully read the audience that's turned out some dark and stormy night to savor the first presentations of your new play in a reading or workshop production.

Phase 1: During the Performance
The operating phrase here is, silence is golden. Unless you've written a comedy, but even then, the only thing breaking the silence should be laughter.

When audiences are captured by a script, you can hear a pin rattle down the aisle.

The Noises of Boredom
Whenever you start to lose audiences, they'll let you know by the rapid increase in the universal signals of discontent.

1. Coughing, nose-blowing, sniffles, throat-clearings, and yawns. Trust what this is telling you. It's never the flu season.

2. Seat-shiftings, leg-crossings, head-lollings, knuckle-crackings. Nobody's figured out how to build a really comfortable theatre seat and it's a safe bet that the seats in small theatres used for readings and workshops are the least comfortable of all. If a play lets go of the audience, their bodies will take advantage of the chance to wiggle away some of that discomfort.

3. Silence following your jokes. There's nothing deadlier than a bad joke. A bad joke is anything the audience doesn't laugh at. It's true that audiences vary and what's funny in Peoria may not get a ripple in Los Angeles, but if more than a few zingers get the deep silence of the sort that might follow grandma announcing the death of the dog, there's nothing golden about this silence no matter where you are.

4. People walking out. This is the worst thing that can happen short of the theatre losing it's electricity or a raid by the Fire Marshall just before your obligatory scene. People walking out make a lot of noise, even when they're desperately trying to be nice by being as quiet as possible. There's nothing subtle about this signal. It's the ultimate vote of dislike short of booing (thankfully that only happens in opera nowadays). There can be extenuating circumstances here: If it's only one person (or two who were sitting together), it may simply be a medical issue and have nothing to do with the play. It may also be that the subject matter, language, or theme is far outside the comfort zone of this audience.

Best Practice: *To read the audience well, it's essential to sit in the back.*

You'll be able to sense what's happening with the audience far better if you plant yourself in one of the last two rows and ideally the last row. From this perch, you can see what's happening in the audience as well as hearing and feeling it.

Phase 2: During the Audience Discussion
In nearly all development programs, the audience gets to have its say after readings and workshop performance. This can be gruesome without someone who knows what they're doing leading the discussion. Never lead the discussion yourself. Most literary managers know how to control this "talk back" process.

Tips for Surviving Audience Discussions
Think of this experience as a kind of ritual, a reward for the audience that took a risk to see the first presentation of your new play.

1. Take notes. This gives you someplace to look – and someplace to take out your aggressions – if you have the bad luck to get one of those types who's determined to turn your play into his play before he'll let you go home. You'll hear some helpful ideas from the director and performers. Write them down so you don't forget. This is one of the most stressful times for playwrights so having a few notes to jog your memory the next morning is a good idea.

2. Never argue with the audience. Remember the Stoics and that story about the kid with the fox chewing on his gut. It may feel the same way, but you're not here to argue – you're here to listen. If the audience doesn't get it, arguing with them won't solve the problem.

3. Don't pay much attention to the specifics. You may end up being bombarded by love letters for the play, but that's rare enough that you need to be prepared for the opposite. The more critical the audience is of what you've written, the more specific the suggestions for fixes will be. In fact, when hearing all this criticism, the more specific the suggestions get – "You've really got to have the dog sing Amazing Grace here" – the more essential it is to look for the subtext of their criticism.

In both stages, ask yourself this simple question (simple to ask, but complex to answer): *What about my play is prompting these responses?*

That's the question you want answered. In most cases, the audience won't be able to articulate what's really bugging them about the play no matter how long this discussion goes on. You'll need to read their subtext to unearth the answers. No matter how wrong-headed their comments may seem, it's nearly always the case that in the subtext driving those comments they'll have their fingers on the pulse of the play.

Best Practice: *Remember that this is your play – and it's always possible this is not your audience.*

Some clever playwrights put on their own readings for invited audiences – not waiting for acceptance into a development program – and have discovered how to short-circuit the "talk-back." They post an online questionnaire for the audience to fill out when they get home. That makes the audience feel rewarded and involved and may actually produce more thoughtful responses to a script.

59. SUBMITTING SCRIPTS TO THEATRES

The point comes when the ship has a bow and the stern and sides and a deck. So you launch it. And it either sinks without a trace, or it floats.
        -Arthur Miller

The first step in the submission process is getting a copy of the TCG *Dramatists Sourcebook* or the DG *Resource Directory.* These publications (see Chapter 62 on Professional Support) are the most practical way of knowing where and when to submit scripts to theatres and competitions.

The Script Submission Package
All parts of the submission package should be in 12-point type (Times New Roman or similar serif font) on 20-pound 8.5"x11" white paper.

> **1. Letter of inquiry.** An inquiry letter is sent when asking a theatre if they are interested in seeing a script based on an attached synopsis of the play. A slightly different version accompanies the full script, saying that a script is enclosed.
>
> **2. Playwright's résumé (or bio).** This is about your writing, not what would be used to apply for a day job with salary and benefits.
>
> **3. Synopsis of the play.** Theatres may also ask for a small sample from the dialogue pages (usually no more than 10) of the script with the synopsis. If the theatre accepts unsolicited scripts, it's a good idea to include the synopsis even if they haven't asked for one.
>
> **4. Bound script in manuscript format.** Unless guidelines require submission of a synopsis first and then to only send the script if requested. Keep in mind that some theatres and competitions may require unbound scripts.
>
> **5. SASE (stamped self-addressed envelope).** A minimum of 9.5" x 12.5" for a 90-page script with enough postage for it to

be mailed back to you.

Paper clip the letter and bio (and anything else the theatre or competition asks for) on top of the front cover of the script and mail the package by Priority Mail.

Note that if a theatre or competition says in its announcement, "Write for guidelines" – do it before going to all the trouble of putting a script package together. Include an SASE (business envelope size) when asking for guidelines. Some theatres will accept email requests for guidelines and will reply with these by return email.

Never send a script submission package as an email attachment unless the theatre or competition specifically requests electronic transmittal. The day may come when all of this may happen over the internet, but the theatre business is still a long way from that point. Theatres and competitions will often list an email address in the *Dramatists Sourcebook* or the *Resource Guide*, but that should not be taken to mean that they will accept scripts sent electronically instead of by snail mail.

Letter of Inquiry

A letter of inquiry should be short and to the point: One-page maximum.

Be interesting. It would be nice to say there's no pressure here, but when your submission package is pulled from the envelope, this letter is going to be the first glimpse a literary manager will have of you. Don't be cute, don't be clever and – most importantly – make it read well.

While literary managers may occasionally cut a playwright some slack on the writing in a letter, agents will often make a decision on whether to read a manuscript based solely on the quality of that letter. They argue that good writing is good writing and if the letter is poorly written then there's a high probability that the manuscript won't be worth their time to read.

There are seven basics parts to the letter – keep in mind that one-page maximum – so combine several of the parts into each paragraph or even within a single sentence (#1 & 2 could be combined into one sentence; #3 & 4 could be in the same paragraph).

1. Say what you're sending using the title of the play.

2. Say why you're sending it. Possible options: a) It's for their competition; b) It's in response to a published request for certain kinds of plays – like the one you've written; c) It's for a special program the theatre has; d) The literary manager asked for it; or e) You're sending the synopsis of your play and a dialogue sample – if that's all the theatre initially accepts.

3. Say something interesting about the play. Possible options: a) It's had a reading or workshop. b) It's had a college/university production. Say who did the production since if it's had a production with professional performers and director, many regional theatres won't be interested in the play. They normally only want to work on plays where they'll be presenting the first professional production; c) You've produced it yourself in a small theatre. Most literary mangers won't see this sort of self-produced production as conflicting with their interests in presenting the premiere professional production – assuming you've done this on a very small scale and without much publicity; or d) It's won, placed, or been in the semifinals of a competition.

4. Say what the play deals with: Your theme and that one-sentence summary of the plot or both.

5. Say something interesting about yourself as a writer, but only if you don't have enough yet to create a separate bio. If you have a track record, mention that your bio is attached. Be discrete here, just giving a few facts without embellishment: a) Your other work has placed or made the semifinals of competitions, b) You've had other kinds of writing published, or c) You've had an interesting job or avocation that's led directly to writing this play,

6. Say thanks for their looking at your work.

7. Mention the SASE is inside the back cover of the script.

Occasionally imaginations can get the best of playwrights early in their careers when writing letters of inquiry. Don't embellish what you've accomplished professionally as a writer or what's happened to the play. The theatre is a very small world and if you slip across that line, someone's bound to call you on it – or they'll just toss the script.

Besides serving as a quick intro to you and the play, the letter of inquiry provides a paper trail of what you've sent where. Keep copies of these letters as part of your record keeping.

The SASE

The SASE is an essential part of this process if you hope to get scripts returned, requests to see your work from literary managers, or guidelines for competitions.

A full-length play of 90 pages or a bit more normally needs a 9.5" x 12.5" envelope for safe mailing. Fold the SASE in half the short way (across the 9.5" axis so it's now 6.25" wide) and staple it inside the back cover of the script. This way, it won't get lost in the months the play may float around a literary manager's domain.

Most scripts of 90 or more pages will need Priority Mail postage on the SASE. Have the script weighed at the Post Office to be sure how much is required for postage both ways. Stick the postage on the envelope or have the Post Office do it – don't just paper clip the stamps to the envelope. The Post Office offers a reasonable deal on mailing something the size and weight of a script package: For $4.95 (in 2011) the package can be sent anywhere in the U.S. in a Priority Mail Flat Rate Envelope (9.5"x12.5" size available at the Post office – and these are free). Check to be sure the bound script and the rest of the submission package will fit.

Given the frequency of changes in postal rates, it's a good idea when first sending off scripts to bring the script package to a friendly postal clerk and see what rates are available. This is especially important if your script is noticeably over 100 pages.

For requesting submission guidelines from theatres and competitions, a standard 9.5" x 4" business envelope is usually ample with a first class stamp.

Some theatres and competitions won't return scripts even with an SASE attached and while this may appear to reflect a less than welcoming attitude toward playwrights, no nefarious plots may be afoot. A competition's volunteers may have strained a lot of backs lugging 400 to 1,200 pounds of scripts to the post office every year and they may not have the staff or enough volunteers to stuff all those plays back into SASEs.

The practical response is not to rule out competitions that refuse to return scripts. The only real reason – other than sentimental ones – to get scripts back is to send them off again. Unfortunately, most of the time between being thumbed by readers and slammed around at the Post Office, they'll be banged up so badly by the time they come back that they won't be usable without a lot of cosmetic tinkering. At the very least, put on a new cover and Title Page before it's resent.

> **Best Practice:** *Don't let the condition of the script telegraph to the next theatre that it's just been rejected by some other organization.*

Don't send scripts by Express Mail or Fedex unless requested to do so by a theatre – it costs a lot more and the few days you save in transit will make no difference in the response to your script (unless the submission deadline is tomorrow). And avoid using a Return Receipt Requested form – theatres don't need the extra work that involves.

A Caution on Mailing Scripts in the U.S.

Mail scripts at the Post Office. For security reasons in the U.S. in the wake of the 9/11 attacks, there are restrictions prohibiting mailing of packages from drop boxes if they're over 1 pound – the weight of a basic submission package with a 90-page script.

Multiple Submissions

Sending submissions of the same script simultaneously to different theatres and competitions is standard practice, but it pays to be sensible. There's nothing to be gained by encouraging unnecessary rejections. Try to figure out which theatres or competitions might be most receptive to the style and subjects of your plays before sending them out. The TCG and DG guides are the best sources for what particular theatres or competitions may be looking for.

Record Keeping

Keeping records is something else you won't like doing, but somebody's got to do it.

Mailing a script package to theatres and competitions is not cheap. About half the cost is tied up in each copy of the play and after a while it will seem like these are worth their weight in silver. That's why – among more important reasons – it's comforting to have a record of where these packages have gone (this also insures against sending the same script to a theatre that's already seen it).

Here's what a tracking system needs to record for each play or synopsis that's send out:

1. The theatre or competition. And the person you may have been asked to send it to.

2. The date it was mailed. So you can figure out how long each copy of the script has been out in the world.

3. Their notification date. The estimated date they've said you should hear back from them, figured from their stated response time. This will vary from a few months to a year. The average runs about three or four months. You don't gain points by being ham-handed with theatres that miss their response deadlines – even if they deserve it. Give them at least a 6-week grace period before you drop them a note. And think of the note as a way to get them to read the play in the event they've overlooked or misplaced it, not just to send it back.

4. Their response. Even if they didn't leap at producing the script, some literary managers may ask to see your next play if they liked your voice. When you send the next play, here's how you'll remember who asked to see it – and to remind them that they asked.

Track all of this on 3x5 cards or with software like Excel. It won't take long before you've got much more than can ever be kept in your head or even as notes in the TCG *Sourcebook* or DG *Resource Directory*.

60. WRITING THE SCRIPT SYNOPSIS

In a way, tackling the problem of writing a play about the Holocaust was to not write about it, but to write about what it has done to us. There are no stock SS guards in the play, no facile sentimental ending. What I wanted to do was dramatize the problems inherent in both remembering and forgetting, and to see what this insoluble problem has done to succeeding generations.
-Donald Margulies

Some time ago, director and critic Paul Gray sent a minor ripple through the nation's literary establishment with his claim that you should be able to summarize the plot of any great play (in this case, Sophocles' *Oedipus the King*) as a headline for the *National Inquirer* or the now defunct UK tabloid, *News of the World*:

KING SLEEPS WITH MOTHER, TEARS OUT EYEBALLS!

He's right in a way. The closer you can come to summarizing the combined suspense and emotional plots of a play in a single sentence, the surer you can be that it may work on stage. And the closer you'll be to writing a good synopsis. If you can't do this easily, it means one of two things:

> **1. Brevity is not the soul of your virtue.** You're just not good at summarizing – which has nothing to do with being a good playwright. Unfortunately it does have a lot to do with writing a good synopsis.

> **2. There are structural problems in the play.** The usual culprit is not having a suspense plot. If you can't summarize the script (and you're not missing the summarizing gene) that probably means you don't have a story with a clear beginning and an end. To write a good synopsis, you need the bookends of a beginning and an end (what the suspense plot provides).

Rules for a Good Synopsis
The first rule of writing a synopsis is to accept the fact that you'll

hate doing this. It's even more un-creative and annoying than manuscript format – and it's all uphill from there.

1. Keep the synopsis to about half a page. A full page if you can't find any other way to do it using single or 1.5 line spacing.

2. Start with that one-sentence summary. But just keep this in your head as a guide.

3. Give us a sense of where and when the play is happening. A sentence at the most should do it.

4. Focus on the central character. Or two central characters. Forget the minor ones – just attach a copy of the Character Page for those.

5. Think of the synopsis as having the structure of a monologue. You're telling a story. It's nice if it can end with the equivalent of a curtain line that will make us want to read the script. This is not easy to do so don't force it.

6. As Jack Web used to say: Just the facts. Never offer your own critical assessment of the play.

Note what else these theatres or competitions may be asking for. If they're asking for plays set in the Northwest, make sure the synopsis lets them know yours meets this requirement.

A Sample Synopsis

PULLIN' 'EM OFF THE RAFTERS
Synopsis

Summer, 1964. A 400-acre Iowa farm seen in seventeen scenes like old B&W snapshots. No nostalgia, no romance. This is the past, nothing more.

Casey Briggs, called Case, has seen what few understood then: He's auctioning his dairy herd and renting out the land. For a livelihood, he and his wife, Nan, have bought a local steak house. And they've convinced themselves they'll like this new life. But as the auction begins, Case holds back the bull, trying to keep open the option of a return to farming.

As the herd goes on the block, Case's brother-in-law, Donny Lewis, arrives from Boston with his wife for a claimed vacation. But Donny has come staking everything on asking Case for work on the farm, driven by the worsening economy in the East and his shrinking milk delivery route. In return, Donny offers Case the use of his main possession, a .45 army pistol.

Donny's dream is destroyed when he realizes Case has sold all the herd, but the bull. And Donny's wife, always hating the farm, taunts him with the futility of what he's done. In desperation, Donny shoots the bull, thinking it too has been mocking him. But his shot is wide.

Case is left knowing he must kill the wounded bull and by doing it, kill the remnant of his futile dream with Nan of a return to the farm.

Your Name
Contact Information

The Dialogue Sample

A dialogue sample is often asked for as part of the synopsis package, usually consisting of between 3 and 10 pages from the script as a quick way to see (hear) your voice as a playwright. If they then ask to see the full script, it's because they like the idea of the play and your voice based on those sample pages. It's a good idea to start with Page I-1 for this. Never send more or less than they ask for.

SASE for the Synopsis Package

Include an SASE (letter-size) for them to easily let you know if they'd like to see your full script. Or even better: A plain self-addressed postcard. Use the kind you can buy from the Post Office. On the back, put the name of the theatre (so you'll know who returned the card) and a reasonable "send it" phrase with a box or space for a check mark and the title of your play:

___ We'd like to read WHITE ALICE.

Don't fold all of this up and cram it into a standard business-size envelope, even though it will fit. Spend the extra change to send the package in a 9" x 12" envelope. Literary managers get hundreds of these things and you want yours to be among the easier ones to read.

61. THE PLAYWRIGHT'S RESUME

I wanted an axis in New York that would do my plays without picking and choosing the ones that might make money and might not. The experience of having a play produced in New York is still unequaled.
 -Tom Stoppard

The résumé or bio is only a brief summary of what's noteworthy about you as a writer. One page maximum. Half a page is better. It's a subtle way of saying to a literary manager that your play is worth the time to read.

If you're just starting, you may not have much that's appropriate for a playwright's bio, but don't look down on recognition you've gotten in other areas of performance or writing. Use this in the meantime until your plays begin to gain notice.

The "Include List" for Bios

As your writing career grows, so does your résumé – but still, one page.

1. **Awards.** For any kind of writing or performance.

2. **Fiction or poetry.** Published (but not self-published unless it's been wildly successful) or presented in public readings.

3. **Non-fiction articles or books.** Published in newspapers, magazines, respected blogs and Web sites, or by publishers in the U.S. or abroad. Books and articles self-published on Kindle, Nook, iPad, and other platforms are worth mentioning, but only if they've had notable reception.

4. **Film, television, or radio scripts.** Optioned or produced.

5. **Other kind of writing.** Selected for anything that suggests you're good at putting words together.

Forget about *What Color is My Parachute* and other how-to-get-a-real-job books when it comes to bios in this business. Playwrights do these as a short third-person narrative, similar to what's printed in theatre programs.

Be brief. Be clear. Remember that you don't have to win a competition to have a flag to wave. Placing in the semifinals of a competition is worth a lot in the early stages of building a bio.

If you've only got a few things to put in a bio, don't try to stretch those into paragraphs. Instead, devote a sentence in the inquiry letter to this. Literary managers know that intriguing new playwrights won't necessarily have amassed a professional résumé yet and most are always interested in discovering an "undiscovered" playwright.

Playwright's Bio Example

HESTER PRYN

Hester Pryn's A FULL EVENING'S WORTH was presented in a workshop production by The Rep Company in 2008. It has also received staged readings at Leesport State University as well as The Washing Machine, an alternative arts space in Nashville, Tennessee.

Her one-act, JUST THE KNEES, was a semifinalist in the 2001 Actors Theatre of Louisville National Ten-Minute Play contest. A children's play, SWELL BUGS, has been performed in six Lestertowne, MA, schools by The Moveable Children's Theatre and is scheduled for production in the Fall of 2012 by the Brook Street Ensemble as part of its New Plays for Youth series.

Her screenplay, BOSTON BLUES, is under option by the Sure Thing Production Company. Several of her poems have been published in *Border North Review* and *Flash Lit*.

1642 Boston Common
Boston, MA 02101
hester@lettera.com

Structuring a narrative bio with a subtle build is worth trying – don't bury the most notable achievements in the middle. Think of the bio as a monologue with an inciting incident starting it off. Save something good for the end as a curtain line encouraging literary managers to be curious about your plays.

62. PROFESSIONAL SUPPORT: DG & TCG

A lot of very good plays are being written now. They're being produced; they're even being published. The only thing they're not is easier to write.
-Terrence McNally

Many cities in the U.S., Canada, and the UK, have formal and informal support groups for playwrights. Writers' groups are helpful in offering opportunities to get together on a regular basis with other playwrights to share insights and offer critiques of current work. Joining one of these can provide extra motivation for putting words on paper and since contacts help, the more people you know in the theatre the better.

If you can't identify a local group specifically for playwrights, many organizations geared primarily for fiction and non-fiction authors will welcome playwrights.

The Dramatists Guild

The Dramatists Guild is the professional association of American playwrights (www.dramatistsguild.com). The DG represents the interests of playwrights particularly by developing standard contracts for commercial (Broadway) and non-commercial (regional theatre) productions of new plays. The Guild also works to protect the rights of dramatists in relation to producers – and more recently, directors and literary managers.

This is one of those cases where writers get what they pay for. Consider joining the Guild at the associate membership level when your plays begin getting positive responses from literary managers or making it to the semifinals (or beyond) of national competitions.

It's hard to find a produced American playwright who doesn't belong to the Guild. Student memberships are offered at half of the Associate membership fee.

DG Annual *Resource Directory*

Similar to TCG's *Dramatists Sourcebook*. The *Resource Directory* makes an extra effort to screen out theatres or competitions that seem not to have the best interests of playwrights at heart. Non-members of the DG can get the *Resource Directory* through Amazon or Barnes & Noble (online).

When ordering online, make sure to get the latest edition by sorting title search results by date of publication. The DG *Directory* is published annually so it's more likely to be current on submission deadlines than the TCG equivalent since the *Sourcebook* is only published once every two years.

Theatre Communications Group

TCG (www.tcg.org) is the service organization representing nearly all nonprofit regional theatre companies in the United States. Since these theatres present the first professional productions of most new American plays, TCG also publishes the biennial *Dramatists Sourcebook* as well as the essential magazine for playwrights, *American Theatre*. Here's what TCG offers playwrights:

1. **Books and scripts.** TCG publishes a large number of books including new plays, translations, and others on performance theory and professional theatre practice.

2. *Theatre Profiles.* The guide to America's nonprofit regional theatres. It's another way to know the production interests of these theatres without traveling the country. Most important are statements of philosophy from artistic directors. Available on the TCG Web site under Tools & Research. The Canadian equivalent is The Theatre Listing available online from the Professional Association of Canadian Theatres (www.pact.ca).

3. *This Month On Stage.* The monthly listing of plays in production at regional theatres offers a good way to tell which of these companies might be interested in the subjects and style of your plays. Available on the TCG site under Tools & Research > Theatre Profiles.

4. *Theatre Facts.* The annual summary of the financial health of the nation's nonprofit theatres is both sobering and helpful in understanding the non-artistic forces that may influence the selection of seasons and the new plays regional theatres produce. Available as a pdf download from the

TCG site under Tools & Research.

TCG *Dramatists Sourcebook*

The *Sourcebook* is a biennial listing of opportunities for American playwrights. Note that it's published every two years, so the second year of each edition will be out of date on specific submission deadlines and some guidelines. Here's what's in the *Dramatists Sourcebook*:

> **1. Essay:** A well-known playwright (for some time it's been Tony Kushner) briefly discusses craft, format, and script submission issues.
>
> **2. Script submission opportunities:**
> *Production*: Lists of theatres wanting to read new scripts – or at least look at a synopsis. Includes information on subjects and styles a theatre prefers, whether they'll look at one-act plays, full-lengths or both, and response times.
>
> *Prizes*: Information about nearly every major new play competition in the country. Includes subject interests, prize amounts, and response times.
>
> *Publication:* Magazines and publishers interested in scripts. A few will consider publishing unproduced plays, though usually these are pieces for children or family fare aimed at dinner theatres and the like.
>
> *Development:* A listing of workshop and new play development programs with submission information.
>
> *Career opportunities:* Listings of agents, fellowships and grants, emergency funds, state arts agencies, writers colonies and residencies, membership and service organizations.
>
> *And:* Publications of interest, A submission calendar showing deadlines, and theatres and competitions listed by special areas of interest (subject, length, author ethnicity, gender, and adaptations).

Large bookstores may stock the *Sourcebook* and it's also available online from Amazon or Barnes & Noble, as well as direct from TCG.

When ordering these DG and TCG guides online, it's essential to sort the title search results by publication date ("newest to oldest"). The old editions will still be listed for sale on these sites and aren't good for anything but nostalgia. E-reader availability of these guides may expand in coming years, but in 2011 TCG and the DG still only offered the current editions in paperback with e-reader versions limited to out-of-date editions.

UK *Writers' & Artists' Yearbook*

If you're writing in the UK – or a U.S. playwright thinking of the other side of the Atlantic – the equivalent of those American guides for the UK is the annual *Writers' & Artists' Yearbook*. It has listings on script opportunities in theatre, television, film, and radio. The *Yearbook* is usually not stocked in U.S. bookstores, but it can be ordered online from Amazon and Barnes & Noble.

TCG *American Theatre* Magazine

American Theatre Magazine is one of the best ways to stay current with the regional theatre scene without traveling the country. Playwriting is a business and as in any other field it pays to know what's happening beyond the walls of wherever you're putting dialogue on paper. Features include monthly news on theatres, plays in production, interviews with playwrights and artistic directors, and trends.

Most important is the Playscript feature, the full scripts of new plays recently produced by TCG-member theatres and often before release in book form (some of these scripts may never be published in any other form). Usually six of these scripts appear in the magazine every year. Since you need to be reading what's current in the theatre, this feature more than pays for TCG membership which includes a subscription to the magazine.

TCG also publishes Dana Singer's *Stage Writers Handbook: A Complete Business Guide for Playwrights, Composers, Lyricists and Librettists*. It has nearly everything you'll need to know – and a lot you'd rather not – about the business of being a playwright. It's available online from Barnes & Noble, Amazon, and TCG. Coverage in her guide includes agents, subsidiary rights, issues with directors, and the complications (and how to avoid them) of collaborating on the development of musicals.

63. PLAYWRIGHT'S PRODUCTION TEAM

The main response to the staged reading of RENT was that the show was unclear and structurally out of balance. In theatrical time, the first act took the longest; yet it was only one night of the story. The second act was much shorter, almost by half; but a whole year of the story took place. So there was an incredibly long setup, and a compressed wrap-up, but no center.
-James Nicola

If you've spent a lot of time behind the curtain, this chapter is unnecessary, except perhaps for the opening section on literary managers. If your experience with theatre is mostly as part of an audience, this will be a helpful introduction to the new play production process.

Playwriting is a solitary art – until you stop putting words on paper (and unless you're part of a collaborative theatre group). From the moment a theatre expresses interest in producing a play, it becomes a collaborative process, but unlike the compromises screenwriters routinely have to swallow, your word is law (or rather, your words are law). Literally. Nobody in the theatre production process can change a word of the play without your approval.

While that's true, some common sense is called for. The play you've put on paper may only be a shadow of the one in your head. Theatre professionals usually know this business from years of experience, so their suggestions will be worth considering and may help in understanding the play you really intended to write. Needless to say, they do have the ultimate brick to bang on a playwright's head – if you're overly stubborn, they can just decide not to do the play.

Literary Manager

Literary managers play a significant role in bringing new work to the American stage by overseeing the review and selection processes for new scripts submitted to regional theatres. At major rep companies running new play competitions or accepting unsolicited scripts, this may involve the screening of 2,000 manuscripts a year.

These are the professionals who also run new play development programs. That makes them the primary gate-keepers of productions and the royalty payments that make up the financial rewards for playwrights.

Most literary managers have graduate degrees in theatre history or dramatic literature and work as dramaturgical consultants to the playwrights whose writing intrigues them – or intrigues the artistic directors they work for (those tastes aren't always aligned). The risks of this sort of development process can be high for playwrights and for the theatre doing it, but so are the rewards.

Dramaturg

Literary managers in the U.S. are often referred to interchangeably as "dramaturgs," a job originally developed in German theatres – a title for which there is no good English translation. To split a very fine hair, dramaturgs may work on new plays but usually concentrate on revivals of older plays, often the classics like Shakespeare or Chekhov, developing the concepts and styles of productions in collaboration with directors and designers.

Literary managers usually focus on developing new and as yet unproduced plays as well as assisting in development of the slates of plays for upcoming seasons. Insight into the work these pros do at regional theatres can be sensed through the Web site of their professional organization, the Literary Managers and Dramaturgs of the Americas (www.lmda.org).

Artistic Director

The Artistic Director is the primary creative officer of the company and normally the chief executive of the entire operation. Everyone else on the theatre's payroll ultimately reports to this position even if it's via other layers of management.

It's the artistic director who give the ultimate green light on going forward with developing or producing new plays. If you're not actively involved with a theatre's artistic director, you can expect the AD to drop in on rehearsals.

Director

Directors make plays work on stage and they have special skills in selecting and working with performers. While playwrights have the power to approve casts, exercise this right with great care unless you've been working in the theatre world for a long time.

Performers are a director's business and for your own sanity let them be your intermediary with the cast. You'll need this interpreter. When performers say to you, *This is such an awesome play!* what they often mean is, *You've written an awesome part for me!* This single-minded focus is what makes them good at what they do, but it also makes them not so good at assessing a play as a whole – and that's one of the points where a director's skill is necessary.

Designers

Designers are capable of matching the words in a play with startling visual and aural images. What they do is an art and a craft as specialized and arcane as that of playwrights. All good designers will want a playwright's feedback on their initial concepts. Rely on the director to mediate these sessions. Designers speak a wondrous language of their own, so if you haven't spent your life in the theatre, you'll need an interpreter.

Working with the Production Team

Before dreams of royalties comes the production. In addition to performers, this is the crowd you'll be living with for anywhere from three to six weeks or more. And you may spend months before that with the literary manager getting the play ready for rehearsals.

1. **Scenic designer.** You've probably said nearly everything they need to hear from you at first on your Setting & Time Page. They'll get almost everything else they need from the script and through discussions with you and the director. The more realistic you want the set to be, the less reason there is for you to look over the scenic designer's shoulder. The more abstract and suggestive the concept is, the more the designer will need and want a detailed collaboration with you.

2. **Lighting & sound designers.** These magicians tread in mystical realms. Until you're an old hand in the theatre, what they do will seem as logical as figuring out how many

angels can dance on a pin. Answer questions they may have, stay out of their way, and assume you'll be amazed by the results. In all likelihood, you will be.

3. Costume designer. Most of your time with designers will be spent here. Costume designers tend to want the most continuous collaboration with playwrights and may end up working through a dozen versions of the "look" for a central character before they think they are ready to deal with cloth. Again, if you're not an old theatre hand, a lot of the costumer's art will be a mystery to you, especially the tremendous difference between what a costume looks like in front of your nose compared to being worn by a performer under stage lights and seen from the middle of the auditorium.

4. Stage manager. Stage managers handle all the production logistics and represent the director once the show opens. They may read the stage directions in initial readings with the director and cast. Your life is in this person's hands. If you've got to be a grump, do it with somebody else.

There will be others coming at you as well, among them the theatre's public relations staff working to generate pre-opening night press coverage and the managing director who handles all of the business aspects of the theatre.

Even if things get a bit rough – and they sometimes will in the confines of rehearsals – remember that professional designers, performers, directors, and all the other players in this project want to come out looking like winners. They all know that won't happen unless everyone wins and they also know they're all dependent on your work as a playwright.

64. AGENTS & MAKING A LIVING AT THIS

An agent asked me why I "limited" myself to writing about Latino themes. He felt that I knew and was able to tackle "more mainstream subjects". I thought about this and realized it wasn't a matter of writing about what I knew – I was basically writing about what I loved.
 -Luis Santeiro

Having an agent – or "representation" as it's called – is essential to making a living from plays, but before walking away from your day job, keep in mind what that really means.

Needing to make a living from writing and being represented by an agent will add substantial pressure to your writing output. It may seem wonderful to imagine a time when all you do is write, but there's a reason for the cliché of the heavy-drinking writer – in case you're wondering, bending their elbows with that glass is not what made them great writers. In fact the reverse is nearly always the case.

Pressures of Writing Success

Both your bank account and your agent will always be asking for that next play – and the one after that. Your fingers will have to work overtime at the keyboard to keep everyone happy, especially if you're also writing that screenplay you've been hired to do as a result of the success of your plays. Your agent will also be asking about the next screenplay – and ideas for another half-dozen after that.

The more successful your work becomes with audiences and critics, the more pressure agents will apply. They'll be doing this for your own good (not to mention their own bottom line). In the theatre business, when you're hot, you're hot. And when you're not, you're – (you know the rest).

There's always a concern – and a legitimate one – that your style or subjects may fall out of favor with critics, artistic directors, and audiences or that you'll lose your voice as a playwright. If you're not continually producing new plays, the pros may begin to wonder where you are – if success has simply gone to your head – or if you've written yourself out.

Agents

Playwrights are a tough business for agents, so you need to give them something to sell besides your raw talent lurking on the pages of a script. Among other things, that means coming up with lots of ideas for plays and screenplays and being reasonably good at meeting your original time lines for delivering drafts of these.

For novelists and screenwriters, having an agent is essential for production or publication – publishers and film producers assume you're not worth a serious read if you don't have an agent – while literary managers don't expect new playwrights to have representation.

Best Practice: *Production comes before an agent.*

If a regional theatre wants to do a production of your play as part of its main stage season, look for an agent as soon as a contract is in the offing. It's possible that agents may come looking for you if that first production will be at a major regional theatre.

This is also the time to join the Dramatists Guild – don't sign that tempting contract until the Guild or your agent reviews it for minimum DG standards. More than a few playwrights have been burned by neglecting this step.

If your first production is by a relatively unknown theatre, the best sources for agents willing to look at unsolicited plays are the TCG *Dramatists Sourcebook* and the DG *Resource Directory*.

If you have a production in hand or pending, many agents will be open to looking at your script, but be prepared for some of them passing on the opportunity to represent you. It's chemistry again. Agents will be thinking about a long-term relationship with anyone they consider representing and most will want to feel a real connection to the subjects, themes, and especially voice of a playwright. They (and you) will be looking for the right match.

If you can't find an agent, but have a production pending, the Dramatists Guild's Business Affairs office offers a contract review service.

Making a Living At This

It's possible to make a living at this business of playwriting, though after a while the odds may seem about the same for sword-swallowing. That's why most produced playwrights also write for film and television.

> **Best Practice:** *If money is your primary motivation for being a playwright, don't do it.*

The only reason to be any kind of creative writer is because you're compelled to put words on paper. Nothing else will provide enough motivation to write that 90-page minimum required for a full-length play – and do it again and again.

You can make a living at this if you're good – and lucky. Needing both talent and luck may seem unfair, but that has always been the artist's lot. As a playwright, you'll need to rack up enough productions by regional theatres and commercial producers, as well as film adaptations of your plays, and sold screenplays to provide whatever you think is enough income.

Royalties

Regional theatres will take a small percentage of future royalties if they do the premiere production of your play. They use this to pay the rent. The theatres deserve what they get. They will have given you a good royalty for their premiere production (a 5-figure number in the largest regional theatres for a six week run) and invested a lot of money in the premiere of the play.

If all goes well, the risks they took should lead to other regional theatre productions for you, a commercial Broadway production, and possibly a film version. For all they've done, the theatre will ask for about 5% to 20% of your take for a limited number of years. In most cases, you won't miss it since this will usually be passed on to succeeding producers to pay (that's one of the talents agents have).

At the other end of the royalty scale from regional theatres are non-professional community theatres, college and university drama departments, and high school theatre programs. Royalties here may run about $15 to $50 per performance, with 3 to 10 performances being the norm for a production. Don't look down on these nonprofessional rates. They may be small, but there are thousands of producing operations in this category. It's possible to bring in enough from multiple productions in these venues to make a car payment if you can do without a Mercedes. The bad news is, few of these venues will leap at plays that haven't gotten notice on the regional theatre circuit or with commercial producers.

A Caution on "Collaboration" with Directors

Just because a director of the premiere production of the play is of immense value in making the play work on stage and even in revisions you have made doesn't mean they deserve a piece of your financial action.

> **Best Practice:** *Directors get paid for directing. Playwrights get paid for writing.*

But not all directors agree.

Don't get talked into any agreement that gives a percentage of your royalties to the director for contributions to the script, no matter how much you think you owe them. You don't. Good directors know that. They also know that making you look good as a playwright makes them look good as a director. So everybody wins when this business runs the way it's supposed to.

The Dramatists Guild insists that playwrights do not owe a percentage of royalties to any member of the production team – including directors and literary managers – for contributions they may make to scripts. This position is incorporated into the Guild's Bill of Rights for playwrights.

On Taking a Writing Day Job

Despite the potential royalties from productions, the sorry fact is that the majority of produced playwrights need a day job to make it work. That's life in America for all kinds of artists. Only a small percentage in any artistic endeavor make enough from their art to support themselves.

That's why television series work is such a seductive lure for playwrights. Hollywood has lots of writing jobs once you've gotten recognition from major competitions or productions. More than a few playwrights view the fees they earn from this as playwriting fellowships, buying them time to write the plays that are their real interest.

Putting words on paper is an odd business, no matter how or where it's done. Taking a writing day job, whether it's in journalism, television, advertising, or technical writing, may satisfy that compulsion to write. The danger is that it may do this to such an extent that you'll never feel up to starting that next play.

65. PRODUCING IT YOURSELF

For the theatre, I write something that fascinates me and I shop it around. In television, you're told what to write and then you hope it becomes fascinating.
      -Nicky Silver

It helps to have an ego slightly larger than the average barn for playwrights to successfully produce their own plays. That's especially true if it's your first play.

Vanity or self-produced productions of new plays don't carry the nasty reputation this still has for authors of novels or non-fiction books. In that world, self-publishing is typically taken to mean authors don't have what it takes to make it professionally, though successful self-publication of e-books is slowly changing those attitudes. To be blunt, in the world of fiction and nonfiction, vanity is still death.

Fortunately, that's not the case in the theatre. Playwrights who produce their own new scripts are thought of as enterprising souls who really believe in their plays. And literary managers know it's a good shortcut to that essential chance for new playwrights to hear their words spoken by performers.

Playwright-Founded Theatres

A few playwrights have founded their own theatres – including putting together a company of performers – to get their first plays presented. Tanya Saracho is one of the best know of these recent playwright-entrepreneurs in founding Teatro Luna in Chicago. It's worth a lot of grief – though this doesn't necessarily have to be part of the package – to get that for yourself.

If you're coming to playwriting after a considerable immersion back stage, you probably have all the contacts necessary to self-produce your plays. Self production can either be a one-shot effort to get your first play on the boards or with a longer term goal of creating a company to present your plays and those of like-minded playwrights.

Making Self-Producing Work

If you've never given in to the lure of greasepaint and bright lights, there are ways to make the production process easier – though it remains difficult without the experience of theatre in your bones.

1. Enroll in a theatre or drama department. At a university or community college. You need to know performers to make this work and how productions are put together. Some college theatre programs encourage the production of plays written by their students.

2. Volunteer at a theatre company. Make sure they have a history of presenting new plays before giving away part of your writing time. By doing something valuable for them, they may return the favor, but even if they don't, you'll know some performers and directors after being there for six months or a year. By that time – and if all goes well – you'll be thought of as part of the "family." That's important because theatre companies think of themselves as supportive families and they like to help the relatives – even distant ones.

3. Find a writers group to join. One that also includes playwrights. They'll all be interested in putting together small productions of their own work so help them do this and ride their bus to a production of your own play.

4. Set up your own development process. Plan a reading of the play with the cast at least 4 weeks before rehearsals begin, using the intervening time to revise what your ears tell you needs work. Trust your instincts.

5. Find a director and a space. Then put a casting notice in the local paper or online. You may be mobbed by a lot of dreadful talent, but let the director deal with that. Most young-and-hungry directors will do this sort of thing for the experience and they usually know a lot of young-and-hungry performers. It goes without saying that these directors will need to seriously love the play to take this on without a fee.

6. You don't need the bells and whistles. This is a hard lesson to learn. Too many new playwrights think their scripts would really work with audiences if they only had those four realistic settings, elaborate lighting, and all their characters in Armani. The reality is that if a script doesn't work on its own, it won't work any better with all those enhancements. For self production, all that's needed (the bare minimum) is an empty room large enough for at least 30 folding chairs for the audience, enough light to see the performers, costumes put together from whatever the performers have in their closets (offer to pay their dry cleaning bills), and a few pieces of furniture (probably yours). Audiences have wonderful imaginations when they're in this kind of performance environment.

For most of these options, you'll need to put up some cash, whether it's for the rental of a space and chairs, or props absolutely necessary to make the play work. Done carefully, the outlay can be kept to a few hundred dollars. Resist any urgings from a director to invest an extra $1,000 or more in lighting and sound equipment rentals to "make the production sing" – see #6 above.

Beware of Hubris

That's what did in Oedipus. Don't take on a theatre larger than 100 seats. You're going to have to find the audience for this production and you'll quickly run out of relatives and friends (including the cast's) trying to fill the place even if it's only for three nights a week. And it's a great idea to have at least half the seats filled when (and if) the critics come.

PART SIX – SCREENWRITING

The longer you're in this film business you realize that the end of the first stage is the script, and the minute you take that material to the next stage, you are doing a translation that you have to turn into visuals, and often the visuals afford you great economy; you don't need all those words. The audience gets it.
   -Joan Tewkesbury

66. REALITIES: THE SCREENPLAY TRADE

The purpose of a screenplay is to tell the story so the audience wants to know what happens next, and to tell it in pictures. Movies are basically about plot. They're about the structure of incidents, one incident causing the next to happen. A play doesn't have to be that. It has to have a plot as some sort of spine, but the spine can be very simple: two guys waiting for Godot to show up.
    -David Mamet

A major newspaper once asked the question (in large type), Is There Anybody in America Not Writing a Screenplay? The answer is no secret and the only thing that's changed since then is that the U.S. population has continued to increase.

Playwrights vs. Screenwriters
In the theatre, words matter and so do the playwrights who write them. Nearly all the famous names in theatre are playwrights.

In film, images matter and so do the directors who create them. Nearly all the famous names in film are directors. (Performers are always famous regardless of where they appear.)

On the other hand, screenwriting is a fine way to pay the mortgage, but a caution about those visions of wealth. If paying that mortgage is your only motivation, you'll never make this work. Screenwriting is a demanding discipline and being fascinated by the idea of visual storytelling is an essential part of the stamina film requires of writers.

Your Role in the Hollywood Machine
The fact is that writers are paid a lot in Hollywood, but they're valued very little. That's the rap a lot of screenwriters lay on the industry – and a lot of playwrights as well who have worked in film. The reality is, they're valued very little compared to bankable film directors and bankable stars.

The machine won't work without screenwriters, even though they're only a cog in the mechanism. That's the primary reason nearly all established screenwriters try to parlay their ability with words, images, and story into becoming directors. That's where the real power sits in this industry.

Competition in the film industry is intense, to put it mildly, and that's regardless of what part you want to play in it. For screenwriters it's ferocious. The Writers Guild of America registers some 30,000 new screenplays, treatments, and related material each year. Hollywood studios produce about 100 feature films a year (the optimistic estimate is about 300). You may not want to do the math.

Working Both Sides of the Theatre/Film Divide

Playwrights turning to screenwriting is a basic fact of a life in dramatic writing now. Everybody's doing it and for good reason. Film is a fascinating form to work in and – to be crass and materialistic for a moment – that's where the real money is.

A growing number of contemporary American playwrights have figured out how to live in both worlds. In England, they've been doing this for decades and their ability to work both sides of the fence has finally become the norm in America.

The best recommendation is still to earn recognition as a playwright and then mount your assault on the film industry with a horse that has a good chance of carrying you over those Hollywood Hills.

The Stage vs. Screen Story Rule

Even with all the years the film industry has been influencing the theatre, two rules remain unchanged – at least in America:

Rule 1: Playwrights tell stories verbally. Edward Albee nailed it: *A play is a heard thing. I learned, to my wonder, that there is an enormous difference in time between a comma, a semicolon and a period, for example. And that a playwright notates very much the way a composer notates a score.*

Rule 2: Screenwriters tell stories visually. Charles Fuller nailed it: *When I write plays, I write what I like watching when I'm sitting out there. Movies, on the other hand, are written from something in my mind's eye that keeps running. The movie was written with me sitting down in front of a yellow pad, writing down picture by picture what was going to be on the screen. I see all the shots and write what I see.*

The visual storytelling of film places much less reliance on the special voice of a writer compared to playwriting. That's not surprising. And it's not surprising that many playwrights can write well for film, while screenwriters are hardly ever able to return the favor in the theatre. This can be dismissed as the influence of money, but hardly any screenwriters seem to have the interest or, more importantly, the voice for playwriting.

Steve Martin and Woody Allen are among the few screenwriters who have managed to leap over the divide between film and theatre in the last several decades and do it successfully. In both cases, they had performing in front of live audiences in their bones before they ventured into screenwriting and then playwriting, thus developing a playwright's voice and how to use language with live audiences. Ethan Coen is the most recent to attempt the journey from screen to stage, so we may see an increase in accomplished screenwriters testing their skills in the theatre.

What screenwriters have is a powerful visual voice that makes them extremely good at what they do. That visual voice – a second voice – is one playwrights need to develop to write well for film.

Film & Its Parent

Film and theatre seem like they should be similar, much more similar than two sides of the same coin. All the pieces are superficially the same including dialogue, characters, conflict, plot and the other structural elements of plays. Both use settings, costumes, sound, and lighting to support the stories they're telling – and of course, performers and audiences that buy tickets. Until recently, we always went to see both in theatres with lots of other people. (Having a large group is especially important in comedy for getting audience reaction – this is the genesis of laugh-tracks and more recently live audiences for sitcoms.)

Historically, the pioneers of Hollywood came from the theatre and many of the first screenwriters – especially following the introduction of sound – were playwrights with Broadway credentials. As the new entertainment medium evolved, it began to develop a language of its own, though even today it's a language with the DNA of theatre.

That's why playwrights have an advantage in becoming accomplished screenwriters. Part of it is having a strong verbal voice to combine with that critical visual voice required for screenwriting. But those voices are so different that they may seem as if they're from two opposing solar systems.

67. VISUAL VS. VERBAL STORYTELLING

*One of the themes of the film is to examine the myth of objectivity.
I never think in terms of this kind of conflict: between the
individual and the mass. I'm not a sociologist. I never make a
political thesis. I would prefer it if something like this comes out of
it. If I put a character against a landscape, there is naturally a
relationship.*
     -Michelangelo Antonioni

The openings of Michelangelo Antonioni's film, *The Passenger*, and
Ariel Dorfman's play, *Death and the Maiden*, demonstrate the
differences between visual and verbal storytelling. One is a classic
of political film, the other a major example of political drama, but
the core of both is similar:

    1. Strong, complex, central characters. Both male and
female.

    2. Violent political intrigue. And defiance of authoritarian
regimes.

    3. Literate dialogue. With a strong writer's voice.

    4. Suspense plots hinging on elusive truth and identity.

    5. A highly visual point of attack.

Even with all these notable similarities between the scripts, the
visual storytelling of the film overwhelms the visuals of the play.

    On the next page is a breakdown of the opening movement
of Antonioni's film followed by the opening of Dorfman's play.
Each breakdown ends with the first line of dialogue and a summary
of dialogue word counts, measuring the gulf between these very
different approaches to storytelling.

Opening of Antonioni's *The Passenger*

Image 1: The desert.
Image 2: Houses in the village.
Image 3: People going by.
Image 4: Soldiers in the street.
Image 5: A street in the village.
Image 6: Men talking in front of a house.
Image 7: An old car.
Image 8: LOCKE [the central character] inside the car.
Image 9: Tape recorder and camera case on the car seat.
Image 10: LOCKE watching the men.
Image 11: The men uneasy with him there.
Image 12: One of the men leaves.
Image 13: LOCKE getting out of the car.
Image 14: LOCKE following the man.
Image 15: LOCKE catching up to him at the corner.
First line of dialogue.

Word count: The longest line of dialogue by a single character in the film is 14 words with the average line about 6 words.

Opening of Dorfman's *Death and the Maiden*

Sound 1: The sea.
Image 1: PAULINA [the central character] sitting in the living room.
Sound 2: Car approaching.
Image 2: PAULINA getting up, looking out the window.
Sound 3: Car braking right outside.
Image 3: Car headlights hit her.
Image 4: PAULINA gets a gun from a drawer.
First Line of Dialogue.

Word count: The longest line of dialogue by a single character in the play is 61 words (47 words more than in Antonioni's film) and the average line is about 15 words (9 words more per line than in the film).

Dialogue vs. Images

This extreme difference between the quantity of words and images between Antonioni's film and Dorfman's play is typical and captures the key difference between screenwriting and playwriting. That difference is clear despite the fact that Dorfman's play has a far more visual opening than is typical of contemporary plays.

The difference in the quantities of words of dialogue in theatre and film is so extreme that it also governs the script formats for screenplays and stage plays: The widths of margins for dialogue and stage directions (scene descriptions) are reversed from one to the other. The length of a dialogue line from margin to margin in screenplay format is about half that in play script format and the length of the equivalent of a General Stage Direction line in screenplay format is nearly double that of play format. In both formats, one page equals about one minute of playing time.

Despite the notable differences between theatre and film, the adjustments necessary for screenwriting are a matter of emphasis and degree when this visual form is approached from a playwriting base. You're not starting from scratch. That puts you far ahead of everyone attempting spec screenplays without the advantages of a playwriting background.

68. MAKING SCREENPLAYS WORK

I'd been working and working on the screenplay, and I was looking forward to it actually being fun. It's not fun unless it gets made. And unless it gets made, you're never going to feel legitimized. An unproduced script is not publishable, and you can't get a bunch of your actor friends to put it on as an Off-Broadway show. A film script is good for only one thing. Otherwise, it's dead. And in many cases you don't even own it.
    -Ted Tally

The visual language of film developed out of 19th Century American melodrama, but while they started out as twins they quickly went their separate ways. One of the results of this divergence is that theatre is referred to as "the business" while film is "the industry." Playwrights never work in something called the film business – you're in an industry now with all that word implies.

For playwrights who don't have the patience to wait for Hollywood to call, the metaphorical trip to Los Angeles is mostly about craft adjustments once the concepts of playwriting are in hand.

19 Adjustments for Screenwriting

The adjustments that follow assume you're taking on a Hollywood feature film and all that implies as opposed to an independent film and the relative creative flexibility that other world offers (see Chapter 76 on the Indie Option).

1. Read screenplays. Good ones. Before writing that first screenplay – and before that see Chapter 70 on Reading Professional Screenplays. Get to know what they look and feel like before starting to write. Seeing movies is not the equivalent of reading screenplays.

2. Use professional screenplay format. It's a must. In the theatre, literary managers joke that with all the talk about the importance of format, the next new play they do will probably come in written in pencil on tissue paper. In Hollywood, if a screenplay is not in proper format it won't be looked at (see Chapter 71 on Format for Screenplays and Chapter 72 on Screenwriting Software).

3. Hold the script to 120 pages. In screenplay format. Commercially distributed feature films typically run between 90 minutes and two hours. Most production companies won't look at a freelance (spec) script that's over this magic number and a lot won't look at anything over 100 pages. Before selling that first script, anything beyond 120 pages is death.

4. Use a 3-act structure. With a crisis or turning-point in the story at the end of Act I and Act II. Screenplays are continuous – don't label the acts. The act divisions are your secret, though the pros will know where to look.

5. Control act lengths. That's important. Make Acts I and III about the same length with Act II about twice the length of Act I. A typical page allocation for a 120-page script: I=30; II=60; III=30. Note how different this act structure is from that of three-act plays. This concept – first proposed in Syd Field's *Screenplay: The Foundations of Screenwriting* – has some controversy floating around it, but it remains a good starting point.

6. Tell the story visually. With just enough dialogue to fill in the cracks. Even if it's an emotional love story. Remember that difference: Film is a sequence of visual images; theatre is a sequence of verbal images. Take another look at Chapter 67 on Visual vs. Verbal Storytelling.

7. Keep lines of dialogue short. Even in the most play-like of films, dialogue is extremely brief. This is not true of European films, especially those made in France, Italy, Germany, and Spain. If you get to do a screenplay there, you'll have the luxury of being able to write like a playwright.

8. American films are about what happens next. The technology of cutting from one image to the next has a lot to do with this. European cinema is the only market for character studies similar to stage plays, though some U.S. independent films embrace this as well (see Chapter 76 on The Indie Option).

9. Establish a strong suspense plot. Film doesn't cope well with the mild suspense plots that work well in plays, at least by mainline Hollywood standards. Suspense plots in film can consume as much as 90% of the script (see Chapter 25 on Plots). The one genre exception to this is romantic comedy.

10. It's nice to have an emotional plot. But it's not essential (except in a romantic comedy). Though the films that win Best Screenplay at the Academy Awards usually have well developed emotional plots even if the real driver is the suspense plot.

11. Put the hook in the first two pages. In theatrical terms, the hook is the inciting incident. If you're still unproduced as a playwright and writing a spec script, get the hook in by the bottom of page 1 (see Chapter 24 on Inciting Incidents). Most Hollywood pros won't read past page 1 of a spec script if there's no hook by the bottom of that first page.

12. Keep scenes short. Two pages is a good absolute maximum before cutting to a new location. Romantic comedies and relationship dramas can support long scenes, but in nearly all other genres a quarter page to a page is a more typical length.

13. Use less subtext. In mainline Hollywood film, subtext floats to the surface of the dialogue much more often. Some playwrights think that's because Hollywood has a dim view of the intelligence of its audience. Even where that may be true, the real driver is the overriding force of the suspense plot which keeps pushing subtext to the surface.

14. Incorporate an emotional pattern. At least in the obligatory scene. These patterns are particularly effective in film (see Chapter 32 on Emotional Patterns).

15. Aim for a happy ending. Or something close. It's the norm. Film – at least most Hollywood film – has to attract a mass audience to pay the freight of production and distribution. Audiences like happy endings and they seem to help encourage positive word of mouth, a key determinant of a film's financial success though these endings are less successful in garnering critical acclaim.

16. Avoid using a narrator. There's a long if spotty history of successful Hollywood films using narrators going back at least to the Graham Greene-Orson Welles classic, *The Third Man*. Mike Mills' *Beginners* and Woody Allen's *Midnight in Paris* are recent examples, but narrators remain an uncommon device in feature films. It's best to have an industry track record before going this route, mainly because narrators nearly always work better in the screenplay than on the screen. Hollywood pros know that. If you simply have to do this in a spec script, make the central character the narrator and confine narration to the opening and closing sequences of the script.

17. Do a detailed outline. Before writing the script. Nearly all screenwriters do this. A screenplay is even more of a construction than a play and it's essential to make sure the supporting structure is firmly in place before adding the dialogue. More than a few playwrights find this a killer – once they've done the outline, they feel like they've already told the story – and their drive to write the actual screenplay floats away like smoke. That can make writing the script pure drudgery.

18. Be prepared to do a treatment. A 20-50 page narrative of the story. Some producers may want to see this before looking at a screenplay.

19. Forget limits on the number of characters. Screenwriters have the luxury of calling on nearly unlimited numbers of characters, but be sensible. When writing a first screenplay, keeping large numbers of characters in your head (or on sticky notes all over the walls) may be more than you need to cope with.

The Rom Com Option

Now take a real risk with your second spec script. The first script with that strong suspense plot will show producers you understand the craft of Hollywood screenwriting. Since you've gotten this far by having the instincts of a playwright, now write a romantic comedy (often shortened to "Rom Com" in Hollywood, as if the genre is a U.S. military command group).

This genre is as close as it gets in Hollywood to the balance of emotional and suspense plots in plays. Romantic comedies are often driven entirely by their emotional plots and have little or no need for a suspense plot. What passes for a suspense plot is a simple question: Will they get together in the end?

There are technical reasons for why this romantic comedy approach can work in film, but not in theatre. Part of it has to do with the subtle suspense generated through the editing process for film and the unexpected cutting from one image to the next and from scene to scene. But you can be more adventurous within this genre. Aline Brosh McKenna has recently created a notable stir in Hollywood by adding suspense plots to her rom com screenplays, the mild versions typical of many contemporary plays: Will the heroine get that promotion? Will she save the TV series?

There's an advantage to having a romantic comedy as a second script since it can demonstrate your ability to create more complex and emotional characters and to sustain extended emotional scenes. More importantly, many producers still like the genre even if it seems that Hollywood is consumed by action sequels.

Contemporary romantic comedies, despite the genre's name, can have serious themes and events, more like the serious comedy approach in playwriting, so the genre can allow you to almost be a playwright while writing a screenplay.

69. ADAPTING YOUR PLAY FOR FILM

I usually start with an idea and discover where it's heading as I go along. This has been giving me problems working in Hollywood, where they want you to pitch an idea with a conclusion before you start work.
                -Christopher Durang

If you've taken the hints about timing in earlier chapters, you'll plan on making your Hollywood move after getting that first production of one of your plays. It's good to be wanted as a screenwriter in Los Angeles. Being wanted earns respect and one of the best ways to become wanted as a screenwriter is through professional notice as a playwright.

There's a prime advantage – besides professional respect – that comes with being asked by a film producer to do a screenplay instead of having to peddle one on spec. Odds are that first offer will be to do a film adaptation of your play that has attracted notice.

That's an incredible position for a playwright turned screenwriter to be in. In all likelihood, you'll be given your head – at least for the first draft – and the producers and potential director will be more than willing to talk you through the specifics of film structure and technique as they apply to the play.

"Opening Up" A Play

Before starting the first draft of the adaptation, you're guaranteed to hear about the need to expand the confined theatrical setting of the play. The first thing the producer will say – even before you've put down that pen used to sign the contract – is the need to open up the story. There's a good reason for this.

Nearly all contemporary plays have a very tight and contained setting, usually indoors, and even plays with a strong cinematic feel through the use of a series of short scenes tend to have limited locations. Theatre thrives on this constraint. The farthest we get out of the house in the Pulitzer Prize winning *August: Osage County* is the front porch. Even in a multiple scene play like Michael Hollinger's *Opus* set in a number of different apartments, greenrooms, and stages, the characters are always indoors.

In fact for theatre audiences, it's not even particularly important to telegraph those changing locations. They follow the story and locations of a play through its dialogue far more than its visual settings.

Film (with rare exceptions) doesn't take kindly to confined locations. What producers will want to see is the story of the play brought into the world surrounding the original setting. Some of this opening up may feel arbitrary – and even unnecessary – until you see that first cut of the film.

Opening up a play requires thinking logically about where else those original scenes could take place beyond the play's setting or adding new scenes that will take the characters into the outside world.

Be cautious about taking existing interior scenes from the play and arbitrarily placing them in some other location. While this may seem like an easy way to open up the play as well as a clever approach to preserving its dialogue, your original concept for the setting will in most cases have had a subtle influence on the conflict and dialogue. As a result, this kind of arbitrary relocation of scenes – especially of interior scenes to exteriors – can lead to an odd disconnect between what audiences see and the dialogue they hear. In nearly all cases, it's better to rewrite scenes in their new locations, trying to hold the original conflict and subtext, but allowing the dialogue to be influenced by what now surrounds the characters.

Time Expansion

To complicate matters, your producers may also want to see the time frame of the story expanded with the most likely direction for expansion being prior to the play's point of attack. Film doesn't take as kindly as the theatre does to extended exposition so rather than having characters tell us what happened prior to the original point of attack, they may want you to show us the most critical of those events.

You've probably sensed the dangers involved in moving the point of attack earlier in the history of the story. Those dangers include the potential loss of conflict along with the necessity of moving the inciting incident – or finding a new inciting incident – to hold audiences during this time period you originally thought would be handled best through exposition.

Keeping It Your Film

To make this process easier, think of the adaptation as an opportunity to retell the story in a completely different medium. Your characters are there along with as many more as you'd care to add. And it's still the same plot. But now it's a film.

Playwrights make a devil's bargain here. In return for money – and the chance for the story to be seen by more people than have seen most of Shakespeare's plays in the four centuries since their premieres at the Globe – they agree to create a visual version of the original story. Cooperation is a good watchword since the last thing you want to have happen is for the producers to hand the adaptation to a seasoned screenwriter, or even worse, scuttle the whole project.

Hopefully, you'll be one of the lucky ones with producers who will let you keep most of the play in the film. You don't have to worry about why they may be doing this. Odds are it's because the play created an artistic stir and producing this "art house" film will earn the producers prestige in Hollywood even if it doesn't do much more than break even at the box office. This is a playwright's fantasy, though it's happened a number of times.

Tips for Making it Work

If these aren't your producers, there are three mental adjustments that may help.

1. No matter what the producers tell you, they want to make a film. Not a recording on 35mm stock of your original play.

2. Everybody loves everybody in Hollywood. Which means you've got to peer through the smoke to see how far your power over the script really extends. It won't be far. Don't be misled by everyone saying how much they love you and your play. Remember #1 above.

3. End the love affair with your own dialogue. It's probably marvelous (seriously) because you've gotten a production that was received well by critics, but resist the urge to fall on your sword or a very sharp pen over favorite lines of dialogue. What the producers love – now that they're moving the project toward production – is the story and characters, not all the dialogue. Remember that you're not a playwright anymore. You're a screenwriter now and with that title change you've given up control over all those words you wrote.

Persuasion can help maintain the integrity of the script, but keep in mind that what really matters – assuming you still want a screenwriting career after this Hollywood experience – will be the opportunity to write a first screenplay that's not an adaptation for these same producers.

70. READING SCREENPLAYS

I've begun to believe more and more that movies are all about transitions, that the key to making good movies is to pay attention to the transition between scenes. And not just how you get from one scene to the next, but where you leave a scene and where you come into a new scene. Those are some of the most important decisions that you make. It can be the difference between a movie that works and a movie that doesn't.
    -Steven Soderbergh

Since you're coming at screenwriting as a playwright, the first step is a crash course in how the pros do it. Reading about 10 screenplays – at least initially – should provide the minimum necessary to get started. But before you get started, some suggestions.

Knowing the World Beyond Film
Hollywood and the world of commercial feature film can give the impression that from an intellectual standpoint it only feeds on itself, that the pros in the industry think of the arts and literature as limited to seeing movies and reading screenplays. At least at the top end, that is far from the reality. Producers and directors from that world are often supporters of classical music, opera, art museums, regional theatres, and other kinds of so-called "high culture" organizations.

This interest can be dismissed as another form of social climbing, but in fact the commitment and passion for the arts is in most cases serious and real and it can have a subtle impact on their professional choices of film projects to green-light.

It's not just a cliché to say that to write effective screenplays, you need to know something – actually much more than something – about what goes on beyond the walls of the film industry.

Many years ago, George Lucas gently faulted his university film education for not introducing students sufficiently to great literature and music, a deficit he didn't realize he had until he went to work for Francis Ford Coppola. Lucas may have shared some responsibility for that deficit by the elective courses he selected, but he was making a very important point: The best of the pros in this industry typically read widely in fiction (often literary fiction) and nonfiction as well as pursuing interests in music and the fine arts.

Coming to screenwriting from playwriting means you may already share some of those interests.

With that in mind, remember that reading screenplays is about sharpening your tools of the trade. All of your other reading and interests beyond film are about sharpening an understanding of the world. It's that broader understanding that will help generate inspiration and intriguing visual stories to tell and lead you to be more daring than the average Hollywood screenwriter.

Contemporary Classic Screenplays to Read

To begin, read some contemporary classics so you'll start with the gold standard. These often have the feel of a play in terms of dialogue (brief as it may be), voice, and complexity of characterization.

1. *Chinatown.* Robert Towne's script is among the best that have been done in Hollywood in many decades.

2. *The Godfather.* (Part One of the three films in the series.) Francis Ford Coppola's script ranks among the most successful American film adaptations of mass market novels – and hardly anyone comes away from the resulting film saying they liked the novel better.

3. *The English Patient.* Anthony Minghella's script is a fine example of successful adaptation of a complex novel in the literary fiction genre.

4. *Moonstruck.* John Patrick Shanley's script is a wonderfully romantic, bizarre, and moving original by one of America's noted playwrights.

5. *Manhattan.* Marshall Brickman's romantic masterpiece for (and with) Woody Allen.

Once you've read the high end of the form, look at four or five scripts of films released in the last several years. The best choices will be scripts of films you've liked. Slot each of these into a genre as practice for what's to come (see Chapter 74 on The Hollywood Hustle) and include on your reading list at least a few scripts in a genre you think you'd be comfortable writing.

Reading vs. Seeing in Film

Reading screenplays is a far better way to learn the adjustments necessary for screenwriting than seeing films. That's another way theatre and film are alike: Scripts tell us much more about technical craft issues than productions.

Reading plays and screenplays require very different approaches. In screenplays, the "stage directions" – in industry parlance, "the action" – are everything. You're not reading so much for dialogue and voice, though the very best screenwriters will have that, but for the sequence of visual images that tell the story. Read slowly enough to allow the time to see each image in your mind's eye.

Draft vs. Shooting Scripts

To get the full benefit from reading screenplays, read actual scripts instead of those published in book form. It's important to read a script as close as possible to how the screenwriter actually wrote it. That means in a version called a draft before its conversion to a shooting script. What you're after is a script that's close to what the producers originally bought, not a record of the film in its final edited form.

Hundreds of screenplays are now easily available in downloads from sites on the Web with the best of these sites indicating what versions (draft or shooting script) of the title they have. To get to these sites, do a search for screenplays or search directly for a film title with screenplay added in the search box.

As with plays, the format of published screenplays has little resemblance to professional screenplay format.

Shooting scripts are serviceable for seeing how the pros tell visual stories, but they're also misleading about how much visual description screenwriters include in their early drafts. It's easy to tell a shooting script by its first page: Each scene heading (or slug line) is preceded by a number:

34.   EXT.   ITALIAN ROAD   DAY

Draft screenplays have no numbering of scene headings at the left margin.

On Seeing Films

It hardly seems necessary to say this in America, but you also need to see a lot of films on the wide screen – or as wide as they get in most movie theatres nowadays. What home screens provide, even with the sound cranked up, is only a meager substitute for the real larger-than-life experience.

It may be hard to remember after watching so many films on television and computer screens, iPads, and smart phones, that part of the impact of film comes (or at least used to come) from its image size. That close shot of the heroine's face from chin to eyebrows can be 15 feet in a large movie theatre, the kinds of theatres that are an increasingly endangered species. The reduction in screen size fueled by electronic devices has impacted projected image sizes in nearly all multi-screen movie venues today. How this will affect screenwriting and moviemaking in the coming years is an open question. It's possible audiences will simply adjust to these small – and even tiny – images. Perhaps only those living in the nation's largest cities will have the opportunity to see films as directors and screenwriters intended.

It can also be helpful to see a few films you wouldn't have considered in the days when you were concentrating on writing plays. It's amazing how many uninteresting films appear every year. Stanley Kubrick took an important lesson from this:

> *I was aware that I didn't know anything about making films, but I believed I couldn't make them any worse than the majority of films I was seeing. Bad films gave me the courage to try making a movie.*

Sampling the typical run of feature films may supply the motivation to try moving the Hollywood needle a few notches once you have a track record to support taking that chance.

71. FORMAT FOR SCREENPLAYS

There is a big difference between a play and a movie, and everybody needs to respect that and be aware of that. The idea is not so much what the production looks like onstage but what we believe the potential is in a whole different medium, which is a movie. They are completely different. A play is a play, whether it has film potential or not. A book is a book. However, a screenplay is just 120 pieces of paper. Respect that what you've written may be simply a great play. It may not be a film.
　　　-Anne Carey

It doesn't make sense any more to dive into a screenplay without using screenwriting software (see Chapter 72). Screenplays can still be written in professional format with Microsoft Word or Google Docs if you're prepared to give your fingers a lot of extra work. If you're not sure if you have a driving interest in visual storytelling, try writing a first screenplay as a test without laying out the cash for the software.

What follows is how screenwriting format works. Even if you plan on getting screenwriting software, knowing the basics will make it much easier to cope with the instruction manuals for these programs. It may help to look at the Page 1 of a screenplay on page 297 of this chapter.

Paper & Fonts
In the U.S. use only white 20-pound 8.5" x 11" paper. Duplicate scripts on the 3-hole punched version of this.

For font and type size, use Courier (or Courier New) 12-point type – it's the industry standard. This is a typewriter font so don't be startled by the differences with the proportional fonts you've probably been using for word processing.

Title & Preliminary Pages
These are nearly identical to stage play format (see Chapter 53 on Title & Preliminary Pages) with the following exceptions for the Title Page:

1. Title: <u>UNDERLINE</u> this and in all caps, centered on the Title Page. The rest is like a play title page: Under the title, "by" or "a screenplay by" and your name centered below that.

2. WGA Registered: This is optional and doesn't need to be put on your title page – it's assumed nowadays. If you feel particularly paranoid, put it in the lower left or right corner of the Title Page, though if you're really that paranoid, the film industry may not be the best environment for you (see Chapter 75 on Professional Support for more on script registration). If you include this, the WGA recommended wording is as follows: "WGAW Registered" or "WGAW #_____" (without the quotation marks). A caution: There seems to be a growing sense in Hollywood that putting the WGA notice on a title page is the sign of an amateur.

Screenplay Format by the Numbers

The format margins and spacing below comes courtesy of the Academy of Motion Picture Arts and Sciences:

1. Page Margins:
Top margin: 0.75" - 1.0" & Bottom margin: 0.5" - 1.5"

2. Description (slug line and scene description):
Left Margin: 1.5" - 2.0" & Right Margin: 1.0"

4. Dialogue:
Left Margin: 3.0" & Right Margin: about 2.3"

5. Character directions:
Left Margin: about 3.7" & Right Margin: about 3.0"

Scene & Dialogue Pages

1. Title. Center your title in all caps and in quotes at the top of page 1 of the script (the first Scene & Dialogue page): "SCREENPLAY TITLE"

2. Page numbers. Number consecutively in the upper right corner beginning with the first Scene & Dialogue Page. Numbering is best done in the Header using the Flush Right tool.

3. Character names. In all caps (beginning at the centerline) over dialogue lines and in caps/lower case within scene descriptions. Sometimes names are capitalized in the first scene description where a character is initially introduced.

4. Character directions. Put in parentheses as in stage play format for Character Stage Directions, but the initial letter is not capitalized: (laughing)

5. Scene headings (slug lines). Beginning flush to the left margin in all caps. Use EXT. for Exterior and INT. for Interior in the following order:

EXT. ITALIAN ROAD   DAY

INT. TINA'S HOUSE   NIGHT

You can use many variants for the location and time of day. Insert one space between the Scene Heading and the following scene description. Insert two spaces between the end of one scene and the Scene Heading for the next scene.

6. Scene Continuations. When a scene continues on to the next page of the script, put CONTINUED in the lower right corner. Do the same next to the character name on the following page if the same character has a continuous speech that runs over to that next page.

Page 1 of a Screenplay in Format

Following is a page of a screenplay in professional format, though keep in mind that in real life the page would be printed in 12-point Currier font on 8.5" x 11" paper – thus noticeably larger than a page in the *Handbook*. In this reduced size, its main purpose is to show the relationships between the elements of the format.

"WHITE ALICE"

EXT. VIENNA COURTYARD NIGHT

Shadow and dampness comes off the surrounding walls and pavement. A single
street lamp casts a shimmering pool of light. JOAN and LARKIN on the edge of the
light. She's in a tan trench coat. Larkin wears a sweater with a scarf around his
neck. Only a slight sound of tires on wet pavement in the distance.

                           JOAN
              How are you?

                           LARKIN
              Fine.
                    (pause)
              Fine.

                           JOAN
              That's not what I was asking.

                           LARKIN
              No?

Joan takes out her phone and checks a number. Larkin watches her. He glances
around, sees nothing.

                           LARKIN
              Everyone who maters in this is dead.
              Or nearly so. At least we accomplished
              that much by doing nothing.

EXT. STREETS NIGHT

A dark car driving fast. We can't see who's in it. It turns sharply, the driver nearly
losing control.

INT. LARKIN'S APARTMENT NIGHT

City light filters through the drapes. A key sounds in the lock. Sharp light cuts
across the floor from the open door and we see Larkin framed. In the middle of the
room, a chair upended, papers scattered on the floor. He takes this in, starts to back
out, struggling to get the key out of the lock. It won't come. He's breathing fast, not

CONTINUED

Screenplay Covers & Bindings

Unlike stage play covers, the Hollywood standard turns a screenplay into a lethal weapon. Maybe that tells you something about this industry.

Covers for screenplays are 8.5" x 11" 3-hole punched card stock in the 67- to 80-pound range in a light to medium color. Don't use term paper covers or clear plastic covers. Center the title in caps and your name on the cover as with a stage play.

Get a box of 2-inch solid brass fasteners (ACCO makes these) from an office supply store. Don't use the brass washers they'll happily sell you. Only use two brads, one in the top hole and one in the bottom hole, leaving the middle hole empty. Note that the brads have pointed ends and they can draw blood or rip the pants of careless readers.

72. USING SCREENWRITING SOFTWARE

I've come to view screenwriting assignments as playwriting grants, because they provide a considerable financial cushion. However, they can also be extremely time-consuming. Film projects tend to drag on and on, which takes me away from the theatre, and then they don't get made. At the same time, the screenplays that have come my way have been quite challenging, for the most part, and even enjoyable.
-Donald Margulies

Screenplay software does all the heavy lifting as you're writing a script and there's far more heavy lifting in executing screenplay format than in the relatively simple version used for stage plays. These programs are the norm now for writers of screenplays and teleplays.

Advantages of Using Software
Software formatting packages remember all the intricacies of spacing, capitalization, and the rest without the screenwriter needing to know much about it, even spelling out character names if you give them a hint by hitting the first letter.

Most important, when you go back to edit that first draft – or as is often the case, that second or third or fourth draft – the software automatically adjusts the CONTINUED indications as you move pages around, insert scenes, and cut or expand dialogue. That may sound like the most modest of perks, but it solves one of the major headaches that used to plague screenwriters when they moved from the first to subsequent drafts.

Script formatting software may not be worth the trouble for stage plays where this part of life is simpler and literary managers usually won't toss out your script if you've got the margins wrong, but pros in Hollywood expect you to have this down cold. The weather may be warm in Lotusland, but it's a tough town when it comes to scripts.

The leading programs also stretch the length of a screenplay to that 100-page goal if the conflict in the story fails to drive you much beyond the high 90s, or shrink it to 120 pages if you've sailed beyond that magic number – and without having to do any editing to get there. But if you're more than two or three pages off that 100- or 120-page target, edit the script to within that range and then use the fancy shrink/expand function.

The Industry Standards

Final Draft and Movie Magic Screenwriter are generally thought of as the industry standard, but there are always competitors coming on the market so explore the field before you buy.

Final Draft (www.finaldraft.com) says it's the best selling screenwriting program in the world. Movie Magic Screenwriter (www.screenplay.com) says that something like 80% of writers nominated for Academy Awards and television's Emmys use their software – or at least the production companies they work for have bought it. There may be a bit of Hollywood spin floating around these claims, but there's no question that a lot of writers for film and television use one of these two programs.

Both of the industry standards include templates for nearly every U.S. television series going. It's important to use these if you're trying a spec script as a way of getting onto a series writing team. Final Draft also offers BBC format templates.

Prices change over time, but currently Movie Magic runs about $200 for pros while Final Draft is about $250 and both have rates in the $120-$130 range for students with proof of enrollment. Both offer free time-limited downloadable demos or the equivalent return deal so you can try them. Selecting software is a bit like finding that special chair to write in: It's all in the feel.

Most suppliers of formatting software also offer specialized help in outlining story ideas, character development, and story structure, though you'll usually need to buy additional packages to turn your computer into a writing coach. Stage play format is either built into the software or available as an add-on download.

Writing for the BBC

If you live in the UK – or anywhere else for that matter – and want to break into the BBC with scripts for radio or television, visit the BBC Writer's Room (www.bbc.co.uk/writersroom). Formatting for plays, screenplays, teleplays, and radio drama is generally different in the UK from formats used in the U.S.

73. WRITING FOR TELEVISION

I have been approached now and again about sitcoms, but, with very few exceptions, one simply needs to move to L.A. for at least a year or two these days if one wants to develop a series – which is what writing a pilot means. I've also been approached about writing episodes for sitcoms, but in order to do that one actually has to watch sitcoms. Life's too short for television, and I don't want it on my actual gravestone, He Stared at a Box for 10,000 Hours.
                                        -David Ives

Increasing numbers of American playwrights have been doing television series work in recent years as a way to make a living with their words. In fact, a contemporary playwright who doesn't do some writing for a television series is the exception today.

Besides the money, most of them doing this find that TV work sharpens their skills in shaping plots, writing dialogue, and even using subtext (most playwrights work at the high end of the medium). And those who have not had more than a few productions at regional theatres enjoy writing for a medium that regularly puts their work in front of audiences.

Increasing Quality of Television Writing

Playwrights have also been motivated by the marked increase in quality of the upper end of American television series concepts and writing on both commercial and cable networks. In turn, that rising quality has encouraged producers to look more seriously to playwrights for their writing teams and where producers look is to the pool of playwrights with regional theatre productions in hand.

Television series writing is grueling work. Those who love that life really love it, but know that it's tough. If you need eight hours of sleep a night to function well, this is probably not the world for you where writers often work well into the wee hours of the morning and do it under tremendous pressure.

The demands for speed and repetition can be disconcerting for playwrights as well as writing as part of a team – often with five or six other writers – and working within strict formulas for the show's characters and plots. Those formulas are enforced for a reason: They're partly responsible (along with the performers) for the commercial success of the shows. Grumpier playwrights have compared the series writing process to making Pintos at a Ford plant: You stamp out the body (with lots of help) and somebody else puts in the headlights.

If you take on television series work, you'll make a ton of money – if the series is a hit and gets that magic 5-year run. Even if you don't get that magic run, you'll still make a quarter-ton and if you're like most, you'll figure that maybe then you can afford to write plays. But be aware that you may have lost (or at least misplaced) some of your playwriting skills if you haven't kept one hand in the theatre at the same time you're writing for television.

On the other hand, Theresa Rebeck, probably the best known American playwright working in television, has little patience for this concern, saying *Going to TV doesn't ruin your writing. You know what ruins your writing? Not writing.*

Making it Work

One of the clearest keys for making television work for a playwright is keeping a hand in the theatre – or at least a finger. Theresa Rebeck and Jon Robin Baitz (another playwriting star in TV) have figured out how to move back and forth between television and playwriting and do it successfully (Baitz developed the ABC series *Brothers & Sisters* which had a five-year run ending in 2011. Rebeck is executive producer of the 2012 NBC series, *Smash*). It's possible to do both well if, like them, you can write for the top end of the industry.

Some playwrights working in television admit – and this may be a self-discipline issue – that they only think about the plays they'd like to write someday. When you write for TV, you may feel the only time left for that real writing you want to do is when you're sleeping, but Rebeck – in addition to executive producing a television series in 2011 – managed to have three new plays opening in the 2011-12 season, two in regional theatres and one on Broadway. Playwrights working in television (and writers in many other genres) can be pros at whining, something that uses up a lot of energy much better spent on writing plays.

Software & Series Templates

The leading screenwriting software programs give you the variant TV series templates with the click of a mouse. Typically, they include templates for 50 or more TV shows in the U.S.

If you live in the UK or just understand that world, try writing for BBC television – check out the BBC Writers Room.

But if playwriting is your passion – and visual storytelling isn't an overwhelming urge – think about getting a "real" job and writing plays in the hours you'll have left every day. Then when you've gotten some recognition as a playwright, you'll have a better shot at picking what you'd like to do for television and getting paid enough so you'll still have time to write plays.

74. THE HOLLYWOOD HUSTLE

You have much less control in film because when you write a movie you're an employee. If you're hired to write a movie, they can hire and fire you 37 times. If I had sold THE HEIDI CHRONICLES to a movie studio, as opposed to independent producers, and they decided they didn't like my script, they would have the right to fire me and take me off the project and say, Why is this woman an art historian? Why doesn't she become a pilot? DAYS OF THUNDER did really well; why doesn't she become a race-car driver?
    -Wendy Wasserstein

If you've exercised some artistic self control and waited until Hollywood asked you to write a screenplay or adapt your play for a film version, you can skip this chapter. (On the other hand, morbid curiosity may prompt you to read on to see what lies ahead for spec screenwriters.)

If you've gone ahead anyway and written that spec screenplay without being asked, what follows is a primer on mounting the barricades of the film industry. They haven't put up these obstacles out of meanness: It's self-defense against the avalanche of scripts flooding into Los Angeles every day.

The LA Story

The first thing you can do is repent, and go back to playwriting until you get that first production or place in that first significant playwriting competition. The odds of getting noticed as a playwright are far higher than breaking through the avalanche of spec scripts clogging Hollywood's arteries.

The surest way to get into screenwriting is to be a produced playwright first, but that kind of restraint is tough to come by with a new screenplay sitting at your elbow.

12 Steps of the Hustle

Playwrights have to sell themselves to some extent, but they enjoy the advantage of having their scripts do most of the talking. Spec screenwriters don't share that advantage.

1. Register the script with the WGA (see Chapter 75). As soon as its done. And definitely before you show it to anybody except your lover. Copyright protection is recommended though there is some question about how valuable that may be for screenplays.

2. Move to Los Angeles. It helps to be there. Hollywood and its film world is an international industry, but a lot of it is driven by personal relationships and chance encounters. Get involved with a writers group and find an apartment in the heart of the "town" – Santa Monica, Beverly Hills, West LA, Hollywood – but ideally no farther away than the close-in portions of the San Fernando Valley. Save Malibu for when you're famous.

3. Practice your answer to, "So tell me, what's this about?" In one sentence. This is what's called a log line in the industry and in many cases it's all that prompts producers to ask to read a screenplay. If you can't do this easily – or if the mere idea drives your blood pressure up more than a few points – stay with playwriting. A path to an effective log line: Lead with the key character tied to the suspense plot with a bit of the emotional plot (if you have one) woven in. Keep it to about 30 words maximum – you need to be able to rattle this off in one easy breath. In the next breath be prepared to tag on a comparison with two other recent (and financially successful) Hollywood films, as in *It's Bridesmaids meets Inception.*

4. Practice your pitch. These come in two sizes – short and long. For the short pitch, take that log line sentence from step 3 and add two more sentences: The first fleshing out the key character or at most two key characters and the last expanding on the plot, ideally ending with a kind of curtain line phrase that will lead a producer to ask for the long pitch. Don't try to sneak in any more with a fourth sentence. The long pitch is a 10-minute synopsis of the screenplay (or outline, if you haven't written the actual screenplay yet). That's the equivalent of five pages, double spaced in 12-point type, read aloud. If you're gutsy and an accomplished story-teller, you can push this to 20 minutes. The theory of a synopsis for a play holds for the long pitch (see Chapter 60 on Writing the Synopsis). The goal is once more to end with something resembling a curtain line leading to that producer now wanting to read the screenplay – and paying you for the privilege. Since pitches are usually presented verbally, they should feel and have the rhythm of how you talk. Never memorize a long pitch word-for-word unless you have a performer's ability to make it seem absolutely natural. There can be opportunities to email pitches so it's a good idea to have a version for that purpose as well.

5. Practice your answer to, "What kind of story is this?" The right answer: "It's a [insert genre here]." Hollywood thinks in terms of genres: Comedy, drama, horror, thriller, romantic comedy, action, adventure, western, crime/gangster, and more. The concern for genre is driven by the need to determine marketing and release strategies for feature films and it's not some strange invention peculiar to the film industry. The U.S. publishing industry uses the same approach (with some variation in the names of its genres) for its fiction lists, likewise motivated by marketing and positioning requirements. Somebody (actually, almost everybody) who matters in the film industry is guaranteed to ask you what the genre of your screenplay is. They won't be impressed if you say, "Well, it's a lot of things, a bit of a drama, sort of a thriller, but there's comedy and a guy on a horse." But you might get away with mashing two genres together as in, "It's a romantic comedy with the heart of a thriller."

6. Enter the Nicholl Competition. An alternative to moving to LA. The Nicholl Screenwriting Fellowship is sponsored by the Academy of Motion Picture Arts and Sciences. These fellowships currently carry a $30,000 award. If you make the finals, move to LA. Making the Nicholl finals should nearly guarantee you an agent, and even the semifinals (on average, the top 60 scripts) may get you representation or at least get agents to give you a meeting. For everything you need to know about the Nicholl Fellowships, go to the Academy's Web site (www.oscars.org) and then to The

Awards. The competition is tough – all the more reason to enter – with as many as 6,000 entries annually (the average is around 3,500). Before you throw up your hands, it's limited to writers who haven't sold screenplays for more than a total of $5,000 prior to submission. The Academy estimates that the screening of submissions breaks down as follows: About 5% of entries advance to the quarterfinals, about 2% advance to the semifinals and about 10 scripts reach the finals. Usually 5 fellowships are awarded. Submission is online only. Go to the Nicholl Fellows page on the Academy's site and you'll find each of the current fellows listed with the title of their screenplay along with that one-sentence log line of what each is about.

7. Be ready for the "Fashion" effect. There's been a belief among artists (and scientists) for many decades that there's a fashion in creativity that results in the same ideas being developed by people separated by thousands of miles – and who have no contact with each other. It's not in their imaginations that there's something in the ether other than ESP that prompts these similar ideas. The Fashion impacts screenwriters with peculiar regularity. That great inspiration you got out of the blue for a story never before told? By the time you get to the end of page 1 of the screenplay, there may well be five other screenwriters who have the same idea. Or worse, have just finished their screenplays on that idea. So don't be surprised if the reaction to a spec script is "We just passed on that idea" or worse, "We just bought that idea." Even if they say one of these things, they may still like your writing enough to ask to see your next script.

8. Prepare for rejection. There's an old and cynical Hollywood quip: *If you say No all the time in this business, most of the time you'll be right.* Sad, but true. Those who make it in this industry beginning as spec screenwriters have skins like a rhino when it comes to deflecting the impact of rejections. That's important. Ignoring rejection and maintaining confidence in your work as a screenwriter are essential. If you have trouble taking No for an answer, Hollywood may not be a good match for you.

9. Look for representation. And look hard. A good agent

can turn a playwright-turned-screenwriter into a produced screenwriter in ways you could never do on your own. Having an agent will get you past a lot of the barbed wire that fences off spec screenwriters from film producers. A warning: It's tough to do if you don't have a calling card from recognition in theatre, fiction or non-fiction books, or journalism. Check through your family tree and your extended network of friends to see if you don't have some link into the Hollywood scene that could help. Sometimes that six degrees of separation thing actually works (or 4.74 degrees, if you believe the latest research). There are occasionally a few agents who may be willing to look at spec screenplays. If you're going to try this, a script lodged within one of the standard genres is nearly essential – and keep using that one-sentence summary of the story until it feels like the most natural thing to say.

10. Be wary of fee for service deals. Hollywood (and lots of other places) are full of folks just dying to help you get your screenplay sold if you'll only pay them a very large fee. A word of advice: *Don't.*

11. Develop a sense of humor. About the film industry. You may find a lot of silliness and excess in the film industry – sometimes off the charts compared to the world of regional theatres – and it will help to laugh about it. Some time ago, a spec screenwriter handed out business cards reading, *Screenwriting and Light Yard Work.* He had the right attitude.

12. Keep a log of screenplay ideas. This should be a continually growing list with titles and log lines for each entry. Those producers who say they're passing on your script may also say, "What else have you got?" if they've responded to your writing. You don't ever want to be in the position of having to say, "I'll get back to you on that." This list gives you a way to toss out a title with that one-sentence log line – with backups until you hit one that has legs.

And if they say, "OK, let me see it," go home and write like mad.

75. PROFESSIONAL SUPPORT: WGA

It was a film of emotions. The sound was more important than the words, the colors more enchanting than the scenery. Every moment was a cry, the sound of a car engine, a song. It was, I think, my first romantic film. With this film, I became convinced that one must not narrate but express. What the characters did not say was often more important than what they said.
-Claude Lelouch

The Writers Guild of America (WGA) is the professional guild for screenwriters, television writers, and electronic media authors. It's an equivalent of the Dramatists Guild for playwrights.

Unlike the Dramatists Guild, WGA membership comes only with production and is expensive. Writers can join as soon as they sign a contract with a production company that is a WGA signatory. In some cases a production company that bought your script may pay your initial WGA dues – that's a very good deal if you can get it.

WGA West & East

Writer's Guild of America seems at first glance like it's a bicoastal operation, but it's not. WGA, West is based in Los Angeles (www.wga.org) while WGA, East is located in New York (www.wgaeast.org). The East unit handles script registration, offers some of the same resources, and cooperates with its West coast twin, but is a separate operation.

Membership in WGA, East or WGA, West is determined by your state of residence when you get that first industry contract. Writers living east of the Mississippi River join the East outfit and those west of the big river join WGA, West. WGA, West has the most complete resources for screenwriters on its Web site.

The WGA offers unproduced screenwriters other resources including much about contracts and compensation ("Schedule of Minimums"). Look for these schedules on the Web site under Writer's Resources. The writing tools section offers articles and interviews with screenwriters on the craft of writing for film, television, and occasionally multimedia.

Script Registration Service

Most important for unproduced screenwriters is the WGA's essential – and reasonably priced – script registration service for nonmembers.

Upon receipt of your screenplay with the necessary forms and payment (currently $20 for nonmembers) either electronically or by snail-mail, the Guild issues a registration number and records the script in its archives. WGA registration establishes a firm completion date for the draft of the script and can help protect against unauthorized appropriation of your efforts by anyone who sees it after that date. If you're particularly paranoid about Hollywood, you can also register – with a new fee for each – outlines, story ideas, treatments, and synopses.

Access the registration service through the home page of the West or East offices. Note that WGA registration is not copyright protection and does not provide protection for script titles.

There is a lot less unauthorized "borrowing" of scripts in Hollywood than local rumor claims, but WGA registration is a good way to help keep everybody reasonably honest.

The Myth of Story Theft in Hollywood

Story theft has happened in Lotusland, but proven cases are rare enough that these are Hollywood's version of Black Swan events.

The myth of wholesale stealing of story ideas in Hollywood – like vampires – never seems to die. That's because nearly every year the media report on a few cases of screenwriters suing producers who they claim have stolen their ideas.

Most of those bringing legal action for story theft are writers of spec screenplays and nearly all of those they sue are producers of highly successful films (you can draw your own conclusions from this). Many of these suits rely on what might be called a six-degrees-of-separation claim: The writer sent the script to an agent or at least someone associated with the industry who knows someone who knows a director or screenwriter who – (you can guess the rest). The thefts alleged in these cases nearly always fall apart in court.

The fact is that story theft makes little economic sense in Hollywood (though every industry has unscrupulous entities at the fringes so know who you're dealing with). If legitimate producers like certain parts of the story or characters in a spec screenplay, the cost of buying it is next to nothing compared to the budget for producing a feature film. It's frankly too much trouble to steal it when you can buy it for so little.

What may drive most of these cases is probably the "fashion effect" that leads to multiple screenwriters coming up with similar story ideas and characters at about the same time – without ever having met each other.

> **Best Practice:** *Paranoia is neither healthy nor usually warranted in Hollywood.*

But still . . . register your screenplay with the WGA.

76. THE INDIE OPTION

I'm not a cinephile. My films don't reference films. I'm more interested in rhythm and feeling.
      -Miranda July

If the idea of Hollywood curls your toes, consider taking the independent route. Glenn Close may say that "The definition of an independent film is a film that almost doesn't get made," but it's still a world worth exploring – and can be a more comfortable match for playwrights than Hollywood.

One of the advantages of this world is that the industry in recent years has turned to independent film festivals to find out-of-the-box films they'd like to distribute. Admittedly the focus is on the leading ones like Sundance, but an indie film that gets screenings at a number of mid-range festivals has nearly as good a chance of attracting Hollywood distribution.

Distribution is key in the indie world. An indie film can be made for much less than 1% of the production budget of a typical studio feature, but to get national and international distribution, you have to rely on Hollywood. As a result, the festivals have become the R&D arm for the distribution side of Hollywood. The festivals object to the showbiz flavor this has brought with it, but it's great for the film makers and screenwriters who get picked up.

If you have second thoughts now about boxing up your computer and heading for Los Angeles, forget about winning an Oscar for Best Screenplay with that first script – at least for the moment.

Try looking instead for an eager, compulsively driven young film director. The best time to find someone like this is just before they graduate from a university film program, (it's nearly impossible to do this if you're not also a student at that university). It's also true that most film director-hopefuls would rather write their own screenplays, but they may respond to your talent with words, especially if it's free, as it will have to be. As you look for this arrangement, keep in mind that the killer industry app they hope to develop into is a writer-director.

Young filmmakers who take the independent route know their way around a high-end digital film camera and oversee all aspects of the production themselves with lots of help from their friends. And given the way the best college film programs work today, they also know their way around a screenplay.

The Indie Road to Hollywood

Steven Soderbergh's *Sex, Lies, and Videotape* followed the indie route. John Sayles did the same with *Return of the Secaucus 7*. In each case, you know what happened next (both of these now classic scripts offer good lessons in how to write for the indies).

Nobody who knows the industry would claim there's a tidal wave of these success stories coming out of the world of indie production, but enough of them happen every year to make the odds worth taking. Among the latest in this low-budget indie tradition is Malcolm Murray's *Bad Posture* (2011), written by his friend and first-time screenwriter, Florian Brozek.

If all goes well, you'll end up shooting a 90-minute film, funded on credit cards and donations. Production can come in for less than $100,000 if you've written it carefully and with costs in mind. Then you and the director will hustle this at film festivals, hoping for the big one: Robert Redford's Sundance Film Festival (www.sundance.org). The Sundance U.S. Dramatic Competition for "new voices in American independent film" selects 16 features each year from a huge number of submissions.

With luck – lots of it – and talent, you'll end up with agents and Hollywood offers. It happens every year: Among the most famous of these DIY indie productions was *The Blair Witch Project*, done for $60,000 (they never went near Sundance). The odds may be steep, but they're much better than winning the lottery.

Features & Shorts

As a playwright, your main interest will be in writing screenplays for feature films, the cinema equivalent of the full-length play. That's the only thing Hollywood is interested in.

At the other end of the scale are shorts, films lasting anywhere from about 5 to 20 minutes (Sundance caps them at 49 minutes), the equivalent of one-act plays. The short form is worth considering because they tend to have more film festival submission opportunities than features. Shorts share all the constraints of one-act plays (see Chapter 38), but they have the advantage of being much less expensive to shoot. In film, time is money.

The gold standard in short film festivals is at Sundance every year. To get a sense of this kind of writing and filmmaking, go to the Sundance Festival Web site and do a search for Short Film at the Festival. In most years there are close to 100 shorts available for streaming. Scripts of shorts are difficult to come by, so seeing shorts is practically the only way to "read" the form.

Writing for the Indies

If you're up for venturing into the world of independent film making, forget nearly everything you've ever seen from the Hollywood studios. If you loved classics like *Titanic*, *Star Wars*, and the *Terminator* epics, this indie world is probably not your line of work.

Thinking in Indie Time x 11

If deep in your soul you're still fascinated by playwriting – and if you're drawn to films coming out of Europe and Australia – here are 11 adjustments for indie screenwriting.

1. Hold the script to 90 pages. Pages are money in indie land, real money that you and the director will have to beg, borrow, or max out on your credit cards – and something in the 90-minute range is all that's needed to make it in this world with a feature.

2. Rely on character centered stories. Indie films are often much closer to plays than Hollywood features.

3. Use subtext. The indie world is open to subtext in the way playwrights use it and there's often (though not always) an appreciation for complex characters.

4. Back away from what happens next. This still matters, but keep it at the much lower level of the suspense plots used in playwriting (unless you're writing in the horror genre – there is an indie appetite for that). Emotional plots work well in the indie world and emphasis on them can approach that 90% level typically found in plays.

5. Emphasize interiors for locations. It's money again. You save a lot by not having to lug all that camera and sound and lighting equipment from one location to another and interiors are easier setups than exteriors. It takes hours to set up that equipment – even for a scene of less than a page – and while that's going on, time on the clock at the equipment rental shop is flying by. Interiors also solve the weather problem. Even when it rains, that equipment rental meter is still running on everything sitting in the van.

6. Use only a few locations. Locations are money. The fewer you have, the less it will cost to produce the film. John Sayles' breakthrough film, *Return of the Secaucus 7*, used only about six locations and roughly 80% of the action took place in the rooms inside a farmhouse.

7. Set the story in a location you know. Preferably where you live now or grew up. That helps insure the script will have the "feel" of the region, often an important element in indie success.

8. Be more generous with scene length. Since indie films tend to be character centered and often rely on one primary location for much of the story, scenes can easily run four or five pages without anyone thinking you don't get it.

9. Avoid special effects. These are death on indie budgets. No buildings blowing up, no elaborate car chases, no underwater shots, no kids morphing into werewolves.

10. Forget about genres. The indie world isn't necessarily opposed to thinking in genres, but you'll find much more interest in what your story is than what the genre is. Even if you have to fudge a bit, it's good insurance to have a genre – or a genre pair – ready to wave if asked.

11. Remember you're writing as part of a team. It's you and the director working on this together and it needs to be a real partnership for both of you to come out well at the end.

Indie Screenplay Competitions

When the script is finished (at least to your satisfaction) and if you haven't found a director to take it on, here are two options:

1. See if your state has a Film Office. (Also called a Film Board.) Many of these operations sponsor state-wide screenplay competitions. Recognition from the Virginia Film

Office competition led to feature production of Megan Holley's first screenplay, *Sunshine Cleaning*, released in 2008.

2. Enter the Sundance Institute's Screenwriters Lab competition. Submissions are currently accepted February 15 – May 1 for the following January lab. Submitting early in this timeframe is a good idea. As with everything in film, the competition is intense: About half of the 12 scripts selected come though this open submission process – the rest come from industry-related recommendations. The current $35 entry fee is well worth the price. (www.sundance.org/programs/screenwriters-lab)

Sundance says it's looking for the kind of script your playwriting DNA will probably lead you to write, one that "represents the personal vision of an artist and challenges and engages audiences in a truly original way." That sounds like the description of a playwright at work.

AFTERWORD – QUOTES ON CRAFT

Novelists, poets and playwrights make literature; screenwriters make changes. This is called collaboration. But someone has to go first, and the screenwriter hopes that the people who go second and third and fourth will remember the person who first stared down a blank page.
    -Scott Z. Burns

77. Playwrights & Screenwriters on Writing

I kind of worship at the altar of intention and obstacle. Somebody wants something. Something's standing in their way of getting it. They want the money, they want the girl, they want to get to Philadelphia – doesn't matter. And if they can need it, that's even better. Whatever the obstacle is, you can't overcome it like 'that' or the audience is going to say, "Why don't they just take the other car" or "Why don't you just shoot him?" The obstacle has to be difficult to overcome. And that's the clothesline that you hang everything on: the tactics by which your characters try to achieve their goal. That's the story that you end up telling.
　　-Aaron Sorkin

I began this collection of quotes on craft while writing the first edition of *Playwriting Seminars* and I've continued adding to it, drawing from playwrights, screenwriters, directors, producers, and a few ringers. The emphasis is on the U.S. though the UK and other European countries are also represented. The quotes range from those early in their careers to seasoned professionals.

The collection is included here as a source of inspiration, encouragement, and cautions from those who've been involved in the business of theatre as well as the film and television industry. Many of the quotes underscore concepts presented in *Playwriting Seminars 2.0*, but more than a few are purposefully included for offering alternate views on the craft of playwriting and screenwriting.

The collection is probably best approached as a series of Haiku-like lessons on dramatic writing and may be more helpful if sampled at intervals.

The Collection: 475 Quotes on Craft

'. . . writing is sometimes like going around poking at lifeless things to see if they move. At least for me. Other times, it's like digging to China, while simultaneously trying to reduce in oneself the sense of any enormous undertaking or burdensome obligation of really having to get there.' *Carole Eastman*

'I'm interested in people's darkness, and humor in the darkness, the humor in the shadows. I'm not literary, and I'm not academic, and I don't think like a poet, so my stuff will never be like that. I'm obsessed with how people talk.' *Tanya Saracho*

'I had a very simple idea and I think, through cowardice, I kept not seeing that through. I wanted a birth and a death and some allusion to the middle.' *Will Eno*

'It kind of screamed out for the gangster genre. It was kind of a mafia family. There was nothing that can take this guy down. The Hussein family almost mirrored the Corleones and that's how I framed it in the film.' *Lee Tamahori*

'After I learned how those old, well-made plays worked, my writing got so much worse. We know so many of those tricks already, they're in our subconscious, so I had to put the rules out of my head entirely. But then after that I went through a period where I was like, "Screw all the rules." I tried to be as weird as possible, and that was even worse – it was much less interesting.' *Annie Baker*

'The generation of my family that had young children in 1955 was filled with things that couldn't be spoken and I had to grow up piecing the stories together. There's something very exciting about having a dinner table conversation where the violence is all happening inside of "More potatoes?" All playwrights are subtext junkies and that gives me a lot of opportunities to work with.' *Jordan Harrison*

'This guy was not a hero [IN DARKNESS], yet he ended up doing the right thing, which to me is the true version of heroism. It's a difficult thing, almost counterintuitive, and yet people do it. We'd all like to think we would know what to do. But if I were in his shoes, would I have done those things?' *David Shamoon*

'Of course you care [about reviews]. I don't read them, but you don't really have to – you know what they are with the way people respond. There's nothing in the world more silent than the telephone the morning after everybody pans your play. It won't ring from room service; your mother won't be calling you. If the phone has not rung by eight in the morning, you're dead.' *David Mamet*

'Everyone thinks I was a sneaky girl who had this play produced over there [in London] because it was controversial. The fact was, the opportunity arose. I had acted in the director James Dacre's play three years before. I e-mailed him [THE MOUNTAINTOP], and a couple of weeks later he e-mailed me and said he'd convinced his theatre to do it. At the time I was working on a bare-bones workshop production here. After the workshop I flew to London and two days later was working on a full production – in a theatre over a pub.' *Katori Hall*

'I make my living now as a screenwriter! Which I'm surprised and horrified to find myself saying, but I don't think I can support myself as a playwright at this point. I don't think anybody does.' *Tony Kushner*

' . . . I was curious to see how close you could stick to real life without enhancing it or condensing it and still have it be viable as a piece of theatre. . . . I really wanted to stick as close to the truth as I could. Because that's kind of what [THE WAVERLY GALLERY] is about, that the main character is trying to make some sense of the nightmare that happened to his grandmother for which there's no comfortable answer, and he's just trying to get it down right as he tells it to the audience, at least try to do that. And in a way the whole play is about: what do people do in the face of something they can't do anything about?' *Kenneth Lonergan*

'. . . when I decided to be a playwright, I decided that I wanted to get black stories up on stage. And there are many, many, many stories, not just one. Not just everybody living in the delta South, or in the urban North. There are all these different variations in between. So to me, that is my responsibility: just getting all those stories up there, and not negating my voice.' *Kirsten Greenidge*

'I'm an undergrad . . . .. I read *M. Butterfly* by David Henry Hwang. I read *Six Degrees of Separation* by John Guare. I read *Zoot Suit* by Luis Valdez. I read that last one over and over. All three plays teach me about fluid dramaturgical structure, the evils of blackouts, and the need to meet media-saturated contemporary theater audiences on their own multi-faceted terms.' *Kristoffer Diaz*

'No one really wants you to tell them how it's done any more than you want to know how a card trick is done. If you want a recipe for banana bread, I'll leave three things out.' *Tom Waits*

'The toughest part [at the Sundance Theatre Lab] is winnowing the 30 semi-finalists to the end. I have to consider such things as balance, geography, genre diversity, the number of men versus women writers. Choosing those last seven or eight plays is very tricky. Something might literally grab me. I look for work that is very personal. I love language.' *Philip Himberg*

'When I read the article, I was touched by the tiger's death in a way I couldn't locate. I thought it was a tragic thing, which was strange because there were far worse things going on at the time. . . . Any fears about the ambition of [BENGAL TIGER IN THE BAGHDAD ZOO] had more to do with dramaturgy than politics. I've written a surreal story, so that allows me leeway as an artist to explore Iraq in my own way.' *Rajiv Joseph*

'I've been on a journey of exploration of self, through every piece that I've acted in and every play I've written. If I accept that my presence, because of the color of my skin, has some type of political meaning, wherever I enter, without having said a word, then with all of my work, what I've attempted to present are fully fleshed out human beings that break stereotypes, characters that anyone can see themselves in. Is that political? I think so.' *Regina Taylor*

'I'd been a playwright and for me, television had become essential to make a living. . . . But it really is a different experience. It requires you to think in a different way about the entire process of dramatic writing. Good theatre is so difficult to attain because there is so much fake-seeming theatre. Playwriting is the hardest kind of dramatic writing and it is the hardest for an audience to receive.' *Will Scheffer*

'I love writing movies, and they certainly help pay the bills, but if someone were to tell me I could never write another play, I'd quickly end up in the loony bin.' *Beau Willimon*

'When you decide to major in playwriting in college, aunts and uncles say, "Oh I hope one day we'll see your plays on Broadway." But the way you build a career in Chicago is very different. You don't necessarily think of Broadway as the light at the end of the tunnel.' *Lydia R. Diamond*

'I am a feminist, both by temperament and intellect, and my films are shaped by my outlook on life. However, I don't put political or moral lessons in my films. . . . The women in ANTONIA'S LINE are thoroughly themselves and not defined through their roles as wife, mother or daughter. Of course, the film is also a fairy tale.' *Marleen Gorris*

'There's a load of stuff in names.' *Michael Ondaatje*

'Theatre, film and television are all modes of storytelling, and many of us are fortunate enough to move freely among them without feeling that we've "left" or need to "go back" to one or the other. In fact, if the theatre is to avoid a brain drain, this kind of fluidity is increasingly necessary.' *Theresa Rebeck*

'[OPUS] came very quickly. I think part of the reason is it takes place in a contemporary world – one that I know well, one that I'm very passionate about – so I didn't have to, as I've done with some of my plays, do five or ten years of research on it. I like that this play followed Tooth and Claw, which took nine years from conception to production. I had to learn all sorts of biology and something about evolution and travel to Galapagos and do research on the various creatures there. It's got Spanish in it and Latin. Finally I thought, "Okay. Let's go indoors. Four chairs, five people, a world that I know."' *Michael Hollinger*

'I have rewritten [NEXT FALL] a bit. I've been working on the play for four years. I'm artistic director of Naked Angels and I'm so blessed to have that company at my disposal because it's allowed me to develop this play and rewrite and rewrite. I'm a big rewriter, tweaker. So I worked on it a lot over the four years. After every reading we did, every workshop, I just went back to the drawing table and refined and honed it.' *Geoffrey Nauffts*

'I think action should be revealed through character, so if you have a plot problem, it's probably a character problem. It's fun and easy to write language, but there were things I loved [in WE LIVE HERE] that I had to get rid of because they are no longer carrying their weight. My rewriting process has been a lot about taking away the explicit and letting the subtext speak for itself.' *Zoe Kazan*

'. . . my characters speak in subtext. In traditional plays, we're still in this moment of psychological realism that we've been in for a very long time. In that world, characters say one thing, but their intentions are different. So when actors are taught how to act, it's "Okay, so you're saying this, but what are you PLAYING? You're PLAYING the subtext." There's none of that in my plays. There's a unity of what the characters are thinking, feeling, and doing. They're acting on pure id.' *Thomas Bradshaw*

'I'm developing two new narrative features and one documentary feature. And shooting commercials because it's nearly impossible to make a living as an independent filmmaker.' *Malcolm Murray*

'The right and the left are always filled with self-justification. Writing about politics and belief is difficult because those of us who want to criticize politics are caught up in the very thing we're objecting to. We are that thing too.' *Lisa Kron*

'There's still a part of me that thinks, "And then we'll just go into this black-box theatre and put it up." That's probably why I'm so adamant in terms of the scenery. I feel like: "Just because I have a budget now, I don't want rotating sets. Please strip it down." I'm essentially trying to create a black-box [in a large theatre].' *Stephen Karam*

'I can feel the instrument blunting. I don't know if we could create SOUTH PARK today. We have it, and it's cool to build upon. But creating it? That takes the energy of a 25-year-old.' *Matt Stone*

'I can't answer [about the meaning of life] now, but give me some time to write a very long play in which nothing happens.' *Siri*

'It's such an old gripe, but you can have a really brilliant idea, and you can write a brilliant script, and you put in lots of material from your own life, and it just doesn't happen. Then TV people say, "But we'd love to hear what your next idea is. Can we have another one?" No, you can't. I'm not that kind of human.' *Nina Raine*

'People think that the only thing my plays are about is exposing hypocritical liberals and what's usually missing from this assessment, among other things, is that I'm something of a hypocritical liberal too. So I'm not just trying to unmask them. I'm trying to unmask me. I'm part of what I'm trying to expose.' *Bruce Norris*

'I have a cousin who lives a kind of transcendentalist, hippie kind of life. And he lost a friend about two summers ago, actually in a rafting accident. I really adore this cousin, and I was really thinking about this experience that he was going through – of being so young and suffering such a major loss. And I was also interested in just the way he's chosen to live his life kind of outside the mainstream. And then the other thing is that I have a grandmother who is in her 90's, who lives in the West Village by herself, and she has this very New York, older person's existence that I'm also really interested in. We're very close. So starting with those two characters I invented this play [4000 MILES], which was not at all based on any events or anything like that, but it was inspired by those two people.' *Amy Herzog*

'Today, [theatre is] more likely to be consciously not aimed at the public, but at a more sophisticated or educated public. . . . The result is that some of the sheer humanity has leaked out of the enterprise.' *Arthur Miller*

'I used to be very repressed about like, discovering stuff. I just thought the script was the script and the actors should be playing the actions written in the script. And as I've gotten older – and a little more experienced and a little less concerned with being great or something – I've had a lot more fun. And I think the worlds that I've been involved in with my plays have gotten a lot more interesting to me.' *Adam Rapp*

'Near the beginning of the play, on a very minor level it's actually a risk for Ben and Mary to have Sharon and Kenny over for dinner. That's the first instance where we see people stepping out of their comfort zone. It's exhilarating and terrifying to take a risk, and I actually think that regardless of what it leads to, the character ends up in a really interesting new place. In [DETROIT], a lot of these risks happen at a small, seemingly innocuous level. These characters often say yes before they think about it, find themselves in a new place, and are forced to readjust.' *Lisa D'Amour*

'The nice thing about a play is that you can luxuriate in dialogue, in a way you can't in movies. My concern in movies is to keep it moving.' *Andrew Bergman*

'Acting teaches me so much about theater. I played George in WHO'S AFRAID OF VIRGINIA WOOLF? in Atlanta. That's a play I have known intimately my whole life. But until you really crawl inside of it and see how it works, it's not part of you. I know I'm a better playwright as a result of acting.' *Tracy Letts*

'All the characters [in OUR CLASS], even the "villains," have profound human emotions. One can commit brutal violence and love his family. One can be a victim and not a very popular person. A survivor can turn into a bitter person, while one can become ashamed of a heroic deed.' *Blanka Zizka*

'When I was a student at Julliard, my teacher Marsha Norma told us, "Write about the thing that frightens you the most." I was in my 20s and didn't know what scared me. Then I got married and had a son. And when he was three, I heard about friends of friends who had children die suddenly. And I understood fear in a profound way. And Marsha's words came back to me. And that became the seed of [RABBIT HOLE].' *David Lindsay-Abaire*

'I have a new script that is at the beginning stages. I love being a writer/director and making art and graphics – all of these things at once. With BEGINNERS it was so amazing to be a writer director. I loved being able to write what I am filming and telling.' *Mike Mills*

'I read something a while ago that suggested that it's nearly impossible to write a theme. In my experience, that's true. You start out with a good story, and if things fall into place, the similarities and common threads sort of stand out on their own, and if you're lucky and have surrounded yourself with the right people, poof! It materializes on its own. (I make it sound easy, of course, as the threads usually only reveal themselves after far too many sleepless nights and chewed fingernails.)' *Chad Beckim*

'This kind of documentary theater work, to us, is about the subjects telling their stories in their own words. Our job is to shape the material, to give it dramatic structure, to turn conversation into dialogue and interview material into a play. But these are not our stories. They are the stories of the Iraqi civilians who we spoke with [for AFTERMATH], and our trying to insert ourselves into the material would have seriously undercut the very nature of the work.' *Jessica Blank & Erik Jensen*

'[ASUNCION is] about a writer obsessed with big issues but who doesn't do anything about them. I do what I like to do, explore parts of myself that I am embarrassed by. I grew up in an apolitical household. I never left the country. When I became an adult, I started traveling and became interested in politics, and I probably talked about things in a silly, ignorant way. So I explored this in myself and exaggerated it for comedic effect.' *Jesse Eisenberg*

'It was the idea of trashing places that I hooked on [for POSH]. It has a real metaphorical purity to it. The idea that I can go somewhere and do as much damage as I like because I can afford to pay for it afterwards seemed completely alien to me as a person, and to the class I come from. The characters are people who have been said "Yes" to for most of their lives. And the play puts them in a position where someone is saying 'No.'" *Laura Wade*

'I think that movies have changed the way we dream and therefore changed the way psychoanalysis works to interpret dreams. I think the form of cinema has penetrated people's heads so much that you have dreams where you have editing, you have soundtracks. You have things that wouldn't have existed in dreams before.' *David Cronenberg*

'As much as I wanted to write a really scathing, cynical and bitter play, the characters wouldn't let me. This thing about people helping other people kept coming in and eventually one or two other characters appeared and I realized that there's as much anxiety in one trying to form a new relationship as the horror of one ending. They both have their share of anxiety.' *Robert Glaudini*

'The origin of [36 VIEWS] was from the Japanese artist Hokusai's 36 Views. So the play actually started from an artifact from the Asian art world. From that I began to think about the issue of authenticity, not in terms of fake or authentic woodblock prints, but authenticity in a larger sense that includes issues of identity, love, and relationships with culture. The fact that Hokusai's project was to examine and depict the mountain from many different perspectives really spoke to me. There was something intrinsic in that effort, suggesting it is impossible to see something clearly and completely head on.' *Naomi Iizuka*

'If you just walked into a play called "That Pretty Pretty," that's a more decorative name than the play is actually. If it was just "The Rape Play," that sounds like a date-rape play. I struggled with the title for a while. Finding a title that was multilayered felt right – or at least a title that competes with itself.' *Shelia Callaghan*

'It's the worst plane flight in history, with 12,000 stopovers – Planes, Trains and Automobiles meets As I Lay Dying – I had never pitched a [TV] show before, and I had no idea what to do. I literally acted the whole thing out; I think my greenness sort of helped me.' *Rolin Jones*

'I'm about the least likely playwright possible. I did not grow up in a family of artists. I did not grow up watching theater. But when I saw my first play, I found the experience absolutely searing. . . . I'm not sure if I'm a born artist, but I think I was born with a couple of qualities that make being an artist possible. For one, I'm able to spend hours completely absorbed in my own thoughts. This doesn't make me a lot of fun, but it does enable me to cobble together made-up worlds, word by word. I also have a really strong imagination. In fact, the people and places I imagine can sometimes feel more real to me than real people and places.' *Julia Cho*

'I am the story. . . . The well-told partial truth to deflect the private raw truth.' *Spalding Gray*

'When people hear about this play [BLUE DOOR], they'll think, "Why would I pay money to feel beat up?" It was very important to me to put so much humor in the play because in the black community, there is so much humor, a great comedic tradition whether it is Richard Pryor or African American folk tales.' *Tanya Barfield*

'One [character in WEEKEND] represents this notion of freedom and struggle and fight against the mainstream, and one represents security and a comfortable life, just wanting to be like everybody else. . . . The root of the film for me is two characters trying to work out who they are and what they want from life, how they're going to fit that into the world around them and show the world they are those people. These issues aren't just about being gay. They're about how you define yourself in public and in private.' *Andrew Haigh*

'They're things in all the characters that come from my life. On the surface [Mitchell in The Marriage Plot] resembles me the most. But a lot of things that Madeleine does come from my life, or a lot of the things Leonard does and thinks comes from my life as well. They're just better disguised.' *Jeffrey Eugenides*

'I write for a few hours first thing in the morning, before I shower even, wearing clothes from the previous day, so that I can get as much done as possible before my brain turns on and stops me, by filling with doubt, brooding about the past, or coming up with ideas for things I can do with the rest of my day; I spend the rest of my day doing those things.' *Itamar Moses*

'No amount of great animation is going to save a bad story.' *John Lasseter*

'A lot of the subject matter [in THE DESCENDANTS] is heavy and tragic and sad and you have to counter that a little bit with some release . . ..' *Nat Faxon*

'[I wanted] to lift my eyes from my navel and look out into the world. . . . We're supposed to write three-character plays, with all white people, sitting in a room, talking about Mom. But I want to make an event.' *J. T. Rogers*

'I gave [film] audiences what they wanted – a chance to dream, to live vicariously, to see beautiful women, jewels, gorgeous clothes, melodrama.' *Ross Hunter*

'You know, when you're writing, you're always an absolute beginner. Each time . . . you sit by a blank page, you start from scratch.' *Leonard Cohen*

'With this script, I saw the cuts and the visuals better than before. Usually it had been about capturing what's on the page as faithfully as possible, but starting with ZOO it was about telling the story with visuals as well.' *Cameron Crowe*

'In general, the surface of TV is too flat, and there's no time for subtext.' *Richard Vetere*

'[Guillermo del Toro] has flourished by exploiting the dark side. He's also someone who very much is an optimist, a happy ending guy.' *Jeffrey Katzenberg*

'. . . above all, a work for young people must not talk down to its audience, because they can always tell. Kids are tougher than any theatre critic. They will easily expose a playwright who doesn't deliver a story that is tight as a trap but also lyrical, focused while being fast-moving, believable but still fantastic, while it challenges them and makes them question . . ..' *Frumi Cohen*

'I chose the title [YOU ARE ALL CAPTAINS] for its musicality, but for me it's a film about the cruelty of creation, which is undemocratic. We are all captains or have the right and opportunity to be, but it will be some more than others.' *Oliver Laxe*

'A lot of the research I did [for J. EDGAR] was to go to gay men living in Washington, D.C. who are in their 80s and 90s now and have them describe to me what the code was at that time. What you couldn't say, what you did to replace the hole in your heart where dating and love would have gone. If anything was consummated, it was not discussed because it was just too dangerous.' *Dustin Lance Black*

'We had never performed in a space bigger than a hundred people. If 100 people don't like your show, that hurts, but 640 people not liking your show? I didn't know if I'd be able to psychologically survive that experience.' *Greg Kotis*

'I'm getting a lot the question, "Why are you so interested in flawed protagonists?' I scratch my head at that because I think, aren't all protagonists flawed – the interesting ones anyway? Oedipus, Othello, Michael Corleone.' *Alexander Payne*

'There are things that happen in this film that are difficult to watch, but I don't want people to think of them as just devices. . . . [TYRANNOSAUR] is about the complexities of survival and the faces we put on to survive every day. You walk past people in the streets, or they serve you in shops, and you know nothing about the horrors they may be living with. You can't be too quick to judge. These people are heroic to me and I want to treat them that way.' *Paddy Considine*

'The question is, what are appropriate words and inappropriate words for network television, and what's the context? Was this appropriate in this context? Or are you creatively trying to find a way to use that word on the air?' *Don Ohlmeyer*

'Marriage is trivial compared to finding a good director.' *Erika Ritter*

'A television series is almost never the product of one writer locked in a room, banging out pages. It just doesn't work that way. That's a very romantic view of writing – in fact, it's certainly the view of writing that I always had growing up, wanting to be a writer.' *Steven Bochco*

'. . . what happened, of course, was that I was writing a play set in the 1940's that was supposed to be somehow representative of black American life, and I didn't have any women in there. And I knew that wasn't going to work.' *August Wilson*

'There's a big difference for the [theatre] audience in an evening that runs 3 hours and 25 minutes and one that's 3 hours and 5 minutes.' *Gordon Davidson*

'But there's another dynamic. It has to do with selling the screenplay. The people who are reading it have even less ability to visualize it than you do, and if you underwrite it, they won't get it at all. You have to learn how to write to be read.' *Danny Rubin*

'Do not think your story [for a one-person show] is unique. . . . your story is the same as millions of others. But that's o.k. You just need to find the one or two things that makes your story interesting enough to justify someone leaving their apartment and exchanging currency.' *Julie Halston*

'The issue in the entertainment field is profit, not race. For the powers-that-be in movies, television, and sports, the only criterion I have ever encountered in observing the decision-making process is money: what will bring the audience in and put people in the seats.' *Wallace Collins*

'Scriptwriting [for film] is the toughest part of the whole racket . . . the least understood and the least noticed.' *Frank Capra*

'The anger is there. But you can get your message across much stronger, I think, through humor and showing humanity. That's the only way an audience is going to come in. And if you're not going to get an audience, at the end of the day, your play is a dead duck.' *Ayub Khan-Din*

'If I'm feeling solitary I prefer fiction, but if I'm feeling public I prefer plays. But I tend to write both at the same time. I've written fiction longer and I can't conceive of not writing fiction. I can conceive of not writing plays. I don't think I would write plays unless I knew that there was a place where I could take them and have them produced. A book is a book, even when it's just on the page. But a play isn't finished until it's on its feet.' *Jim Grimsley*

'The first scene that got written was the strip club. I had this girl who is a stripper and I had this guy. I found out who she was; I found out who he was. I had two instruments, but the play didn't sing with just two. At one point, there were three couples, and then I realized I didn't need three; I needed two for a string quartet. It's kind of if A meets B, and then meets C, how's D going to feel about it? Some critics of the play have said it's algebra and not true to life. Of course it's not true to life; it's a play. It's kind of virtual reality.... I think that's why the play is called CLOSER, because it was the idea that the closer you get to someone, you might feel your own solitude more deeply.' *Patrick Marber*

'But usually, I'm the only audience in the room and I try to write just for me. As a result of some 19 years of teaching, of seeing a lot of plays in development, of being ill myself, and of witnessing death, I have far less patience. What I say has to be said – I call it the now we're two hours closer to death principle. . . . So I'm a little more aware of sort of cutting to the chase at the top of the play. Each time I sit down to write now, I feel a greater urgency. . . . The second I stopped trying to please the dramaturges of this country, the second I accepted that I wasn't going to get through the door – and I still haven't gotten through the door of a lot of places – the more I started writing for myself.' *Paula Vogel*

'. . . playwrights inherit a lineage, a family lineage, of great playwrights. We don't suddenly pop into the world as if we had no antecedents. . . . What one learns are not specific adages. Rather one learns to explore one's own mind, those corners of it which were previously illuminated by those great playwrights.' *Jean-Claude van Itallie*

'What I tell [playwrights] who are interested in joining us [in TV] is that you have to have a flexible spirit. You'll have to give up your disdain. And if you stick with it, you'll get a chance next week to do it again.' *Janet Blake*

'The condition of endless waiting is one that modern American playwrights share . . .. Don't spend your life waiting. You may not be an actor, but that doesn't mean that action is forbidden you. Playwrights can, with very little expense, mount readings of their work; they can band together with other playwrights for readings and discussions; and they can, if they want to, produce their work themselves.' *Tony Kushner*

'. . . I would like to write a piece about the influence, its dangers and its values, of a powerful and highly imaginative director upon the development of a play, before and during production. It does have dangers, but it has them only if the playwright is excessively malleable or submissive, or the director is excessively insistent on ideas or interpretations . . ..' *Tennessee Williams*

'[My screenplays] are not dark. Dark is a code word in Hollywood for un-commercial.' *Paul Schrader*

'I may write a play because I'm so upset about something that I have to say something. . . . I may want to write about someone in my family I love very much and want to memorialize. I may see someone walking down the street in a certain way. I'll imagine a whole life for that person and go home and write a play about this person who interested me because of the walk. Or I may be in a supermarket and hear a phrase.' *Megan Terry*

'Screenwriting is not an art form, it is a punishment from God. . . . I'm too much of a snob to be a screenwriter.' *Fran Lebowitz*

'. . . it was a tough adjustment [to film] because LOVE LETTERS thrives on, depends on, its simplicity. It's simply two people sitting at a desk reading letters back and forth. The fun of going to the play is letting the audience imagine the events they write about. With the movie, of course, you have to show all that . . .. It really became a very different thing.' *A. R. Gurney*

'. . .I found the characters trying to figure out the sort of questions that so many Chileans were asking themselves privately, but that hardly anyone seemed interested in posing in public. How can those who tortured and those who were tortured coexist in the same land? . . . And how do you reach the truth if lying has become a habit?' *Ariel Dorfman*

'Being a playwright of any race is difficult, and Lord knows it gets more difficult the further you get from the middle of the road.' *Suzan-Lori Parks*

'At the theatres I've worked with, people seem more and more convinced that New York theatre speaks only to an urban audience on very particular issues that are of very little relevance outside of New York, and that the issues that are tremendously meaningful in the rest of the country are of no interest in New York.' *Shirley Lauro*

'If some of the people in your family have been erased – for religious reasons or for what they have done – that means that part of yourself has been erased. . . . I was trying to restore [my great-uncle] in the book of life, and, ironically, the only way I could do that was to invent a life for him, a lie of a life, but it's the only life I can give back to this man.' *Sebastian Barry*

'The [solo work] process starts very early on with the initial ideas of what the show is going to be about, who the voices will be, and how those voices come together thematically and rhythmically. So, rather than jumping in when the script is finished, it's very much a cycle – the performer writing, my editing and suggesting, watching them improvising or reading more pages, workshopping it in front of an audience, then doing it all again.' *Jo Bonney*

'Part of learning about writing is learning how to distinguish your good stuff from your bad stuff. I write some perfectly awful stuff . . . . I write bad scenes, I mean, whole scenes that just don't work, that don't build, the people don't sound right. The important thing is to be able to recognize them, so they won't end up in the play.' *August Wilson*

'When they read my plays, people ask me all the time what horrible things must have happened in my childhood. Nothing horrible happened. Just mundane things that I perceived as horrible tragedies.' *Nicky Silver*

'As I get older, I need less and less. I think there are a lot of things I can miss, and I wont miss them. Like a lot of people who felt displaced when they were young, I crave domesticity. It's all there is, really. A warm, well-lit, quiet place, with someone listening and telling you stories at late hours. I can't think of anything better than that.' *Jon Robin Baitz*

'When, like today, I feel I have got a little, little way with a plot and knock off for the day, it is like a climber going up a sheer face who pitches camp on a narrow ledge. Tomorrow he may get no further; he may even roll off during the night.' *Alan Bennett*

'I've heard people comment on a play by saying, I didn't like that moment, it was out of character. I'd say that was probably the best moment, the moment that made that character believable. People have different sides to them, and that's what interests me.' *Edwin Sanchez*

'I've written plays where I didn't want my head to get in the way of my "point." But the only way to battle that sort of irony is to risk going too far. . . . That's the only shocking thing left – it's not nudity, it's not language – the only shocking thing left, frankly, is sentiment, to use our talents to tell the stories that we feel.' *Steven Dietz*

'[My dialogue in THE HOPE ZONE] is not a specific regionalism; it's made up out of Americanisms, a little Eastern Shore, a couple of other Southern things and stuff I've heard. To me, everything begins with how people talk.' *Kevin Heelan*

'I miss the city, but I don't need it anymore. By a certain age you're writing what you already know, and wherever you live, you take it with you.' *Arthur Miller*

'. . . if one goes by that criterion alone – that the more people understand it the better – then one can only reduce the language that you speak in the theatre to the language, for example, of a television series which does take the most reduced language to speak to people: the contemporary shorthand.' *Joseph Chaikin*

'I just wrote them the way that seemed right to me. I wasn't trying to write them in an understated way, a Japanese way. It just turned out to be my voice.' *Kazuo Ishiguro*

'Part of my job is to try and keep people interested in their seats for about two and a half hours; it is a very difficult thing to do . . . .. I want to make people feel, to give them lessons in feeling. They can think afterward.' *John Osborne*

'Though I may think I control my career, if I'm honest I know that what I am in complete control of is the blank paper. What happens there is not luck. I create a problem that didn't exist before and solve it to my own satisfaction. That's the creative process.' *Al Hirschfeld*

'The play is in the novel, it's just hidden. . . . If one is to be lucky in the task of adaptation, first find a novel that has a real play in it, for it's not so much the skill of the adapter as the skill of the novelist that creates success.' *Frank Galati*

'The MacGuffin, a term used by Alfred Hitchcock, refers to that element . . . that is a mere pretext for a plot. The MacGuffin might be the papers the spies are after, the secret theft of a ring, any device or gimmick that gets the plot rolling, The plot, moreover, is simply a pretext for an exploration of character. The MacGuffin itself has little, if any, intrinsic meaning. The MacGuffin, said Hitchcock, is nothing.' *Lorrie Moore*

'THE DUCHESS OF MALFI . . . Sex, murder, betrayal, politics, poison, kings, damnation, and salvation – all the things we really love! A good night out!' *Declan Donnellan*

'We like to label people and suddenly when something about a character doesn't conform with the label, we get somehow irritated. Once you can put a label on somebody, you can put it in a drawer and you are done with it. But when you discover a character has different aspects, that someone you thought was 100 percent bad turns out to be only 50 percent bad, then it becomes very puzzling and we want to argue about it.' *Milos Forman*

'Though obviously in a sense provoked by Miss Helen's story, I've never quite been hooked by it. I'm a fisherman and I know the difference between a fish that's just playing with your bait and one that says, Write! I'm It! and takes your rod down and you sit back and put the hook deep in.' *Athol Fugard*

'If one is making theatre, the issues have to be immediately visible to the audience, so one needs a carrier.' *Peter Brook*

'When I start writing the play – because I don't write from an outline – is when I have an idea where the play is going to arc to or land on . . .. With THE SISTERS ROSENSWEIG I wanted a woman to turn to a man and say "I love you like I've never loved anybody," a woman who's never said this before. That's not in the play, but it's where the play's going. In THE HEIDI CHRONICLES, I wanted this woman to get up at a woman's meeting and say "I've never been so unhappy in my life." Then I know that in fact it's a play, that it's starting somewhere and going somewhere.' *Wendy Wasserstein*

'I think all writers finally make their own rules . . ..When I first began writing, I instinctively knew what an obligatory scene was, but no one had ever told me in so many words what it was. I also found out that what is an obligatory scene to one person may not be the same thing to another person. We all have our own idea as to what that means. You know, the rules are not so mysterious.' *Horton Foote*

'I think it's an American thing that we're afraid of dark feelings. Americans don't like to confront the other side of things. Americans want to be entertained. I'm not interested in providing laughter, even though I like to laugh . . ..' *Jamaica Kincaid*

'I'm always exploring the rules. I want to know which ones are breakable and which ones are not. I'm convinced that there are absolutely unbreakable rules in the theatre, and that it doesn't matter how good you are, you can't break them. . . . The audience must know what is at stake; they must know when they will be able to go home.' *Marsha Norman*

'All my films have the same themes, albeit in different forms. My evolution is in the way I excavate the same themes. I suppose there's some autobiography, but it's totally deformed. It's fiction that interests me. But for this fiction to work, it is fed by distant experiences that return to the surface.' *André Téchiné*

'We're more reluctant to offer cues as to how the audience is supposed to react in different situations, which confuses certain people. It's not a question of not being willing to follow conventions . . .. It's just that there's nothing interesting to us about being as formulaic as a lot of Hollywood movies.' *Joel Coen*

'. . . people come to the theatre to be told the truth. I think that's where theatre's future lies. Whether they know it or not, people will continue to see theatre at its best as a place where the idiosyncratic voices of American dramatists can speak to them in a way which cannot happen in any other medium – not in cinema, not on television.' *John Weidman*

'In my work people are always trying to find a way out . . .. Some people complain that my work doesn't offer the solution. But the reason for that is I feel that the characters don't have to get out, it's you who has to get out. Characters are not real people. If characters were real people, I would have opened the door for them at the top of it – there would be no play. The play is there as a lesson, because I feel that art ultimately is a teacher.' *Maria Irene Fornes*

'I'd been writing plays for nearly 30 years when I wrote SERIOUS MONEY. . . . When I went off to write the play, the newspapers went on being full of City [Financial District] news and in particular the scandals involving the takeover of Guinness, and Boesky, the American arbitrageur. When I got the idea to write the play in verse, it gave me the theatrical purchase on the material that made it possible to write it.' *Caryl Churchill*

'In my writing I have looked back in time, at my parents and at my grandparents, who lived in Japan. I figured that if I told their stories I could move on to my own generation, and then on to speculating about what life might be like for the next generation of Japanese Americans.' *Philip Kan Gotanda*

'The play for me was so much about intermission, the terrible canyon between the two acts, and the film [adaptation] looks for what was in that canyon.' *Jon Robin Baitz*

'. . . I wasn't thinking in terms of cinema, but in terms of Shakespeare. He was never bothered by the fourth wall and realism, a thing I'm always trying to bust out of. He had scenes that lasted one page, two pages, a few lines here and a few lines there. He could move from place to place at will, and cover a lot of time. I think it's a model for how stories can be told again.' *Octavio Solis*

'I recall a time when for me theatre was an escape, a place where new worlds better than the real one could be imagined and built . . .. Then I discovered Ntozake Shange, Woodie King and Joseph Papp; Douglas Turner Ward, Barbara Ann Teer, Amiri Baraka – folks carving out new spaces, or reclaiming old ones but on new terms, their terms. Suddenly theatre wasn't a means of escape, but a viable tool for confronting issues and causing change to occur.' *Ricardo Khan*

'. . . there was no problem intermingling time frames or epochs. The golf course was one of the first few scenes that came to me. What would two doctors from different epochs be doing but playing golf?' *Lisa Loomer*

'We had an ending and a beginning to LA BAMBA which . . . seemed right on paper. . . . it was a stepping back and looking at the fifties from the perspective of the eighties. Our audiences told us they didn't want to come back into the eighties. They wanted to stay in the fifties. I had been trying on some level to alleviate the pain of Ritchie Valens' death, but audiences told us, Leave us with the pain. So that's where we left it.' *Luis Valdez*

'I'm a cancer, and every fortune-teller I've ever been to has told me that if I want to be truly creative I should be living by the water. (One even said that if I wasn't living in such a place, at the very least I should put a glass of water on my desk. I did, of course. For years.) The biggest problem, the one no fortune-teller ever gave me good enough advice about, was that for most of my life not only couldn't I afford to live by the water, I couldn't even afford to live within miles of a habitable shoreline.' *Larry Kramer*

'When I first started I read [every review]. Now I skim or ask to be told. Reviewers don't have time or space to do anything very meaningful so I've stopped looking for that. Frankly, it's only about good or bad business. . . . If reviews are good, they're never quite good enough, because they're not complex enough. If they're bad, they're just discouraging.' *David Rabe*

'Yes, there are farcical elements, but anybody who's had a tense family experience inside a small home knows what it means to have something going in the bedroom while something's going on in the kitchen. I really wanted to focus [in SONS OF THE PROPHET] on that pressure cooker time.' *Stephen Karam*

'By now, I am obviously aware that I have a predilection for . . . dealing with the painful and frustrating aspects of certain family and love relationships. . . . Those who have an affinity for these subjects – the low key description of strong emotions – will see them as variants on a theme. Those who are bored with them will say that I repeat myself.' *François Truffaut*

'Clearly even white mainstream theater could be more interesting, and more honest, if people of color were integrated into the drama rather than used as walk-on stereotypes.' *Anna Deavere Smith*

'. . . when the line/got too long she'd reach/one sudden black foreleg down/and paw at the moving hand . . .' *Philip Levine, A Theory of Prosody*

'As a playwright, I think you learn more from staged readings than from productions. You learn that if the words can't tell the story, all the other stuff is meaningless.' *Jack Heifner*

'I have never been about the business of doing feel-good theatre. I don't think all black plays need to be celebratory. I love and admire BRING IN DA NOISE, BRING IN DA FUNK, but I like dealing with darker aspects of what the African American experience has been for a lot of people. When so much of the male population is in prison, how can we be so celebratory, you know, when there are so many individual tragedies being lived and played out?' *Robert Alexander*

'For creation you need isolation. A certain piece of you has to stand still and listen. . . . The process of creation is an intimate and miraculous thing.' *George C. Wolfe*

'That little [play] was . . . the first text that I wrote in the same way in which I would later write all my novels: rewriting and correcting, redoing a thousand and one times a very confused draft that, little by little, after countless emendations, would assume definite form.' *Mario Vargas Llosa*

'Sometimes I'm not able to find the trajectory of an idea and carry it through to the end. [My director] is a truffle pig to an idea. He just ruts it out.' *Jon Robin Baitz*

'I'm in my prime right now [at 50]. I still have energy and some degree of youth, which is what a filmmaker needs.' *Alexander Payne*

'In this culture we want to simplify everything. U. S. playwrights work so damn hard to avoid criticism. That's why we avoid metaphor – because critics might say, Your play is so ambiguous. But that might mean it's rich in meanings.' *Steven Dietz*

'I think in recent years we've gotten to the point where plays can't be straightforward, where we're not even allowed to tell a story. We've gotten away from the simple, clear things in life. I don't think you can go wrong when you deal with that. When you're trying to be cryptic and super-intelligent, a lot of times what you're saying gets lost. There was one time when a reviewer said about OLD SETTLER, He's not a groundbreaking playwright, but he's a good storyteller. What's a groundbreaking playwright? Not that I aspire to be one, but I have no idea what one is even if I did!' *James Oseland*

'The reason I write, is my need to find out what I think and feel. Writing what I see, in a way that incorporates my reaction to what I see, helps me to live life.' *Amlin Gray*

'The audience was different in the 1930's. They expected a three-hour play, and in [J. B. Priestley's DANGEROUS CORNER] there was a lot of 'As you know . . .' The play doesn't need all that, and it still plays absolutely well.' *David Mamet*

'Before I wrote PICASSO AT THE LAPIN AGILE, I'd been going to the theatre in New York and every time, I could feel a little surge of energy. I hate to say it was a challenge but it was, to get those laughs, to even get those silences in the theatre. I also thought, What is it that I do best? Listen to the audience. . . . On a first play there's no ego at stake. If it's no good you can always throw it away.' *Steve Martin*

'I do a lot of history plays. But for me, history is a metaphor because things haven't changed. I wish these plays were archaic, set in time, but they're really set in transported time because we're still dealing with the same issues . . ..' *Carlyle Brown*

'The play writes itself. The first draft writes itself anyway. Then I look at it and I find out what is in it. I find out where I have overextended it and what things need to be cut. I see where I have not found the scene. I see what I have to do for the character to exist fully. Then I rewrite. And of course in the rewrite there is a great deal of thought and sober analysis.' *María Irene Fornés*

'With experience comes an ability to handle complex themes. You grow up and do mature work. . . . It's true that Hollywood is run by young people who see it more as a business than an art, and they will still market movies to 14-year-olds, but we [older directors] are a very powerful presence.' *Martha Coolidge*

'My only salvation is to write.' *Adrienne Kennedy*

'I'm what you call a pressure-cooker writer. I give myself ten days to two weeks to write a first draft because it's too terrifying to have an open amount of space. I make myself start on a given date and then I have a first draft.' *Naomi Wallace*

'. . . you [film critics] always overstress the value of images. You judge films in the first place by their visual impact instead of looking for content. This is a great disservice to the cinema. It is like judging a novel only by the quality of its prose. I was guilty of the same sin when I first started writing for the cinema.' *Orson Welles*

'You know absolutely everything about what you're creating, better than anyone else can ever know. . . . It's that thing, too real to be crammed into [a screenplay]. And yet, the only tools you have to relate it are sound and images. How those tools are used is what should be critiqued, but never the idea; that's when criticism becomes personal. . . . It is no longer a critique but an opinion.' *Darnell Martin*

'I've quit writing screenplay [adaptations]. It's too much work. I don't look at writing a novel as work, because I only have to please myself. I have a good time sitting here by myself, thinking up situations and characters, getting them to talk – it's so satisfying. But screenwriting's different. You might think you're writing for yourself, but there are too many other people to please.' *Elmore Leonard*

'. . . I felt that making her one-dimensional would be an insult to the audience, and also not as interesting. All destructive people have an inner side to them, and the more three-dimensional your characters are on screen the more compassion you can open up in an audience . . .. To me, that involves the audience more, it stimulates them and asks more of them.' *Richard LaGravense*

'I start on page one. I don't know where it's going to go, except in the most general sense. I didn't know how GEORGIA was going to end. I knew certain of the characters were going to be there . . ..'
Barbara Turner

'I usually write very few stage directions. I think a lot of that is a waste of time. The art of screenwriting is in its terseness, saying a lot with a little. I have no patience when I read a script where the writer describes this guy and what he's wearing and his glasses and his hair.' *Scott Frank*

'as a poet in the American Theater/ i find most activity that takes place on our stages overwhelmingly shallow/ stilted & imitative. that is probably one of the reasons i insist on calling myself a poet or writer/ rather than a playwright/ i am interested solely in the poetry of a moment/ the emotional & aesthetic impact of a character or a line. for too long now afro-americans in theater have been duped by the same artificial aesthetics that plague our white counterparts/ "the perfect play," as we know it to be/ a truly european framework for european psychology/ cannot function efficiently for those of us from this hemisphere.' *Ntozake Shange*

'Character arcs always seem to be a big issue with [film] studio executives . . . so the inevitable questions were posed: What was her emotional journey? How does she change? Is she a rich little snob who learns to embrace the less fortunate when she becomes penniless or is she a racist who becomes more liberal when she . . . yawn yawn yawn.' *Elizabeth Chandler*

'I'm interested in the way that the language of labor has been suppressed in our culture, the way it has disappeared from our vocabulary and is never heard on stage. . . . I'm better at writing than I am at organizing [political action]. SLAUGHTER CITY is my small contribution. If it gives people a voice it is worth something. So often we forget what we are no longer hearing.' *Naomi Wallace*

'. . . every time I went through U.S. customs, I was stopped. I'd tell them I worked in theatre. They'd search my bags as if I were involved in some illicit pornographic activity. I've given up now. I say I work in movies. No problem! Welcome to the U.S.A.! Good Luck!' *Stephen Daldry*

'. . . strange and fantastic things really happen. During a rainstorm in Australia, fish fall from the sky; several Southern states consider legislation that would make the licking of toads illegal; Lisa Presley marries Michael Jackson. You read these things and you think to yourself that realism may not be the best medium through which to express the real world.' *Karen Joy Fowler*

'I definitely write from a need to try, in my own two hours, to right a wrong. My little play is inconsequential in terms of whether or not we have health care, but it may affect the way people who see the play think about the issue.' *Lisa Loomer*

'The nervous system of any age or nation is its creative workers, its artists. And if that nervous system is profoundly disturbed by its environment, the work it produces will inescapably reflect the disturbances, sometimes obliquely and sometimes with violent directness.' *Tennessee Williams*

'The first time I went over to [my director's] house, he said to me, This is a very strange play. I was pleased that he reminded me of that. [He] understands [VENUS] intellectually and emotionally and the humor, the funny bone.' *Suzan-Lori Parks*

'. . . I don't really think of myself as a director. I started directing plays because nobody would direct my plays.' *Richard Forman*

'Be honest and accept the consequences; be creative and accept the consequences . . .. And above all, if you choose the path of the artist, understand that life is a risk.' *Jesús Urzagasti*

'. . . I felt I was finally in a position to affect not only the artistic content of the American theatre, but also its institutional structures. This has been an important goal of mine, as there have always been a variety of issues – artistic freedom, author's rights, access by minority groups – which have concerned me and even influenced my decision to become a playwright in the first place.' *David Henry Hwang*

'Belonging to the Dramatists Guild Council where, with my fellow dramatists, I can directly affect (and protect) the professional lives of all American playwrights has always made me feel that I am returning as much to the theatre as I withdraw. Because only playwrights can ensure the well-being of playwrights. No one else will do it for us.' *Peter Stone*

'In some plays, there's a buildup, growing and growing, and you really don't want to break it. In that case, eliminating the intermission is advantageous. It's about wanting to engage people, not letting them go.' *Richard Nelson*

'Very few people who met my adoptive mother in the last 20 years of her life could abide her, while many people who have seen my play find her fascinating. Heavens, what have I done?!' *Edward Albee*

'Unless I write something, anything, good, indifferent, or trashy, every day, I feel ill. To me the only good reason for writing is to try to organize my scattered thoughts of living into a whole . . ..' *W. H. Auden*

'Sometimes I'm sorry I ever came across the magic realism label. I just think of it as an interesting approach to theatre . . . an extra tool in the box, an incredibly effective and poetic method of accessing a character, of getting at the truth. . . . If you choose the details of everyday life carefully enough, and examine them with enough clarity, they can seem magical on their own. Like Garcia Márquez says, the human condition is so absurd, and people are so outrageous, that insane things happen on a daily basis. All you really have to do is record them.' *José Rivera*

'I don't consciously start writing a play that involves issues. After it's done, I sit back like everyone else and think about what it means.' *Suzan-Lori Parks*

'My style as a human being is to indulge people who need to escape, yet I insist on confronting them as a playwright. It's quite embarrassing, it's quite unpleasant, it's quite awkward.' *Wallace Shawn*

'How you get work done is by exploiting yourself and your feelings, and sometimes people get in the way.' *Carrie Mae Weems*

'I know lovely people, but I see their faults. I see their mistakes. If I would write a story about them, I would show it all. I would not censor myself in order to make a group happy. . . . Writing about people implies faults as well as admirable qualities. The exclusion of one from the other for the sake of satisfying desperate people is preposterous, or worse.' *Silvia Gonzalez S.*

'We live in an age where quantity is seen as preferable to quality, and many people tend to work in a horizontal line: next, next, next. But if you do that, you never investigate the vertical line – the depth of the piece.' *Simon McBurney*

'In all, I've had 18 plays produced, but I'm still considered an emerging playwright. I haven't been served by the mainstream theatre at all. . . . I do theatre because I'm passionate. Believe me, I've wanted to quit as many times as you have, but I haven't given up. And I'm not going to.' *Robert Alexander*

'There's nothing personal in it. I'm not ever inclined with any of the plays to say, This is about that, because plays are about the whole event that they are. . . . I was certainly wanting to write a play about damage – damage to nature and damage to people, both of which there's plenty of about. To that extent, I was writing a play about England now.' *Caryl Churchill*

'I haven't had a single moment of terror since they told me [I was dying]. My only regret is to die four pages too soon. If I can finish, then I'm quite happy to go.' *Dennis Potter*

'During the life span of baby boomers . . . we have come to be ruled by a shadow (now no longer secret) government of spy agencies, right wing billionaires and military fanatics. Our oceans have been turned into chemical dumps, half the world's rain-forests have vanished, holes have appeared in our ozone layer, and our hopes for the future have been buried under a steadily mounting pile of unimaginable weapons. During the same period, a single topic has dominated the American stage: personal relationships.' *Joan Holden*

'In writing HOMER G., I let myself go. The play is an archeological dig. It's also a personal journey, and a personal yearning I've had about the sensitivity of severance. . . . I wanted to do a piece that begins a reweaving, that looks into our most ancient past to the Homeric story of Troy – and to do it in a hip-hop way.' *Ifa Bayeza*

'For me, writing plays is far more an act of the mind than of the emotions. It's a very different kind of impulse than fiction writing.' *Jim Grimsley*

'This was a very mean play when I wrote it. It's still mean, but what I learned along the way, mainly from my wife, was that the other side of the coin had to be expressed. So the character of the Rabbi, who represents moral objection to violence, legitimizes that position and gives the issue balance.' *Ernest Joselevitz*

'. . . the highest meaning in life for me is to do the kind of theatre that touches people, that raises people's consciousness, that inspires. But I work in an industry in which you don't always get that kind of opportunity. So, in terms of working in Hollywood and elsewhere, I see myself doing mercenary work. I suit up wherever they need me, I go around and make the money – then I come back hopefully to try to realize the dreams that I have about touching people's lives with true art theatre.' *Shabaka*

'I like having to deal with the facts of the case. I couldn't make up who the Klan and the Nazis are. I had to look the real devil in the face and say, 'Who are you?' I felt that if I could make this story powerful on stage – and that can be very hard because sometimes real life is not as theatrically exciting as what you can write – if I could distill and juxtapose and theatricalize this story well enough, the impact would in the end be stronger than if I'd made it up.' *Emily Mann*

'[Their journey in *The African Queen* is a symbolic] act of love.' *James Agee*/'Oh, Christ, Jim, tell me something I can understand. This isn't like a novel. This is a screenplay.' *John Huston*

'Prolific? I don't experience it that way. To make a film every year is not such a big deal. It doesn't take that long to write a script. I write every day. I'm very disciplined. I enjoy it. It takes a month, two months to write a script. . . . I have a perfectly sedate life. I wake up, do my treadmill, have breakfast, then I write and practice the clarinet and take a walk and come back and write again and turn on the basketball game or go out with friends. I do it seven days a week. I don't travel much. I could never be productive if I didn't have a very regular life.' *Woody Allen*

'TV and film work is pure craft. It's like building a table. No matter how well you build it, how well you carve the legs, it will always be a table. Because I have to outline my TV and film work, because I have to write scripts to the page count, I tend to be less structured in my playwriting. I simply let myself go where I go.' *Sally Nemeth*

'The hardest thing for me as a playwright in the early days was to figure out how to be a poet and a writer for theatre at the same time – to write in a way that involved an interrogation of language, and also was germane to what was going on in the world. If art's not contemporary, then it's geezer theatre; it's embalmed from the start.' *Mac Wellman*

'Well, what I really wanted to do [in THE DYING GAUL] was to write a tragedy. There have been many critical discussions about whether it's possible to write a tragedy within our culture since we don't believe in fate the way the Greeks did nor in tragic heroes the way the Elizabethans did. So I tailored the idea of a tragedy to my own sensibility, creating a character who is potentially noble – in my view, not Shakespeare's or Arthur Miller's view – and then I constructed a sequence of events that lead to this character losing his soul, which is my idea of a tragedy.' *Craig Lucas*

'I'm drawn to [directing] plays and screenplays that are about people in situations, not situations that simply have people in them.' *Scott Elliott*

'I don't believe in a message. I think it would be disastrous if you could say what the message of HAMLET was. Even with a minor play, everyone is going to come away with something different depending on if they've just left their lovers or if they've just had a child or if they've just been fired.' *Beth Henley*

'. . . the trouble is, show business peddles the sentimental piety that you can always get over your problems. To go to the theatre and be told, No, there are certain problems which you cannot get over – grief, separation, loss, aging, the need to part from people you love – to go to a play where these things are faced seems to me to be a bracing way to spend an evening, not a depressing one.' *David Hare*

'I see something, find it marvelous, want to try and do it. Whether it fails or whether it comes off in the end becomes secondary. . . . So long as I've learned something about why.' *Alberto Giacometti*

'[Rewriting is] a whole other art form; it's about craftsmanship.' *Sam Shepard*

'What is absolutely true is that any good [television] series has a specific voice. And I think that voice is almost exclusively the domain of the executive producer. . . . As a staff writer you're not being called upon to be the great creative person. You're sort of called upon to understand the characters and their voices and put them through certain paces.' *Howard Gordon*

'If you're a writer on a [film] set and make a suggestion, it's treated as if the caterer had made a suggestion. But if you're the director . . . then that's it. Actually I didn't like that so much. I wanted to pull opinions out of everybody.' *Doug McGrath*

'No comedy, no matter how many jokes you put in, will work if it doesn't have a story. . . . Make it real, then make it funny.' *John Markus*

'I have a little problem when [TV] shows are about nothing. After a while, minutiae can be stretched only so far.' *Matt Williams*

'[The producer] said, I want you to write a family [TV] show with kids and animals. I thought, Oh, great. The two things they always warn you about.' *Pam Long*

'Every film I have made has corresponded to a very special moment of my life. I like to think that if someone wanted to reconstruct the story of my life, they can just see my movies and know what I have been through.' *Bernardo Bertolucci*

'[The director's idea for the film was:] A young American or English girl goes to Tuscany to visit English expatriates. She is on a mission to lose her virginity. That's a mission easily accomplished, if that's the only mission. The story had to be more complicated than that. Because there is so little happening dramatically, there had to be something to keep you curious.' *Susan Minot*

'I had no agenda in writing this play except expressing myself. . . . It later occurred to me that I was not only announcing things to my family; I was announcing it to the world. Of course, if the play had been a flop, only my family would have known.' *Mart Crowley*

'Cinema is a literature of images. Theatre is a literature of ideas. . . . If you go 20 seconds without dialogue on the stage, you've had it.' *Peter Glenville*

'I wrote to write, out of my guts and my heart. I wanted to cause some kind of wonder in the minds of people. I don't rant or rave about the terror of our racist society. It is never directly stated, it is just there.' *Lonne Elder*

'I was so mad at my agent. I had polished and polished and polished [the play], and he referred to it as a draft. I wrote him a bitter letter: How can you call this a draft? I don't do drafts! By now I've done 18, and its turning, in the rehearsal room, into a 19th.' *Cynthia Ozick*

'I was talking to one of the writers about our target audience, and he was insulted that I used that term. But if you're given $60 million to make a film you'd better know who your target audience is. That's who's going to pay back the bills you run up.' *Michael Bay*

'Writing dialogue, playing with words on a page, has almost the tactile pleasure of molding clay. It's not the concrete word per se that has meaning for me but its infinite possibilities, like building blocks in the hands of children. With words I can create metaphor which is my way of shouting to the world.' *Rachel Feldbin Urist*

'Independent films will probably kill themselves off by virtue of their own success. With a crossover hit like PULP FICTION, the criteria by which art-house movies are produced and marketed and exploited have changed. With studio money and overheads and budgets and deal-making machinery, a certain kind of narrative structure and popcorn-type payoff start infusing themselves.' *James Schamus*

'I want to say something about people, not necessarily about male-female relationships – although that's where people often show themselves most clearly. Between the lines, I want to say something general.' *Sönke Wortmann*

'Heroes? Don't believe in them.' *Sam Fuller*

'What is a screenplay? 120 pages of begging for money and attention.' *James Schamus*

'It's hard to give a dramatic shape to even the most dramatic life. . . . you are forced not just into selectivity, but into alteration, distortion and outright lying about what did and didn't happen.' *James Toback*

'I don't write [screenplay character] biographies beforehand. I usually go in knowing some sequences: this is where I want to start, this is where I want to end.' *John Sayles*

'I've always been drawn to writing historical characters. The best stories are the ones you find in history.' *Tony Kushner*

'Most people spend their lives trying to avoid criticism, but criticism is part of the game. The only way to avoid it is to stick your play in a drawer and not show it to anybody.' *Marta Praeger*

'Most television shows are not written; they're rewritten, by a crew of 12 different writers.' *Sam Henry Kass*

'I was taught to lie at a young age. . . . I think that [A PARK IN OUR HOUSE] describes what people make out of their reality in a totalitarian system like Castro's. They take flight and move into the imagination in order to transcend their immediate reality. I had to write this play. It helped me understand my own loss of innocence.' *Nilo Cruz*

'When I got to the end of this play, I realized I was trying to make Angel do something that had not been justified by the characters and by their story . . . .. I kept trying to force it, but that doesn't work. So I had to come to terms with what it meant for me to create a character who doesn't triumph.' *Pearl Cleage*

'I think in this country we're committed to developing plays, and many plays I've seen have been rewritten too much. The scenes are tight, the play ends at the right time, you know exactly what the scene is about, but it seems flat; you can almost see that too many hands have been on the play. The individual voice is gone.' *A.R. Gurney*

'. . . don't rewrite unless you know what you're trying to do.' *Craig Lucas*

'The play is really a kind of nightmare. It ought to flow rapidly and effortlessly from one moment to another. In London, we had difficulty with the set, which required too much effort to move around. Having gotten the benefit of seeing it done once, I wanted to work on the script, to make it sharper and more pointed.' *Arthur Miller*

'However much I may like to talk about or be interested in a more philosophical or moral agenda, [film] is, ultimately, about narrative. And it's about telling stories that are engaging and dramatic.' *Ed Zwick*

'. . . I wrote a letter to Thomas Pynchon asking, Can I have your permission to try to make an [adaptation] of your book? And I had no idea that he would answer me, because he's pretty elusive. But he did send a letter back that said, Yes, you can do that as long as the only instrument in the opera is a banjo. I thought, That's an interesting way of saying No.' *Laurie Anderson*

'. . . the whole idea of WHAT HAPPENED WAS . . . is not about dating. It is more about people who are not committed to who they are or are indifferent about their life in general, which is how I felt about myself when I wrote it. I had turned 40 and I was unhappy and I wanted to write about that. Dating just became the framework.' *Tom Noonan*

'I'm not interested in [producing] formula films. . . . The great problem of the job is that you say no to 98 percent of the stuff. We have to spend 60 percent of our time on stuff we're planning to make, and 40 percent on rejecting the rest.' *David Aukin*

'TRUST took as its starting point the question, What would happen if a movie took the character of a teen-age girl seriously?.' *Hal Hartley*

'[Hollywood] studios are handing out money to make independent films now, but they all want the same thing. They want the style and the deadpan delivery of RESERVOIR DOGS or FARGO and so they imitate those movies. They want PULP FICTION, but they get it all wrong! They get the detachment, but that's it. And then it's all about style, and in the end what do you learn about the characters? Nothing. You learn you wasted two hours.' *Stanley Tucci*

'I firmly believe in and support everyone's right to freedom of artistic expression. STEEL MAGNOLIAS is my artistic expression, and it is my right to say that its female characters be portrayed by women. The concept of a play set in a beauty parlor where men portray women is a terrific idea. If that is someone's artistic expression, I encourage them to write their own play as soon as possible.' *Robert Harling*

'I do not make films which are prescriptive, and I do not make films that are conclusive. You do not walk out of my films with a clear feeling about what is right and wrong. They're ambivalent. You walk away with work to do. My films are a sort of investigation.' *Mike Leigh*

'This is a craft where the only pure version of the movie is the one that exists in your mind when you write your first draft. For that golden time, it's yours, and you see this movie that no one has seen and nobody knows about. Unfortunately, that is not the draft that is going to be filmed.' *David Newman*

'All my fiction – short stories, novels or plays – began as personal experiences. I wrote those works because something happened to me, because I met someone or read something that became an important experience for me. I am not always aware of the reasons why a particular experience remains in my memory with such vividness, nor why an experience gradually becomes a source of encouragement to invent or fantasize about.' *Mario Vargas Llosa*

'The strange power of art is sometimes it can show that what people have in common is more urgent than what differentiates them. It seems to me it's something that theatre can do, but it's rare; it's very rare.' *John Berger*

'I thought Jane Austin would be a good collaborator because she writes, you know, superb dialogue, she creates memorable characters, she has an extremely clever skill for plotting – and she's dead, which means, you know, there's none of that tiresome arguing over who gets the bigger bun at coffee time.' *Douglas McGrath*

'The avant garde is somebody rediscovering the classics.' *Robert Wilson*

For the collection, I am like a painter or a writer. I may or may not be a character in my own story.' *Sonia Rykiel*

'. . . what drew me to theatre was precisely the opportunity it provided to join word and image, word and action, to force language to encounter the three dimensions of the theatrical space.' *Beth Herst*

'People's relationship to what they want from theatre is changing. People, including me, are still looking for the next STREETCAR NAMED DESIRE. And people can't or won't write that anymore.' *Austin Pendelton*

'I get frustrated and I leave the theater, but I come back because I know there's an audience to whom I have an obligation. There are people who desperately want to hear something that clarifies reality for them, that lights them, that makes them cry. They want to cry. They want to feel. They want to see themselves on the stage. And I keep coming back, I guess, because I – when I leave, I become a part of that audience and then I want it, too.' *Ntozake Shange*

'In five days we had the [TV series] pilot pitched out. We had seven characters fleshed out. . . . This kind of thing takes a certain amount of good fortune, and lots of money. I wouldn't recommend the process to just anyone.' *Diane English*

'The dramaturge is the [playwright's] best friend. That doesn't mean you get to walk down the aisle.' *Jack Viertel*

'. . . as far as the regime is concerned, well, the play is sheer terror for them. Because they feel, How dare, how dare anybody lift his or her voice in criticism against us? We have the guns. Their level of paranoia and power-drunkenness is unbelievable.' *Wole Soyinka*

'One of the things about what . . . I do – writing plays – is that a poll is not taken before you say, Well, I'm going to write this because I think that you're going to like this and therefore you'll buy a ticket for this.' *Wendy Wasserstein*

'[Henry] James is much more complex than Jane Austen. That's why it's not so easy to adapt him. People expect a nice period piece, but that's not always the case. There's a deep human mystery in his work.' *Agnieszka Holland*

'There are times when the people you have nurtured come up with a play that is not necessarily their best work. But they feel very strongly that it should be seen, and you've nurtured it in the development process, and you become slightly blinded to it, because you believe in [this playwright]. Yet the public doesn't understand that some writer's trying something new and you want to support that. It's the downside of the development process.' *Carole Rothman*

'[Using humor to explore serious issues] disarms people. It's a way in. It's gentle, but at the same time it's subversive, and I like that duality.' *Lisa Loomer*

'I now know that to do a worthwhile family history I must interpret the past without falling into either demonizing or unquestioning acceptance. . . . As a playwright, what I object to right now is any form of fundamentalism, whether it's nationalistic, religious or ethnic. . . . I think it is ridiculous – and fundamentalist, by the way – to say that I am not changed by the culture around me.' *David Henry Hwang*

'The most important playwright's gift is to hit your time and speak to your time.' *David Hare*

'On their own, each [character] is a victim of no importance. But when you bring them together, they become a dangerous weapon. Jeanne is the vowel and Sophie the consonant. Psychologists know this phenomenon well. Each individual is harmless, but together they create an explosive chemical reaction. It's like Bonnie and Clyde, like Thelma and Louise.' *Claude Chabrol*

'The plays I find most interesting are the plays I don't understand when I read them on the page.' *Marcus Stern*

'I was not interested in doing the plot of OEDIPUS in blackface. I did wonder, what would these people have been like if they hadn't been in that situation? . . . One could look at Oedipus, or at my character Augustus, as a cynical schemer who did everything because he was hungry for power. But that's just too easy. I'm more interested in how humans can embody conflicting goals and emotions.' *Rita Dove*

'It's interesting during these lean times that one of the jobs of playwrights and directors is figuring out how to do huge epic things, and then solving everyone's problem of: wait, I need both of these characters but we do not have the bodies because we cannot afford the bodies or we don't have the rehearsal space.' *Alison Carey*

'You have to decide at what point you're willing to please people in order to get your play on and at what point you don't care if they do it or not.' *James Houghton*

'White male playwrights' works continue to dominate production slates. Sometimes it seems easier for them to have the texts of their driver's licenses produced than for the female or non-white playwright to have her best play produced. The reality is, they are more often given that all-important opportunity to fail than the women's play or ethnic play.' *Velina Hasu Houston*

'I always thought that playwriting was supposed to be a lonely process. That's why they invented alcohol – liquid balm for poor shlubs like Sophocles . . .. Those, of course, were the good old days when . . . it was presumed that you knew what you were writing about. They respected your voice. For some reason, partly to do with money, partly to do with the influence of Hollywood, and partly from an arrogance inherent in the patronage system, playwriting has become more like screenwriting, a group exercise.' *Steven Leigh Morris*

'Now, creatively, what is the result of adapting my own plays for the screen? . . . I have been able to create the characters and write the scenes taking place in locations I only referred to on stage. What have I lost? Some favorite dialogue and the length of some scenes.' *Richard Vetere*

'When I'm asked whom I write for, after the obligatory, I write only for myself, I realize that I have an imaginary circle of peers – writers and respected or savvy theatre folk, some dramatic writers and some not, some living, some long gone. . . . Often a writer is aware as he works that a certain critic is going to hate this one. . . . You don't let what a critic might say worry you or alter your work; it might even add a spark to the gleeful process of creation.' *Lanford Wilson*

'So here's the tough question. Is all this [development] activity making great plays and great playwrights? With notable exceptions, I submit to you that it is not. . . . Play development leaves playwrights at the mercy of directors, producers, actors and dramaturges who are ill-prepared to do more than give subjective responses to the play – and playwrights are ill-prepared to sift though this feedback.' *Roberta Levitow*

'I thought if I can do something more playful and light like my play BEYOND THERAPY, it might be a money maker. I think one of the reasons BEYOND THERAPY has legs – it's been very successful for me around the country – is because it's a friendly play, rather sunny.' *Christopher Durang*

'I'm back in fashion again for a while now. But I imagine that three or four years from now I'll be out again. And in another fifteen years I'll be back. If you try to write to stay in fashion, if you try to write to be the critics' darling, you become an employee.' *Edward Albee*

'And how deeply do I let business considerations affect [screenwriting] choices that might otherwise be more or less esthetic? . . . Do I choose the upbeat rather than the downer ending because I know it will score better at the preview? Can the idea be sold in a single sentence? Can it compete with space aliens and tornadoes and missions impossible?' *Edward Zwick*

'The fear of a work becoming dated is one of the most effective tools for keeping people from writing political work.' *Tony Kushner*

'I am not a historian. I happen to think that the content of my mother's life – her myths, her superstitions, her prayers, the contents of her pantry, the smell of her kitchen, the song that escaped from her sometimes parched lips, her thoughtful repose and pregnant laughter – are all worthy of art.' *August Wilson*

'I always believed that when you wed passion to craft, there was a certain alchemy. For me, that has only happened in playwriting.' *Luis Alfaro*

'I am very, very aware of my place in the continuum that goes back two thousand years. I'm very proud to be like one of the soldiers in the army that Aeschylus started. Some of the greatest learning experiences I ever had were simply reading classics, reading Brecht and Chekhov over and over.' *José Rivera*

'. . . passion and commitment and humanity, those are the things that get you to write seventeen drafts of a play.' *Edit Villarreal*

'If this were a [Hollywood] studio film, I wouldn't have pushed my father into a table, I would have beat him up. My father wouldn't have kissed my girlfriend; he would have raped her.' *Noah Wyle*

'What was once a cottage industry dedicated to the discovery and development of new voices and works has become instead the raison d'etre for many a playwright's existence . . .. And since readings have become playwrights' main source of exposure, the nature of playwriting has changed to fit readings' needs. Investigation into what is eminently theatrical has been substituted – more and more these days – by what can simply come across and read well.' *Caridad Svich*

'I know there are writers who get up every morning and sit by their typewriter or word processor or pad of paper and wait to write. I don't function that way. I go through a long period of gestation before I'm even ready to write.' *Wole Soyinka*

'[Nixon] reduced the meaning of his life to nothing but power. In the film, we gave this sad figure consciousness of what he was. We weren't right to do that – I don't think he did have that consciousness. But we did it for movie reasons – to create empathy.' *Oliver Stone*

'It's very hard with cutbacks not to feel that our theatres, our work, is not as important as it should be. . . . But I also know that nothing creates vital theatrical energy like anger.' *Wendy Wasserstein*

'I'm mixed about [Elia] Kazan. The argument is about two rights, which is much more interesting than a wrong and a right, because then you're just beating someone up.' *Mark Kemble*

'I thought if I was going to live a life in this land I was accidentally born on, I must people it; I must have a history. . . . I'm looking for these people inside me, wherever they may be; that is my form of research.' *Sebastian Barry*

'I'm a little compulsive and not too messy, so there may be 30 drafts before I'm through. . . . When I start writing, I have a quiet panic that I won't remember how. It's important to leave off knowing what I'm going to say the next day.'' *Susanna Moore*

'Even some of us who make movies underestimate their influence abroad. American movies sell American culture. Foreigners want to see American movies. But that's also why so many foreign governments and groups object to them.' *Irwin Winkler*

'Character interests me more than narrative. I make the narrative up as I go, which is more fun anyway.' *Mac Wellman*

'. . . when they say that [Hollywood] studios don't care about quality, that studios are stupid and couldn't tell a good-quality script from a bad-quality script, that's facile and not accurate. The focus of our efforts has got to be on the mainstream. The size of these companies, the amounts of money you spend to make and market a film, our agenda of distributing these films all over the world – with the size of the staff we have – puts the bulk of our attention on making movies that will be accessible to as many people as possible.' *Joe Roth*

'You have more and more people coming into the tent with the creative guys [on Hollywood films]. You have marketing and concept testers, advertising people. What you find gets the high numbers is easily appealing subjects: a baby, a big broad joke, a high concept. Everything is tested. The effect is to lessen the gamble, but in fact you destroy a writer's confidence and creativity once so many people are invited into the tent.' *James L. Brooks*

'I'd been reading Daniel Defoe's *Journal of the Plague Year* when the riots broke out and I began to see them both – L.A. and the London plague – as the same event. A time of crisis. A time when rich and poor get thrown together – and, suddenly one sees alternatives. I began to think about what happens when the containment of a presumed danger through the regimentation of space breaks down, such as when South-Central L.A. began to invade Beverly Hills.' *Naomi Wallace*

'Nobody goes into [Hollywood] to sell their soul. The truth is, people give it up for free.' *Emma-Kate Croghan*

'We're one of the last handmade art forms. There's no fast way to make plays. It takes just as long and is just as hard as it was a thousand years ago.' *Steven Dietz*

'I thought I would write something that would make some people uncomfortable. . . . What intrigued me, I think, was the idea of women of my own generation who were successful, intelligent, coming to power and suddenly in the public arena. I started to think about what they are allowed and what they are not allowed.' *Wendy Wasserstein*

'I was presenting an ideal of society that was completely lost to many people in today's audience. . . . Audience members who lived though that period were crying, while younger people had no idea that such a level of idealism existed – the show was a history lesson for them. And yet there were plenty of laughs, for the humor of the show is based in story and character – the intellectual, powerful man, the impulsive, intuitive woman, and the observer. It helps that all three are based on real people, but they're also classic types.' *Linda Griffiths*

'Traditional notions of what constitutes a solid screenplay involve setting up events, making them pay off later, measuring when to resolve what story line – in other words, a large part of it is mathematics. Playwriting seems to me the very opposite of screenwriting: One keeps going at an idea, chipping away at its surface, not much concerned with how claustrophobic or confined something might be. One keeps looking for new approaches to the thing.' *Jon Robin Baitz*

'My frustration with a lot of new writing is that it's so unambitious for the form of theatre. It may or may not be good writing; that's perhaps immaterial. But it's been written by people you feel are happy with the wrong, traditional, conventional theatre form or, indeed, disappointed by the theatre, a bit cross, and would rather be writing a film than writing a play.' *Deborah Warner*

'. . . I think the theatre is a place for community discourse on important matters, ethical and moral matters. The play doesn't judge the scientists. It doesn't tell people what to think about making or dropping the bomb, or about World War II, but it does invite them to think. Ultimately, it isn't about science, or about the 1940s. It's about men, and competition, and hindsight. It says a lot about bonding. It says a lot about being so enmeshed in an exciting project that you don't think about its consequences.' *Russell Vandenbroucke*

'It is a political film, but not a political language film. Even if you don't care about politics, you can care about these people. I wanted to make a film about real people who are trapped by circumstances.' *Bruno Barreto*

'I want to seduce the audience. If they can go along for a ride they wouldn't ordinarily take, or don't even know they're taking, then they might see highly charged political issues in a new and unexpected way. . . . The theatre is now so afraid to face its social demons that we've given that responsibility over to film. But it will always be harder to deal with certain issues in the theatre. The live event – being watched by people as we watch – makes it seem all the more dangerous.' *Paula Vogel*

'I try to make films that move people when they are in the theatre and make them think only after they leave.' *Claude Berri*

'There's an insane desire [in Britain] to find new playwrights, but you need talent to show there is more to life than misery, pain, and degradation.' *Dominic Dromgoole*

'. . . usually, the biggest problems of adapting plays into screenplays is that they stick too close to the play, and I think film is a completely different medium. I think a novel is much closer to a film.' *Arthur Miller*

'We get a huge number of plays about collapsing society. Perhaps that's why people choose to write plays in [Britain]. Because they're opposed to the status quo. But the plays are not political as such. There's an ideological vacuum, indeed a disbelief in a larger society.' *Jack Bradley*

'. . . I have written a couple of screenplays for studios, and each time has been less gratifying than the last. In my experience, they want no real representations of homosexuality, they want no complexity, they are terrified of ambiguity and unanswered questions – they don't know what they want, except that they want to make lots of money. The only freedom I've ever had as an artist has been in the theatre . . ..' *Craig Lucas*

'. . . I heard the opening lines of the play in my head. The son, who has been HIV-positive for some time, says, I can't stay long. His pragmatic mother says, No, no, we know. Temporality and the acute knowledge of it. The entire play was in those two lines, and I wrote it in four days.' *Tom Donaghy*

'In a painting called Moonlight [by Edvard Munch], a full moon illuminated a dark, almost barren landscape where a picket fence surrounded a lone cottage; the figure of a woman stood nearby. Although not visible in the painting, I sensed the closeness of the ocean and the icy dampness of the cold night air. But the woman, dressed in black and standing alone at the gate staring off in the distance, seemed not to feel the cold, as if numb to anything but the pain so clearly expressed on her weary face. Suddenly, I understood the cause of her grief . . .. I took this spark of a story and lifted her spirit from the painting, and I placed the woman I would come to know as Kathleen on a blank piece of paper.' *Mary Hanes*

'So the task of the translator . . . as I see it, is to hear the language of the original, not simply to see it on the page, and then to write a play in English that will produce, when staged, the same or analogous effect that the original may be said to have on [its intended] audience.' *Paul Schmidt*

'When baby ducks and geese are born, they imprint on the first thing that they see, and that becomes their mother. An audience is like that. They imprint on what you give them in the first few minutes of the play, and they will follow it. In those first moments you can do anything, because hope springs eternal. The lights come up and you've got them until you start to lose them. . . . With a play, you're trapped there; it's got to keep giving or people turn on you. They resent you.' *Constance Congdon*

'Whenever you think you're writing what other people want to hear from you, and that it'll be commercial, you're doomed to disaster. Writing has to be as truthful and specific as we can make it. The minute we think that we're reaching more people and pleasing them, we get general. And audiences sense that and turn away, shun us.' *Terrence McNally*

'All autobiography is fiction.' *Sandra Tsing-Loh*

'I wrote a draft of a play that was sort of like Pete Gurney's THE DINING ROOM, about the Standard Club. A different family appeared in each scene of the play, and this family from Ballyhoo was just one of them. Ultimately, I decided to focus on just one family.' *Alfred Uhry*

'All plays stem from personal experience. I was reading psychoanalytic lit for a couple of years, obsessively, in depth, and I got involved in analyzing everyone around me. . . . Eventually, all my friends' eyes began to glaze over when I started talking this way, and I got the hint that there might be something comical in it.' *John Patrick Shanley*

'I thought, This is fabulous. It sent shivers up my spine. I thought, What kinds of people are these that would produce this kind of music in a camp? All the prison camp stories I've seen, and heard of, were about the heroism of men. As I researched this and heard the music, I realized that women were heroic too, on just as grand a scale. And their treatment was just as appalling.' *Bruce Beresford*

'When I have an idea for a story, it's usually because I have met or heard of someone who interests me. I then work a bit like an academic, digging into the material, going back for more exploring. It takes a long time, but it interests me. I think I am above all a writer. And when I write, there is always the famous I who is the narrator, which is why I often finish up appearing in my films.' *Danièle Dubroux*

'[The play is] a journey from Wilde's public into his private persona. I had two major objectives, to tell the story – a story – of Oscar Wild, and to understand how theatre can communicate history.' *Moisés Kaufman*

'Our volume of [commercial] production has fallen to nothing. In Broadway's heyday, you'd have 60 or 70 new productions each year, of which 12 to 15 would survive, and of those several would be pretty good and 2 would be brilliant. The failures gave birth to the successes, and out of it came some of the best, most exciting theatre in the world.' *Robert Whitehead*

'People have always turned to plays [for films] and will continue to turn to plays because Hollywood is a great gigantic maw looking everywhere for ideas and stories. And they are hard to come by. A play has, in a sense, already been tried out. You've already put that story up on a stage, seen how it works, seen how audiences have reacted. You can't do that with a new movie script. A play puts you a step ahead.' *Thomas Rothman*

'You can lose the play in the translation [to film]. They are two different mediums and very rarely can material succeed in both.' *Frederick Zollo*

'Movie makers buy plays because it makes them feel smart. Acquiring a play that has been well received makes them feel incredibly worldly. But the irony is that plays are about words, and here in L.A., they like to make movies about lava flowing down Wilshire Boulevard. A play reveals itself through dialogue. In a movie, the dialogue is likely to be, "O.K., shoot him."' *Anonymous Hollywood Executive*

'. . . it is true that language and forward movement in the cinema are jolly hard to reconcile. It's a very, very, difficult thing to do. . . . There is still a place in the cinema for movies that are driven by the human face, and not by explosions and cars and guns and action sequences . . . there's such a thing as action and speed within thought rather than within a ceaseless milkshake of images.' *David Hare*

'There are a lot of plays that are just about how well you use the English language. [In others] the writing is spectacular, but it feeds into an emotional story. And I think that's the key to a successful transition from play to movie.' *Jonathan Weisgal*

'I love problems. That's why I like drama; telling a story is recounting a series of problems. That's probably why I love Paris, because of its conflicts. . . . I wanted to show Paris the way it really is, as one lives in it, not the cliché of lovers kissing by the river. The city, with its differences between the young and the old, has become much more multiracial. Modern life creates a kind of ghetto orientation where men stay with men, women with women, and races and ages don't mix easily. What's striking in Paris is that people don't really connect with each other, although there is a sense of community.' *Cédrick Klapisch*

'I know what it's like sitting on the other side. The most important thing I can tell you is that literary managers are not your enemies. It's just that we are inundated by scripts all the time.' *Nathaniel Graham Nesmith*

'One of the best ways to lose a play is to talk about it too much. Talking a play is not writing a play, and what works as chatter never works any other way, I find. So, I'd say "pitching" a play can kill it.' *Julie Jensen*

'I'm told that a few critics asked whether presenting my satire on the religious right in a theatre amounted to preaching to the converted. On the one hand that's a fair question . . ... On the other hand, I think it's a stupid question. If theatergoers may indeed be more liberal than, say, the people who voted again for Jesse Helms in North Carolina, what then is my option in order not to preach to the converted? Contact the Republican National Committee and say I have a play I want you to put on? Well, obviously that's not going to work. So is my option simply not to bring up topics that supposedly liberal theatergoers agree with?' *Christopher Durang*

'I feel that if an audience leaves a play and they don't know which side I'm on, then the point of the play did not come across. Which is not to say that I'm telling them that they have to agree with me, but they should definitely know where I'm coming from. . . . I would rather make sure that my plays have a clear point of view than worry about them not being dramaturgically sound. I don't want to feel that literary handcuffs are keeping me from saying what I really need to say.' *Kia Corthron*

'GOOD AS NEW was born out of the idea of writing a play where the stakes were high and the collisions were of a verbal nature. Also I wanted to write a play where people were smarter than I was, and more alive than I feel normally. I became interested in the idea of characters who would surprise me. I guess one could argue that nothing comes out of you that wasn't within you to begin with, but maybe there are ways to trick yourself into becoming more an observer or an advocate for the characters.' *Peter Hedges*

'. . . I do think that deep down, a lot of my work is about people trying to make reasonable accommodations of situations that are insane or absurd. . . . At first I thought the events had power in themselves, that I would just present them. I really wasn't aware of the things that finally became central issues to me – the shifting alliances, the way people hardly even know they've shifted. That part of [A QUESTION OF MERCY] is very familiar to me in terms of my other plays.' *David Rabe*

'All reviews should carry a Surgeon General's warning. The good ones turn your head, the bad ones break your heart.' *David Ives*

'I don't have an idea for a play until after I've finished writing it. I write first, and come up with what it's about later. My technique could be compared to having a large canvas and coming in every day and putting a dot on it somewhere, and after several years – literally – I begin to say, That reminds me of an elephant, so I think I'll make it one.' *Wallace Shawn*

'Essentially what we did was we took the relationship between the crime boss and his lieutenant, which we felt was the most interesting thing about the [Dashiell Hammett] novel, and sort of wrote a story around that. . . . I think if something is sort of out there in the culture, it's fair game for anyone who wants to use it in any way that they please . . ..' *Joel Coen*

'A good play is a good play. If you want to chalk up your rejection letters to the fact that you're a woman, that's your choice. But often you get a rejection letter because your play isn't ready. Or the time isn't ready for your play. And that has nothing to do with gender.' *Jane Anderson*

'[I was] particularly eager to give voice to the women of my mother's place and generation, who grew up in turn-of-the-century, privileged New England households, who really never had a chance to flower and assess themselves and find out who they were. More than anything, I wanted to give voice to the sort of anger that women of that generation could never express for themselves.' *Tina Howe*

'In BENT, I use one of the great weapons that a playwright can use, which is intermission. The play radically changes between Act I and Act II, but you don't have that in film. It has to be all of one. . . . Most plays are claustrophobic, and that's why they are so hard to turn into film. Theatre is by its very nature not real. Whereas film gives the illusion of reality' *Martin Sherman*

'I don't believe in inspiration. Inspiration is for amateurs. Some of the time you know you're cooking, and the rest of the time, you just do it.' *Chuck Close*

'I just had an eye-opening experience in London – it seems that there, directors don't think it's their job to throw a lot of rewriting notes at you. Here I think directors think they're not doing their job if they don't offer you major dramaturgy. Sometimes it's been helpful, but I've made changes that have hurt my soul and that I still regret, even if others might have deemed the change successful.' *Neena Beber*

'I do think the challenge, in a way for me, is to write a narrative film and when you finish watching it you feel like it's a collage. You tell the narrative, you tell the story, but you feel like you've created this tapestry. But it also has a shape, a story. So I think there's a middle ground I try to strike . . . away from where everyone else seems ready to go, which is, setup, payoff. You know, He's afraid of water, oh, and at the end he's swimming in water Oh, my God. I hate that stuff.' *Shane Black*

'I always start with a political impetus, and then the characters come to me next and then I slowly form the story.' *Kia Corthron*

'I love to play with language; make it do tricks, turn a word inside out to see if it's got a hidden meaning tucked away somewhere, or perhaps find that it's capable of an extra entendre or two. . . . Plotting is nothing I did, or do, naturally. It is the hardest part of the writing process. No matter how many times you plot a script successfully, the next one, representing new and uncharted territory, convinces you that you really don't know how to do it at all.' *Larry Gelbart*

'The big difference is you can always fix a play, especially a comedy that's playing before an audience. You're trained to go home and rewrite. You figure out the texture of what's comedic in front of an audience. In films, you have no audience response. Screenwriting is very spare. In a play two people can sit down and say how unhappy they are, and they can talk for two hours with each one saying, I'm more unhappy than you, and the other saying, Yeah, but let me tell you about my mother. In a film, you literally have to move from scene to scene, you have to pare everything down. The emphasis is on telling the story, moving it forward. What I learned is that you can learn something about a character by going in on them with a camera.' *Wendy Wasserstein*

'It's not [autobiographical]. But it's a legitimate question because I play the leading role, and as Truffaut said, one always makes the same film about oneself. Truffaut is in his films, so I, too, am in my film. I really wanted to speak about heartbreak, because it always surprises me that one pays such a high price for love. I don't know why. Perhaps it's an old Catholic thing inside me, the idea that happiness has a price, that one gets nothing for nothing. I have had my heartbreaks. I have had younger lovers. But the age difference is not the point of the film.' *Brigitte Roüan*

'I felt, if I'm going to take on some of the most overdone material, which is men and women and affairs and betrayal of friends, I had better have a new take on it. I think my films come from a desperation not to be boring.' *Neil LaBute*

'I think of a plot, I think of an idea, and then I wonder, How can I get that onto the stage? . . . Whatever devices you use should always be there to serve the theme. If the theme has been overtaken by the device, then something's wrong.' *Alan Ayckbourn*

'Write plays that matter. Raise the stakes. Shout, yell, holler, but make yourself heard. It's time for playwrights to reclaim the theatre. We do that by speaking from the heart about the things that matter most to us. If a play isn't worth dying for, maybe it isn't worth writing.' *Terrence McNally*

'Producers are still willing to break their necks to put good material onstage, and we have playwrights who are afraid of nothing. But plays of this kind of substance are essentially going the way of the dodo bird [on Broadway], because the money is going to grand spectacles featuring special effects. So we turn to our nonprofit theatres for these kind of adventurous productions.' *Alexander H. Cohen*

'Producers [of film and theatre] are afraid of controversy whether from the left or the right. Everybody's scared and not even necessarily of offending groups – they're afraid of offending one person.' *Jonathan Reynolds*

'As you write plays, you discover what you believe. And until you know what you believe, you can't write a play.' *David Hare*

'There is a trend in the whole culture toward making things shorter. People have been watching too much television, and they have a television mentality. I think people really are wary of sitting in a theatre too long. They're not used to it.' *Rocco Landesman*

'I believe you shouldn't force the audience's interpretation of a character or a story. The more you explain things, the less intriguing and imaginable they are for viewers. . . . Film to me, in its essence, in its ultimate nature, is silent. Music and dialogue are there to fill what is lacking in the image. But you should be able to tell the story with moving pictures alone. For my next project, though, I'd like to make the kind of film where the characters blabber all the time.' *Takeshi Kitano*

'Things were kind of lean. I was in that position where it's like, What do I really want to write, do I trust myself enough not to care about the marketplace or anyone's expectations and just reach further into myself than I've ever reached? I said what I wanted to say, and it made it to the screen intact, and luckily it was a hit.' *Gerald DiPego*

'I have always been pro-choice, but my feelings became less matter-of-fact after I had children. That made me very nervous. Does that make me pro-life? The play is my internal argument made manifest.' *Wendy McLeod*

'If you've got time to waste, you might as well waste it listening to people.' *Martin McDonagh*

'The title's so upfront. It gives fair warning about the play's content. I'm writing about a kind of disenchantment, an anger, but quite a cool 90's anger, at a time when we're not very good at openly being angry. . . . I don't think I ever thought the title was titillating. I thought it was incredibly catchy. If the play is about the reduction in human relations down to a consumerist rationale, then thematically, the title is entirely linked into the thesis of the play.' *Mark Ravenhill*

'[HOW I LEARNED TO DRIVE] is a complicated, troubled love story. Basically, I wanted to respond to *Lolita*. I wanted to know if a woman writer, a theatre writer, could attempt a take on *Lolita* from Lolita's point of view.' *Paula Vogel*

'[Action's] a Western thing. We think of the hero going into battle, rebelling against a government or an oppressor, but [in KUNDUN] action is nonaction or what appears to be nonaction. That's a hard concept for Western audiences. . . . We wanted to show a kind of moral action, a spiritual action, an emotional action. Some people will pick up on it; some won't.' *Martin Scorsese*

'I wanted to make a very spontaneous film. So I thought, if I follow the dress, at each stage I am free to make the choice of what new characters I invent. It was a way of not becoming a prisoner of the story. But I consider myself a realist because I don't show things that are impossible. I just have the curiosity to follow strange details.' *Alex van Warmerdam*

'The ideal time for writing a [TV] script is four days, though sometimes it has to be two or three days depending on the deadline. If it's two days, sometimes there are things I see that don't work as well. If I have two weeks, the scripts get kind of flabby and lack the adrenaline that a sense of deadline fills you with.' *David E. Kelley*

'. . . the cruel part is that, to let the play live, you have to surrender control and let your characters go. You have to let them stumble, fall into walls and be mute, let them drift and be lost. If you hold the reins too tight, they won't spring to life.' *Tina Howe*

'I like all those fringy, weird, nonverbal, quiet, tiny little things, those powerful interchanges between people, things that go unsaid, that people know are happening all the time but nobody wants to talk about. That's what I want to make movies about.' *Tom Noonan*

'I don't write for a target audience. I write for myself more than for anyone else. . . . Psychological problems and journeys are what happen to interest me. The problems of the poor are not generally psychological. Obviously, the more affluent the person is, the more time they have to spend on their imagined unhappiness. It wouldn't be in my nature to write STREET SCENE. It isn't that poverty doesn't interest me. Poverty, politically speaking, certainly interests me, but that makes for a more didactic play than I'm prepared to write.' *Nicky Silver*

'An excess of development can undermine the most ephemeral but distinctive tool a writer possesses: authorial voice. A writer's voice is as individual and marked as a thumbprint, and is a playwright's truest imprimatur. It is as innate as breathing, and can be as unique as any genetic code. By its very singular nature, it is seldom born in the act of collaboration. True authorial voice always pre-dates the first rehearsal of a text. And it is – and will always be – an author's most distinguishing and valuable feature.' *David Wright & 34 members of New Dramatists*

'The play is a very simple idea really; someone needs some support and consolation, and she finds a place where she gets it.' *Conor McPherson*

'I don't know why I'm working off all these historical pieces – I never thought of myself as an historian. People say you should write what you know, but I write what I don't know. If I knew about it, I wouldn't have to write it.' *Charles Smith*

'As a TV writer, you're faced with a constant sense that someone can switch the channel. You want people to say, Hey, this is good. These are interesting characters. And you want to hold their interest so they won't wander away.' *Andy Wolk*

'I don't know if playwrights are good storytellers any more. I think in the post-Beckett generation, we've sort of dissed stories and dissed plot. I don't think it's a sign of commercialism to create a good story.' *José Rivera*

'I had a plot connection that nobody understood for this fourth character, and decided, Oh, nobody gets it, that's all. I'll write another draft to make her make sense. It took me awhile to learn that these three people were the core of this play, which seems so obvious now.' *Richard Greenberg*

'I survive as a playwright by focusing on the people who support and respect my work and the people who do work that I respect. And trying to put the rest of the wonderful world of theatre out of my mind so it doesn't turn my heart to stone.' *Y York*

'Hell, I tried to sell out, but no one would buy. I lasted one year on television. I hated the process. I didn't control anything. I had to do all my thinking out loud in a room with others. It made be nervous.' *Julie Jensen*

'I started out with this idea of someone going back in time. I woke up crying one night from a dream about my grandfather, who is dead, asking me to take him home, and I knew when he said home, he meant home, back to slavery, to that place where it all began for us in this country. . . . But the play began to form a few years after that, when I began to wrestle with the idea of trying to figure out what I would have been like and where I would have fit in the past. All of me. Not just my blackness, not just my irreverence, and not just my sexuality – but all of me. What if I went back?' *Robert O'Hara*

'So somehow, things that seem extraneous to the play in reality are not. The scene lasts 37 minutes, and you only need 12 minutes of that for the plot. But if you pull the rest of it out, it's not my play.' *August Wilson*

'I respect the decision of many of my colleagues to avoid writing for pay in [film & TV], but I need to make a living, and am grateful I can do it this way. It is necessary to keep a balance, and when the balance is struck, I feel very lucky – the TV stuff keeps my theatre writing more pure and honest, the theatre writing keeps the TV writing from sucking out my soul. Basically, the for-hire stuff is a job, and a job I usually like; the theatre stuff is life.' *Neena Beber*

'When do I say No? I say No when I feel that the intention of the play, or the spirit, or tone – or text – is being knowingly changed. Fortunately, this has happened only once. Next time I would say No earlier, and definitively. Otherwise, ultimately, the only No you have is No, you can't open the play. And that No is very, very hard to say.' *Lisa Loomer*

'I wanted to finally write my chinky Oriental play, because they love that stuff in regional theatres. So, as a writing exercise, I started a story about the Peking Opera. But then my true nature took over, and I started critiquing the Orientalism in that kind of theatre – and that's how this play became about art, commerce and politics.' *Chay Yew*

'. . . I was told . . . that when I write I should always take the white gloves off. That piece of advice would never have been given to a man because a male writer wouldn't wait for that kind of permission. I was writing nice little plays, and after I got this sense of permission, that changed.' *Wendy MacLeod*

'I do choose to write for a living in addition to writing plays. I no longer write sitcoms, and I no longer feel shame.' *Lisa Loomer*

'I very much write from characters. Those people start speaking, and then I have them in the house with me and I live with them. Then at some point, it's time to get them out of the house. You can only live with someone like Dr. Georgeous Teitelbaum from THE SISTERS ROSENSWEIG for so long, and then it's time for her to go. But it is very like having the company of these people and trying to craft them in some way into a story.' *Wendy Wasserstein*

'I'm drawn to very large texts that are mammothly popular in different parts of the world but are almost unknown here [the USA]. They're safe bets; if they've been around for 2,000 years, there's a reason. It's often a title or just a phrase within the text that will compel me to adapt it.' *Mary Zimmerman*

'I, too, am deeply concerned with an overarching idea that dramaturges are now authors . . . .. I am not taking the position that all dramaturges own copyright, deserve special billing credit, or should receive remuneration akin to that of the playwright. I know from my years at the Dramatists Guild that almost everyone a writer encounters has suggestions of how to write and rewrite the play or musical to make it work.' *Dana Singer*

'I hope people understand what I'm talking about. But, seriously, I don't make the connections beforehand. The process is less intellectual. I have a feeling that comes up around an image, and with that feeling comes a series of conversations, and out of those conversations comes the play. It usually takes a couple of years for the work to complete itself.' *Marlane Meyer*

'There's something in the Zeitgeist now. A lot of [film] scripts I get have these very dark themes, a cornucopia of dysfunction. You know, Jane is a 13-year-old anorexic who lives with her parents and has been raped by her father. And this is a comedy.' *Christine Vachon*

'Within the film community there is an increasing pressure to become edgier and edgier, to sort of separate yourself from the pack and to shock. There may be a form of one-upmanship going on, you know, Let's find a new genre of human depravity.' *John Sloss*

'What makes screenplays difficult are the things that require the most discipline and care and are just not seen by most people. I'm talking about movement – screenwriting is related to math and music, and if you zig here, you know you have to zag there. It's like the descriptions for a piece of music – you go fast or slow or with feeling. It's the same.' *Robert Towne*

'THE DYING GAUL is a Hollywood satire. But Hollywood is not the real subject matter here. My play uses that world of high-rolling big money – that crazy-making business – to examine a whole range of subjects.' *Craig Lucas*

'The pressure we get is making the [TV] show racier, not less racy. There's a huge amount of impetus to make things edgy, to try to do something that hasn't been done before, not to avoid sensitive subjects.' *Christopher Lloyd*

'What I've concluded is that, like it or not, the development process has become a permanent fixture in this country and, while it runs the gamut from being extremely beneficial to totally disastrous, most of us simply have to learn to live with it.' *Buzz McLaughlin*

'I've wanted to write a play about Chelsea, the 5,000-person town I live in. Recently, the big issue is whether we get a trailer park or whether we don't. Also, I'm helping a friend through a rough divorce, and it fed the play. I'd also read a lot of Lanford Wilson, a lot of Sam Shepard, and a lot of David Mamet. I really tried to understand what it is they do and do so well. They crank up the tension and make the audience sit in this room with these three characters who cannot leave until the drama is resolved. The tension gets tighter and tighter. I wanted to crank things up as high as I could before they snap.' *Jeff Daniels*

'[TV executives] feel much more at ease with the guys and gals they went to school with. They also feel that the older you get you're less in tune with your wit and sexuality. You can't write love scenes. It's beyond your ken. [TV] is one of the few businesses where the more experience you have, the less useful you are.' *George Kirgo*

'I wrote for SANFORD AND SON and I wasn't black, I wrote for Shari Lewis and I wasn't a puppet. You don't have to be the age, sex, race of the thing you're writing about. You have to be a talented writer.' *Saul Turteltaub*

'I never get to . . . the index cards. I've never done that. I should, probably. I start with theme and character and, sometimes, ideas for scenes and dialogue, and I get a sense thematically of what I want to explore and accomplish. Basically I'm too immature to actually work it all out in my head before I start for some reason. So I actually start and just let the screenplay sort of guide me as to where it's going. . . . I also find that by approaching writing that way as opposed to [outlining], you come up with incredibly original work, because you're not using formulas and you're not mapping out plot lines that can't help but be sourced from a million movies you've seen.' *Richard LaGravenese*

'I'm sensitive about the criticism [for not producing new playwrights], yes. But I'm hip to it as well. I read 500 new plays a year, and 99.99 percent of them are not good. I see no reason to do a new play just because it's new. It's like kissing your sister, a virtue, but so what? It seems to me more worthwhile to take a proven playwright and say, Write something for us.' *Gregory Boyd*

'My mother and aunt were both up in years when they decided to live together. They would bicker about every little thing – it didn't matter what. Bicker, bicker, bicker. I would sit there and laugh at them. I thought to myself that I wanted to capture that love, to be able to share that love with others.' *John Henry Redwood*

'There's a sense of a jazz riff that I wanted all the way through. I didn't want to be hemmed in by chronology, and I didn't want the arc of the story to be a diorama. It's an emotionally driven structure, and I wanted to let it unfold the way a nice set does in a club. In a good jazz solo, you begin by stating the melody, and then you start to do riffs and go farther and farther out, or one guy in a combo will play a figure that will cause another guy to jump back to a solo of 30 years ago. But you always come back . . . and resolve and go out with the melody, and there may be a coda. There's definitely a coda, Clifford's monologue at the end of [SIDE MAN], after the emotional story is over.' *Warren Light*

'Lots of my friends and family belong to churches, and some of them are part of the so-called Christian Right. In this preacher, I wanted to show a good man struggling to reconcile his commitment to the community with the political agenda of his church. He does not see that as a dilemma, but I do.' *Lanford Wilson*

'Work with good directors. Without them your play is doomed. At the time of my first play, I thought a good director was someone who liked my play. I was rudely awakened from that fantasy when he directed it as if he loathed it. . . . Work with good actors. A good actor hears the way you (and no one else) write. A good actor makes rewrites easy. A good actor tells you things about your play you didn't know.' *Terrence McNally*

'I'm giving up acting. . . . I'm 66 and there are a number of celebrations I've got to get down on paper, and acting doesn't allow me to do that. It was a hell of a drug, performance. It's a great thrill, especially for a storyteller. But it can go. Directing can go. Writing can't go. And in terms of what lies ahead, I want to have a burning focus almost like smoke coming up from the paper as I write.' *Athol Fugard*

'Writers go through periods where they get into terrible trouble with themselves. And [my agent] never backs away from that – never backs away from the awful, infectious loneliness and free-floating failure that just goes with the territory. When I retreat into a long, long period of quiet work without coming up for air and I isolate myself, it's sort of comforting to know that [he] checks in a lot, he doesn't forget. . . . I can't ask for anything on my own behalf. I can barely get coffee for myself without feeling incredibly guilty about it, and I don't think I'm alone in that. I don't want to learn the point system, nor do I particularly want to know how to handle some of the more rabid producers in the world – I don't want to learn that skill. I want to muddle through a few plays and occasionally be sort of reasonably paid to try and write a movie, and [he] makes that life style choice not impossible to maintain.' *Jon Robin Baitz*

'Some can just knock it out and some have to lock themselves in a room and get to a fever pitch of self-loathing before they turn in a first draft. . . . each writer's process is screwed up in its own way.' *Warren Leight*

'Usually I decide on the title of a play about halfway through the writing process. Before that, I change titles almost every day and trust the right title will come.' *John Murrell*

'This is about the daily ins and outs of a marriage. I don't want to give away the ending, but they are trying either to make the marriage work or make the separation work. Our job is to make that interesting.' *Rob Reiner*

'When you get old enough in this [screenwriting] business, they figure you can fix all the mistakes made by the kids.' *Marc Norman*

'I went in right up front and said, This can't be about some guy in bandages. I didn't even want to do a horror movie. I took the concept and made a romantic adventure film. I like action heroes who don't take themselves too seriously. I wanted to make everyone take the mummy seriously, but it couldn't just be a guy in bandages. But the main thing was to build in surprises. That's one of the great things you can do with special effects.' *Stephen Sommer*

'People think I write fantasy, but I don't. Some things may be exaggerated or distorted, but they're realistic figures. . . . There's nothing incredible about it.' *Joe Orton*

'I thought if I wrote more quickly and worked harder, things would start happening for me. But I realized that my time was too precious. I wanted to make sure not only to do things, but to do them right. I finally said to myself: Sure, I can work on four plays simultaneously, because I have the time, But should I? I didn't want to end up like the Tasmanian Devil, whirling around and around in a frenzy of activity, generating huge clouds of dust, but ultimately nothing more.' *Melanie Marnich*

'. . . you have to write your own stories. I'm such a big advocate of working with people, but at the same time I think it's important to write the story you want to write. In graduate school, you sometimes get more feedback than you can handle. My first play at school was a one-act, and during the production process it changed over and over again. About a month or so before the play opened, I suddenly realized that I had written a play based on everybody's feedback. The trick, I learned, is to take feedback and cull what is useful to you.' *Kathryn O'Sullivan*

'I see [SNAKEBIT] as a comedy. So much of suffering is hilarious when viewed at a distance.' *David Marshall Grant*

'I work sometimes from outlines, which are immediately abandoned. Sometimes, when I'm trying to find the characters, I'll sketch things out a bit. Sometimes, outlines help me aim a little bit, but I tend to find it's usually much more interesting, especially with the first draft, to spew it onto the page. I used to get very nervous that, if I write this first rough draft and I die that night, whoever finds it might think that I thought it was good. For me, it's much more important to get some general shape onto the page and later take all the time I need to refine it, fix it, and rewrite it.' *Paul Rudnick*

'I write in order to understand the images. Being what my agent . . . somewhat ruefully calls a language playwright, is problematic because in production, you have to make the language lift off the page. But a good actor can turn it into human speech. I err sometimes toward having such a compound of images that if an actor lands heavily on each one, you never pull through to a larger idea. That's a problem for the audience. But I come to playwriting from the visual world – I used to be a painter. I also really love novels and that use of language. But it's tricky to ask that of the theatre.' *Ellen McLaughlin*

'I'm like a blue-collar writer. I just sit down every day and I write.' *Philip Kan Gotanda*

' Harvey [Weinstein] didn't want to release [MY SON THE FANATIC]; he held it for two years because he wanted a happy ending, although I don't know what that means. Does that mean the taxi driver leaves his wife or doesn't leave his wife? I think it has a happy ending.' *Hanif Kureishi*

'Actually, who hasn't been through the ghastly experience of sitting in front of a blank page, with its toothless mouth grinning at you: Go ahead, let's see you lay a finger on me? A blank page is actually a whitewashed wall with no door and no window. Beginning to tell a story is like making a pass at a total stranger in a restaurant.' *Amos Oz*

'The dream of a writer is to be surprised by his characters. All of a sudden, they are living their own lives; they are not prisoners anymore. . . . Tati taught me how to observe, how to sit in a cafe in Paris and to look at the passersby and to guess what their story is, even a little moment of their story . . ..' *Jean-Claude Carrière*

'[VIA DOLOROSA]'s pushing Broadway as far as it can be pushed. I stand before you as a reporter, and you have to decide whether I'm an honest reporter or not. And if you're convinced that I am honest, then I think that you will listen to me in a way that you wouldn't have listened to a fiction where scenes are made. . . . I've thought quite long and hard about what I want to say in this play. And if it means that every single sentiment that I produce is put minutely under an ideological microscope, that's fine.' *David Hare*

'A play gets on Broadway by fluke. And you don't even start out with that ambition. When I do a play, the intention is just to put it up somewhere.' *Richard Greenberg*

'Broadway remains the closest thing we have to a national theatre, the place where the greatest number of people can potentially see new work. For an American playwright to say it doesn't matter is simply to capitulate to the current situation.' *Tony Kushner*

'[Intercutting the past and the present] seemed to be a way to tell the story that kept the audience engaged, trying to reconcile how these women who, in Scene 1, talk about their boyfriends and are strangers, result in the woman in Scene 2, describing this beating. How did they get to that point? I wanted people to be able to make that connection throughout the play. When I'm in an audience, I really want to feel that I'm doing something, that I'm not just there to indulge the writer's need to impress me with the use of language or with one-liners that can make me laugh. I always appreciate it when the writer asks me to put things together myself, or to have an opinion about a character that may not be the writer's opinion.' *Diana Son*

'Talk isn't work. Work is when you have pages in the evening that you didn't have in the morning.' *Frederic Raphael*

'It's a movie, OK? I went to see GONE WITH THE WIND, but did I really believe there was a guy named Rhett Butler who said, "Frankly, my dear, I don't give a damn"? No. Movies need heroes and villains, and real life doesn't usually have heroes and villains. Real life has a lot of shades of gray, and movies have black and white even when they're in color.' *Don Hewitt*

'I'm a difficult playwright to interpret for audiences and for actors. That's because the thing that comes first for me is the emotions, the feeling. Life to me is feeling. I try to tell a story, but I think that my kind of writing aspires to the condition of music.' *Tom Murphy*

'What is so American about American [film] comedies is that the underdog has to triumph at the end. What is quintessentially French about THE DINNER GAME is that Villeret's character has his revenge, but remains as annoying at the end as he was at the beginning.' *Mark Urman*

'. . . the soap opera in a very real way is a morality play. In a soap opera, you reap what you sow and when you as a character do something wrong, you pay for that. The viewer knows that. And that is one of the attractions to the viewer. The only question is when and how, and I will admit it sometimes takes a long time.' *Robert L. Wehling*

'I am the same artist with the same nagging questions I had in my early 20's. What's real and what isn't? How do we tell what's real in our lives? How do we see things as they are? What is my role in life? If the Signature hadn't forced the issue by devoting its season to my plays, I could at least believe I had changed. Really, they're all the same! What is SIX DEGREES OF SEPARATION but THE HOUSE OF BLUE LEAVES with money?' *John Guare*

'Consider: for all the gobbledegook [film studio] executives spout about backstory, all that we, the audience, want to know is what happens next. That's the only thing that's going on. . . . Character is nothing other than action, and character-driven means the plot stinks, and you'd better hope the star is popular enough to open the movie in spite of it.' *David Mamet*

'There's this sense of being strange, which is at the heart of every creative person. Every writer, every actor, every director knows who Ripley is. We've made careers and lives out of pretending, making things up, inhabiting other people's stories and lives. That's what I do every day. . . . The story is so audacious and subversive: a central character who behaves badly and isn't apparently caught. That intrigued me no end.' *Anthony Minghella*

'Real life has always let me down. That's why I do the monologues. I have always said I would rather tell a life than live a life. But I have to live a life in order to tell one.' *Spalding Gray*

'Writing makes you lonely because you have to exile yourself. But deeper than that is an inborn native loneliness, a spiritual voice that words, for some reason, help fill. I would say that every writer I have admired, like Faulkner, whom I love, and Joyce, or Emily Bronte, Sylvia Plath, Chekhov, Beckett, regardless of their particular daily history, has a loneliness and a depth of feeling that cannot be corresponded to, and that's why they write.' *Edna O'Brien*

'What I find interesting is how close you can run the laughter along the seam of seriousness, and occasionally cross it, so that half the house genuinely doesn't know whether to laugh or cry. Custard pie humour is fairly universal, but at the other end, which I'm more interested in, there's the humour that hovers on the darkness, that walks in the shadow of something else, not always that obvious.' *Alan Ayckbourn*

'I am one of those writers who started on Broadway and who was immediately spirited away to Hollywood to become a very well-paid television comedy writer. . . . Despite the perils of the theatre, it is only in the theatre that the writer enjoys any kind of meaningful creative control. Producers can, of course, coerce the writer by threatening to pull the financial plug. In television, however, whoever pays the bills dictates every aspect of the show, including the cast, your script and who rewrites your script. The theatre is hard, mainly because you don't get your money up front; you make money only if the show does. Obviously, it's more attractive to get paid a ton of money whether or not your show is a hit. . . . As for being a playwright, I remind myself: nobody asked you to be a writer.' *Ernest Chambers*

'Writing a film – more precisely, adapting a book into a film – is basically a relentless series of compromises. The skill, the "art," is to make those compromises both artistically valid and essentially your own. . . . It has been said before but is worth reiterating: writing a novel is like swimming in the sea; writing a film is like swimming in the bath.' *William Boyd*

'There is no language in a screenplay. (For me, dialogue doesn't count as language.) What passes for language in a screenplay is rudimentary, like the directions for assembling a complicated children's toy. The only aesthetic is to be clear. Even the act of reading a screenplay is incomplete. A screenplay, as a piece of writing, is merely the scaffolding for a building someone else is going to build. The director is the builder.' *John Irving*

'What I was looking for with Jeffrey was his psychology, what he is obsessive about, what drives the man, why he did what he did. You don't look for how this man is like everybody else; you look for how he's different. The film [THE INSIDER], as it relates to Jeffry, has one and only one motive – to put you under the skin of Jeffrey, walking in his shoes, through a dramatized battlefield and minefield of the heart. We don't pretend to be, nor do we want to be, the complete historical record.' *Michael Mann*

'Humour is about context. If you're reading DORA, you wouldn't think Freud's first line, Good evening gentlemen, is particularly funny. When you're in the audience, and you've watched Freud come on, shuffle his notes, nod at several people in the audience, look very carefully at the others, glare at a woman in the front row, and then start his lecture, Good evening gentlemen, the context makes people (usually women) laugh. Humour in a black comedy or a satire is also about directing people's attention. By the third word, as well as making the audience laugh, it's also established Freud as an unreliable narrator.' *Kim Morrissey*

'Most of my plays are mysteries or have a mystery element in them. AGNES OF GOD certainly did. I wanted to write a play that people would talk about afterward. . . . BOYS IN WINTER is structured very much as a kind of "why-done-it." With SLEIGHT OF HAND, I wanted to attack the thriller form head on. I think it's absolutely the most challenging form to write for the theatre.' *John Pielmeier*

'But I don't really write to honor the past. I write to investigate, to try to figure out what happened and why it happened, knowing I'll never really know. I think all the writers that I admire have this same desire, the desire to bring order out of chaos.' *Horton Foote*

'Whatever you do, when you're sitting on that platform facing the audience [after a staged reading], resist the impulse to defend your work. Resist the impulse to answer back to someone who bruises your feelings or insults your baby. You probably don't know who that person is. He could be the artistic director's boyfriend. She could be a member of the board and might have something to say about the budget for next season. . . . In my experience, your best option is to respond with, Hmm, that's interesting. I'll think about that.' *Jeffrey Sweet*

'Regarding pushing the form, ideas interest me more than form. I think you can write a very subversive play in a three-act structure. The content makes the play. I feel the form is simply dressing, because ultimately, you want to communicate to the audience, and sometimes the best way to do that is to present a provocative idea in a format that is comfortable for them to receive. Then the idea will come through directly, right in the solar plexus. After all, I want to make a living as an artist, and that means speaking to the audience in a form they can understand.' *Caridad Svich*

'I've always been interested in people, perfectly intelligent people, who seem to have some sort of grasp on life but go around acting in a self-defeating way because they are expressing some neurosis – either sexual or spiritual. The guy who saves a President's plane from terrorists isn't terribly interesting to an artist. . . . The goal of any artist – somebody else said this, but I'll take credit for it – is to attempt to sell out but fail. By that yardstick, I've done pretty well. Though at some point the product becomes unworth your time and effort. [Martin] Scorcese and I went through this with BRINGING OUT THE DEAD. At the last minute, we received notes from the producer trying to simplify the main character's struggle to more of a problem-solution situation. But life tends to give us dilemmas, which are never really solved. Marty and I wrote the producer back, saying that, true or not, you see character as an instrument of elucidation, whereas we see character as an instrument of mystery.' *Paul Schrader*

'One [of the two ideas for PROOF] was to write about two sisters who are quarreling over the legacy of something left behind by their father. The other was about someone who knew that her parent had had problems of mental illness [and that] she might be going through the same thing.' *David Auburn*

'I had seen that wedding films did very well at the box office; look at FOUR WEDDINGS AND A FUNERAL and MY BEST FRIEND'S WEDDING. I saw that films about middle-class African-Americans, like SOUL FOOD and WAITING TO EXHALE, could be profitable. A wedding film about African-Americans was, I thought, overdue. I was just tired of not seeing people I could relate to on the big screen. In too many movies the black characters are marginalized and stereotypical: the black friend who imparts wisdom to his white co-star, the black prostitute, the thug, the side-kick. They tend to be one-dimensional. I wanted to go beyond that. I was just trying to tell a story [in THE BEST MAN] that was close to my own experience, about people who have been to college, people who are pursuing careers and getting on with their lives.' *Malcolm D. Lee*

'If a playwright cannot handle negative criticism he or she ought to get out of the game. After all, once people pay money to see the work, they have every right to say anything they feel about it. I have never worried about whether I would be criticized or not. . . . Critics I listen to from time to time, but not nearly as much as I listen to the audience. I am in the back of the theatre listening to people shift in their seats, move their feet, talk, cough, get up and go to the bathroom. Those are the signs that tell you the play is not holding their attention.' *Charles Fuller*

'It wasn't a question [with WIT] of navigating upstream and starting up this branch, then coming back down and starting up that branch. The play was always clear in my mind. The play that's on now is the play that was in my mind. It just had more parts to it. The first reading around the dining room table was completely recognizable. There was not a change in tone or anything. It was just too long. Even when it was first in my mind, there wasn't a start in this direction, then a start in that direction. It was straight through all the way. I was writing a play about a person who's being treated for advanced cancer and who's a professor of John Donne. A synopsis I would have given on the first day would have been accurate.' *Margaret Edson*

'You have to keep in mind what you want from the film pitch. What you really want in a pitch is to set up the next meeting. It's always about the next step. And you've done that. You've hooked me. I want to know what happens next.' *Marcus Hu*

'Even in the things that look most frivolous there has to be the threat of something quite painful to make the comedy work. I suppose the play of mine that's best known is NOISES OFF, which everyone thinks is a simple farce about actors making fools of themselves. But I think it makes people laugh because everyone is terrified inside themselves of having some kind of breakdown, of being unable to go on. When people laugh at that play, they're laughing at a surrogate version of the disaster which might occur to them.' *Michael Frayn*

'I don't expect to find anybody here [at the International Film Financing Conference]. That would be a miracle. But it's so hard to get somewhere in this business that what I try to do is explain to people the dos and the don'ts. Just being a good filmmaker does not mean you know how to sell your idea. But to succeed, that's exactly what you're going to have to do, over and over.' *Joe Pichirallo*

'There's a lot of hyperventilation that takes off before the [Sundance Film] Festival, a lot of buzz. Every year we hear, this is going to be the new this, this is going to be the new that, and it never is. The buzz just doesn't mean anything. I'm glad it doesn't. Because I think the festival shows that what succeeds is content.' *Robert Redford*

'I had a phone call from an agent who was trying to steal me from my agent and he said, What do you want? If I can give you what you want, what do you want? I said, I want to write stories and see them come to life on stage and on screen. He said, No, really, what do you want? I mean, it is unbelievable to some that one would want to be a writer. . . . Creating entertainment for a live audience is the nobility of it. There is something very noble about writing plays.' *Douglas Carter Beane*

'Plays are literature: the word, the idea. Film is much more like the form in which we dream – in action and images (Television is furniture). I think a great play can only be a play. It fits the stage better than it fits the screen. Some stories insist on being film, can't be contained on stage. In the end, all writing serves to answer the same question: Why are we alive? And the form the question takes – play, film, novel – is dictated, I suppose, by whether its story is driven by character or place.' *Israel Horovitz*

'There's very little in the substance of [THE LADY IN THE VAN] which is not fact though some adjustments have had to be made. Over the years Miss Shepherd was visited by a succession of social workers so the character in the play is a composite figure. . . . A composite too are the neighbours, Pauline and Rufus, though I have made Rufus a publisher in remembrance of my neighbour, the late Colin Haycraft, the proprietor of Duckworth's.' *Alan Bennett*

'The central event in [COPENHAGEN] is a real one. Heisenberg did go to Copenhagen in 1941, and there was a meeting with Bohr, in the teeth of all the dangers and difficulties encountered by my characters. He almost certainly went to dinner at the Bohrs' house, and the two men almost certainly went for a walk to escape from any possible microphones, though there is some dispute about even these simple matters. Worse disputes have surrounded the question of what they actually said to each other, and where there's ambiguity in the play about what happened, it's because there is in the recollection of the participants. Much more sustained speculation still has been devoted to the question of what Heisenberg was hoping to achieve by the meeting. All the alternative and coexisting explications offered in the play, except perhaps the final one, have been aired at various times, in one form or another.' *Michael Frayn*

'Some people think I am an issue-oriented writer, but I've never said to myself, I'm gong to write about such-and-such an issue – that would make for incredibly boring writing, at least to my taste. Creating someone I don't know and her made-up world shows us more about who we are – is actually a better mirror – than if I were to parade in front of you an instantly recognizable person in an instantly recognizable situation. I'm not saying, Let's make it all abstract and weird and difficult and thereby you will know more about yourself. My process is much more organic than that.' *Suzan Lori-Parks*

'I guess I'm just arrogant enough to imagine what it's like to be in different people's heads. I mean, yeah, I do research – everyone does that – but it really comes down to liking the characters and sympathizing with them. Not turning them into caricatures. Really putting them across. As a writer, the minute you start questioning your ability to do that. . . . Well, you might as well pack it in.' *Jason Sherman*

'I think the hardest thing for playwrights who want to write for television to accept is that they must relinquish that sense of authorship we pride ourselves on when writing for the stage – but it's necessary for the form. I truly believe no one person can write twenty-four genuinely funny one-act plays one after another in the time we have. For the kind of plays we need – where you laugh out loud twice a minute for twenty-two minutes – you have to get in a room with other writers. . . . The most frustrating thing for me is that every script has to be exactly the same length: twenty-one minutes and forty seconds, which is down from twenty-two minutes and nine seconds last season. That doesn't seem like much, but let me tell you, I can think of something in just about every episode – some wry aside, maybe – that gets lost to a commercial because of that thirty seconds less!' *Joe Keenan*

'My work for the RSC has been very large in scope. Not many people write in a larger scale. It's economic suicide. TWO SHAKESPEAREAN ACTORS has been done at the Royal Shakespeare Company, on Broadway at Lincoln Center, at the National Theatre of the Czech Republic, and at a boy's school in Scotland. That is the extent of the productions – period. Many people love the play, but not many can do it. As all of us in the Dramatists Guild know, you make your money from the royalties of future productions and not from the first production. However, with a big play, a first production is usually all you're ever going to get. Writing on a large scale is a very dangerous thing to do, but it's one that I've enjoyed doing and need to do.' *Richard Nelson*

'I usually base my characters on composites of people I know. One trumpet player in SIDE MAN is really a mix of four different guys I knew growing up. Patsy, the waitress, is a mix of about three different people. I like doing it that way. I start with the characters, as opposed to plot, location, or some visual element. I write more by ear than by eye. I always work on the different sound of each character, trying to make sure each has a specific voice and speech pattern, which some writers could care less about.' *Warren Leight*

'Yes, the first draft is the key. That's why I put so much energy, focus, and attention on the first draft, because I respect that first go at the story. If I don't have the key in that first draft, I invariably won't get it in subsequent drafts, though I can craft around it.' *Caridad Svich*

'All my plays are accidents. I never sit down to write a play about anything specific. I never construct it ahead of time. Sometimes, I sit down to write, and something comes up through the writing. Sometimes, I write a monologue, and it opens a world to me. I've had plays come from imagery in my dreams. I've had plays come because I saw something in an art exhibit. One play came from my work experience making boat deliveries from Chicago to Fort Lauderdale.' *Sally Nemeth*

'When I ran the New Harmony Project, I read a lot of new scripts and proposals. Sometimes the subject was compelling and intrigued me, but it was usually the point of view that most interested me. It's exciting for me to read something where the voice of the writer is present, as clear as can be. I may not like that particular play, may not like the content, may not like many things about it, but when there's an individual and creative voice present, it's always exciting. So, it's a question of voice, as raw or as unshaped as it may be.' *James Houghton*

'First, if you're serious, decide which network's movies you find interesting, which ones you feel a visceral connection to. Then really watch them, see what kinds of subjects they deal with, see the patterns in them, and learn to adapt your ideas to what they do. . . . Commercial television has very definite requirements that vary from network to network. A movie at CBS, for example, has to have a seven-act structure, while at NBC it's eight acts. Where NBC wants to be in the story by the end of the first act is different from where CBS wants to be. At NBC, a scene that goes more than one, maybe two, pages makes people nervous, whereas at CBS, they're more leisurely – sometimes you can get by with a scene that's three and a half pages long!' *Larry Strichman*

'The culturally specific, in particular, the American porch play that American writers have cherished and loved for many years in terms of their new writing, has seemed to have very little relevance to a much more fast-flowing, abstract, experimental drama that has been emerging in [the UK]. The porch play, not to mention that thing of, Oops, I wasn't loved enough by my father, somehow didn't have the relevance in this country.' *Stephen Daldry*

'I'm a man of the left. In the 1950's and 60's, I did pamphlet-style, schematic, speaking-to-the-converted, black-and-white theatre. Then I realized that things are more complex and indirect, and art has its own language.' *José Sanchis Sinesterra*

'I didn't consciously think through how to tell such a story. When I'm writing, I think where, emotionally, does this need to go next? What would take us further through someone's journey? In this play, it felt like a straight, linear narrative wouldn't make sense because of Samuel's having to go back and piece through these events again. The first section is straightforward storytelling. It settles you in. Then I wanted to do something that would blast that apart – something more fragmented, jarring, visual and theatrical. I wanted to create a visceral experience of what it was like to be in Samuel's head.' *Heather McDonald*

'I saw a book called "How to Survive Your Ph.D. Dissertation" in the library, and one of the things it suggested was playwriting. They shouldn't have books like that in the library.' *John Henry Redwood*

'The point of departure was the family story. I wanted to explore the links that necessarily exist between intimate affairs and politics. Private life is never really private. Everything we experience has to take the social environment into account. In the family there is a natural hierarchy between the father and the son. The idea of the film was to look at the workplace, and see how that hierarchy could be reversed.' *Laurent Cantet*

'. . . while there may be no harm in being treated like a screenwriter if you're paid like a screenwriter, it's certainly dangerous to be treated like a screenwriter if you're paid like a playwright.' *Ralph Sevush*

'The usual wages of screenwriting in Hollywood are money and oblivion . . ..' *Aljean Harmetz*

'We were interviewing an author, and we started talking about how so many of them – Salinger, Shaw, Fitzgerald – were really an odd bunch. They put a barrier around themselves, and not many people got through it. This was the spark that I really latched onto – someone who could break through the barrier. Of course [FINDING FORRESTER] really began to take shape when I began to wonder, what if it was a young person?' *Mike Rich*

'I never had an original idea in Hollywood. Well, I did, but no one ever liked them. . . . To make myself feel better, I repeated my mantra over and over, The check is good. The check is good. It's the mantra of all L.A. screenwriters once they find out that after years of hard pitching, writing, rewriting, and silly story meetings, there is no movie, no audience, no satisfaction – or that there is a movie but it has little in common with the script they wrote. Screenwriters write for money; playwrights, as Zoe Caldwell says, write to get well. If you are one of those thousands of screenwriters who would like to get well, perhaps it's time to write a play.' *William Missouri Downs*

'I saw a TV news report on a book about neurological disorders. The author talked about this kind of amnesia where, when you go to sleep, you forget everything you've remembered during the day, and when you wake up you're a blank slate. I thought of the first scene and then the very last one. Otherwise, [FUDDY MEERS] unfolded itself to me as it unfolds to Claire – as a series of surprises. I tried not to know where I was going with it. When the masked man stepped from under the bed, I didn't know who he was or what he was doing there. Later on I had to go back through the script and tinker with it like a Rube Goldberg contraption.' *David Lindsay-Abaire*

'Yes, I am one of those people who feels that most of my work is adaptation of one sort or another. For me, it's a way to jump-start the engine. For example, some people use the technique of basing a character on a friend. They start writing with his or her voice, then at a certain point, the character takes off on his or her own. It probably no longer resembles the model, but it helped the author to get going. I find that's true of form, too. For every play I've written, I know what play I was trying to imitate. That helps me get going.' *David Henry Hwang*

'[In development programs] there are too many chefs in the mix way too soon. I'm trying to take the emphasis away from fixing and doctoring plays and to encourage writers to listen to the impulse that's inside them and to honor that impulse. Across the country plays are being developed to death. I'm encouraging a notion of play evolution versus play development. I want to let a play find itself and to let a writer find himself within a play.' *James Houghton*

'I don't write agit-prop because I think the point gets across much stronger if the audience feels something rather than being told something intellectually. But every play of mine starts from a socio-political issue. Police brutality was my original impetus to write [FORCE CONTINUUM]. While I was writing, I felt first of all that it would be very easy to write a play about white cops beating up a black man, which we know happens. I decided to complicate it by focusing on a black cop and those contradictions. But also I really wanted to find solutions. I didn't want to say: This is a problem. We all know that. I wanted to see if there's a way to bridge the sense of black people not trusting the police, police not trusting blacks – if there's a way to go beyond that.' *Kia Corthron*

'So I went to this wax person and I just found it hilarious to lie on this slab getting my hair torn out by the roots – and paying for it! The woman who did it happened to be Russian, and we had this amazing conversation about Chekhov and Tolstoy while she was pulling. I thought, I've got to put this in a play. . . . Human relationships are so difficult and mysterious to me. I called this play THE WAX because it's about stripping away. It's about the ridiculous pain and hilarity of modern life. And the woman who waxes, who represents another world and another culture and another century, is meant – in a humorous but serious way – to bring a certain perspective on this little hothouse.' *Kathleen Tolan*

'One simple rule of preparation I've learned the hard way: if you have so much as one rehearsal before the reading, use a director to guide the rehearsal. Don't do it yourself. Be the writer. Be the expert on the story. Be the one to answer all those questions that come flying from the actors. Be the voice of authority on the dramatic intent of a scene. . . . You'll have enough on your mind as it is without worrying about the performance of your material.' *Gary Garrison*

'I grew up in southern Utah, and most of my folks sound like my characters, even if the characters are not living there. To be honest, my characters sound a lot like my sister. She's very bald verbally, out there, and funny. So, the language comes from the vestiges of what I can hear in my head of the folks I grew up with. After that, the place is a strong influence, the weather, the season, the time of day.' *Julie Jensen*

'So, right from the beginning, before I knew what the story [of Y2K] was, I knew that I wanted to see what it was like to take a couple who were no better or worse than anyone – they weren't perfect. But I knew that there was nothing in their past for which they should be brought down, no drunken evening when they hit somebody in their car, nothing that the Gods could strike them down for. They were just going through their lives . . .. They would be brought down very, very swiftly before they had even the ability to recognize what was happening to them. And it was the swiftness and the sureness of it with which they would just be undone. One of the main images that I used, that helped organize it was the memory of being in an earthquake in Mexico. . . . That was astonishing. Because what was solid was not solid.' *Arthur Kopit*

'. . . the movie business flattens everything in its wake like an ancient dead tree falling from an immense height into a particularly soft spot of moist, dumb green grass. . . . I suppose the only things that have ever seemed to hold my interest in life are the stories we tell one another, the things overheard and unsaid, the choices people make, their desires and fears and dreams. But it's very difficult to pursue that interest in the movies of today, perhaps to pursue that interest in the America of today. Because in the America of today, the sole arbiter of nearly every kind of art (or even entertainment) is not what it provides but only what it makes.' *John Malkovich*

'All these teachers and [screenwriting] books mean you see movies that have been worked over by more committees wielding more rules, that all originality and authorship is lost.' *Paul Schrader*

'. . . I had the structure of [PROOF] from the beginning. I knew what was going to happen in each scene. . . . in the first draft, the father had a monologue at the beginning of the second act in which he gave a little math history lesson. I knew that was the right place, structurally, for him to talk a little bit. It was the right moment for a longer speech from him, but that was not the speech. It was generic. In the revision, I took that out and replaced it with the current speech, which is about his not being able to work and what he does all day, looking at the students in the bookstores. Finding moments like that, moments more specific to each character's situation, was most of the work of the revision.' *David Auburn*

'Part of the fun is trying to guess what the ending might be. The challenge was to let the audience know in a way that wouldn't upset them that there wasn't going to be an ending. To switch off the expectation. . . . To mesmerize the audience, I had to experiment with rhythm. Too slow and the film would become indulgent. You would see the wheels turning.' *Peter Weir*

'. . . mostly I've found observing people to be the source of most of my inspiration. I studied photography for about five years, and I constantly find myself drawn to tense, awkward moments that I see – similar to what I would be compelled to photograph – these pictures I see between different people. It's usually what these people are doing physically, as well as what they're actually saying to one another that I watch – the way the react: sometimes with aggressive violence, at other times playing with each other coyly. I feel driven to know what these behaviors could mean to these other people and find a great challenge in fictionalizing the reasons behind their impulses.' *Crystal Skillman*

'I took many notes, more than usual before I sat down and wrote Act One, Scene 1. I had perhaps eighty pages of notes. . . . I was so prepared that the script seemed inevitable. It was almost all there. I could almost collate it from my notes. The story line, the rather tenuous plot we have, seemed to work out itself. It was a very helpful way to write, and it wasn't so scary. I wasn't starting with a completely blank page.' *Charles Busch*

'I've never written a fiction before about real people. . . . I read everything that I could find by people who met them and tried to get some impression of them, but as always when you write fiction, even if you have completely fictitious characters, you start by thinking of what is plausible, what would they say, what would they be likely to do, what would they be likely to think. At some point, if it is ever going to come to life, the characters seem to take over and start speaking themselves, and it happened with [COPENHAGEN].' *Michael Frayn*

'So often the challenge [in film] is you have two people and you know they're going to get together. It's just a question of how and how interesting the journey will be to get there.' *Ken Kwapis*

'Write whatever you want, as long as there's a love scene and the girl jumps in the volcano at the end.' *David O. Selznick*

CPSIA information can be obtained at www.ICGtesting.com
Printed in the USA
LVOW07s2133030814

397360LV00011B/180/P